THE
BUTTERCUP

CAT RIPPON

Tellwell Talent
www.tellwell.ca

ISBN
978-0-2288-9015-7 (Paperback)
978-0-2288-9172-7 (eBook)

A psychological thriller spanning two decades. Five people's lives that are tragically intertwined with impact on the lives of their families as fate twists and turns. One thing and one thing only holds the secret, the key to the mystery.

What is the secret of the simple buttercup that holds it all together?

Dedicated to my sister, Nicolette, who assisted in editing this book and to those who believed in me and said I could do it…. And so… I did

TABLE OF CONTENTS

PROLOGUE

1996

Have you ever seen a buttercup standing proud and tall in a field amongst the weeds and tufts of grass, its delicate petals bright yellow, smiling up at the sun and swaying ever so slightly in the summer breeze?

The sight evoked memories of years ago - that slim girl in the yellow dress and matching sun hat. Her arms stretched out with a smile that lit up her face as she twirled under the hot summer sun. Her skin shining and there was an innocence unmistakably of the young. Her laugh held by the breeze just for a second before drifting away.

From the window Fran watched as the little girl laughed into the sun. Her hat dislodging, falling to the side unleashing a mass of red curls which tumbled over her shoulders glowing with a life of its own. It was her laugh that she remembered more than anything, it carried on the breeze, unleashing happiness that swirled around and around - she hadn't felt that way for a long time.

She heard the child's name called; what was it?.........she knew it, but yet it wouldn't come to her. The name played in her mind, like a song once heard but still it wouldn't come and when it finally did, even then, she couldn't be sure.

Perhaps she should have paid more attention, but time was ticking by and there was somewhere she needed to be. Where she couldn't quite remember.

She reprimanded herself; wasting time was shameful when there was so much to get done, but it had felt so good, watching, and listening. She could just hear her, but the sound kept drifting away, "Mummy, mummy, look at me mummy". One more look wouldn't hurt but she couldn't see her anymore, where did she go? She peered through emptiness and then she heard her again but this time there was no laughter, a cold chill went down her spine as the words sounded more desperate "MUMMY!" Then the sun went behind a cloud and the world was all that little bit greyer.

2019

The rain poured and the sky was black with ominous clouds.

Fran looked out of her car window, drops of water dripped down in a continuous stream.

She just wanted to be home. It had been a long tiring day and it seemed to be taking ages.

A sudden blue and red light came up behind her with sirens blaring. It made her jump, sending shivers down her spine. Not again! Please God not again!

She stared desperately out of the window, but the police car sped past on her inside and weaved in and out of the traffic and Fran let a long slow breath out.

Twenty-three years had passed and yet her anxiety seemed to have got worse.

Lost in thought, a horn sounded behind her and her driver moved slowly forward raising a hand in apology to the person behind. Ahead the blue and red light angrily flashed and a policewoman in her waterproofs, flashlight in hand, waved them on - a diversion in place.

She just wanted to get home and they were still at a standstill. Fran slumped in her seat, her head pounded, and she leant her brow against the window trying to ease the throbbing pain, and there it was, standing alone, struggling as the rain battered the delicate body, bowing down under the weight of the water, its yellow petals grimy from dirt splashed up from the road. The lonesome flower bobbed its tired head as if to say, "I'm done, get me out of here". Fran knew exactly how it felt.

Finally, the cars began to move, and Fran pulled her eyes from the buttercup, whispering a silent goodbye, watching, as it lost its battle with the elements. Soon she would be home and she would be safe.

Still the rain kept pouring.

The orange headlights weaved their way along the dark streets; one behind the other until the turn off. There the road snaked to the left and the congestion of the motorway fell away and Fran was driven down the familiar winding road into the village of Little Stockton.

The streetlights threw shadows across the road as they turned into her street, her gut clenching with apprehension, as it always did; settling again as the car, slowed and turned into her driveway. As always, she admired the pretty cottage with its welcoming smile and the anxiety of the day slipped away.

She was home.

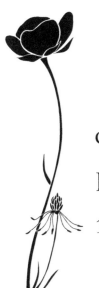

CHAPTER 1

LITTLE STOCKTON
1990

It was a beautiful summer's day in Little Stockton. Fran stepped from the bus at the top of Church Lane. She could, she told herself, have got off two stops further along but she felt like walking the cobbled stone path all the way down to the village centre. Fran grew up here, she liked to think that she knew every nook and cranny, but she could see that it had changed over the last two years. Many of the family-owned shops had gone and had been replaced with modern facilities that had no customer service with bored teenagers at the checkouts. She felt the loss of the charming personalities that had greeted her as a child.

"How's your mum Francesca?" "Did you have a good day at school"? This was no more, and the streets seemed strangely quiet with non-descript houses holding blank expressions.

Families had moved away in the hunt for employment opportunities or better high schools for growing kids and although charming, Little Stockton was not exactly the financial Mecca of the world. Nevertheless, Fran still felt that it had that village charm which was marred only by a new type of inhabitant. The village, only an hours' commute from London was ideal for business minded couples; mostly with no kids and definitely with a preconception of country living; the quintessential two dogs and four-wheel drive. They felt that this was their serenity from the hustle and bustle of city life, and donning wellington boots and jackets, once home, would walk said dogs. They took ownership of the village bringing their expertise to Shire council meetings and for those who had children, the local school P&C. Several had joined the local amateur theatre group stating they had been "semi-professional" in London and thought themselves an integral part of village life. Of course, they were but the true life of the village were those families that had been there for generations and who had chosen to stay to live out their lives at a slower pace. Fran's family was such. Her mum, a local teacher at the primary school, and her dad, the local mechanic, had lived in Little Stockton all their lives; they'd met at school and had no intention of leaving. Her brother Tom, who worked in the family business with their dad, and heavily pregnant girlfriend, lived two doors up from the local pub and life went on.......but Fran had been different.

As much as she had loved her family and where she lived, she had dreamed of travel and adventure and once school was finished, instead of joining others at university, she travelled around Europe. She found a love for fabrics and colour whilst in Italy and on her return she studied Interior Design in London and now worked for Mackenzie Taylor, a boutique company in Notting Hill. Nowadays there was very little time for home visits but today was different. Today she had returned home as it was her mother's 50th birthday and a huge village party was the order of the day. Fran's mother Mary had decided that all the village should be invited to her celebrations and the village green now held a huge marquee covered in fairy lights with chairs and tables within, it looked glorious.

As Fran walked towards the village green, she could see the marquee and felt a thrill of anticipation. This was going to be such a perfect night and for some reason she felt that something magical was going to happen.

As she got closer, she heard the band practicing and the familiar sound of her father yelling out instructions and ran through the gates with a broad smile on her face.

It was Tom who saw her first, calling out her name and as her dad joined them she was swept right of her feet and swung around like a little girl. "Hello Frannie, love, good to have you home". She felt 6 years old again, laughing as he gently lowered her to the ground. "How's Nancy, Tom? She is due any minute isn't she?" Fran's big hearted brother laughed "She's fat!" then dodged a punch in the arm from his sister "Come on you two stop messing around" her dad said with a cheeky grin, "there is still a lot to do; Frannie, love, can you go home and keep mum busy and by busy I mean don't let her out of your sight, we want this to be surprise" "Of course dad, see you at 6 0'clock" and with that she left.

The sun was still hot, which was unusual so late in the afternoon, and Fran stopped to remove her cardigan. She really wasn't paying attention as she undid the buttons and stepping off the curb she walked straight in front of a motor bike heading down Downer Street. Swerving, he narrowly missed her but clipped his wheel on the curb as he righted the bike back across the road. Fran stood still and watched as a man got off his bike and ripped his helmet from his head; "What were you thinking? If you were thinking at all! I could have hit you or worse." All of this yelled in Fran's direction as he walked towards her. "I'm sorry" Fran stammered, "I didn't see........" she didn't get to finish her sentence as he launched into another stream of abuse, ending with that it was painfully obvious that she didn't see. Fran saw red. It had been an honest mistake after all.

"As I said, I am sorry- the streets are much busier than I remember and yes, I should have taken care....." she took a deep breath "but there is no need to lose your nana over it. There has been no injury and that...." she pointed to the bike, "that danger to society has not got a scratch on it". Her voice rose as she grew more indignant.... "You don't own the roads you know"! She knew she was being unreasonable, maybe it was the shock, but she was behaving and looking like a small angry child. Her small stature radiated defiance as she looked up at an equally irate driver.

To her surprise, the man threw his head back and laughed. He continued to laugh as he put his helmet back on and turned to Fran saying, a little more gently, "just take more care, hey?"

With that he straddled his bike and drove off saluting her as he left.

"Well! What a cheek, who does he think he is!" It was more of a statement than a question. She knew she had done wrong but honestly...... Fran watched as the bike disappeared up the road, his sparkling blue eyes and infectious laugh had not escaped her, neither did his pronounced Australian accent but she told herself that now was not the time for having these sorts of thoughts; she was on a mission, and he, she decided, was insufferable .... probably a womaniser trying to impress woman with his stupid bike.....but those eyes. She turned and continued down Dennison Avenue, towards No. 5 and by the time she had got to the pretty, slightly run-down family home, she had completely written him off. Now to keep her mum busy.

MARY

Mary had lived in Little Stockton most her life. She had gone to the same primary school that she now taught at, which she loved. It had never been important to her to travel elsewhere and even going into Upper Stockton, made her tired, with all that traffic and people. She liked that she knew most of the families; seeing babies grow into toddlers who then became old enough to attend her school. She was proud that she was part of their development and this gave her immense pleasure. She belonged to the local church group and assisted with church activities Wednesday evening and of course Sunday morning. Book club happened on a Thursday, where talk with her girlfriends saw little literacy and usually ended up in hysterics with the consumption of several bottles of wine; and recently she had joined the new gym that had just opened in the village centre. She had hoped that her husband, Joe, would come with her but he had just given her that slow smile, shook his head and patted his rather rotund stomach saying that he had worked hard for his physique and that he was a fine figure of a man. Mary had laughed and mimicked him, dodging a playful slap. She wouldn't have wanted him any other way.

Joe had moved to Little Stockton when his father became the new parish vicar.

He was 17 years old and when 15 year old Mary and her mother had assisted with the church flowers, there was an instant connection. There was never any doubt that they would end up together and even when Mary went to university, they managed to maintain their relationship, getting married the year she qualified.

Now here they were, 28 years on; she couldn't believe how time had flown by and liked to think that they were a great deal wiser. They were proud of their two beautiful children and God forbid they were about to become grandparents to Tom and Nancy's first child and today...... today she had turned 50 years old. She stared in the mirror moving her face this way and that, frowning and then releasing her forehead..... she didn't look too bad, did she? Over the years she had maintained her weight, well almost and although there was grey in her hair, the hairdresser had done wonders. She continued to stare at herself lost in the face looking back at her and didn't hear Fran come up the stairs behind her. "Mum you look beautiful" and for the first time all day, the face looking back smiled.

CHAPTER 2

THE PARTY

1990

As the church bells rang out six strong chimes, which resounded across the village, 6 o'clock, Joe looked across to the entrance of the green. He had strung fairy lights over the wrought iron gates and trees, giving a magical glow to their surroundings. Turning, he looked back at the marquee with its gold and purple decorations and smiled, knowing that hidden behind the veils of white were the people invited to celebrate is wife's birthday. Where had the time gone.... he could hardly believe himself to be 52 let alone his sweet Mary turning 50. He turned back to the gate and there she was. He still had that feeling in the pit of his stomach whenever he saw her; it had always been like that from the very first time. He had been cleaning the pipes of the organ high above the pews when he had heard voices

"Mary, can you take the Lilly of the Valley and put them in each vase, and I will go back to the car to get the Fuchsias and ferns". "Okay mum". Her mother had left her on her own, and Joe watched as the young girl scooped up the flowers and glided up the aisle as if a bride. Her measured steps walked with purpose and her head, bowed from side to side as if she was acknowledging her guests. He was mesmerised and looking back that was probably when he had fallen in love with her right there and then; her golden hair hung down her back and the smattering of freckles and rosebud smile lightened up her face, but it was later when he got to know her at school that her green eyes had totally won his heart. The green changed colour - warm green when she was happy; almost amber when angry and emerald when she loved.

Today, with her beautiful hair wound around her head which gave her a Grecian look, her skin fresh with minimal make up and her outfit flattering her body made him feel the luckiest man in the world. He watched as she walked toward him, laughing at something their 23-year-old daughter had said. Fran, the spitting image of her mother and had thrown back her red hair and laughed out loud, then stopped to watch as her father opened his arms which Mary glided into, fitting perfectly.

"Get a room" Fran said as she walked by laughing.

Joe and Mary walked up toward the marquee hand in hand and just as much in love as they had been for years. He bent to kiss her, "Happy birthday beautiful girl", and her eyes sparkled as she looked up at him. As they entered the marquee, the guests clapped and cheered, yelling Happy Birthday and the music started. Mary smiled and squeezed Joe's hand as they took to the dance floor and their quiet moment was gone with many of their guests clapping Joe on the back, so reminiscent of their wedding day.

Anyone looking back on that night would remember so many beautiful memories: the cake, the lights, the band that played music from the 50's and 60s with nearly everyone twisting and jiving the night away, even Doris Jones with her Zimmer frame or maybe it was the speech given by Fran and Tom that had them all laughing and most definitely no one would forget the beautiful sentiment that Joe, who normally wouldn't say boo to a goose, put into his speech which had ladies dabbing their beautifully made up eyes and men feeling ever so slightly uncomfortable that they themselves hadn't thought of that.

For Fran it wasn't just being back home with her family, which was always special or the warmth and love around her with people sharing the happiness. It wasn't seeing people sitting in groups or dancing on the green or standing at the make-shift bar chatting with the air filled with laughter.... No, it was something else, something she had heard. She first heard it when she and Tom had done their speech........that laugh, that throwback your head guffaw of a laugh. It was unmistakable. It was quite a blur when she looked back how quickly she had felt so comfortable in his arms, those blue eyes looking down at her. "Are you looking where you are going tonight, or do you need a hand?" he had said. His hand had stretched up and helped her off the stage, which, surprisingly, she took. He was tall, much taller than her." So, do you fancy a dance." he had said, and she, surprisingly, said yes. As he walked her to the dance area, her mum yelled out over the music, "Ah Robbie, I am so glad you could come, oh and thanks for popping into school Friday, I knew it wasn't broken but you never can tell........So you know my daughter then?" The conversation cut short as Joe whisked her away for a dance, her laughter floating in the air.

"No, but I hope to, and thank you for the invite." he called after her. Fran looked up at him and taking a deep breath said, "My name is Fran; Francesca actually- are you a plumber or something?" He laughed again and was just about to speak when he was clapped on the back by Fred, who owned and ran 'All Electrical and More' with his wife. Both had lived in Little Stockton for most of their lives and were a jolly pair. They always had a story to tell, and Gladys, Fred's wife, was known as a bit of a gossip, albeit a kind one. Robbie turned, getting his hand warmly shook vigorously, "Hope you are settling in Doc, my missus talks very highly of you".

"Yes thanks, I am and so glad she is feeling better".

"If you need anything you just give me a bell, that surgery needs a bit of sprucing up if you ask me" He nudged Robbie, "You see that is the More". When there was a look of confusion, Fred chuckled, and in doing so every part of him wobbled, 'All Electrical and More, that's the More! I can turn my hand to anything.......just give me a call, I'll see you right" and with that he merged into the crowd and was gone.

Fran was laughing as she spoke, embarrassed "Oh Robbie, I am sorry, I thought when mum said she knew it wasn't broken; I thought she meant a pipe or something". "How long have you been the village doctor, and when did Dr Crabbe leave"?

"Crabbe retired a month ago and I took up the position....I am here as a 6-month locum, from Australia... I have to say it's totally different. I like the whole village feel and being part of something that makes a difference. The whole village has been most welcoming....well nearly all; Doris Jones has given me a run for my money.........but she made me a cup of tea, when I fixed her cough and her light bulb issue, I think that may mean that I'm in." They both laughed. Doris Jones, Fran explained, was formidable in her day and truth be known was still a little scary. Robbie continued, "So where have you turned up from? I am sure I would have noticed you before."

Fran giggled "Well every now and again, I make it a habit of popping up in front of stray motor bikes".

"You gave me a right scare, one minute the road was clear and then...." said Robbie.

"And then I jumped in front of your bike. I am sorry Robbie".

They continued chatting comfortably as they walked over to the dance area. He learnt about her passion for textiles and the company that she worked for. She heard about Perth, in Western Australia, where he lived and she watched as his blue eyes twinkled when he spoke of the sun and beaches and no, there weren't kangaroos absolutely everywhere. He asked for a dance, which she accepted and when eventually they stopped for a breath, she felt comfortable walking hand in hand to the bar.

Although they found that they had nothing in common, they found everything to talk about and most of all they had fun. Fran hadn't felt like this for a long time.

It didn't go unnoticed. Mary and Joe nudged each other whilst others gave the all-knowing looks. Some of the single ladies felt rather peeved that so much attention was spent on one, but Robbie and Fran were oblivious. In the years to come, Fran not only remembered the party but could pin-point the exact moment that her world changed. The last dance was called, and Robbie put out his hand. Enveloped in his warm embrace, they danced as one and when he bent to kiss her, just lightly brushing against her lips with his....she knew she would never forget this night, not ever.

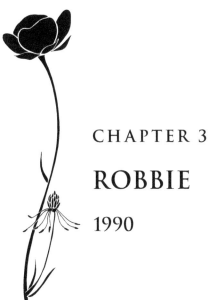

CHAPTER 3

ROBBIE

1990

Over the next few months Robbie and Fran saw a lot of each other and suddenly visits home became much more interesting and very more frequent. Robbie was looking after a stray; an excitable dog called Digger, named for obvious reasons. He had turned up at his doorstep, starving, and after the first feed, hadn't left his side. Digger now looked considerably better than when he first arrived, and they had taken him for long walks which often became journeys of discovery about each other. She knew he came from Australia and that like his father he had qualified as a doctor. He hadn't been sure at the time if that was want he truly wanted to do, but it had made his father so proud to have another doctor in the family. He told her that he had always wanted to travel, and he was envious that she had had the freedom to do so at such a young age. Now more travelled himself, they compared notes and endless stories around the various cultures that they had come across.

On another walk, he told her that he was an only child and that sadly after a short illness his mother had passed away and with his dad needing support, he had gone to university locally when most of his friends had gone abroad or interstate. He had gone very quiet after that particular conversation and Fran instinctively knew to give him that time, realising that they were both comfortable in each other's silence and walked hand in hand lost in thought. Another time she had spoken about her life in textiles and her job at McKenzie Taylor. Fran spoke earnestly and in depth when talking about her dreams of how one day she would break into the market with her own designs. She had a good eye for colour, often taking amazing photos of rustic flora; reds and orange often on the turn of brown that were found in the surrounding countryside, because, as she said, you never knew when it may be needed. He in turn had taken several good photos of Fran. Her beautiful russet curls that tumbled over her shoulders; rosy cheeks and her button nose which was home to a smattering of freckles. It was, however, her piercing green eyes that had first caught his attention, like her mother's they changed colour with her mood and danced merrily when telling a story or explaining the latest colour that inspired her.

They were both conscious that Robbie only had limited time left in Little Stockton and would be leaving for Europe in three months. The thought hovered over them, like a spectre of doom, with both doing their best to push it away. It was perhaps why the relationship moved so quickly to another level, and why, whilst laying in his arms, Fran found herself falling in love; a deep soul searching, heart fluttering type of love which held no boundaries.

Robbie caught himself catching his breath, when she suddenly looked up and smiled, her green eyes intense, bewitching.

Why now? He asked himself. There was no choice but to move surgeries as a new GP had been recruited, a family man looking to settle down. That had never been for him, he wanted freedom and travel, riding his bike, and living, working wherever he landed.

Why now? He would catch himself, lost in thought when he should have been working..........maybe he could look at a surgery near Fran........maybe that might be the answer, but did he want to be constricted by city life, but more importantly could he lose Fran?

He looked down at the mass of curls sprawled across his chest, her body warm and giving against his. They had made such passionate love earlier; he knew he loved her. God, why was life so complicated?

She murmured sleepily as he pulled her towards him, and eventually, in each other's arms, fell into a restless sleep.

It was strange how the powers of the universe worked.......in the end it was not a difficult choice to make, in the end the decision wasn't entirely theirs.

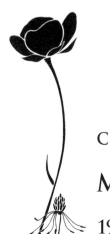

CHAPTER 4

MACKENZIE TAYLOR
1990

Running up the stairs, Fran knew she was late for the big weekly operations meeting. It had been so difficult leaving Robbie and getting out of bed. He hadn't wanted her to leave but she had had a train to catch. They had repeatedly promised that neither would get in the way of their individual careers, but it was getting harder. Robbie had stated on several occasions, just in passing, that it would be so much nicer if they could be together every day for breakfast, but of course that couldn't happen. Her phone vibrated. She cursed the big bag she carried and although she dug deep her phone seemed invisible. Eventually finding it between two files, she was relieved as she looked at the incoming message. It was from Robbie: "The bed is cold without you, come back and keep me warm...." Fran hurriedly wrote a message back. "I am far too important for that, but I do already miss you". It would be a long week she thought to herself as she ran up the long corridor to the meeting room.

The heavy glass door loomed in front with its gold italic "Mackenzie Taylor" embossed on the glass. As Fran hurried into the board room, ten heads turned, nervously to look at her, taking in her disheveled panic. Richard Taylor, CEO, slowly turned- "Thank you, Francesca, for taking the time to join us", his clipped South African tones emulating his displeasure. Her colleagues, feeling uncomfortable, put their heads down looking back at their laptop screens intently. The only person not fazed by Richard's obvious annoyance was Suri Lo, a rather ambitious member of staff, who sat there with a smirk on her face.

In the competitive market of interior design, Suri had come from a rival company and had been tipped for promotion from the second she arrived. However, it was Fran who had achieved the status of Senior Designer by majority vote, and it was well deserved for her colour matching and beautiful designs were winning admirers and requests for her particular rustic style had grown. At the time Suri had been outspoken in her competitiveness, saying that Fran's ideas were outdated as she favoured the more geometric block colour; this suited some, in particular the young up and coming yuppies that she associated with, but it wasn't to everyone's taste. It was, however, her lack of customer service which had been her downfall, with Fran's customers giving glowing reports. It was, therefore, no surprise that there was no love lost between them, and somehow Richard encouraged this competition between his top designers, saying that it gave them the edge that was needed.

"Sorry Richard," Fran stuttered cursing the red flush firing up on her cheeks. "I have the new tartan swatches that you asked me to pick up - traffic was awful"

Richard looked across at his young protégé, her hair escaping its tie with curls sneaking free every which way. He controlled a smile that twitched onto his lips; they couldn't be more different with Suri's sleek black hair, hanging straight down her back, never out of place, her Asian features beautiful which were expertly made up and her size 6 figure draped in contour fashion was second to none and then Francesca who had her own unique persona with bright inquisitive eyes, a beautiful smile and oh so much talent, willing to learn and bend with the trends that met her. Both brought that special something and yet that something had changed of late in Francesca and he made a mental note to have a chat with her; in this game they always had to be switched on....

The meeting went on for hours and as usual Richard asked for opinions, on the subject matter presented, targeting young interns as he had done with Fran when she first started.

It was an exciting project one which Fran's particular style of design had been asked for. The owner of a large recently renovated property in Oxford had engaged the firm to work their magic on the interior design; it was a massive undertaking with high profile for the company. There was a lot at stake, namely a huge revenue boost but it was their reputation, if not successful, that could see a company of this size destroyed. It was not going to happen, not on Richard Taylor's watch. Richard had his finger on the pulse every step of the way with every decision made. Today's discussion would show a mock-up of the house and the areas that were being worked on; a computer-generated plan that simulated the real thing - discussion of colours and textures, changed by a click of the mouse. Suri's team was in charge of the bathrooms with its gold taps and ornate and decorative design and the kitchen, sleek in black onyx; Fran's team was to design the main living areas throughout the house and the bedrooms. The owner had been specific in colour schemes but had allowed for creative license and that certain 'je ne sais quoi' that he knew they could provide. Textiles and materials were passed around the room to be examined, and ideas were bandied back and forth. Richard was scathing about some choices and enthused about others. The meeting finally ended with him saying that they had 30 days to get the final look ready to present adding quite menacingly that there was no room for error. Fran and Suri went back to their desks, Richard's words running around in their heads. The meeting had left them stressed and further meetings were called with their individual teams. As Fran had predicted earlier this indeed was going to be a long week, a hell of a long week.

ONE WEEK TO GO....

The following weeks were a blur, weekends home became a luxury and where possible, although begrudgingly, Robbie came up to London. They were both conscious that their time together was ebbing away, but Fran's workload had increased with days blurring into nights. Her stress levels were high and often tempers would turn into tears and she needed Robbie to soothe her when things got too much.

Suri, however, remained calm. There were no sudden dashes to the factory and certainly no long nights at work. Her team, however, looked fragmented and in a panic. Most were fresh out of university and none had worked at this level. With one week to go, a member from Suri's team sidled up behind Fran's messy desk- he stood back watching her as she discussed a fabric with a young intern called Alice; she was smiling and reassuring as she went through material swatches and congratulated her when the right colour jumped out. Fran had noticed him standing there and as she finished with Alice, she called him over.

"Are you spying on me, stealing my ideas?" she asked, slightly teasing him, smiling a winning smile. "It's Marcus, isn't it?" Fran signaled for him to come over, "What's up?"

Marcus looked behind him and then side to side before moving forward.

"It's ok. Come here Marcus, I don't bite". Then she paused, realizing the issue behind his reluctance, added more gently, "Suri isn't here, do you need her for something?" Seeing his reaction, she continued "Have you got a problem you would like some help with?"

It all came out hurriedly and without, it seemed, a breath. Suri seemed to be the problem and the interns working for her wanted out. They didn't want to let anyone down but the pressure they were under was ridiculous and..........

Marcus carried on talking until there was nothing more to say and Fran reassured him that it would be sorted, and that there was no need for anyone to leave.

Later, when Fran spoke with Richard, he knew it wasn't done in spite but with concern and he had told her that he would deal with the problem.

Later, with a scotch in hand, he thought about the conversation that he had had with Fran. He remembered how worried she had been and how she'd babbled on about how Suri was brilliant in her vision but that the interns, like she had been, were the future of designing and we needed to engage them, not scare them out of the profession. He had agreed and for once had no smart-ass answer. As she left, she turned back and smiled and mouthed the words "Thank you".

Fran's forward thinking and her passion had impressed him from the beginning, she had something that he hadn't seen for a long time. Her understanding of every thread, living through the colour, and believing in the essence of her creations was second to none. He had only seen it once before, a long time ago, - a student of his called Mackenzie James. She had put the light into the frame, the energy into design and made him love what he was doing. Years later, after she had qualified and he had stopped lecturing, they had met again, and their love of the industry developed into a love for each other. They married and set out on an adventure to create Mackenzie Taylor but that was history, painful, sad, history and now their company was well known, and growing. It was just a shame that she never got to see the success, her light had faded suddenly, without much notice; dying far too young and he was now alone, doing what she said he did best. He raised his glass to the ceiling, blew a kiss and poured himself another whiskey.

His thoughts reluctantly came back to the present- Suri! It wasn't anything that he hadn't seen before; an over competitive designer who would tread over anyone and anything to get noticed. Well not in his time and it would get sorted! Mackenzie Taylor had a good reputation as a training institute with a consistent waiting list of interns; first, second and third year, some of whom were chosen to stay on gaining a Mackenzie Taylor Scholarship. He wasn't prepared to lose his good standing and for what? Some smart arsed businesswoman, who, yes, had a future in design but who didn't understand the values of their business. Not on his watch, not at Mackenzie Taylor. His wife would never have stood for it.

During this deliberation, it crossed his mind that this deal meant everything to him -It could make or break the company and all that they had worked for. Why now! His focus should only be on this current deal, not some spoilt bitch that thought of only herself.......

Richard downed his drink and slammed his glass down. He would deal with it, he always did.

Two days before the presentation the teams were once again in the board room, facing Richard. Today everything needed to be in place with all details down to the last thread loaded into the program. There was excited chatter between them, with some very nervous expressions. To the interns, it wasn't just the upcoming design but the prospect of a scholarship, which would see them hold down a lucrative position; they had the right to feel nervous; there was a lot at stake.

Fran sat amongst her team, confident in her presentation. Her interns had worked hard and together she felt that they had captured the essence of the design required. Suri, however, walked in 5 minutes before the start, flicked her hair over her shoulder, removed her sunglasses and sat slightly to the side of her team, crossing one beautifully shoed foot across the other; her team's chatter unlike Fran's, stopped.

Richard cleared his throat and brought the room to attention –

"Welcome! Today either makes or breaks! You are either a worthy designer or not!

After your presentation any changes will be mine, which, must be completed by close of business today". They all knew it would be another late night for some.

The presentation commenced by zooming into the kitchen and Suri stood to speak. Richard put his hand out and waved it down indicating her to sit. She did, with one risen eyebrow and a look of surprise. Richard continued, turning to one of the interns, "Clare can you give us a run down on the fixtures and fittings used?" Clare flushed red and stood nervously but gave an accurate description, answering any questions fired at her. When she finished, she sat, feeling relieved. Next Marcus was asked to discuss surfaces and flooring, once again, although, stuttering and nervous, he gave an accurate account with Jason following up with the textiles and colour pallets. With very few alterations, relief was felt by all. However, they still had the three bathrooms to discuss; the ordeal wasn't over. Richard handled this in the same way, with Suri looking on showing obvious discomfort. After the second bathroom he asked the interns to sit and thanked them for their hard work. He informed them of the improvements he could see and that the innovations used were individually brilliant; there was very little to redo. Richard then turned to Suri, "Suri"! She turned slowly in her chair to look at him. "Please stand and carry on". He indicated the screen which showed the opulent master bathroom.

As Suri stood, the room fell silent. She felt strangely nervous, a phenomenon she was not used to. She had done this before, why, then, did she feel so uncomfortable? She looked at the screen and turned to the room, seeing expectant faces looking back at her. As she started to speak her mouth was strangely dry. "This is the master en-suite, you will see that we have continued with the same flooring but added tiles with gold fleck and a mosaic border with contrasting colour picked up in the towels, flannels and bathroom wear." All agreed that it was beautiful, stunning. She continued, "The bath is free standing, hand crafted and inspired in a contemporary style by the Italian designer....." she stopped; heads turned. She reached into her bag and got out a sheaf of notes- flicking through, looking for the designer's name. Richard looked at her interns, "Anybody?" Clare raised her hand, "AQANI - a new but up and coming designer. The contemporary lines are designed around the shape of the human, making it one of the most ergonomic designs of its time, the hidden jets activate on temperature and ...." "Thank you, Clare......Suri, the vanity, and mirrors please"!

Richard's voice was strangely cold, and his eyes bored into Suri's as she continued to frequently falter on brand names and the rationale behind each purchase. General discussion broke the atmosphere and sitting down gingerly, she indicated to Jason to describe the textiles used. The sass with which she had walked in with had gone.

All in all, the first part of the morning was successful. Richard liked what he saw and made very few changes. He dismissed Fran and the interns, giving them a break, telling them to be back in an hour. As Suri stood to leave, he indicated for her to sit, which she ignored and turning to face him, she crossed her arms and stared at him.

Richard spoke quietly, noting her defiance. "Suri, how do you think your interns went today"? She walked to the screen, and tapped it with her pen, "They did good, but they have a long way to go". Richard chuckled, "Suri they did more than good. They knew their stuff, but you gave them no credit for their hard work. Why was that"?

"Because they needed pushing to get to here" again she tapped the screen, "and I will continue to push them to be the best we can be".

"No Suri, you will not push them anymore"!

She turned towards him, her eyes flashing – "Do you think I got to where I am by being hugged and supported? Do you think I am good as I am because I was molly coddled? Huh? No, I was pushed and look at me now! I am the best you have got, and I get results". She sat down, crossing one long leg across the other, looking down and examining her beautifully manicured nails.

"Suri, you see this is the thing – there is more to interior design than the end result. To be successful, the designer, in this instance you, needs to feel every product, know it inside and out and not leave that to interns, who are still learning. The encouragement given and knowledge imparted should give them a feeling of team, instead you threw options at them and left them without the support that they needed. All in all, I am disgusted at your behaviour and I am not sure how I feel about that". Suri flinched at the harshness of his words, his clipped South African accent enforcing the coldness in his voice. Richard continued "Having said that, your interns, all of them, even Marcus, showed an amazing amount of knowledge and you should be proud of them! Your neglect of their needs does not fit Mackenzie Taylor's values, and that although I have no doubt that you are an excellent designer, you are not the sort of designer I want to work alongside." Suri's head pulled up sharply. "What are you saying Richard? You surely are not going to listen to some sniveling intern! My methods, in pushing them, obviously worked and yes, it was hard, but it isn't easy out there and there won't be someone holding their sweaty little hands. I wanted to prepare them". Suri had stood up and was facing Richard, her voice hardened and low as she spat the words out. Richard walked to the glass doors and held the handle, he turned as he spoke –

"It is with great regret that I must tell you that your services are no longer required and as you are within your six months' probation, your contract will cease immediately. Please grab your personal items and leave the building"!

"Richard, you cannot be serious! You won't manage this contract without me"!

"We will, I assure you! Your services are no longer required"!

Suri, slowly looked at Richard and, slipping on her sunglasses, turned without speaking and headed towards the exit. As she reached the heavy glass door, she spoke, her face so close to Richard's that he took a step back, "Richard Taylor, you will live to regret this! One day I will destroy you"! Leaving, she marched down the corridor towards her office, her heals clicking on the parquet floor and her long black hair swinging from side to side.

Richard took a deep breath, reached for the phone, and called security, "Please escort Miss Lo out of the building, she will not be returning".

Fran looked up as Suri swung into her office, box in her arms and a bag swung over her shoulders," I hope you are happy Fran! I hope you've got what you wanted"? It wasn't a question but more of a statement. "Sorry? Are you okay Suri"? but as Fran spoke, Leonard from Security loomed up behind Suri, and with her eyes narrowing she hissed "As if you didn't know"!

She watched as the slim, stylish Suri walked ahead of Leonard, his bulk and height obscuring most of her as they walked out of the designer floor. Fran sighed, she knew Suri was ruthless and there was bound to be trouble but checking her watch, Suri would have to wait.

Leaving her office, she walked towards the glass doors, took a deep breath and readied herself for her presentation.

An hour and half later Fran and her team, and the remainder of Suri's team completed their portfolio with precision but unlike the earlier discussions, Fran introduced each of her three interns and interacted with them on each and every detail. As with the earlier sessions, Richard liked the presentation, there were, as before, changes to be made but all in all – it was good, really good and Richard was impressed.

Of course, it was obvious that Suri was missing, and worried faces looked for reassurance. On closure, Richard informed them that the project would now be coordinated by Francesca and that all interns would work with her to complete the final details. Suri was not mentioned again but Fran smiled at Richard, nodding her head towards him in acceptance of his offer and acknowledging the difficult decision that he had made.

In return he inclined his head toward her and then leaving the room, she watched as he strode down the corridor to his office.

The excitement in the room was palpable and ideas were being thrown between the teams, this was going to be fun, and Francesca was ready for the challenge.

CHAPTER 5

MR. MAUNG CHOO
1990

Two days later at 9 am all were back in the board room. The atmosphere was tense, there was no chatter this time and anxiety had no noise.

At 09.15 Richard walked in with Mr. Maung Choo and his wife, Mo Mo Choo. Whereas Mr. Choo was round and smiling nodding at conversation made by Richard, Mrs. Choo was tiny, not even coming up to her husband's shoulder, her face like stone. Francesca noticed that although pale, she was exquisitely made up with her lips drawn in and painted bright red. Mrs. Choo looked around the room with distaste, her eyebrows raised, giving her a haughty look and took the chair offered to her. When introduced to Francesca, she did not take her proffered hand, instead turned her head to look at her husband, who moved to her side. Once both were seated, Richard gave an opening introduction. The room was silent as his words resonated around the conference room

The blinds were closed and in the dim light the screen was slowly lowered adding to the tense atmosphere. Fran felt an uneasiness; a feeling of nausea and her skin felt clammy. She had done presentations before, but this was the biggest and meant so much for the company. She had studied Suri's plans all night and felt that the interns had it in hand, but just in case they faltered she needed to be there and support them. What if they didn't like any of it! What if all their hard work had been a waste of time; the cost wasn't worth thinking about!

She tried to steady her nerves by thinking of something else and thought of Robbie.

Robbie whom she hadn't heard from for two days and realised that the nerves in the pit of her stomach were not only because of the presentation, but more the uneasy feeling that something had changed, and it had haunted her. It was so unlike him. Perhaps he knew she would only give the hurried one-word answers that he'd been getting from her lately. Perhaps he felt it better to leave her alone, but a few words of encouragement would have been nice, or maybe some flowers for good luck; a call or something! Fran spoke sternly to herself, "Not now Fran, keep it together Fran" but the niggling feeling hadn't stopped nor had the nausea. She noticed that from her seat how straight-backed Mrs. Choo was sitting, and how there was little or no interaction between her and her husband. She couldn't see facial reactions or expressions and apart from an occasional slight lean in when discussing something-there was nothing to hold on to. She turned to the teams around her and made a thumbs up sign, mouthing "We've got this" and then she saw Richard, his jaw clenched, one eyebrow raised and pallor to his face. He nodded at her, as if to tell her they were starting the presentation and somehow, she got up to speak. Each of the interns presented as they had done before, but with clearer determination. Fran linked the areas together with beautiful commentary and Richard noticed how her smile touched her lips as she herself explored the possibilities as if seeing them for the first time. They presented from behind - allowing the full impact of the plans to ebb and flow in front on the large screen; Fran was rather pleased about that, but she still felt unsteady. She cursed inwardly that she should have eaten, but then this morning she hadn't felt well or maybe it was just the lack of sleep!

She came out of her thoughts just in time to hear Jason talking about the textiles and count thread of the towels, the hand-made ceramic bathroom ware made by a local potter and the beautiful gold fleck picked out throughout. It was almost lyrical the way he spoke, and Fran could not have been more proud - he would, one day, be a great designer. She rounded up the first half of the presentation with gratitude for their time, and then Richard ushered Mr. and Mrs. Choo out of the room for morning tea; Mr. Choo smiling and nodding and Mrs. Choo still stony faced. There was no indication whether they had liked it or not and the team held their breath as they exited.

There was 40 minutes to kill before the second half and although confident in the product, Fran flicked furiously through the slides, making sure nothing untoward would happen.

The noise of relief erupted in the room "I thought I was going to die!"; "Did you hear me muck up the designer's name, can you believe it?" "You were so cool!" "What do you think, did they like or not like?"; "Who bloody knows". It went round and round, with the noise escalating. Fran stood "Guys, you did really well but keep it focused and real - we still have the longer session to go, and I need the same intensity". Seeing some frowns, she added, "Suri would have been proud of you all, as am I, now go - get some air! See you back no later than a quarter to, ok!" They filed out, leaving Fran alone with her thoughts.

What was wrong with her? She felt disconnected and focus was required. Something felt so wrong and although she had checked her messages prior to the meeting, they had not brought her the reassurance she was looking for. There had been one from procurement; one from her mum, wishing her well, and one from her brother, Tom. She pictured him holding her new niece in his strong arms. Little Katie was funny and so sweet, which made her smile, but there was nothing from Robbie. Her niggling worry took flight again and with it the nausea grew stronger. Grabbing her bag, she made a dash for the door, reaching the toilet just in time. She sat on the floor in the cubicle cold and shivering and checking her watch she saw that there was only 20 minutes left before the presentation commenced again. Gingerly she stood up and walked to the basin, where she splashed her face. Looking up she saw her reflection in the mirror and instead of the happy glow that should have been there, she saw dark rings circling her eyes and clammy pale skin. The nausea her hit her again like a wave and she stood holding onto the sink, taking deep breaths, until she felt slightly better. Fran washed he face again, and patted it dry with a paper towel drying her face and neck. She wiped the pander bear mascara from around her eyes and adjusted her lipstick. Her thick curls had stuck to her face and looked lank without its usual bounce and so she brushed it back into a hair tie at the nape of her neck. The face looking back mocked her, as if to say, come on, think, you know what it is! Fran looked back. "No, it can't be"! In a panic she urgently pulled out her diary and checking the little squares allocated to each day she counted back the days. "No! No! No!" She flicked through the little book, flicking pages backwards and forwards but there was no red P. Maybe, she told herself, she had forgotten but she knew she hadn't…. "Oh God"! Her head hung down over the sink, her thoughts lost. She looked up at the mirror and spoke to her reflection "Now what the hell am I…………." But that was a conversation she was to have another day as Alice crashed through the door. "Fran, we're on"!

Fran dragged herself back into reality and somehow delivered a hell of a presentation using her interns as before. As she came to an end Mr. Choo stood and turned. He walked towards Fran with purpose and put out his hand. Fran reciprocated.

"We are very honored to have you design our home, we thank you".

He then turned to his wife who joined him as they left the room, Fran couldn't be sure, but a slight smile had touched Mrs. Choo's lips as her head nodded towards her. Richard turned on his heels and followed them out but as he ushered Mr. and Mrs. Choo out of the door, he turned back and gave a thumbs up and a wink at Fran.

Once again, the room erupted, and this time Fran joined in.

It seemed ages before Richard returned. He told them there were some structural changes that needed to be made by the architects whom they had met with yesterday, but the Choo's were satisfied overall with not one, but all the interior designs shown that day.

Mr. Choo had been happy to leave his whole account with Mackenzie Taylor and Richard told them that the contracts were signed with a hefty deposit negotiated. The cheers erupted and everyone was ecstatic, particularly when Richard gave them all the Friday and Monday off.

No one noticed as Fran left the room, picking up pace down the corridor, except Richard. That chat was long overdue but today the firm had the backing of the Choo Dynasty and he couldn't ask for more.

CHAPTER 6

WHAT MEMORIES ARE MADE OF

2019

It was still raining but Fran was finally home. She entered the cottage and immediately felt her anxiety decrease. She did not like the drive at the best of times but today was not a good day.

A wet nose and wagging tail greeted her, and although it had only been for a day, he had missed her and needed immediate attention. She tousled the top of his head and two loving brown eyes looked up at her as she said his name.

Rupert, her chocolate Labrador was great company and with his unconditional love, she could be herself. He didn't judge her or ask questions other than "when's dinner or are we going for a walk?" It was easy and just for once life became uncomplicated, normal.

Walking through from the garage, she listened. It was quiet apart from the ticking of the grandfather clock and the hum of the fridge. Dumping her shopping at her feet, she flicked on the light and then the kettle. It was the same routine every day. It was better that way.

Her home, Holly Cottage, was situated on the outskirts of Little Stockton, about 20 minutes from her parents' house, where her 80-year-old father lived. Mostly Fran worked from home in a large workshop at the back of her property but once a week she would travel the hour and half to London to make a delivery or pick up more material. The local suppliers all knew her, and she had several chosen contacts who she felt comfortable with.

It was a quiet life, and that suited her. She didn't ask for much, just to get on with life the best way she could. Walking through her house to the large master bedroom at the back, she continued her routine: blowing a kiss at the photos along the way and touching the handle of her door three times. Her feet stepped over the threshold and peace and normality returned. The room was beautifully designed and with calming colours. Mint green and rose infused throughout with different shades in damask, wool, and silk. Matching cushions and throws were strewn onto the bed and the small settee in the corner of the room. Fran dropped her bag, and did what she always did, walked in a circle, touching each item and then went to the small dresser, sitting down on the matching stool. She unclipped her earrings and brushed her hair with long strong strokes, shaking out her red curls, now sprinkled with grey. Staring into the mirror she noticed dark circles of tiredness around ~~her eyes and~~ gently touched the lines which indicated her maturity. Her undeniably green eyes stared straight back at her; piercingly green, which gave her an impish look. When she smiled, they twinkled, sparkling with flecks of light but that smile… that smile was rare these days.

With a sigh, she stood. There were still boxes to get out of her car; it was all too difficult… "Breath" she told herself, "just breath".

An hour later, with her parcels safely on the table, she started to open the many boxes. It was, as it always had been, the most anticipated and thrilling part of her day. She breathed in the smell of the gold lined paper as the lid of the pink and white candy-striped box came loose. The lid, a work of art itself, slid on to the table. She looked at it, taking in the velvet gold initials embossed on the top, so familiar, a constant reminder of the life she had lived and her life as it now was. She traced her finger over the slightly raised letters - the M and T entwined like two lovers who could not separate.

To most the letters symbolised the international business that Richard Taylor had built up over the last 30 years but to those who knew his story, it meant so much more.

Fran drifted off to a different place, a memory returning, and found herself walking, nearly running down the corridor, which led from the famous boardroom of Mackenzie Taylor. Celebrations were in full swing having just procured a huge lucrative account, which had changed the face of the business, putting them on the Interior Designer radar. Although exhilarated, the nausea that had been troubling her all day was relentless. She had left the room, and looking back saw Richard looking directly at her, questioning silently her exit.

That night, on her way home, she popped into the local chemist. She already knew what the result would be. The habit of the last 12 years or so was not easily broken and she had not put the tell-tale red P into her a diary. The thought acted like a trigger and bile sprung up into her mouth. She stopped, leaning against a wall, breathing hard. She righted herself and paid for her goods. She had no idea how she got out of the shop and onto the bus to take her home, but she found herself sitting nervously on the edge of the bath in her little flat, waiting for a sign. She had tried to ring Robbie more than once that day and had been dismayed that he had not returned any calls or messages. There were, however, several messages on the answering machine from her mum; and one from her brother.

15:00 "Hello love, I expect you are busy, you always are, but could you give me a call when you are free?"

15:08 "It's me again.....I hope all went well, I am sure it did, all that hard work. I said to your dad, I get worried about you, but he says you are fine......give me a call"

16:23 "Ring me love, ok"

16:30 "Hi sis, mum said you had a huge presentation today, hope it went well. Katie, say hello to Auntie Fran." Some gurgling baby sounds followed, making her smile. "See you Sunday... oh and Digger is with us... so don't worry."

Why had her brother got Digger?

17:10 "It's mum again, and dad." "Can you call now love. We need to speak to you, it's about Robbie."

"Mary, you'll scare her." Dad again, "Frannie, it's really nothing to worry about but do call."

It was 18:03. She had been so busy of late; she hadn't had time for anyone and now hearing these messages she was worried........ Robbie! Panic began to rise, something was wrong! That damn bike!

There had been a few other calls left in the morning and one message that she couldn't really hear with a lot of background noise and so couldn't be bothered to listen to. She rang her mum's number and felt relief when she heard her familiar voice. "Hello love, you all finished for the day?"

"Mum what's happened? Where's Robbie, I can't get hold of him".

"Oh, it's been dreadful here, everything happened so quickly and ....." Fran cut her off. "Mum!"

"He tried to call you last night, but he said you weren't listening, being interrupted all the time, and you told him you would ring back. Did you? No of course you didn't. He said he had left you a message this morning, but he didn't want to upset you before the presentation, so he didn't try again - and it was such a shock to your dad and me... ."

"Please mum just tell me what's happened." Fran's voice was now verging on tears. "Just tell me please!"

"I am sorry love, but he has gone back to Australia. He left this morning....He rang dad as he was desperate to talk to you, but time was ticking, and he had to leave."

Fran went quiet, the nausea was creeping up again and she felt herself sink to the floor knocking the little test kit back into the bath. She was crying now, why hadn't she made the time for him....

"You their love? … Frannie?"

"Yes mum.... here..., but why what happened? We still had two months left....why?" Her voice had become quite shrill and as her mother spoke, her tears began to fall.

"You see Robbie's dad had had a massive heart attack and had to be admitted to a hospital in Perth, that's in Australia. It was touch and go and Robbie being his next of kin was needed immediately. He tried to tell you but there had not been a lot of time, what with getting his passport and ticket organised, and he pretty much left as soon as he could. In the end he asked us to tell you and that he would call when he got to Australia."

There was a pause, it was silent…

"Fran, are you alright, love"?

When there was no more to say, Mary hung up. Fran sat on the cold bathroom floor, head pounding and the realization that Robbie had gone!... She hadn't even said goodbye......

She thought back to the failed conversation the night before. She had still been at work and it had been late. With the hive of activity around her and with the many interruptions, she hadn't listened! She hadn't bloody listened! She couldn't even remember saying she loved him! She had been so distracted that she couldn't remember any of what he had tried to say. The whole team relied on her, they had needed her.....Fuck, fuck, fuck, Robbie had needed her.

Tears cascaded down her cheeks. She rolled into a ball holding on to her tummy tightly. Rocking slightly, she felt the pain of her loss consuming her. The phone rang. Grabbing it she leapt up, "Robbie?" But how could it be, he was somewhere over an ocean somewhere…

Richard's familiar voice came over the phone. "Are you okay? You left in a hurry. We are heading downtown to Henry's for a bite to eat, to celebrate", When there was no reply, he added "Are you coming - shall I pick you up?"

Fran took a deep breath and, trying to sound normal but failing, replied "Sorry Richard, I think I've eaten something that doesn't agree with me…feeling really off…will miss this one… but …but well done all of you", and with that she hung up. A sudden mad dash to the toilet took away the right to think anymore; she hung on to the bowl, her head, cooled by the porcelain as she gave in to the nausea, remaining that way on and off for the rest of the night.

The kit, forgotten, lay in the bottom of the bath and there it was, the pink cross evident. When Fran finally picked it up, after her shower, she already knew what the result would be and threw it angrily into the bin. Now what? She felt alone and scared.

Crawling into bed, she lay there, eyes wide open. Half of her believed that Robbie would come back, that this baby would cement the foundations of their love but the other half…it wasn't worth thinking about, she literally couldn't bear it. She was so tired, but something was niggling at her. She mulled over the conversation that she had had with her mum…words so many words…shit! What was it …? "He said he had left you a message on the answering machine this morning". Fran jumped out of bed and switched on the answer machine. She pressed the button going through all the messages until she reached it. This time she strained to listen through the inaudible distortion and then suddenly:

"Hi Frannie, my dad's ill, actually very ill. I am at Heathrow now. I tried to tell you last night but...and then this morning you didn't pick up. It is all a bit surreal, and I have been seriously busy sorting things. The keys for the house and surgery are with your parents and another doctor is coming Monday, so it's closed until then. Oh, and Digger, he's with you brother. The thing is I don't know what will happen." Here she heard his voice break... "I am all he's got, you see, babe...I will call you when I land." It went quiet, and Fran stared at the phone, willing for more. Then his voice, quieter and not so rushed. "It's like this Bean, I love you, you will never know how much I love you...I will find a way - I promise! Got to go they are calling the flight.....love you Bean....Shit! Nearly forgot! How did it go- bet it was brilliant! Bye.... gotta go.....love you."

Fran continued to stare at the phone, she wanted to hear more. She played the message again and again, tears falling, pain overwhelming her. Bean, a nickname he had given her when on a cold windy day, she had worn a bobble hat to keep warm. She could hear his deep voice mocking her. "Love the Beanie," he had said, and then seeing her confused expression he told her it was one of the many Australian colloquialisms used.

The name had stuck...............she loved the name.

Rupert barked. He was hungry and demanded attention, the sudden noise pulled her back to reality. She looked down at the coloured material that she had purchased and hurriedly removed the boxes that had evoked so many memories... .

The smell from the oven indicated that Mrs. Thompson had been in to put the dinner on earlier and it was nearly ready, and she fed Rupert, who greedily ate the contents of his bowl. Two headlights appeared through the window and she poured two glasses of wine. Good timing. He was here!

CHAPTER 7

LIFE GOES ON

1991

When Fran told Richard that she was pregnant, his initial reaction wasn't the best....

"Great timing," he had said. "There is a lot on at the moment and it's so busy." But then seeing her worried expression he managed a reassuring smile. She reminded him that they were not living in the dark ages and that she had two hands and a heartbeat and eventually he relaxed. He didn't say anything when she told him that Robbie wasn't in the picture and although she was smiling, he could see the pain in her eyes. He had heard that Robbie had gone back to Australia, but he didn't like to ask what had happened. What he said and what he thought were two different things, but he knew for sure that he would look out for her.

Now five months later, Fran glowed; her smile was bright and in Richard's eyes, was more beautiful than ever. She worked just as hard if not harder as Mackenzie Taylor was certainly growing, and with it came more responsibility. Clare, the young intern, was now permanent as were others, having finished all their studies which was a great help.

Richard knew he would be lost without Fran and had discussed the possibility of her working from home whilst on maternity leave, she had jumped at the chance but realised her flat in London was too small and as much as she loved her walk to work and being so close, she didn't want to bring a baby up in the city. With her parents' help she found a small cottage on the outskirts of Little Stockton; it was slightly run down but nothing that couldn't be fixed, and her dad promised he would help. It was perfectly liveable and more importantly it had a great workshop space at the back.

She went to Richard for advice as to whether she should buy it, and with thumbs up it was decided that it was a great investment. Richard offered to pay for all the renovations for the workshop, as after all she would be working for the company, and although Fran had argued it was eventually agreed on and Richard set about renovating a rundown space into a workshop. As a surprise, he added a rocking chair for when the baby arrived.

A week after he had left, he finally phoned, apologising for not calling before but that it had been a terribly upsetting time and so very hectic. He had spent days and nights beside his father's bed who was still unconscious. He said he would be back soon but wasn't entirely sure when.

When he told her that he loved her and missed her, they were the words she needed to hear, and they gave her some hope that he would return.

Then after a month of sporadic calls, his father had passed away. There was a funeral to arrange and the estate to deal with. Robbie told her he had started working at a local medical centre on a six-month contract but that when it was all over, he would be back. He missed her terribly, he said. But to Fran, something wasn't quite right, and she felt that he was just saying words that she needed to hear and that he had in fact settled back into his former life far too comfortably.

He hoped she understood but it was a difficult and busy time for him and perhaps there would be a chance of her coming out to Perth to join him. "Bean I miss you." he had pleaded.

Of course, she couldn't. She was extremely busy at work and 12 weeks into her pregnancy still feeling so very sick and totally exhausted. Her workload had expanded and now was not the right time. She didn't actually know why she was making all these excuses, or why she hadn't told Robbie about the baby, but she knew at this time, she couldn't.

However, when the scan showed a healthy embryo, Mary insisted that Robbie had the right to know. Fran made up her mind to tell him, but the phone calls had become fewer and with the time difference, more difficult. Eventually when she tried to call the number the operator told her that the number was no longer connected and with that, a dead end, with no means to find him.

Richard after the initial shock had been most attentive and caring, which was surprising but lovely all the same. Over coffee she spoke to him about the "Robbie situation" as she called it and asked him what she should do. Richard had given her a strange look and said that her parents were right. Robbie had a right to know but she should be prepared to be let down. The obvious fact was that Robbie, had very clearly gone back to his life in Australia and although he had loved her, which she agreed was probable, he had, after all, only been in England for a very short time - four months wasn't it? It had seemed so much longer to Fran and seeing her expression, he chose his words carefully. "Maybe Fran, you need to move on, but do tell him first, so there are no skeletons in either of your cupboards." "Move on? I look like a bloody whale, and in four months I will have a baby, who the hell would have me then?"

"Just ring him Fran!"

"I will, tonight, promise." And with that she stood and gave Richard a winning smile, and just as she left his office, she made a whale like pose and putting her hand on her hip said, "Who wouldn't want this?" Laughing she left.

He watched her walk down to her office, chatting with Justin as he showed her some material and calling Claire over for her opinion. God he was going to miss her. Who would want her? He wanted her and it took all his restraint not to tell her. He slipped on his suit jacket. He needed to get out and think.

The next day at midday Fran sat in her office, her mind on anything but work and jumped as the phone started to ring. Picking up the receiver she was surprised to hear Robbie's familiar voice.

Hello Bean, sorry I haven't called of late; You know how it is, life runs away with you and I have been incredibly busy. What are you up to, busy building Richard's business for him?"

She interrupted, it always annoyed her when he spoke in such a derogatory manner about Richard. "Robbie, I wanted to phone you I have something I need to speak to you about, but it seems your phone has been disconnected."

"Are yes, I meant to tell you about that. After dad passed away, we were getting all these calls and so I changed the number. What is it?"

"What is what?"

"What did you want to speak to me about?"

"Hang on, who is we? Anyway, never mind, you see it's quite obvious that you are not coming back and what we had, although magical, I now realise was simply a holiday type romance, do you agree? .....And I am okay with that but there is ......"

Robbie interrupted her. "Oh god that is a relief.... I will always love you Bean and if dad hadn't well died....I would probably still be with you but, you see things change and I've met someone!" He paused and it went very quiet. "Bean? I am sorry; I should have told you sooner." Still Fran said nothing. Filling the silence Robbie continued. "For ages I kept thinking how or when I would come back and truthfully, I always imagined our lives together. You know the quintessential cottage, Digger, how is he by the way? Kids and all that but life threw a curve ball.........shit... I am sorry! Bean, talk to me......."

Fran stared at the receiver. What now?

"I am very happy for you" she said. Robbie let out an audible sigh of relief. "Digger is fine and still as mad; he lives with Tom and Nancy.

"I must call them, I felt so bad not coming back, and just leaving him there".

"Robbie, please listen to me! There is a reason why I called.....there is something I need to tell you......apparently you have a right to know......I'm, we're pregnant.......and the baby is due at the end of May......It seems you didn't completely leave Little Stockton after all."

It was Robbie's turn to go quiet, and not knowing what to say, Fran said nothing either.......

"Are you sure?"

Fran looked down at the ever-increasing bump and put a protective hand on her stomach. "Oh yes, quite sure and before you ask, I am quite sure who the father is too."

She wanted to scream out that unlike him she had stayed loyalty and faithful, but she didn't.

"Shit.......how did that happen?"

"Well, you're the doctor. One would hope you would know. Look, mum and dad felt you had a right to know but I want you to know that I don't need any help. Actually, I don't need anything at all but if you like I will let you know when it is born but I guess that is up to you....."

"Shit Bean, that's all I needed."

"What? It's not actually that much fun for me either".

"No, I mean, it's a shock and well, there's Vanessa to think of..."

Fran threw the phone down. She had a name! Anger and tears welled up; she hadn't wanted to tell him and now, it seemed, he didn't even care. She could and would do this alone!

She put her head in her hands and sobbed. He had always been so loving; they had spoken about marriage and children but now this betrayal. God, she had loved him so very much and this was just too much to bear......

She was so distraught that she didn't hear Richard walk into her office, "Fran?" She sat up not caring what she looked like. Seeing the concern on Richard's face, her tears fell again, and she grabbed for a tissue. "Sorry but...." the words wouldn't come out.

Richard put out his hand. "Come on, let's get out of here - you need air and a shoulder."

Gratefully she stood up, and because she was a bit wobbly on her feet, he steadied her putting an arm around her waist. She leant into his arm and felt his warm body against hers and they walked out of the office. She didn't care what people thought and she realised that she **didn't** feel awkward at all. In fact, she felt quite comfortable. Fran sighed, under any other circumstances this might have been the start of something beautiful, but instead she was 5 months pregnant, her ankles were swollen, she had red eyes with her makeup smeared god only knew where and she had just been unceremoniously dumped. The tears fell again.....

When they reached outside Richard opened the door of his car. "Robbie?" he asked. "Vanessa," she replied. He gave her a quizzical look, jumped in and they drove off whilst she explained between sobs the whole pitiful story.

CHAPTER 8

WELCOME EMILY GRACE

1991

Rose cottage was a hive of activity and with the workshop up and running Mackenzie Taylor had come to Fran, who now worked from home. Today Claire and the team had come for a meeting, bringing all sorts of textiles, swatches and ideas accompanied by excited chatter. They had just been awarded a new account for an ultra-modern hair salon which was opening quite near to the city office. The meeting with the owner, Chris Divine, had gone really well with only a few differences of opinions, namely colour schemes, which could be easily altered but on the whole everyone involved seemed on the same page. Ideas were prolific and Fran sat back listening and enjoying the teamwork that she had created. Discussions around the three-dimensional graphic designs, the colour palette, extreme but fabulous, and the metallic light fittings, which were extortionately expensive, created an end result which was stunning.

The meeting clarified some areas of doubt, ironing out changes that Mr. Devine, "simply must have". It was the last meeting Fran would be involved in for some time and reluctantly, as it came to a close, she realised that she would have to not only say goodbye to this project but also to her protégés until she returned.

As she awkwardly stood up, signifying the close of the meeting, Claire took her hand. "Just before we go Fran can you do us a favour please?" "Yes of course," she said. Justin stepped forward and quietly added, "Would you mind shutting your eyes?". Fran did so, giggling as Justin tied a piece of material around her eyes. He then asked her to take a step forward. She was guided out of the workshop between Justin and Claire and across the small path to the main house. She couldn't see anything and stumbled slightly but trusted those around her who were stifling giggles and whispers. Inside her home the familiar smells permeated her senses, and she was asked to sit. She could hear something being dragged across the floor and placed in front of her. She was then told to keep her eyes shut as the blindfold was removed. A collective shout of "Open" rung in her ears and she opened her eyes seeing in the middle of the floor a beautiful Victorian cradle with a lace canopy and quilted bedding. A handmade mobile hung from the peak and the soft cashmere blankets blended beautifully in soft aqua and lemon. Standing awkwardly next to it was Richard, holding a huge bouquet of flowers and everyone cheered and clapped. Fran's hands flew up to her face and tears sprang to her eyes. Their generosity overwhelmed her "I....I...don't know what to say" and with that she dissolved into tears. Claire took her hand and spoke "Fran, you have done so much for all of us and the company, we just wanted to say thank you." Others joined in with their own gratitude. Looking around the room at their faces, she saw the love shining from their eyes and her own filled with tears again. She would miss the energy of her team and when she really thought about it, she was quite terrified of going on alone without the refuge of work. Her eyes rested on Richard, and she smiled, he had been a constant figure in her life since being abandoned by Robbie, and she knew he could be relied on for help for he had offered it more than once. He had been brilliantly supportive over the last few weeks, helping with the set up of her work from home. He often stayed the night in the spare room having had one too many wines at dinner and nothing had been too much trouble. Fran looked affectionately at him. It occurred to her that maybe if it had been another time she, they might have made a go of it but that wasn't worth thinking about now.

He was looking intently at her, smiling at her blushing cheeks. She was stunning with a radiance that engulfed both inside and out. He knew that he was in love with her, but she had been so independent, and he was sure she only saw him as a friend. He put out his hand to her and she gratefully took it. "You look done in, my love." She agreed as Richard put a protective arm around her, and she leant in feeling at ease and safe. He guided her to a chair, and she sat down, hands on belly and leaning back. She was tired and felt the baby shift and gasped as it took her breath away. She could hear Richard taking charge, quietly and efficiently moving people out of the cottage, each blowing Fran a kiss as they left, their chatter followed them to various cars and there in the beautiful silence she at last relaxed. It had been lovely seeing everyone but in the sanctuary of her own home, an overwhelming tiredness hit her, and she slipped into a peaceful sleep. One hand on her protruding belly and the other above her head.

When she woke an hour later, she could smell cooking from her kitchen. It permeated through the house and carefully she stood and wandered through. Totally engrossed in pots and pans and listening to classical music, Richard stood stirring a pot and unaware of Fran's presence, he lifted his hands and conducted a mythical orchestra, dripping sauce all over the oven top. He then swirled an imaginary partner round the kitchen table until he came face to face with a bemused Fran. Covered with embarrassment he made an attempt to stop his dance but, instead, he stumbled into her arms as she collapsed against him in fits of laughter. Full of embarrassment, he adjusted himself, standing upright and awkwardly spoke" You're awake then?"

"Well obviously.....actually we both are." She indicated to her extended tummy. "What are you doing?"

"I thought I would make you dinner, but I have made so much you may have to eat it for weeks" he smiled a lopsided grin and shrugged his shoulders "I am quite good at cooking."

"I'm sure you are, thank you, I really couldn't have faced it tonight". Smiling she took a seat at the kitchen table. He gave her that boyish grin again and turned to continue stirring. She watched him and once again, under different circumstances, realised that this could have been a thing, whatever "this" was. The baby shifted again, and Fran gasped, there was still 3 weeks to go but tonight there had been quite a lot of sharp pains. She made a note to speak with her obstetrician in the morning. She breathed deeply and put a protective hand over her child. Her child, it seemed so odd, but already there was a bond, and she the protective mother.

Richard turned and saw that Fran had shown some discomfort. "You ok?"

"I think so". She said, not entirely sure.

"Do you have much to do with Robbie, these days?" he asked and watched as she formulated her answer. He loved the way she rubbed her nose, when thinking and then picking up a titian lock of hair she twisted it as she spoke. "Not really. His girlfriend knows about the baby but it's the elephant in the room really. I said that I would let him know when the time comes. It's quite amicable, I suppose"

"Fran, I have to ask, do you...um…"

"Do I what? Do I miss him? Do I still love him?" she snapped.

Richard started to apologies; it hadn't gone how he had wanted it to. "Sorry, I shouldn't have, it's just that........."

"No, Richard, you shouldn't. Let's just say whatever was there, isn't anymore, apart from this." She pointed to her stomach. Tears coursed down her face and Richard rushed over to her and put his strong arms around her shoulders.

"I am sorry, so sorry" he rocked her into him. "It's just that..." He took a deep breath.

Fran turned to look up at him. He towered above her as he looked into her beautiful eyes. "It's just that I love you. I want to take care of you….. I always have."

For a moment all was quiet. Fran searched his face but only saw love, "But the baby".

"Fran, the baby will not know any difference. We can bring this little bundle into the world together…I love you Fran and maybe, in time, you could learn to love me too…….what do you think?"

Fran awkwardly stood. It was an answer to her current situation and in her own way she loved Richard but was it the right decision at this vulnerable time?

Staring at each other across the table, she saw Richard's desperate expression…….

"Say something, please Fran!"

"I think……" A spasm of pain crossed her again and she bent over. "I think…." she gasped and held onto the table tightly "my waters have just broken".

Dinner forgotten, Richard turned off the gas, washed his hands, expertly picked up her packed bag and got her into the car.

One way or another, he would take care of them both.

Through the next nine long hours, Richard held her hand, marveling at her strength. He left to phone her parents, and came straight back to her, mopping her brow and giving her ice to suck on. She held him tight when the pain got too much and he spoke softly to her, loving her more.

He told her over and over that she could do this and that he loved her. Then there was one big push and the nurse said, "Daddy the head is crowning, your baby is coming…." He looked down at Fran, and she smiled a weak smile and nodded her head. He watched at this miracle and the little girl came tumbling into the world. The nurse put her onto Fran's chest, "You have a little girl". Emily Grace was there and the bond between baby and mother was instant. She looked proudly up at Richard, who had tears in his eyes, and she knew that this was her family- The Three Musketeers.

CHAPTER 9

MEMORIES

2019

Hearing the TV on in the other room, she decided that tonight she would not join him, but instead go into the workshop to look at the fabrics she had brought back from the city. She called out, knowing it wouldn't be acknowledged. "Going into the Workshop" but there was, as she had surmised, no reply. He was probably asleep. He'd been working far too hard. Fran walked through to the back door which led to the workshop. As she did she caught sight of herself in the mirror- a tired face stared back at her, one that she didn't recognize as her own reflection. Her hand ran through her hair; silver mixed with her titian curls; green eyes dulled with pain which no longer danced and her skin pale and taut. She looked older than her years, but it was hardly surprising. She ran a finger down the long scar that ran from her forehead to her chin which had narrowly missed her eye; she was still a beautiful woman, but she no longer saw it and sighing, slowly turned away. The counsellor said it would take time. How long for God's sake! Again, tears stung her eyes and she angrily slammed out of the kitchen and walked up the joining path that led to the workshop.

Just walking through the doors decreased her mounting anxieties and slowed her breathing. Here she felt no aggravation only peace.

Half opened boxes lie open on the table and Fran started to sort the contents. Nestled in the tissue paper were layers of pink and purple taffeta which rustled as Fran ran her fingers over the crisp, smooth weave. It didn't matter how many times she did it, the feeling was still the same, sending thrills throughout her body. It had always been that way, whether smooth or rough, luxurious or otherwise. Textiles were in her blood. She lifted the samples up to the window, twisting and turning them to into the light. The colours blended perfectly and were exactly what she had in mind. As she stared up at them, a memory of years ago was evoked and once again she was lost in a time …

1992

The balloons, tied to the gate, bobbed in the summer breeze, dancing colours of pink and purple. Ribbons curled around the post, waving at passersby. Inside, through the open window, laughter trickled onto the breeze and anyone walking past would feel the happiness that was within. "Happy birthday to you, happy birthday to you…", this accompanied by squawks of laughter.

Fran walked into the front room and on the rug lay Richard with Emily in his arms, raised up above his head and she was giggling which in turn was making him laugh. Who would have thought that in a year her life would be so different?

She had realised, shortly after Emily's birth that any thought of a reunion with Robbie, even just to meet his daughter, was not going to happen. The obligatory congratulation was given without showing any real interest. There were no questions about her hair, the colour of her eyes, which were green like her own, or who she looked like and when a token blue teddy bear arrived, it was given to Digger, telling him that it was from his dad. Digger duly severed the head from its body and the poor creature didn't last long enough to even get a name.

He had told Fran, excitedly, that he was preparing to get married and of course, once the dust settled, he would try and get back. As she reminisced it became obvious that all it had been was a beautiful experience, just a beautiful memory. She closed the chapter and felt at peace.

Where Richard was concerned, his constant support had caused her feelings to change and the cherry on the cake was that Emily adored him. It just seemed to be right, a jigsaw piece that fell into place, but when he asked her to marry him, Fran didn't say yes straight away, much to Richard's surprise and her parents' horror. They suffered three days of an agonized waiting whilst Fran needed the time to work out whether both she and Emily were the right fit, and realising that they were, she had agreed, much to everyone's relief.

They were married in the village church and everyone, so it seemed, in Little Stockton had crammed into the pews to witness the event. Like her mother she had preferred to have a village green reception with everyone invited. The London crowd kicked off their heels and joined in the dances with the local band, who, mostly in tune, played rock 'n' roll till the early hours.

Everyone agreed it was the best wedding they had ever been to and there was not a dry eye in the house when Richard gave his speech.

Since then, he had often told her he loved her and showed it in so many ways that she believed it and felt safe and happy. They were a family.

As Fran stood watching, leaning against the plinth of the door Richard saw her and smiled back at her. "Emily, doesn't mummy look lovely?" Emily clapped her little hands and squealed with delight.

"Come on you two, people will be here soon and you, my little Bean, need to get ready."

Fran whisked her into her arms and swirled her around with screams of joy from her daughter. The doorbell rang interrupting their fun. "It will be mum and dad, let them in love, please".

Fran took Emily into her bedroom whilst excited chatter echoed through the house. As everyone arrived, the chaos ensued with the accompanying noise of several toddlers. Emily was passed around from one relation to another but eventually, overwhelmed, fell asleep in Mary's arms and got put down for a nap.

With the other children taken home, Richard and other family members left the mess and sat, exhausted, on the patio, drinking a well-earned glass of wine. Fran checked on Emily, and as she left to join the others, the doorbell rang. "Are you coming love?" called Richard from the patio. "Hang on there is someone at the door" Fran replied.

Answering the door, she blinked as the sunlight streamed into the darkened hall and there, leaning against the porch, was none other than Robbie. His unmistakable blue eyes, brown hair and tanned handsome face with its cheeky schoolboy smile looked down at Fran, who stood open mouthed and stared at the oh so familiar face.

"So, where's the birthday girl then?"

5.07PM

At 5.07pm Fran's happy world fractured. The hurt that she thought buried climbed out of its hiding place and slapped her right in the face. "What the hell are you doing here?"

"I thought it was about time to meet my daughter," Robbie drawled.

"Without talking to me first.....this is so like you Robbie... absolutely no thought for others".

"Don't be like that babe, it's been a tough year and ...."

"Tough year? You have no idea! Why now Robbie? No word from you and very little interest and now you just turn up? What happened, did you just wake up and say today I am going to be a father? Well, it doesn't work like that!"

"But Bean, just hear me out. I really want to see her, get to know her."

"It's a bit late for that," Fran snapped.

She just couldn't believe it. Her happy world was crumbling around her and the walls so carefully constructed were falling down, brick by brick. Somewhere deep inside a fire started to burn, her green eyes narrowed, and her face flushed; a scream manifested, growing in volume, all those months of pain coming to the fore.

"No, no Robbie, NO! Get out, now! Get out!"

Her raised voice brought Richard through from the back garden, with Mary and Joe closely following. "Fran are you ok love?"

"What the hell are you doing here?" Richard's surprise was blatantly obvious as he took in the situation. He walked quickly towards Fran but just as he reached her side, she stepped forward, shoved her hands into Robbie's chest pushing him right off the step. Losing balance, Robbie fell backwards into the garden. Fran turned on her heel and pushed past her parents, tears burning in her eyes. She was angry, 1 year 9 months' worth of angry. She walked into her bathroom, slamming the door. Sitting on the edge of the bath, tears of frustration cascaded down her cheeks. She loved Richard and her safe world; she just didn't need this interruption in hers or Emily's life.

Mary knocked on the door, "Fran love, can I come in? Franny, please, open the door." Knocking again she could only hear muffled crying within. Mary could only imagine the pain that her daughter was going through. Speaking softly, she told her that she understood but that she was strong and had support of her husband and was not alone anymore. She told her that when she was ready, they would sit down and talk about what they should do. With that Fran threw open the door, her face blotchy and eyes swollen. "What we should do, mum? Tell him to go away and leave us alone. He didn't want to know when I was pregnant, and he didn't want to know Emily when she was born." With a big gulp and tears flowing, she said, "He sent a blue teddy for God's sake, it wasn't even the right colour......and now he walks back in and expects to be part of her life.... no mum, over my dead body!" Her face crumbled, tears beginning to flow again, and she fell into Mary's open arms.

Joe and Richard walked down into the garden and Joe put out his hand to pull Robbie up.

"Time to go lad! It's a bit of a shock, you see."

"Please Joe, I don't want to cause trouble, I just need to see Fran and explain. I know I've made mistakes; huge mistakes and I haven't been here for Emily, but I am back now."

Richard had been quietly listening to this exchange and when he spoke, he did so slowly and deliberately as if to emphasise the point. "So, you think you can waltz in and take over where you left off. You have no idea how hard it was for Fran. I think it would be best for everyone if you left!"

"Thanks, but the only person who can tell me to leave is Fran!"

"I think she made herself quite clear Robbie, now get off my property"

"Your property, I thought this house belonged to Fran."

"Oh it does, or it did. We're married, Fran is my wife, and now if you don't mind I need to see if my wife is okay." With that he turned and ran up the steps.

Robbie looked at the retreating form of Richard, straight backed, slight but tall. He then looked at Joe and with regret he realised what he had lost.

"Married! Well, that didn't take her long." The statement left Robbie's lips before he had a chance to digest its content and was met with Joe's disappointed expression. "On your way Robbie, it's for the best. You left her high, dry, and pregnant, 19 months ago. Now, she is very happy. Well, actually son, we all are. She didn't need this reminder, so please go!"

Robbie turned to go and then turned back "Joe I just need to tell Fran what happened. I truly loved her and was coming back but then dad died and there was so much to do......." Robbie suddenly stopped, and Joe turned to see what he was looking at. Both lifted their hand to shield their eyes from the sinking sun and framed in the doorway stood Fran standing on the step with a sleepy Emily in her arms, her red hair glowing with life in the light. Richard walked up behind her and Robbie watched as she turned to hand him Emily, then crossing her arms she stood fast. Robbie changed his hand into salute and turned away. As he sauntered across the grass and on to the gravel path, Fran watched his familiar stride with mixed emotions. She acknowledged her father, who then walked into the house, clutching her arm as he passed and when she turned back, she saw Robbie walk through the old wooden gate and as it clicked shut behind him, he punched the pink balloon which, although deflated, was still bobbing in the breeze. She watched as the balloon bounced down and up and entwined with the purple balloon like lovers dancing. Fran stood staring at the balloons for a long time until a squeal of laughter from inside pulled her from her thoughts and with one last glance; she went inside and closed the door.

2019

So many memories and with a sigh, Fran started to put the taffeta away. These thoughts had shaken her, and she felt old and tired. It was such a long time ago and so much had happened since. Sliding the boxes into the cupboard, she stood slowly, putting her hands on her back, and stretching up. She let her eyes drift around her precious room, her sanctity, but today this brought no comfort as it normally did. She felt unnerved and anxious. It seemed now that Pandora's Box had decided to burst wide open, tumbling out memories that had been long ago buried. There was no stopping it. The more she tried, the more thoughts champed at the bit to revisit. With a heavy heart she walked to the door and looking back into the workshop, she remembered conversations, love, arguments, and the day that life was never quite the same again. She sighed again and switched off the light and, closing the door behind her, slowly walked up the path to the house. As she entered the house, the familiarity which normally soothed her added to her mounting anxiety. Glancing across to the TV room she could see through the chink in the door his profile, head to the side and body slumped, and knew that he was sleeping. She suddenly felt a shortness of breath and steadied herself at the door but with the familiar buzzing in her ears she knew it was an indication that it was about to happen again. "Please no," she whispered but the cruel twist of fate didn't listen and as the involuntary twitches and convulsions manifested, she fell to the floor, her hand reaching out, banging against the door.

"I've got you! I've got you! My darling, just breathe!" His gentle voice, penetrating through the waves of confusion, did little, in this instance, to stop the tremors that invaded her body, but she knew he was there. He nearly always was. Slowly, she came back, her eyes trying to focus into caring eyes that looked down at her.

"That was a big one, my love. What brought that on?" Cradling her in his strong arms, he saw Rupert, his soft brown eyes showing concern at his mistress's plight. "Come, boy, you are needed." Rupert lay by Fran's side, pressing his body close as if to say I'm here, I won't leave you. Fran's hand rose, resting it on Rupert's back and seeing Fran settled with Rupert, he knew that he had to make the call. She had had too many of these fits lately and he knew he needed help. Fran would hate him, but he just couldn't cope anymore, and he didn't want to lose her again.

She could hear the conversation being held and wanted to stop it but knew she couldn't, she was so tired.........

"Hi, Simon, it's about Franny................no not really...........yeh a big one. Ambulance? Well, that won't please her but yes, I agree. Thanks. .... Yeh, yeh, I'm fine. See you soon".

She saw him walk towards her and turned her head away, sleep, or something resembling it was hovering over her and slipping back in time, her memories and people that had remained hidden for so long, came to visit.

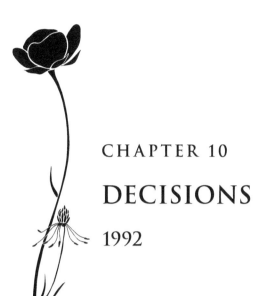

CHAPTER 10

DECISIONS

1992

After a restless night, Fran lay staring at the ceiling. She was angry with herself and thumped the mattress which caused Richard to shift his position and groan. Rather than disturb him, she quietly got out of bed and went through to the kitchen. Making a cup of tea, she found herself lost in thought whilst stirring the boiling liquid and then, spilling some over the edge of her favourite cup, she chastised herself. "Bugger"! She cleaned up the mess but stopped mid wipe, her head running through the events of the day before. He hadn't changed, still handsome with that stupid grin, that lost boy look and annoyingly, her stomach had given that same nervous flip when she first saw him, but then anger had thwarted that. He had abandoned her, and he had abandoned his daughter and that she could not forgive!

Joe had said that Robbie had wanted to explain something to her, and perhaps it would be the right thing to let him do so and Mary, putting a comforting arm around her, said, in her gentle way, that after all he was Emily's father, and what harm could just a chat do? Richard had been quiet throughout this discussion. At first he had been protective and supportive but in the latter hours his mood had changed, and he had become distant. If she was honest, Fran knew why and thought it best to speak to him later. She would give him the reassurance she knew he needed but for now emotion and pain of the last year overwhelmed her.

Sipping her tea, she walked out onto the veranda and sat on the swing seat, which moved gently in the breeze. The fence posts were entwined with roses which continued climbing up over the wooden porch. They smelt divine and the plethora of colour, reds, peach, and harlequin, yellow and pink, danced in a performance that any ballerina would envy. It would be a lovely summer's day but at this early hour it was still quite cold, and Fran pulled the tartan blanket around her. Fran was so deep in thought that the next-door neighbour's cat went unnoticed as he snootily stared at her and, becoming bored, stretched then jumped up onto the seat next to Fran, curling within the blanket, purring with pleasure as Fran scratched his head and stroked his fur.

The pallet of colour normally excited her imagination and then she would snatch up a sketch book as she emulated the mix into a design; but today, her mind was far too confused to take in the glory of her garden. She stared ahead, trying to make sense of why she didn't just send him packing and why she was actually contemplating a meeting. Backwards and forwards went her thoughts until with an exasperated squeal, which sent the cat leaping with annoyance from his resting place, she stood. She let out another exasperated cry and slamming her cup down she stepped into the garden and walked towards the back gate, which led onto the farming land beyond. The fields were covered with daisies but here and there buttercups wearing their yellow bonnets bowed to her as if in greeting. They had not yet turned their little heads up to the sun and it never failed to amaze her how their thin spindly bodies held them upright. The hinge creaked as she opened the gate, and suddenly she was running with arms held wide open, running against the breeze into the meadow which stretched as far as the eye could see. The sun, rising, warmed the land and feeling it on her face, she lifted her head and opened her arms and swung around in a circle, her titian hair splaying out around her as she twirled. "I'm a buttercup and I am free" she shouted to the air and as if joining her, the little flowers lifted their heads enjoying the vision before them. Around and around she twirled, freeing her mind from the horrors of yesterday until dizzy and hot she stopped leaving her arms open, breathing heavily.

Hidden by the trees, someone watched Fran's spontaneity. The beautiful vision of her titian hair as it swirled around her was as he remembered her, so alive and pretty. It was with reluctance that he left his hiding spot, climbed on his bike, and sped off. The sound disturbed Fran and dropping her arms, she turned abruptly to see where the noise had come from, but the rider had long gone. Walking back to the house, she looked up at her bedroom window and seeing Richard looking down, she raised her hand to wave, but he withdrew, and her hand dropped by her side and she entered her home.

CHAPTER 11

THE BLUE CAFÉ

1992

With the sun shining and just the slightest of breeze, Robbie left the bed and breakfast and walked around to the back of the house into the very neat, pretty garden. He took in the sweet-smelling flowers and followed the flight of a busy bumble bee as it collected nectar from the hollyhocks. Walking across the grass to the shed, he was met by Murphy, the resident dog, who set up a show of fierce barking which subsided when Robbie bent to scratch his head. Murphy reminded Robbie of Digger who he still hoped to see although he wasn't sure whether it would be the best thing to do, for hadn't he abandoned him as well?

Wagging his tail Murphy excitedly pushed a ball towards Robbie who dutifully picked it up and threw it across to the other side of the garden. Darting off to retrieve it, he returned disappointed to find his playmate had moved on and lay down panting in the sunlight. Retrieving his hired motor bike from the side of the shed, Robbie put on his helmet and walked it down the path leading out of the back of the property.

"You may leave it around the back," Mrs. Cuthbert had said "but no further than the Forsythia bushes, for I don't want it seen by my neighbour or anyone else that decides to walk by and do not leave by the front gate, you know what awful gossips there are." He had agreed but Mrs. Cuthbert had not finished. "Just remember, that contraption is your responsibility and not mine, so if something happens to it don't come complaining to me! Nasty polluting things. I am surprised, doctor, that you condone it, such dangerous things they are!" Robbie smiled and shook his head as he remembered the conversation. He didn't mind the very house-proud Mrs. Cuthbert, in fact he had a lot of time for her. She was quite the busybody by nature, with a reputation amongst the town folk for gossip but in truth she had a kind heart and having been widowed only a year ago was very lonely. Robbie had been the treating doctor for the family when her husband had died very suddenly, leaving behind his wife and children. It had been a terrible time.

On returning to Little Stockton, Robbie had found that Mrs. Cuthbert had opened her large house as a bed and breakfast, and she had been delighted to have young Dr Robbie as her guest. In her new role as a business owner, she could not wait to tell the townsfolk of his return. The guest house was not only doing exceedingly well but the variety of guests gave her the company she needed.

He wheeled his bike through the back gate and down the back lane. He looked back at the quintessential English garden and thought about his Australian residence, which couldn't have been more different, not only in climate but also the fact that his idea of gardening was native plants that looked after themselves, or a pot plant or two. Once down the lane he hopped on, released the throttle, started his bike and hit the road.

Little Stockton was a pretty village and he enjoyed, as he had before, nothing more than going for a ride. Fields and market gardens and an eclectic style of houses lined the road.

Yes, Robbie thought, this time, he could make a home here.

Turning the bend, something yellow caught his eye, and as he got nearer, he knew it was her. He turned off his engine and pushed the bike into a group of trees, moving closer to take a look.

Her titian hair spun out around her as she swirled round and round. She looked so free and beautiful as he had remembered her. Her face turned up to the sun, she was smiling, and her laughter landed on a whispered breeze and drifted towards him. Robbie reached his hand out as if to catch it, but it was gone. She was gone! He had lost her and yet knowing this he had come back.

Climbing back on his bike, he headed towards the centre of the town. He noticed nothing as he rode through the narrow roads, his mind awash with memories and regret. Reaching the town, he parked his bike and walked into the centre to the Blue Cafe, a place where Fran had met him on many occasions and where they had sat holding hands discussing their plans for the future

Nothing much had changed, the same plastic tables and faded menus, the same barista and probably the same dreadful coffee. They had often wondered why it was called the Blue Cafe because there was nothing that was obviously blue and had laughed as they made up stories. Looking up he saw the same green eyes looking back at him, except these were accompanied by greying hair and a fixed expression. "Hello Mary thank you for meeting me".

"Hello Robbie, Joe will be along in a minute." Then there was an awkward pause, as if words meant nothing and small talk would not build any bridges that were long gone. The silence hung in the air for what seemed an eternity and it was a grateful interruption when Robbie heard "I got you a coffee lad" as Joe joined them, and he sat himself down. He noticed that they hadn't really changed much but the welcoming smiles had gone, replaced with concern and suspicion.

Awkwardly, Mary started the conversation, her soft dialect did not match the piercing green eyes that stared as she spoke." Why have you come back?" Robbie started to speak, and she raised her hand as if to silence him. "It took a long time for Francesca to get over your abandonment of not only her but also your child. The months leading up to the birth were not happy as they should have been, nor exciting.

Instead, they were terrifying and had it not been for Richard........"
Her voice trailed off and tears filled her eyes, but she continued. "They
are a family now and a happy one. Why come back and destroy that?
Nothing you will say can change our feelings.... we lost you from our
family too! Emily doesn't know you. Richard is her daddy now. The
implications of introducing her to another daddy will confuse her. She
is only 1 years old and has known nobody else".

At the sound of his daughter's name, Robbie sat up straight and shook
his head. What a mess, what was he doing here?

Joe had been holding Mary's hand and cleared his throat as he spoke.
"She loved you, lad, don't you see and behind all her anger she still
does, she never stopped!"

"Joe!" Mary pulled her hand away and Robbie's head shot up.

"It's time for truth, Mary love." Joe had never been one for long
speeches but there was something so honest and real when he spoke
that Mary sat back, the stress leaving her shoulders as she listened to
her husband speak.

"That is not to say, Robbie, that she doesn't love Richard. She does and
as you know they are now married. You cannot or must not interfere
with that! But son, you hurt her deeply and you lied to her. That we
cannot forgive! We thought, once, that you would become part of our
family so you betrayed us too in a way, however, I believe, although
others don't," He looked at Mary and took up her hand again, patting
it, "that there must be a story behind this whole mess and we, Mary
and I, are willing to hear your side of the story"

"And Fran?" Robbie asked quietly.

"Maybe, one day, but if what you say isn't worth the breath it takes to
say it, then it will not be with our encouragement."

With a shaky voice, holding back anger and tears, Mary added "You realise that we are going against our own daughter's wishes, Robbie, but we have to think of Emily's future and that of further children." She sat back in her chair, took a sip of her coffee, which had gone cold and placed the cup down shakily missing the saucer and making a clatter. Joe steadied the cup and wiped the spill.

They had spoken and argued about this meeting last night and the night before. Robbie had called Joe and begged for an audience, but Mary had refused. In the end Joe had persuaded Mary that it would at least protect their beloved daughter and grandchild with the truth examined before reality hit home, which he was sure it eventually would. Already a rift had appeared overnight between Richard and Fran, an awkwardness that was obvious. Joe rose, pushing his chair back and went to the counter to order more coffee and on return nodded his head at Robbie. "So?"

As Robbie began to speak, he felt the heat of the Australian sun and the enormity of his return hit him all over again. He took a deep breath and to the enquiring pair of eyes he began.....

1990 - Robbie's Story

The balmy Perth heat hit Robbie on his arrival. Although it was only just spring, the temperatures were unusually high for October and he no longer needed his warm rainproof jacket that he had brought from England. Walking through Arrivals, Robbie stopped at the row of pay phones; he needed to speak with Fran, it was all he could think about, feeling bad that he didn't say goodbye before he left. He would have told her to wait for him, but he didn't get the chance and he reasoned with himself that he had at least tried. Fran had been busy, he knew that, too busy.... god he missed her. Picking up the receiver he began to dial the international code but then realised that it would be the middle of the night in the UK, and he put the receiver back down. He would try later.

Getting into a taxi, he gave his home address and exhausted slumped in the back seat not seeing the familiar surrounding scenery and in giving no response to the taxi driver's endless patter which eventually stopped, he fell asleep. He awoke just before reaching his home and dug deep in the pocket of his rucksack for his front door key and Australian currency which had been tucked away. As the taxi drove away, Robbie stood at looked at the impressive entrance, it was good to be home but there was no outstretched arms, no smiling face to greet him and with a heavy heart he let himself in. Dropping his bag to the floor he was met by loud barking and the rush of feet as a golden Labrador rushed from the back of the house to ward off the intruder, but this turned into excited yelps of pleasure as the dog saw Robbie, who knelt down to hug the old family pet. "Hello old feller, hello my Toby. What's been happening here then?"

"Hello Dr Harvey, you should have let me know when you were coming, I could have picked you up".

The light streamed in from behind the voice and as Robbie looked up he saw a shapely pair of legs and an attractive smile. He stood, conscious of the fact that after 24 hrs of flying he didn't look or smell the best and proffered his hand. "Um and you are?"

"Sorry should have introduced myself." He noticed a strong American twang; she wasn't from around here and then realised she was still addressing him.

"I am Vanessa, Vanessa Brooks. I was invited by your father to assist him on his research paper as we both have a keen interest in Endocrinology. I am studying at Notre Dame where your father was giving a lecture. I am in my final year and, well I asked him if he needed an assistant, and the rest is history." Seeing Robbie's confused expression she continued.

"So what am I doing here.......I have digs at the University but about a month ago, Hugh, I mean Dr Harvey, had a fall. He broke his ankle and when I arrived that day, I found him at the foot of the stairs. ..."

"But why the hell didn't he tell me... I would have come home earlier!"

"He wouldn't let me call you, it wasn't a bad break, but he couldn't weight bear. So I suggested that I act as a housekeeper..." and seeing Robbie's eyes narrow she hurriedly continued....

"Not for payment or anything but genuinely to help out, with cooking; washing etc and of course walking Toby, didn't I fella". Seeing Toby responding to the sound of his name with a wag of his tail.... Robbie started to relax.

"Dr Harvey, Hugh, and I have a great relationship, it was all working out quite well until this set back." With this remark, she stopped, bit her lip and turned away walking towards the kitchen,

"Do you want some coffee?"

Leaving his bags in the hallway, he followed Vanessa through to the kitchen. He noticed how comfortable she was in this environment and for some reason it annoyed him. Why hadn't dad said anything? Was more to this relationship? His dad had never even mentioned Vanessa, let alone his broken ankle and now he may never know. It crossed his mind, briefly, what Fran would make of this and he took an inward breath.

"How is dad now?"

"Stable but hooked up to machines and so bloody unwell" She bit her lip again. "Shit, Robbie, can I call you that.....it was awful. He had had his cast off his ankle and was making progress having hydro and physio, you know all that stuff and more". She dug in her bag for a cigarette, "May I?" Robbie nodded and she lit a cigarette. Taking a long drag, he saw that her hands were shaking as she continued.

"He complained a few days later of a pain in his groin, no one really thought much of it, maybe a strain but it got worse. Then whilst having his hydro session he felt very short of breath, the Physiotherapist was really worried, and I offered to take him to the specialist, but he waved me away and once home took himself off to bed. He didn't come through for dinner and when I checked in on him, he was slumped over his writing desk." She took another drag. "I phoned triple 0 and the Paramedics revived him and took him to Sir Charles Gairdner hospital. That was three days ago, and he hasn't really regained consciousness... well, I am sorry Robbie but it's not looking good. I think you father knew this because….."

Robbie interrupted, "Why, how?" Tiredness and emotion overwhelmed Robbie. "Fuck.......sorry, it's all a bit much to take in"

"Yeh I know... the thing is, when he was worked on by the paramedics, a piece of paper was found in his hand.... here" she turned and opened a drawer and took out a piece of paper. Handing it to Robbie, she continued "I haven't a clue what it means but it had to have been important. Also he had turned a page of the old blue address book to your name and English phone number, that's how I knew how to contact you"...

"Thank you". Robbie looked down at the scrap of paper, eyes misting as he read the old language in his father's sprawling handwriting and smiled, he knew what this meant, and his eyes filled with tears. Looking up into Vanessa's quizzical eyes he excused himself "I need a shower and then I will go to the hospital".

As the hot steaming water poured over his exhausted body, he wept and not for the first time today he wished Fran was with him........

The next week passed and then another there was no real change and Robbie wasn't really sure if his dad knew he was there. He hoped so.....

He had from time to time spoken with Fran but instead of being supportive she had been distant and didn't seem interested. She had said the right things but there was something missing and he realised, well, he realised there was nothing left to say really.

However, there was one constant in his life; Vanessa who waited up for him night after night, making food, which was often left untouched. She sat with Robbie at the hospital as his father's life ebbed away, not intruding and quietly being supportive. Her soft smile and lyrical voice, soothing as she offered him a drink after hours or holding his hand, whilst he prayed for a change that he knew, as a doctor, would never come. Eventually the decision had to be made and Vanessa was there when he talked through the night justifying the agonising decision that only he could make.

He had asked Fran to come to Australia but there was some project she was working on and she couldn't get away, Richard and Mackenzie Taylor had come first again, and he reflected that it always had.

The person he loved and thought he knew was gone and the pain in losing his father was almost too much to bear. Angry tears and drunken words were soothed by Vanessa, who comforted him. Smashed glass thrown at the wall in a fit of despair, was cleared and gentle hands held him as he wept through the night.

The embolism that had travelled through his father's body on its path of destruction had hit its target and the man, that Robbie knew as dad, was no more and he felt broken.

He sat in the quiet room alone, holding his father's cold hand. The beeping machines now silent and the screens black. They would come soon enough to take him but for now there were no words left to say. He dug in his pocket and pulled out the note his father had written, his last message to his only son. The words written in the Aboriginal native dialect translated as "Sorry my son it's time to go." Desperate tears poured down Robbie's face, he should have got there earlier

Of course Dr Harvey had known of his next journey in life or as it happened, death.

A renowned doctor of not only Physiology but was recognised as a Doctor of Philosophy in Aboriginal Medicine and would have known that his Dreamtime was waiting for him.

As a boy, Robbie had been taught by his father about the Indigenous people, their history and cultural understanding. The way of the land, the Narlijia way of life (no bullshit) was how Hugh Harvey delivered his lectures and how Robbie believed life should be. Together they had gone to the Kimberley region in the northern most part of Australia to understand and administer health and vaccines to the children of the Karajarri tribes.

Doc Harvey had been well known and these trips were something that Robbie would never forget. The last trip had been taken on his own, as his father was busy lecturing and although he too, administered vaccines, he never was awarded the mantle of Doc Harvey.

As Robbie grew into man, he learnt to understand the culture and the traditions that his father had held so dear and looking down now he spoke to his father telling him that it was alright to go on his next journey and that the "Sorry business was over". He brought his father's hand up to his lips, murmuring goodbye. Robbie stood and then left the room, a solitary figure walking down a long cold corridor. Vanessa was there when he opened the doors to the car park. She held out comforting arms and he was grateful and fell into her embrace, tears flowing down his face. They held each other as if nothing else mattered.

When he returned to his home Robbie tried to ring Fran but once again she was not available. He didn't recognise the voice on the end of the phone and was told that Miss O'Brien was in a meeting and was there a message. What could he say...."my dad is dead....it's over" He couldn't bring himself to leave a message and said thank you and hung up. Standing, he looked into the mirror, his face grey and etched with pain. In reality Robbie felt he had lost two people in his life. Running a hand through his hair, he asked himself – What now?

The telephone rang and the answering machine picked up the call...."Good afternoon Dr Harvey, excuse the intrusion. I know you are a busy man, but I am from the University of Western Australia, Sarah Chandler is my name......Professor Sarah Chandler...perhaps you have heard of my work? Um.... anyway I wonder if you could return my call. We have an Aboriginal Art Exhibition and would very much like to invite you to open it." Professor Sarah Chandler left her number and rang off.

With a howl of emotion he smashed his hand down on the telephone and pulled the jack from the wall. He didn't want to hear another commiserating message or another enquiry for his father. All he wanted, for now, was peace. Once again it was Vanessa he turned to.

November was warmer than usual, and the skies were blue, Robbie thought of the cold winds of Little Stockton and shivered with the thought. On the day of the funeral a breeze softened the heat of the day and even though Robbie felt sad, he felt at peace. The tribal Elders lined the aisle as the coffin was walked down and his father was remembered by many in an honorary fashion. Vanessa held Robbie's hand tightly as the coffin was lowered and just like that the day was over and life, although just a little sadder, went on.

With Christmas looming, Robbie was offered a position at the local surgery in High Street, not far from his home and he took a 6 month contract. He could go nowhere whilst his father's estate was in probate and it seemed the right choice. This he had tried to explain to Fran, and she had agreed that it was the only thing he could do, yet Robbie felt again, as he had before, that there was an element of disinterest and when asked if she would come out for Christmas, she had declined saying it was a busy time and then continued talking about the new contracts that she was in charge of at Mackenzie Taylor. He had quipped about Richard's empire and her voice had snapped a response and then she said she had to go with the phone abruptly put down.

Although there had been no need for Vanessa to remain once the funeral was over, it somehow didn't matter that she was still around. He enjoyed her company and the lilt of her Californian accent, with her quick thinking sense of humour lightened the mood. He had to admit to himself that she was rather pleasant on the eye and without even trying Vanessa became part of his day to day. So it was a shock when Vanessa, on completion of her studies, told him she would be returning home to California after Christmas and her graduation.

In the weeks leading up to Christmas, Robbie spoke to Vanessa about Fran and told her about Little Stockton and the O'Brien's. He made her laugh when describing Doris dancing with her Zimmer frame at Mary's party and about the people in the village whom he had called friends. Having never been to England Robbie tried to paint a picture of the village green and the local pub and she hung off every word. He didn't, however, talk about how he had loved Fran so very much. How her green eyes changed colour with her mood and how he would tuck her curls around her ear as they escaped from her beanie. He didn't talk about their plans which now seemed all a bit futile and the hurt that he felt each time they spoke, all the time feeling the void in their relationship growing bigger. Maybe all it had been was a holiday romance, but Robbie was sure it had been more, and he thought that they were meant to be together. Sadly it was obvious to him that Fran no longer wanted their union for it had been replaced with a drive to succeed in her career and reluctantly he had to conclude that enough was enough. There was something, someone, waiting for him here and he had to take a chance if he was to have any sort of future.

Running through to the kitchen, he found Vanessa sitting at her laptop at the kitchen bench....

"What are you doing tonight?"

Vanessa looked up startled, she certainly wasn't expecting the sudden intrusion, be it a pleasant one. "Not a lot actually, I have been looking at flights. Gees they are expensive this time of year......but soon be out of your hair" she drawled.

Running his hands through his hair nervously Robbie walked into the kitchen and started to make coffee. "The thing is........do you want one by the way... no, right ok.....the thing is, I wondered if you would like to go out for dinner tonight?"

"Yeh that would be cool – Robbie are you ok?"

"Yes, no, shit I don't know!"

"What is it Hun? You have been through so much in the last month and......." she was interrupted abruptly by Robbie "The thing is I don't want you to go, I don't ever want you to go......so stay.....please!"

In the silence Robbie felt his heart plummet "Shit!" – he turned his back and continued to make coffee, one that he no longer wanted but it gave him something to do. "Sorry Vanessa - I'm a stupid ass...sorry I....I'm just no good at this stuff". He turned, reluctantly, and found Vanessa standing in front of him, she removed the cup from his hand and placed it on the bench behind her. Manoeuvring herself into the shape of his body, she kissed him gently on the lips,

"I didn't want to go either". His arms went around her, and their kisses became more passionate; holding her hand he led her out of the kitchen. Looking back at her, she nodded, and he kissed her again, just to make sure. The pain and emotions of the last three months unleashed itself in a bed of passion, beautiful passion and after their lovemaking, they lay in each other's arms not caring about anyone or anything and just for that split moment Robbie felt happiness return.

The next day, Vanessa telephoned the authorities as her student visa was nearly expired to see if she could extend it or if she would still need to return to California. There were a few options, expensive, options which she discussed later that day with Robbie.

"Apparently, if I take up more study I can extend but really I have had it with the books or I could apply for a working visa, but would need sponsorship and babe, that takes time.....and I would need a sponsor....

there are other options but....that's just too hard. Anyways, I am going to speak to Adele, my agent on Monday and dig a bit further".

"What other options Vanessa?"

"They are not an option!"

"Are you talking spousal arrangements? One of our doctors at the practice is bringing his wife over from India on this visa."

Vanessa cut in quickly.....”Robbie, please don't go there.....I don't want to stay with you on a pity visa, something I may regret later.... done on a whim"

"Vanessa!"

She held up her hand to stop him talking........”Leave it for now, I will talk with Adele Monday"...........

1992 THE BLUE CAFE

Robbie hadn't touched his coffee and coming back to the present, he stared sadly ahead. When he spoke again, it was with an air of despondency – "When I next spoke to Fran she told me that she had realised our relationship was nothing more than a holiday romance, and that she had, although reluctantly, come to terms with that. I was relieved and told her about Vanessa and asked for her understanding. She gave it, she gave it!" Robbie thumped the table as if making a statement, other patrons looked across and Mary put her hand out and held Robbie's fist, until he relaxed his hand back on to the table. It was only then that she then told me that she was pregnant, I guess there wasn't the opportunity before, but hell it was a shock. She said she didn't need anything, but she thought I should know. I asked her what I could do to help, and she told me she didn't need anything that I had to offer and that I should concentrate on Vanessa, she then hung up.

You have to believe me that I tried to keep in touch, but it was difficult, what with Vanessa and the distance between us.

Robbie then stood, pushing his chair noisily back. "We will speak again but.....look... sorry for all of this."

Turning Robbie walked out of the café without looking back. They watched as he climbed back on his bike and pulled away, riding back up the hill.

Mary leant into Joe and he patted her arm. "C'mon on my love, let's go". Gratefully she took his hand and they too left the cafe a little bit wiser and a lot sadder than they were when they entered.

CHAPTER 12

VANESSA BROOKES

1991

The news of Fran's pregnancy was indeed a shock. Robbie felt that he should go back and support her but how would he explain this to Vanessa and anyway what was the point? Fran didn't want him there. She was quite clear about that. God what a mess and with Christmas just around the corner he didn't know what to do.

Christmas came and went, and Robbie tried to celebrate as Vanessa had made so much effort, but the news weighed heavily on his mind. He had tried to contact Fran but either the call didn't connect, or she didn't pick up. Probably, he thought, the latter. Robbie had become distant, and Vanessa was confused by his sudden disinterest even when he gave assurances that it wasn't her fault. "It's not you Vanessa; I just have a lot on my mind"

"What with probate? Have you heard anything?"

"No nothing as yet". Robbie had then held her, and he felt the relief in her body as she leaned into him and his kisses reassured the niggling feelings of doubt.

Vanessa, urged on by Robbie, had, as she said she would, visited the Department of Immigration in Perth. The visa agent had told her to apply for a working visa, but she would have to do that from California unless a firm would sponsor her. She knew she needed, and didn't have, experience for that to happen. She also knew that she didn't want to go home and argued that she had a steady partner who was a doctor and who could support her, but it made no difference.

The agent, a woman in her early 30s, smiled sweetly. She didn't like pushy rich Americans, who flashed dollars and expected answers. They flaunted situations and didn't care what the government policy was. Celia Forrester was there to abide by the rules, and she had seen every trick in the book. She smiled at Vanessa and tapped her pen on her chin as if she was thinking about the next step, but of course this was just a game to her and stalling in conversation was part of it.

"I do understand; I do," Celia gushed. "But Australian law is set and there is to be no deviation to the policy or procedures in place". Celia smiled again and waited before continuing; she had been yelled at, cried over, begged, and suffered abuse but she could not, even if she wanted to, bend the rules. "If it was up to me......but it isn't you see".

At that point Vanessa wholeheartedly hated her, and for a split-second thought of demanding someone more senior but couldn't see the point and so replied, "Of course Ms Forrester, I quite understand"

Celia turned in her chair and reached for a file. Stamped on the index Vanessa saw her name in black block print - 'Vanessa Brookes' and she wondered what could possibly be in the manila file that would magically change the situation.

She watched as Celia busily opened, then turned the pages of the file; she looked up and smiled again. Vanessa in return looked into brown eyes set behind heavy rimmed glasses, which stared at her quizzically. "Can I ask how long you have been in your relationship, with doctor...... Um?" she turned the page again as if searching for the name.

"Dr Harvey....Dr Robbie Harvey" Vanessa replied. It seemed ludicrous to say one month, although it seemed longer, and she could imagine the smirk forming across the red painted lips opposite. "Just under a year." The twitch of lip and a 'tut tut' was audible as it was meant to be, Vanessa wasn't disappointed.

"And a more permanent relationship isn't on the cards?"

"I really don't know at this stage; why would it make a difference?"

"Probably not but you never know." That smile again. "You have four weeks before the end of your visa, who knows what might occur." She winked, which sent a spasm of anger through Vanessa, her steely blue eyes narrowed at the audacity of the comment, but Celia seemed oblivious and carried on talking about the next appointment. "I will see you in two weeks and maybe some sort of decision can be made, yes? Thank you Ms Brookes."

She had shut the file with a slap and now stood, holding out her hand.

Vanessa stood. She felt frustrated but forced herself to shake hands and walk away.

She had said she would meet Robbie, but instead turned and hailed a cab.

"Notre Dame - Fremantle, please."

Vanessa sat back; perhaps she could continue the work that Hugh had begun? She had their thesis which they had been working on before he had died and perhaps the University would sponsor her to continue. Vanessa knew she was clutching at straws, but it was worth a try.

On arrival, she entered through the wrought iron gates and walked across the courtyard to the Dean's office. Notre Dame was an impressive building with stunning architecture but there was no time to admire it today. She didn't have an appointment but was known well enough and was sure she would be seen. After what seemed ages, she was given an audience and explained her situation.

There had been a lot of nodding and sympathetic understanding. This was followed by discussions about funding, which had been lost with the death of Dr Hugh Harvey and how no decision could be made until the next financial year. It was unfortunate and a loss to the faculty that she had missed the first intake, and if she was considering further study she could try again in March. Somehow Vanessa managed a smile and with the obligatory responses she had left.

Walking home, the thought of returning to California tormented her; she had nothing to return too. She had left with the idea of not ever going back; walking out of a life she didn't wish to re visit. Yes, she had money, plenty of it, and a family name that meant something but walking out on her family and what they represented was a big deal. It had all gone wrong, and she needed to think of something fast.

Letting herself in to the house, which she felt had become her home, she hung up her jacket and greeted an excited Toby. She wandered into the kitchen, opening the fridge for a bottle of wine, and poured herself a large glass. Sinking into the brown leather couch, she patted for Toby to join her, which he dutifully did, curling into her; the familiarity of the furnishings and environment made her feel safe, and she shuddered at the thought of leaving. Taking a swig of her wine, she thought of Robbie, and knew she couldn't lose him, not now; she loved him, didn't she? Having already lost one, she would be dammed if she lost the other, she thought, musing at their similarities. Raising her glass, she toasted out loud, "Like father like son!"

Vanessa Brookes had always been used to getting her own way - working with Hugh had been just that. He had been reluctant at first, but her persistence saw acceptance. They had become work colleagues, then companions and eventually so much more. The huge age gap meant nothing to her as it was a means to an end and when Hugh had broken his ankle, the situation played straight into her hands - his vulnerability met with care and empathy. He had asked her to ring Robbie, and he'd seemed surprised that the number was no longer available. However, Vanessa had soothed him saying that maybe Robbie had moved on and left no forwarding number and perhaps he would call when he reached his destination. She had, at that time no intention in calling him.

When Hugh had been rushed to hospital, Vanessa knew she had no choice and had called, but she worried that her good fortune would come to an end. Lady Luck had shone down on her again when Robbie had walked through the door. He was a younger version of Hugh; handsome, gentle, vulnerable, and caring. He would, as others had done before, eventually need her and Vanessa had waited, biding her time. She had been genuinely sad when Hugh had passed away and so very supportive of Robbie's needs, which had paid off but something of late had changed and even though Robbie had reassured her, she had felt a mounting nagging concern.

The sound of the key in the door roused her from her thoughts; she felt so exhausted that she didn't get off the couch to greet Robbie as he came in. She has struggled with nausea all day and closed her eyes feigning sleep, curling into a cushion.

"Vanessa? Ness?"

She heard her name called and snuggled further down. The phone in the hall rang and she heard, as Robbie picked up the receiver, his voice gentle and loving "Hello Bean, how are you feeling?"

"Please don't cry. I will come if you want me too, you know I will."

"I haven't spoken to Vanessa yet, but I am sure she will understand."

"I know you don't need anything from me, yes, yes of course, please ring me, if you need to."

"I am so sorry. You have no idea. Neither of us knew it would work out like this but with dad gone and waiting for all the legal stuff, well it is just a mess. How are Mary and Joe? Are they there for you?"

"Well, that is good. Give them my love won't you. Please don't cry Fran, this is killing me."

"Don't say that, of course I want to know. Vanessa? No as I said, I haven't had the opportunity."

"Yes, I will tell her, but the timing is not right."

"Yes, please call again, anytime but don't forget the eight hours' time difference. Bye, bye Bean."

Then silence. She heard Robbie sit heavily on the stairs and still she waited. Whatever was said, and by whom, she had a good idea, had deeply upset Robbie.

Vanessa laid mulling over the one-sided conversation and started to put two and two together. A plan began to formulate. It was survival after all and quietly she rose, downed her wine, and opened the door.

Robbie's looked up, surprised to see her then looked back at the phone

"So, Robbie, what did you want to tell me? Is now the right time?"

CHAPTER 13

ENTRAPMENT

1992

Robbie sat in Mary's kitchen, drinking coffee. It was a pleasant room, comfortable and welcoming. "Thank you for seeing me again Mary, I hope me being here will not cause problems for you and Joe."

"Richard and Fran have gone up to London for the weekend and Joe is at work. I called you because the discussion last week has bothered me; it has bothered me a lot. Mind you to be honest Joe told me to leave it alone, but I just can't. which is why he isn't here." Mary took a deep breath and carried on talking. What I don't get, Robbie, is how one minute you were here for our girl, in love and making babies and the next you are getting married to someone you hardly knew."

Robbie rubbed his hands on his jeans and sadly looked up, "It isn't as simply at that, Mary. Although I can see why you would think so and, if I could turn back the clock, I would." He picked up his cup and then put it down again, shaking his head. "If only I hadn't listened to her."

"Fran or Vanessa?"

"Fran! She told me that the baby was the result of a holiday romance and she didn't want me to come back as she could manage on her own.

I offered to come back more than once and maybe if I had things would be so different."

"Of course she wanted you back, but our girl is proud, she didn't want you back after you told her that you had met Vanessa. What did you think she would say?"

"We hadn't spoken much and to be honest with all that had happened with dad, my mind was elsewhere. When I did phone, she was never available, always busy at work and we became distant. When she told me that she felt we had been a holiday romance, I had told her about Vanessa, and all this happened, I swear, before I knew of the pregnancy. If I had known that she was pregnant things would have been different. You see, I went back to work whilst I waited for my father's legal stuff to be sorted out and out of necessity I just got back into life, but I have to say I had always intended to come back."

Mary shook her head. It was getting complicated. She stood up and turned to look out of the window. "Damn, it looks like rain. I will have to get the washing in!" She looked at the grey skies and the small sparrow battling the sudden wind and sighed. The silence hung suspended between them as she watched big fat raindrops hit the window and turned back to Robbie, "So what about Vanessa?"

"When Vanessa learnt about the baby, things changed; Vanessa changed.

1991

On hearing Vanessa, Robbie looked up from his position on the stairs.

"So Robbie, what did you want to tell me? Is now the right time?"

Robbie scrambled up, "Vanessa, I didn't know you were home."

"I am sure you didn't!"

Robbie looked at her and he saw betrayal written all over her face, or maybe he just imagined it, but her blue eyes were narrowed, her face taut.

"I think we had better talk. That was Fran on the phone and......."

Vanessa interrupted, "Yes so I gathered, and?" Vanessa's voice cut through the tense atmosphere like a knife. "Perhaps, Robbie, you need a drink before you start; this sounds serious."

He watched as she turned towards the kitchen and remained, leaning against the bannister. He heard her open the fridge, pour a glass of wine and watched as she walked past him, handing him the glass as she did so. She went back into the sitting room waiting expectantly.

Reluctantly, he left the stairs and wandered into the room, where he found her sitting on the old leather couch curled around a pillow. He took a long sip of the wine, although he didn't really want it and looked at Vanessa who stared him, her eyes piercing blue, waiting for answers. He sat down, across the coffee table from her and taking a deep breath he gently told her about Fran and the baby. Once he had finished, he threw back the wine left in the glass and put the glass down in front of him. Vanessa flicked her hair from her face nervously and bit her lip; the silence was palpable.

Eventually Vanessa looking directly at Robbie, spoke, "Why didn't you tell me before? Why keep this from me? It could have made a whole deal of difference had I known."

"I had to come to terms with it myself and what with Dad's death and us... I didn't know what to think. I am so sorry."

"And Fran? You were obviously so much more than friends! Christ, I would never have slept with you if I had known. I am not like that?" She bit her lip again and her eyes filled with tears. "So what happens now Robbie? Are you leaving me and going back to Little wherever it is? Her voice was clipped, her eyes narrowed, and she spat the words out venomously.

"I don't know; Fran doesn't want me to; I don't know what to do!"

"Do you love her?" And as Robbie started to speak, she held up her hand and continued, "You see that would be a problem!"

"A problem?"

"Yes, you see making love to you happened without much thought; you know Hun, spontaneous sex. Remember sexy sultry spontaneous sex....." Seeing the confusion on Robbie's face, she continued. "And since then, I find myself in a bit of a predicament".

"Predicament? What the hell are you talking about?"

"I am pretty sure that I too am pregnant, about 4 weeks!" Robbie's shocked expression said it all and he sunk into the chair as Vanessa continued. "I wasn't going to tell you until I was absolutely sure, and it is early days, but a woman knows. The question is, Robbie, which woman are you going to stand by? The woman with whom you had a holiday romance or the woman who will stay by your side and be a supportive wife and mother to your child?"

"My wife?"

"Well you surely don't want this child to be deported to America, because according to Ms Celia Forrester that is exactly where I am heading. You see babe, without a sponsorship I can't stay in Australia. If we marry, then they cannot deport me, if you can prove that you are able to support me. Don't you see? We can bring up this child together! Robbie, it really is the answer to our problems, my darling. You, me and the baby. It doesn't mean you can't be part of the other child's life - I wouldn't stop that. They will be siblings 8 weeks apart, almost twins."

For the second time of hearing the same news all Robbie could say was "Shit, I don't need this." But unlike Fran, Vanessa put her arms around him and pulled him to her and whispered that she would always love him and together they would get it sorted.

In the days that followed, Robbie was quiet and Vanessa, respecting his privacy, left him alone. He spent a lot of time in his father's office as if to gain the strength he needed to make the right decision, but he could see no way out. It wasn't that he didn't have feelings for Vanessa. He did, but he knew he was in love with Fran and probably always would be.

In the next week, Vanessa had told Robbie that her pregnancy was positive, and she wanted to keep their baby. Of course she should but ......but the question of marriage to her and not Fran was too much to bear, and he could not make sense of it. He wished his dad was here to talk to, for him to advise and support him but this was not possible. He decided that he should talk to Fran again but on phoning her number at Mackenzie Taylor, he was put through to Richard, who reassured him that Fran was doing really well, and that he, personally, was looking after her. There was really no need to telephone her anymore, as the decision had been made and for the sake of the baby and Fran's well-being it was best to leave her alone. When Robbie demanded to speak to Fran, he received a flat NO! The South African guttural voice aggravated his senses.

"Mate you have no right to keep me from talking to her, that's my child."

"Yes, but Fran doesn't want to talk to you, and you should respect her wishes. She needs a new life and, bud; I am going to give it to her so why don't you live your life and leave ours alone"

"Will you just tell her I called.......I still love her you know!"

"How does Vanessa feel about that?

Robbie stopped and caught his breath; he knew about Vanessa!

"Fran is happy for you, bud. She told me that she hoped you would settle down in Australia. No hard feelings but marry your girl and I am going to marry mine." The conversation stopped and the call ended. It was so very final and in processing the information, Robbie put his head in his arms on his father's desk and cried.

Sitting once again in the Department of Immigration office Vanessa hugged herself; her plan was almost complete.

"Good morning Ms Brookes". Celia slapped the manila file onto the desk.

"Ms Forrester."

"So, where are we up to?" Opening the file she made show of reading the previous notes. "Have we made any decision? Time is a ticking."

"Yes, Ms Forrester, I am staying".

"I am afraid that is quite impossible. Under your visa stipulation, you must be out of Australia by Tuesday week. Did I not make myself clear?"

"Oh yes, crystal clear. However, my circumstances have changed."

"I don't really see how they could have changed in two weeks, Ms Brookes."

"Really! Well let me put it this way, a more permanent relationship is most definitely on the cards and not only that I'm pregnant"

"And would this be Dr Robbie Harvey's child?"

"You betcha!"

"I underestimated you Ms Brookes. Well that is a turn up. Of course I will need a meeting with Dr Harvey, alone. When do you think he will be free?"

"He is away at the moment, but he will be back next week. Can I get him to telephone you?"

"That would be delightful, the sooner the better. Here is my card. I look forward to my meeting with the good doctor. My he has been busy! Oh and congratulations!

With that she stood and walked out the office leaving Vanessa alone. She had work to do but first on the list was to get Robbie to propose and she only had a week to do it.

When Robbie came home, he found Vanessa in bed with a flannel across her forehead. Concerned Robbie sat on the edge of her bed and held her hand. Vanessa opened her eyes slowly and smiled weakly.

"Hi babe, what's up?"

"I am just so exhausted. I have been to the Immigration Department and Celia Forrester gave me a hard time." Her eyes filled with tears and she turned her head away sobbing into her pillow. Robbie stroked her hair, "What is it, don't cry?" Vanessa continued to sob, talking through her tears. "It seems without a spousal arrangement; it doesn't matter if we are pregnant or not; I will be sent back for sure and you will miss out on yet another child." More sobs ensued. "It's all my fault, I should have been more careful!" Her crying became hysterical, and her words were lost as she rolled off the bed and walked into the bathroom, locking the door behind her.

"Vanessa open the door, we need to discuss this!"

"No Robbie. It's just all too much for me. I didn't ask for this and I feel so unwell."

"Come on, open up! Vanessa! This is bloody ridiculous!" From inside a muffled voice spoke up.

"Why don't you go back to Fran while you have the chance? There is no future with me, unless you want to visit California." More tears followed and then the sound of retching.

"Just leave me".

Robbie sunk down onto the floor, leaning against the door. He felt dreadful that he had put two women that he cared for through this. A decision needed to be made. He had to face it. He had responsibilities! Fran had made it quite clear where she stood and nothing more could be done, and after all, she now had Richard. The least he could do was to do the right thing for the other. He sat for some time, on the floor when suddenly the door opened, and he fell back against Vanessa's legs. Scrambling up he tried again.

"There you are. Come on. Let's get you back to bed. You look awful. Can I get you anything?"

Vanessa let him lead her back to bed; she really did feel awful. Perhaps, she thought to herself, she really was pregnant. After all there was the nausea, and she didn't feel like wine or have any appetite. She never had had regular periods so it could be and hoped it was. She would go to the doctors in the morning but for now all she wanted to do was sleep.

"Vanessa! Ness!" He gently shook her.

"What is it Robbie? I just want to be left alone.....please."

"I need to talk to you!" Robbie knew if he didn't do it now he would chicken out.

"I don't want you to go back to California. I think we can make it work here. You, me and the baby; what do you think? Vanessa struggled up upon her pillows. She was feeling nauseous again.

"What are you saying? Don't mess with me, Robbie."

"I am asking you to marry me. I am asking you to be my wife!"

Tears poured down her cheeks as she agreed and threw her arms around him. "Yes please, yes".

They laid together in silence, their bodies wrapped around each other, until Robbie finally fell asleep. Vanessa lay awake as she smiled into the darkness. One more hurdle and she would be home free. Nothing would stop her now.

1992

"But why then are you now back in Little Stockton? Mary asked. "How does your wife feel about this trip and what of the baby? It must be coming up for a year in a month's time. Will you be going back then? Because if you are thinking of disrupting Fran's world, only to leave again....it is not on!" Mary looked across at Robbie expectantly and saw tears in his eyes. He put his hands over his face and then scraped his fringe back, taking a breath and letting out a sigh he continued. "The thing is, Mary, there is no baby; there never was and there is no wife, well not anymore." Mary sat down next to him and resting her arm on his, she spoke gently. "What happened, son, do you want to go on?" She looked at the clock; Joe would still be some time. "Let me get some lunch". She busied herself around her kitchen and Robbie continued. It was not an easy story to tell, one that was quite unbelievable but better out than in; it was, after all, why he had come.

"Our wedding was a small affair. Vanessa had no family in Australia and with dad gone, and not being close to any of his side, we just invited a few friends. Vanessa had been desperate to marry before she began to show, and we were also contending with immigration, so the date was brought forward. At 4 months pregnant, she was still slender; she didn't want anyone to know, keeping it, she said, our secret. She had told me that all was well, and the baby was just scanning as small; it had concerned me that nothing was visible, but I had no reason to doubt her.

On the morning of our wedding day Vanessa whispered that we were having a boy before we walked through the doors of the registry office; Mary, I couldn't have been happier, and I truly believed at this time that I had made the right decision. I pushed away that niggle of doubt that never really left and although I had questioned why Vanessa had always gone for scans without me, she explained that I had always been busy, which unfortunately had been true. Shortly after the wedding, I was asked to travel to Broome to vaccinate a community. I had jumped at the chance and invited Vanessa to accompany me, but she had not been feeling well again and after she'd thought about it, declined. She told me that she wanted to continue with stripping the spare room in readiness for the new arrival, and I promised to help her complete it on my return.

At this point, there was nothing out of the ordinary and we were relatively happy."

1991

"Just rest while I am away, and when I come back, we will see the obstetrician together. You shouldn't be doing this alone. I will be back by Friday so try and make an appointment for Monday?"

"Sure, I will. Let's hope I can get one at short notice."

"I can ring before I go if you like. I know David Proust, quite well."

"No Robbie! I will do it today, so stop worrying."

"Well, look after yourself and our boy. I will be back soon." Robbie kissed her and stood up to leave. "Oh and we can finish the room when I return. There is still plenty of time" He smiled reassuringly and then left.

Vanessa went to the kitchen, opened the fridge and poured herself a big glass of wine. She let out a huge sigh of relief and skulled the contents then poured herself another.

She really didn't know how much longer she could keep this up and had to do something soon to prevent suspicion. Robbie had already started to ask questions and her lies were mounting.

Thinking back to the visit at the doctor's, she shook her head, drank her wine and slammed the empty glass down. She had been certain that this time she was pregnant. In fact she had convinced herself that she was. She shut her eyes at the memory and leant against the kitchen bench for support as the conversation flooded back.

"Ms Brookes, the result of your blood tests has come back and unfortunately it is a negative result."

"Are you sure? You see, I have all these symptoms. In particular the nausea and going off food."

"I am sorry but, no, you are not pregnant. There have been some nasty bugs about and a high number of patients have come through lately with a gastric type virus and it is my opinion that is exactly what you may have contracted. However, on the other hand, you could be experiencing hysterical pregnancy, which can echo the symptoms and give false hope."

"Hysterical pregnancy?"

"Yes! When examining your scans, it looks like you have a condition called polycystic ovary syndrome. However, judging by the scar tissue we saw, you have probably known that for some time. Have you been trying to get pregnant for long?"

"My partner and I have been trying for years. Thank you for your help doctor."

"I can put you in touch with a specialist, who can help you," her doctor said, turning to write down the name. She turned back with the information to see Vanessa standing and ready to leave. "Thank you, doctor. That will not be necessary."

With a proposal imminent, nothing could rock the boat. So Vanessa had continued with the lie about her pregnancy even saying that they were to have a boy and now married, the lies had continued and as Vanessa poured another glass of wine she knew she was in trouble.

Finishing the bottle of wine, and quite drunk, Vanessa threw the bottle into the sink. She watched as the glass shattered with a piece bouncing out and falling onto the floor. On picking up the slither, she sliced across her finger and the blood poured. Running it under the tap, Vanessa swore at her stupidity but as she watched the blood splashing into the sink and over the broken green glass a plan formulated. She wrapped up her finger and went to the freezer where she took out Toby's raw meat, leaving it in the microwave. She then went up to the bedroom and pulled back the cover and undoing the makeshift bandage she let her finger drip onto the bed. The cut was deep and pumping blood flowed until a puddle had formed soaking through the sheet and onto the mattress. When enough damage had been done, she took herself to the local hospital in the early hours of the morning. Here she was fitted with a name band and checked in but with no real damage done she was eventually sent home. Although tired she continued with her deception and taking the meat out of the microwave, she strained the meat and took the bowl of drained blood upstairs, pouring the content onto the sheet, which soaked through. She then put on her nightdress and climbed into bed on top of the bloodied mess and, exhausted, fell fast asleep.

On waking she took off the bloodied nightdress and threw it into the bottom of the bath. She then stripped the bed, leaving behind a dark bloody stain on the mattress. The sheet then joined the nightdress. After her shower, she shut the door and went downstairs. Cooking up the lamb's fry, Toby ate the evidence. She made a coffee and smiled. She was fairly impressed by how easy her deception had been and now all that was left was a call to Robbie but that could wait.

CHAPTER 14

DISSEMBLED INNOCENCE

1991

It took a few days before Robbie received the message to ring home as he was in a remote area, treating and educating children and their families. It was what he and his father used to do, and he had felt so much closer to him here. "You young Doc Harvey?" Enquiring voices had asked. "Old Doc Harvey, is with his ancestors, we know, we feel him?" Brown faces and bright eyes, smiled up at him with acknowledgement. Only now would he be known as Doc Harvey, with the mantle passed down. He vowed he would come back and do more in these remote areas, where the people relied on natural medicine to heal. As he had before, he would learn so much more about tribal tradition and natural medicines which coupled with westernised medicine would bring great benefit. This, he decided was his happy place and couldn't wait to tell Vanessa about it.

When he returned to his hotel after four days of remote living, he showered and laying exhausted on his bed he was interrupted by a knock on his door. He was handed a note, thanking the steward, he took it and put it on the desk unopened.

He then ordered room service with a bottle of red and asked for his clothes to be taken and laundered as they were covered in red dust and filth. When his food arrived, he hungrily devoured it and pouring his wine he sat looking out of the window, the view was spectacular. Time, he had always felt, was irrelevant up here and seemed to stop or at least go slowly. He rocked back in his chair, enjoying the comfort and the silence; He thought about the months ahead of him and feeling healed, he felt that he had found the peace he needed to make it work. He smiled to himself as he thought about his son's arrival, his life, their lives would be whole again, it was, he acknowledged, the circle of life. He imagined bringing his son here as is father had done with him, to meet the Elders, introducing his wife to the tribe and their rituals. He wondered if she would like it and admitted to himself that he didn't know her that well. Things had happened too fast.........

His mind drifted back to Fran and wondered if she was well. It still hurt so much when he thought of how she had behaved. He justified his hurried exit from Little Stockton and still asked himself why she didn't understand or support his circumstances. He told himself, as the wine took effect, that he had would have gone back when he heard of her pregnancy but to be told what they had was nothing more than a holiday romance had hurt, it still hurt! Slamming both feet down from their resting place, he poured himself another glass. A day had not gone by when he didn't think of her and the life they should have been sharing. He found himself feeling angry at how Richard had muscled in but then he too had found solace in Vanessa. Perhaps, he thought, he was no better.

Vanessa.... he thought of her warm smile and determination to please him; her beautiful blue eyes and lovely accommodating manner. He had not been fair to her, burying himself in his work just to prevent thinking about the consequences that his actions had caused. He had missed his father's wisdom, and at times he had just wanted to run, and he had, all the way to Broome. On reflection he realised that perhaps he hadn't given himself the time he needed to grieve but here, in Broome, he had. In his solace he had found peace, feeling closer to his father's memory; remembering his love and feeling his presence around him and the wisdom of many conversations he had as a boy. Shaking his head, and finishing the bottle, he held his glass up to the window and marvelling at the red liquid reflecting in the window, he promised that things would change. He would be travelling home tomorrow - another adventure ahead of him and his sigh was one of contentment, not anguish as it had been before.

Remembering the note he had received earlier he walked over to the desk to retrieve it......

Wednesday 27th March 1991

Message from Mrs. Vanessa Harvey
Time: 08:01
Subject: no returning phone number

"Robbie, if you have a moment can you ring me. Miss you and love you -Nessa"

He smiled, looking at his watch it was too late to call her now and there was no air of urgency, as there had been no further messages. It would have to wait....he would be home tomorrow anyway.

With that he went to bed, falling into a deep sleep.

Friday 29th March 1991 - Perth Airport

Looking through the sea of faces, he couldn't see Vanessa's. He took a seat and waited but it wasn't like her to be late. Eventually, having waited for half an hour he phoned home but there was no reply. Perhaps she had been caught in traffic but for some reason he felt uneasy.

Catching a taxi he arrived home and seeing Vanessa's car out front, his concern mounted.

"Vanessa?" Hearing his voice, Toby came through from the kitchen, wagging his tail. Robbie noticed how old he was getting and fussed him, "Where's Nessa my boy?"

"Vanessa, you up here?" Robbie called up the stairs, and then mounted them, two at a time. As he walked across the landing, he headed towards the back of the house to their bedroom, but a sudden noise from the spare room, made him stop. He heard it again, something between a human sob and a kitten's mew, stifled and yet audible. Nervously he pushed the door open, "Nessa?" As the door swung open, he saw the unfinished room and the old beanbag that had been thrown into the corner, he also saw a foot sticking out from it, Vanessa's foot and from it more sobs. "Nessa, what's happened, it's me, I am home".

"Please go away, don't look at me....." with that followed heart wrenching sobbing which filled the room.

Robbie found Vanessa curled up in the beanbag holding a blue teddy to her stomach; her face was pale with dark circles under her eyes; the tell-tale sign of lack of sleep. Her eyes were red from crying, skin blotchy and her hair hung limply. From the sight of her, she seemed to have been here for days. Wearily, realising that Robbie was crouched beside her, she turned and spoke "I am so sorry Robbie...the baby"...more sobs ensued..."the baby.....I had a miscarriage!"

He held her then, in his arms whilst her body shook with tears and the pain of their loss covered them like a blanket. When she settled, he gently spoke, "When did this happen?"

"Tuesday night....I called your hotel, Wednesday but they couldn't get hold of you...I am so sorry."

Robbie then remembered the note, once again he had let her down; two days of dealing with this alone..."Have you been checked at the hospital.....what happened?" Vanessa proffered her wrist to him, showing her hospital bracelet attached.

"I hadn't been feeling well and went to bed early on Tuesday, the cramps started at about eleven o'clock and by midnight I was bleeding. In the hourly hours, I went downstairs to get a drink and as another cramp came I dropped the glass into the sink, and it smashed cutting my finger - I drove to the hospital but nothing could be done. I had to have a D &C and was sent home later that day."

"Oh my darling girl, I should have been here for you. Are you still in pain? What can I do?"

"I am just tired - I am still bleeding but the cramps have now stopped. God Robbie, I am so sorry"

"It is not your fault Nessa these things happen more often than you think! Stay here, I will go and run you a bath". He left with his head reeling. A couple of hours ago he had felt so happy and was planning their future but what were they supposed to do now.

Walking into the bathroom, he saw the aftermath of the miscarriage, the sheet and nightdress left in the bottom of the shower and again he berated himself for leaving her alone. He removed the offending items and turned on the taps, adding bath salts to the water.

He then scooped up the washing and walked through to the bedroom. It wasn't until he saw the stained mattress, did he cry, the reality and enormity of losing his son hitting him hard. Pulling himself together, he collected Vanessa, and assisted her out of her clothes and then into the bath. She asked him to leave her soaking and he reluctantly obliged..... With Robbie downstairs, Vanessa slid under the perfumed water, she loved the feel of the warm water completely covering her with her hair swirling around her under the water, it felt so relaxing and after that performance she needed it. she pushing herself up through the water, she could hear Robbie taking the washing downstairs but also heard his deep sobs, presuming he had seen the mattress and for a moment her heart constricted, then she smiled. She deserved a bloody Oscar for her performance and the sequel was only just starting.

1992

"Oh love, how awful for you! I cannot imagine what you both went through."

Robbie smiled but his eyes were full of sadness. "Thank you Mary, but this was only the prelude of the drama that unfolded, and the miscarriage is not the reason why I returned". Mary had got up and was busying in the kitchen and listened as Robbie carried on. "You see, eventually life got back on track. The immigration department granted temporary visa to Vanessa whilst the paperwork was being sorted. It could take years and was expensive, but we were prepared to wait. Then came the news of Emily's birth. I wanted to visit, Mary, I really did but Vanessa had become very needy and as she was unable to work, had too much time on her hands which messed with her mental health. Together we were fine but if I went away anywhere I would come back to find her in the beanbag staring at nothing.

On the day I got the news about Emily's birth, I toyed with the idea of keeping it to myself, I was worried, you see, as our baby would have been due the following month and whereas I had thrown myself back into work, Vanessa seemed just lost and the smallest thing would send her back into the babies' room, sobbing.

However, when she was told the news, she took it remarkably well, and came down the stairs holding our son's blue teddy. She then asked me to send it to Emily from her brother.

So I sent it and hoped that things were turning round for the better, I thought that she was beginning to heal and in a way she was. Did Fran get it, by the way Mary?

"Yes, she did, Robbie love, thank you. Unfortunately months later it got left at Tom's and unfortunately Digger got it and ...."

"Say no more, it wouldn't have lasted long after that, how is Digger?".

"Mad as ever and very much loved. Oh Robbie, I am so sorry for your loss, it must have been so hard for you both. If only you had told Fran, perhaps then she would have had some understanding, but I suppose in hindsight you were just trying to protect her. I can see that now, and perhaps so will Fran. So where is Vanessa now?"

Life carried on with some sort of normality and in September Vanessa went on a retreat for a ten day break, with her friend. It had taken a lot of persuasion to get her to go but finally she had agreed.

I had decided to clean up the spare room whilst she was away, as a surprise. I thought it would do her good, a new start. I had stripped the wallpaper and then started removing the old furniture. It was quite therapeutic. On the far wall was an old bed side cabinet, it was far too heavy to move and so I pulled out the drawers one by one to make it easier. The bottom and second drawer came away easily, but the top drawer would not budge; getting a hammer I knocked it out and with the first hit, the drawer shot forward and in doing so released an envelope that had been stuck in the runners and which then fell to the floor. Grabbing the envelope, I was just about to open it when I was interrupted by the phone and ran downstairs to answer it leaving the envelope on the desk..........................

"What was in the envelope, Robbie?" Mary said. Robbie just shook his head and ran his fingers through his hair. He didn't reply but nervously taking a deep breath he continued.

CHAPTER 15

AN EVENTFUL YEAR

SEPTEMBER 1991

Picking up the telephone, he heard the voce of Stephen Hockley, a friend from school and who had and was looking after his father's legal affairs.

"Hi Robbie, it's Stephen Hockley here, the investigation and documentation has been completed and the will and its contents is ready to be read. As there are two recipients both are needed to be present."

"Good afternoon Steven, how are you going? That is good to hear, thank you. Just as a matter of interest can I ask who the other person is, as my father had lost touch with his other family members years ago, perhaps he bequeathed to the university or...."

"Vanessa Brookes, do you know her?"

"She was my father's assistant and now she is actually my wife."

"Your wife?"

"Yes, why?"

There was silence….."Is there a problem Stephen?"

"Robbie, I think you should come in for a chat. I can see you in an hour, if that suits, then we can catch up for a beer after?"

The arrangement was made, and the envelope upstairs forgotten as Robbie walked towards Hockley and Brownstead's Solicitors on the High Street. With concern he reflected that Stephen, was a busy man and although friends, wouldn't have suggested an immediate meeting unless something was amiss and although curios felt somewhat apprehensive.

On arrival Robbie was, by a young and efficient receptionist, to sit in the rather plush waiting area. The door open, and Stephen Hockley burst through. He hadn't changed a bit since school and Robbie stood, smiling.

"Havers how the hell are you....good to see you, come through, come through" As he walked through the door to his office, he turned to the receptionist, telling her to hold all calls and there were to be no more meetings for the day.

Stephen indicated a chair, his normally friendly face, turned serious....

"What's this about Stephen?"

"How long have you been married to Vanessa Brookes, Robbie?"

"5 months, why?"

"And your father died in November, yes?"

"You know he did, what's with all the questions?"

Stephen passed a large enveloped across to Robbie and he noticed that it was similar to that which was found in the spare room.... "Open it."

"What?"

"just open it Robbie.".

Shaking the contents on to the desk, the face staring up at Robbie was unmistakably Vanessa, her beautiful smile and blue eyes looking out of the picture. He turned to look at Stephen, questioning the photo who indicate for him to continue.

Robbie turned over the next photo, which was of his father, around his neck arms belonging to Vanessa, both smiling and looking up at the photographer....

"They worked together" Robbie said lamely "and were great friends!"

The photographs that followed were of various poses of laughing faces all smiling into the camera. Robbie was confused, his father hated commercial type photos, he called it an evasion of privacy and yet here, in front of him were several. As he turned the last photo he was faced with two lovers entwined, lips locked, and eyes closed shutting out everyone else ...his father and his wife!

Robbie looked up, confused, into the kind eyes of his friend Stephen. "I'm sorry, there must be some mistake. I just don't understand".

"Your father came to see me earlier last year, March I think and said he had met someone and wanted to change his will; that she was younger than him but that she had given him a new lease of life. However, in August he revisited me asking advice. He seemed anxious and very unlike himself. He gave me this envelope of photos and told me that Vanessa had become demanding, she needed to get married to stay in Australia, and that he had refused owing to his age. The University, he knew, would have been against the relationship as he was the tutor, and she seen as a student. When she didn't get what she wanted she threatened his status by saying that she would show the photos to the Dean at the University. All she wanted, he said, was to be Mrs. Hugh Harvey as she felt it would keep her in the country. He wanted me to keep hold of the photos for safe keeping and then he left.....it was the last time I saw him"

Robbie sat there dumbfounded; it was history repeating itself. Vanessa didn't want a husband she wanted a free ticket to stay in Australia and Robbie had given it to her......

"Stephen, do you feel there was foul play?"

"One can't say and difficult to prove. Unfortunately Robbie, changes to the will were never reversed and therefore remain legally binding and we will need to talk to Vanessa on her return. Although, on your instruction I am happy to investigate further."

"Yeh for sure, do so, if you don't mind."

He went through the motions of having a drink but once home, went straight upstairs and opened the envelope found earlier. It contained, as he guessed it would, more photos but these were explicit, something a son should never see. Thoughts crowded Robbie's head, who the hell was this person, not the Vanessa he knew, or was it? There were so many lies; it just didn't make sense!

That night he couldn't sleep and in the morning went through her bags and drawers but found nothing untoward, in fact everything was absolutely normal. Going into the bathroom Robbie opened her bathroom cabinet and found nothing much, just her hospital bracelet and a few bottles. He picked up the bracelet and held it tight remembering the events of the last few months. A sudden anger washed over him, his tears pouring down his face. The raw pain he felt for the loss of their son and the daughter he was never to meet, came up to greet him, buried for so long. He had never questioned the reason for the miscarriage, it had been easier not to think about it but as a doctor he knew he should have done more, but at the time, considering Vanessa's state of mind, it wasn't something that could be discussed. The whole thing had just stayed buried. Running downstairs he rifled through the business cards that were in the bottom of his doctor bag and made the call...

"Hi, I wonder if Michael Proust is available, it is Dr Robbie Harvey."

"Hold on doctor, I will check........putting you through…."

"Hi Robbie, long time no hear, So, you are back in Australia then, when did that happen?....oh shit! Your dad. So sorry to hear about Hugh, great loss to the profession."

"Yes, yes it is. I thought you knew I was back, Vanessa and all that."

"Vanessa?"

"Vanessa Brookes, well now Harvey!"

"Sorry you have lost me; I don't think I know a Vanessa ....do I?"

"My wife, Vanessa, we were pregnant, she was seeing you, or so I thought, and she lost the baby. She was just over 4 months pregnant and went through the D&C alone. You see I just need to know why......I need to know what happened as I wasn't here when the miscarriage occurred."

"Well these things happen and sometimes there is no reason. Look Vanessa doesn't ring a bell and it should....leave it with me, I see so many people – can I give you a call back?"

"Yes sure, thanks."

Robbie knew what the answer would be, and he supposed he had always known......but still waited for the call, and any explanation of why both he and his dad had been played.

The call came .... "Robbie it's Michael here, look I have checked my records and I haven't treated a Vanessa Brookes or Harvey. I have also checked the hospital and the only Vanessa Harvey that they have on record, is for a cut finger, which was recent. Maybe she saw someone else, sorry I can't help you.... yes... must catch up. Ciao."

Nothing made sense, Robbie looked at the photos around the room, of their wedding and life so far, his anger was palpable, it had all been a lie. He couldn't think and as the days waiting for Vanessa to return dragged on, Robbie behaved pretty abysmally, drinking and not eating. He met up with Stephen again and more was unravelled, and a plan of action was devised. It was such a mess!

By the time Vanessa came back from the retreat Robbie had himself under control and acted normally listening how the holiday had put things into perspective. She was tanned and smiling and said she was ready to try for another baby; it was so beguiling and convincing that it was hard not to believe her. Over dinner and a glass of wine, Robbie told her that they needed to see the solicitor as the probate investigation was completed. He saw how this excited her and two days later they sat in Stephen's office as the will was read. It was fairly straight forward; Robbie inherited the house and a very large sum of money; some shares, everything really.....and a letter that had been added after the will had been completed. He put it in his pocket to read later.

Stephen continued reading "To my love, my exotic orchid, Vanessa, you have made an old man happy. I want you to know that although I couldn't marry you, I did love you......I bequeath you $25000, enough money to assist with your Visa and to continue with your life in Australia....."

There was more, but Robbie heard nothing. He turned to look at Vanessa, who was staring ahead, her face motionless, and the reading was continued......."and for that I will be forever grateful" She stood and walked over to the window and without turning her head, spoke. "We were great friends and colleagues; I had no idea......" she stopped and burst into tears. Neither Stephen nor Robbie reacted. It was a great performance but maybe she did love him, and he had been merely the pawn in her game.

"Robbie, you will need to sign here and here, and I will witness it. Thank you." Stephen made a show of rifling through papers and passed over a pen. "Vanessa, can you please sit down. "Of course," she replied, dabbing her eyes and sitting. She picked up the proffered pen in readiness....... Unfortunately, Vanessa or should I call you Sarah," her head shot up... "I am unable to witness a signature that is fraudulent and before you insult me further by showing me your papers which I am sure came at a high price, I have to tell you that under Australian law, you are now an illegal immigrant and I am not able to release any funds to you." Still nothing was said. "Vanessa, I have let immigration know that you are here on false pretences and you will be deported. Had it been up to me the police would have been called to escort you out of my office, but Robbie has asked, for whatever reason, to speak with you first." This was a Stephen that Robbie had never seen before...... "However, I suspect it will not be long before they arrive. The Harvey family have been coming to my firm for many years and Robbie is a close friend and because of that, I have to respect his decision, but Hugh was a fit man and should still be with us now. Anyone can have an accident but the severity of the fall, shocked me, particularly, as he had visited me with so many concerns, leaving me with the evidence that you hoped to blackmail him with. I now believe that the envelope received was not the right envelope, and that you, in fact have more photos. Am I right Vanessa? I also have reason to believe that your name is not Vanessa Brookes, but Sarah Brookes and your documents are, like you, a fraud."

The colour had risen in Vanessa's face, and turning to Robbie, her voice tremulous, she began to speak, "I don't know what you are talking about! I am so sorry Robbie; I loved your father, but I love you too." Her eyes pleaded with me. Coldly she turned back to Steven.

"This is all fabrication, and you have no proof of this."

"No but I do" Robbie took the second envelope out of his bag and threw the contents out on the table. "For whatever reason, this is what you hoped to use against my father, he obviously loved you enough ....." I said indicating the nature of the photos. "to do this!"

There was nowhere she could hide and as if fed up with the lies and deception, Vanessa started to talk. Her name was Sarah May Brookes, she did have degrees in science, and she was born April 30th. Her life in California had been one of a spoilt only child with her parents, both wealthy. Her mother had died in a car accident and she had got in with the wrong crowd and owed money. Her daddy, disappointed with her choices, would not bail her out anymore and it had been very easy for her to get papers to go abroad, money buys everything.

Her life leading up to Hughes's accident had been happy and Hugh attentive. She was used to getting what she wanted but when she realised that Hugh had no intention in marrying her, they had argued. Overhearing a conversation between Hugh and the solicitor about photographic evidence and his reputation, she had seen him put an envelope containing photographs in his briefcase the night before and whilst he slept had switched them.

Things became strained and with their work nearly completed and the funds for the program coming to an end, she felt she was running out of time. In October, Hugh had asked her to leave, they had argued and when her begging didn't work she had shown him the photographs, having evidence to incriminate or at least sully Hughes's name. Hugh had lurched forward to grab the envelope as she taunted him about it and missed his footing falling down the stairs and the rest is history.

Robbie had stood and was looking out of the window. He quietly spoke, his voice catching, "And the baby, was there a baby?

"I really thought I was pregnant, this time. You were so happy; I couldn't tell you it was a false alarm......Robbie I loved you so much". She stood grabbing at his arm, but the level of deception was too much, and he shook her off pushing her away from him and walked out of the office. He needed some air. Outside on the street, the realisation made him dry reach; shock, anger and humiliation swamped him. Eventually, after what seemed like a long time, he returned to Stephen's office and Vanessa had gone.

1992

There was silence in the small kitchen. Mary stared at Robbie, her face, one of horror and sadness. Fran needed to hear this, as did Joe and walking over to Robbie rested her hand on his shoulder as he continued.

"In the next two months, I left my position at the surgery and I drank. I drank to forget, Vanessa; I drank to forget Fran and Emily, and was out of it most of the time .....and then something happened which changed my perspective on life; Toby, my dear companion, died, he was old, and it was his time and it sort of bought me back to reality. I decided, with nothing holding me in Perth, that I would travel to Broome. There I studied the culture: the art; the medicines used but most of all I lived and believed in the Dreamtime. After 6 months of my nomadic life, a wise Elder told me to travel to the place that made me happy and where I could do good. I went out to the bush and sat asking the ancestors to help me, it was here that I felt the calmness of my father and found the direction that I needed. It gave me the strength and courage to find myself again and as I had nothing left in Australia, I packed up and left, leaving the property in Fremantle to be sold.

I had a child, that needed to be part of my life and made my way back here. It seems Mary, that I am too late and looking into her kind eyes, he realised that he was.

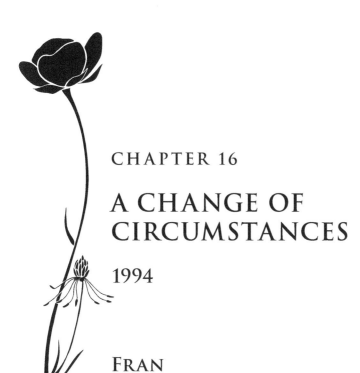

CHAPTER 16

A CHANGE OF CIRCUMSTANCES

1994

FRAN

Fran watched as he walked towards her, the small child sitting up on his shoulders. The little girl with her red curls was laughing and the man, looking up at her as they walked showed his absolute enjoyment in his small passenger. He raised a hand as he saw Fran, and said something to the child, who looked across the crowded marketplace, her little eyes sparkling as she followed his pointed finger and squealing with joy when she found her mother. "Mummy" she yelled and waved madly. In her little hand a gift; a bunch of wild buttercups to present to her.

It never failed to amaze Robbie, that the vision of Fran, still gave him that knot in his stomach and as he reached her and lowered the squirming child down, her brilliant smile that reached those green eyes, once again affected him in a way that no other woman had and smiled back at her. "Has she been good Robbie?"

"She's been an absolute terror haven't you Emily!" The small girl turned from her mother's hug and pulling a face, put her little hands on her hips "No, Uncle Robbie, I was a good girl!" They both laughed and Emily joined in not really knowing why. They walked together towards the Blue Cafe, and as he had done on many occasions before, asked if Fran would like to join him for a coffee before his drive home.

Much to his amazement, she said she would love to. As they walked into the cafe, Robbie noticed that Fran looked tired, very tired and had lost a lot of weight but had learnt not to ask personal questions, or in fact show any form of affection. However, it was Fran that instigated the conversation "I wanted to catch up and talk about this little person's birthday" Emily oblivious of the discussion, continued colouring at the table. "Would you mind awfully if you celebrated it with her when she came to stay, instead of at the house?" Seeing Robbie's quizzical expression, she continued.... "It's just that Richard has been working so hard lately, and we have hardly seen him, and thought it would be nice to have some family time together."

"Am I not family?"

"Bloody hell Robbie, please don't make this more difficult than it already is. Richard is going through hell at the moment, problems with work and the like and......." Robbie interrupted her.

"Will Mary and Joe be present, Tom and Nancy or maybe it's just me that is excluded?" Robbie knew he was snapping but this hurt. The last two years had been difficult but with encouragement from Mary and then Joe, Fran had not only believed Robbie's story but had also became empathetic to his request to see his daughter. However, it was Richard who had caused problems. He had become jealous and unreasonable, even when Robbie had done everything asked of him in order be part of Emily's life including relinquishing the title of father.

"I am so sorry; it's been rather difficult of late!" And to Robbie's distress, Fran started to cry, lifting her hands to her face.

"Mummy?"

"It's ok Emily, mummy is just very tired".

"What is it Fran?...I am sorry I did not mean to upset you"

"God Robbie, it isn't you....It's Richard, he is just awful to live with. Nothing I do is right, He gets unreasonably angry with Emily when she talks about you and on top of that we have been trying for another baby over the last year without success, not that he is home much, yet somehow it's my involvement with you that has caused the issue"

"Me? What involvement? Look I will stay away for a while; go ahead and celebrate Emily's birthday and I will pick her up a week later, ok?"

"I am sorry Robbie, really I am." Fran checked her watched, drained her coffee cup and got up ready to leave. Robbie also stood and put on his coat, blue scarf and hat, whilst Fran grappled with a reluctant Emily. Standing up, Fran indicated for Emily to kiss her uncle goodbye, which she did and then fastened the buttons on her coat. The sudden gesture of Robbie grabbing her arm surprised her, but she was too tired to resist his touch. "If you ever need to just talk, I can meet you for a drink or a walk or something, anything! You know Bean, I am here if you need me". Wearily she thanked him and with a wave to Emily he left the Blue Cafe and sauntered down the road to where he had parked.

Fran watched as he left and not for the first time felt that nervous flutter in her stomach.

"Fran Taylor, you are a married woman" she mentally reprimanded herself, but it didn't stop her having thoughts. His easy stride, that she could never keep up with; his long fingers that combed through his fringe when he was thinking and the earnest blue eyes, which searched her inner thoughts, still affected her. In the last two years all that she'd buried about him, had resurfaced. She had done her best to keep him at bay, but tonight they had broken an unsaid barrier, it had not been easy, and Fran knew she would have to be careful.

"Mummy, I want to go home"......Emily interrupted her thoughts and they set off for home. Upon the table lay a wilted posey of buttercups, forgotten, and like Fran, not surviving without tender loving care and the sustenance required.

ROBBIE

Robbie walked through the Emergency Department at St Luke's Hospital on the outskirts of Stillbridge, where he now lived. He had been working at the hospital for the last two years, being sponsored by the Executive Board who were assisting him towards permanent residency. Recently promoted to Head of Department, he was now responsible for the smooth running of incoming patients and the services that they needed. Robbie loved his job, and had become very popular, always with a boyish smile which staff, particularly the female staff, adored and had a thoughtfulness for others, not just the patients, which was rare. He felt more settled than he had ever been, particularly as now he saw more of his daughter having her every second weekend at his home and all day Wednesdays at Fran's house, until Mary got home from teaching, whilst Richard and Fran were working in London.

Yes, it had all worked out quite well, better than expected or he believed he would be entitled to, but there was a loneliness that never left him. There had never been another woman after Vanessa and he knew he still loved, and always had loved Fran, so he doubted there would be another. His divorce had come through and the sale of his house finalised. Financially he was pretty set up but mentally, that was another story.

At least he saw Emily, the light, that made him forgive the cruel twist of fate, that had befallen him.

Her nickname, Buttercup, said it all - strong resilient with the brightest of smiles that lit up his world. "My name is Buttercup," she would tell people and it filled his heart with pride. He had made up a silly rhyme and they danced a silly dance.....which made them collapse into fits of giggles, the innocence of childhood.

Buttercup buttercup face to the sky
Open your arms stretch out wide
Twirl round and round and do not stop
Until you fall with a great big plop....

With that they would fall over and over screaming with laughter. Emily had told him, that her mummy really loved the song too and she had shown her how to do the dance....

Watching Emily dancing around his sitting room, he was reminded of someone else, in a field, who threw back her titian curls and swirled around laughing at the sun, letting her troubles fade for just that instant.... he had been the one to cause those troubles and he never wanted to hurt her again.

So life went on.....

RICHARD

Life changed when Robbie came back into it. Realistically Richard knew it wasn't Robbie's fault, but he felt that everything had gone sour and he pin-pointed this to Robbie's return.

Mackenzie Taylor had been doing well and between them, Fran and Richard worked to gain respect from the clients and the industry. More and more interest had been shown and their business was recognised both in London and abroad. Fran had never come back to the city to design, choosing to design in the workshop attached to the cottage. She said that she got inspiration from the countryside around them and indeed that was the case with her use of colours and soft lines. They could also afford others designers now and the modern, more geometric line, that was requested was done by others. All in all Mackenzie Taylor was on the map. However, Richard spent more and more time away from home, he didn't complain but without Fran's input he had found it difficult, lacking her natural eye and the easy way she spoke to the clients, beguiling them with her beauty and gentle voice. Her descriptive and obvious knowledge was the sale tool that brought the customer; he felt lost without her.

Just after his beloved Emily turned one, he had asked Fran to return to London to work and although they had spoken about it several times she had seemed adamant that she wasn't ready. He was sure he hadn't imagined the lack of enthusiasm and had often caught her looking wistfully into nothing.

Since Robbie's return there had been a definite change, he had heard her crying but never when near him and when he held her at night, he felt a resistance not there before.

Maybe, if he hadn't been so busy, he could have spoken to her, maybe he could have done more but there was an unspoken void appearing between them which he couldn't fill.

He had spoken to Mary and she had listened and gently said "Give her time, she has had a shock" but he had seen Mary and Robbie sitting in the Blue Cafe heads bent down, talking on more than one occasion, and jealousy mounted. It was easier to stay at work, it was easier to be busy and build their future. He had hoped that in time Fran would want to have another baby, his baby but he didn't push that either, after all Emily was only little and love making few and far between.

The true resentment began after a particular difficult day; Richard had arrived home late to find Mary, Joe, Fran and Robbie sitting on the patio. It had been a balmy night in July, and they were deep in conversation, he arrived very much unnoticed. Walking through the front door, he put his briefcase at the foot of the stairs as normal, when he heard Robbie's voice. To his left was Joe nodding in agreement at something Robbie was saying. He took in Robbie's long legs clad in blue denim, his black T-shirt taught across his chest and his tanned arms. His hand, as usual, combing through his fringe and his face with his chiselled good looks, was animated and he spoke. Richard slowly walked through the corridor, he knew Emily would be tucked up in bed, it was late, so he wouldn't go into her and instead carried on walking into the kitchen. Looking at the empty wine and beer bottles, he deduced that Robbie had been here for some time; he stood quietly listening to the conversation moving to the side of the kitchen bench so he could see more clearly.

Joe was speaking "When Mum told me, Fran, it took some convincing that someone could do that to another person but if your mum believes him then so do I. It must have been a hell of a time lad".

"Yes it was but it is over now, and I just want somehow to be part of Emily's life. I cannot begin to say how sorry I am, for the pain I have caused"

And then his wife, his Fran spoke, "Perhaps you deserved the pain Robbie!"

Mary and Joe looked at each other, together chorusing "Fran!" She held up her hand and continued. "It must have been awful, I agree and no one deserves to be treated like that. You left me high and dry, but I left you too. I didn't tell you I was pregnant straight away because unlike Vanessa, I didn't want to trap you. I pushed you away! I don't know why, and I don't know what I expected really...maybe a fairy tale ending….. "She looked away as if the memory was too painful… "However, I was rescued! Richard is a brilliant father to Emily"…. She went on with encouragement from Mary and Joe, who were in agreement at her statement….. "And in all sense and purposes Emily's daddy. He is my husband and we have made a life together both here and in London…….". From the kitchen, Richard let out a sigh of relief, he felt tears prick his eyes and went to move forward but stopped in his tracks, hand resting on the door handle of the back door as Fran continued "But it seems a cruel parody, if I refused you access to your own daughter, but this I will need to discuss with Richard."

"Discuss what with Richard, Fran?" Richard who could take no more, exploded onto the patio; four pairs of eyes looked up and Fran scrabbled to her feet.

"What is he doing here Fran! ....Get out Robbie, I have said this to you before, you obviously didn't get the message!" Richard advanced towards the table and Joe stood, "Richard, this is not helping".

"Last time I looked, Fran was my wife and Emily my daughter, legally, and hey this is my house and you, Robbie, are not welcome here. You are nothing but trouble, so I ask politely, for the sake of my family for you to leave....or ...or I will call the police!" With his voice raised and angry he stepped towards Robbie aggressively.

"Richard!"

"Keep out of this Fran"......

"That is enough, you don't have any idea what you are saying or talking about Richard. I suggest, Robbie, that you leave so I can fill Richard in but for God sake just stop!"

Fran burst into tears and looking at her mother for support she said, "I can't do this!". As if on queue, Emily let out a bellow and Fran ran inside to calm her.

Mary stood to join her "Well that is hardly surprising" indicating towards Emily's room "all this yelling - Robbie, I am sorry but time to go and Richard, sit!".

At the time, that was how it was left, words left unsaid, and feelings buried but time is a great healer, so they say and in order to move on differences were left behind. In the end Richard accepted that he had no choice and during another meeting it was decided that Robbie would become an Uncle not a daddy so as not to confuse Emily as she grew older, leaving the true bond between father and daughter obvious to those who knew.

However, Fran struggled with having Robbie and Richard in her life and did everything in her power never to be alone with Robbie. Her denial of feelings drove a knife through her own relationship and the more Richard worked, the more she distanced herself from both. It had become a difficult time in the design industry and competitive companies became ruthless in their delivery. Richard, therefore, became anxious and insular in his thoughts and without his wife's encouragement, felt alone.

Fran felt that she now had an empty challis that could not be filled and even when the suggestion of another baby was mentioned, she only went through the motions and not surprisingly the magic of new life was absent.

As the years went by the only stable in her life was Emily and with Emily came Robbie. It was hardly surprising that their pathways would entwine and the loneliness consuming both would be abated.

Robbie, now a successful doctor at Stillbridge General had settled into not only his life but also theirs'. Never assuming and always accommodating, it was so easy to accept him, and the family forgot the misdemeanours of the past and in doing so he became an integral part of all their lives.

Richard however, despised this intrusion and whether he knew consciously or not there was a hatred burning inside which ultimately would manifest with enormous and immeasurable consequences.

CHAPTER 17

INDUSTRIAL DISRUPTION

1995

1995 proved a difficult year for Mackenzie Taylor. The trend towards commodity textiles from other countries increased forcing closure of many English textile companies. The niche market became highly technical based on synthetic materials and a scientific method was adopted in many fields. Mackenzie Taylor felt the push for change and although it was not affected directly, revenue drop was significant with the loss of so many businesses around them.

The change of direction came with the employment of Sanjet Khan, a chemical engineer who specialised in textiles Sanjet, originally from India, had studied in California applying the principles of chemistry to the production of textiles. Since joining, his team had developed newer more sustainable products and with it a new avenue for Mackenzie Taylor advertising the use of organic material, which had not been done in London before. It had been an enormous gamble which thankfully had paid off with interest growing throughout America and other European countries. The M&T branding on designer furniture; fixture and fittings with newer ergonomic designs pushed them in yet another direction but with this more expenditure and although an exciting time, Richard lost sleep and stressed about the company and responsibilities that he upheld. The other serious competitor, Designer Home Textiles undercut many suppliers and designed similar products at cheaper cost, using synthetic materials; not only breaking into the Asian market but competing in the British.

Richard wasn't surprised to hear that Suri Lo was the founder and now CEO. Having removed her from Mackenzie Taylor in 1990, she had done well for herself. Now five years later and married to a multi-millionaire, she could do no wrong, with her bold geometric designs, which now seemed to be fashionable; affordable and very much sort after.

At the Industrial Exhibition, she was introduced to Richard by an unsuspecting organiser and smiling, she simpered "Darling, we have met before." Flicking her sleek hair and dazzling her host with a smile. The organiser went on to enthuse about Mackenzie Taylor's achievements, not realising the obvious tension. Richard noted that her beauty had matured, her clothing, as before, impeccable and her smile, cold, never reaching her eyes. However, there was something quite different about her, apart from the obvious wealth that oozed out of her, and that was confidence and moreover, power. Suri had become a serious contender in the market, and she knew it with every fibre in her body. Richard watched as she slipped in and out of the clientele with chic precision and knew without a doubt this was not only competition, but trouble and he would have to up his game.

Throughout the evening he felt her eyes boring into him and before leaving she sought him out; "Richard how are you and the family? I hear Fran had a little girl." He responded cordially but he could see it was merely lip service and she had no interest. "It must be a worrying time for you with Mackenzie Taylor dropping on the share market. DHT has had its share of difficulties, but we are back on top, I expect you have noticed? There is, as you know, a whole new world out there with the market changing rapidly. There will be a time, when a boutique firm such as yours however, well known, will be swallowed up by corporate firms like mine. Whether you like it or not and with the best will in the world, you will not survive and when you fall, I will be waiting!" She kissed him on the cheek as a photographer snapped a shot..... "Ciao, darling", she left with her entourage following; it was a formidable army and one that left Richard concerned, his gut churned, and for the hundredth time that night he wished Fran had made the effort to attend.

The next day the newspapers headlined in the Business section - "The Industrial competitiveness heats up. Roger Taylor, CEO and owner of Mackenzie Taylor and Suri Lo CEO and founder of Designer Home Textiles go into battle or do we see a merger ahead? Looking at MT share prices, this is a strong possibility! With an injection of funds from DHT, which they can well afford, a new direction might be on the cards - without it, we might be seeing another closing door, only time will tell". Above the blurb were three photos - those interested would see Suri Lo smiling at the camera, a successful, beautiful, businesswoman; a photo of her deep in conversation with Richard, his face clearly troubled and finally the kiss.

Richard's phone was ringing, it had rung all morning. Messages had been left on his desk by his secretary - people were worried; companies were panicking. He threw the newspaper across the room, "they couldn't even get my bloody name right" he shouted to no one.

Pressing a button on his phone he rang through to the outer office, "I want all heads of department in the boardroom in one hour, one hour- got it?".

"Yes Mr. Taylor, I have Mrs. ......" he had already slammed the phone down. His thoughts were interrupted by a knock on the door....

"Yes!"

The door opened, and much to his relief Fran walked in. Seeing her husband's expression she rushed over to him.... "I saw the paper, and I tried to phone...so I thought I should come up, are you ok!"

"I called a board meeting in an hour, you would have been expected to come anyway, well that is if you still have an interest in this firm!"

"Richard!"

"I could have done with your support last night, Sanjet was a poor substitute!" His words were cold and unforgiving. Fran sighed and sat down, why had she thought it would be any different. She knew her husband was anxious, but he had shut her out, spending more and more time in their London flat, than at home with his family. She justified that times were difficult, but they were fast becoming strangers. She tried again "I was at home with Emily, mum had a parent evening at school; dad still has that awful cold, and I couldn't leave her with strangers, particularly as she is so very clingy at the moment"

"And today?"

"I rang Robbie and he managed to change his roster.....he is going to have Emily today and tomorrow at his place, so I can stay over, we can pick her up together Wednesday night."

"Hail the conquering hero.......thank god for Saint Robbie!"

"Oh shut up Richard, what else could I do. Perhaps if you spent more time at home, I wouldn't...."

"You wouldn't what? You wouldn't have to rely on your lover!" As fast as the words came out, he regretted them. What the hell was he saying but still they came..... "whilst I am saving the company, you can continue to play happy families with Emily's father, how do you think that makes me feel Francesca?"

Slowly Fran stood and looked at the man she had married. His fine features contorted and his skin grey with stress, all senses of kindness gone. She turned on her heal and walked to the door... she knew he didn't mean it, but boy it hit home because in reality, at the moment, she enjoyed her time with Robbie far more than she did with Richard.

Stooping she picked up the newspaper strewn across the office floor, turning she looked at Richard, his angry face staring back at her and very deliberately screwed it up, throwing today's news hard into the bin. He was not surprised when the office door slammed shut and with his head in his hands, he wondered what had gone so wrong.

The board meeting was as expected. Concerns for the company were high but even though Richard felt their anxiety and that of his own he came across calm and focussed. He made a joke about Roger Taylor saying that Roger Taylor may have got it wrong, but Richard Taylor had not, and they had applauded his resilience. He reassured them that although the company was going through a difficult patch, there were plans to increase the need for cheaper products working in the synthetic arena. Mackenzie Taylor would indeed go in another direction but would maintain the quality that was their name; another burst of applause filled the room. As he spoke he walked around the table, laying his hands on shoulders, squeezing reassuringly, he had, Fran noticed, rallied the troupe and had then in the palm of his hand. He arrived behind her chair, placing his hands on her shoulders, spoke "My wife and I, will not see Mackenzie Taylor fail. Francesca will head up the organic fibre production of textiles, working from home and in the London office, as before and Sanjet, he clapped him on the back, will head up the new division of synthetic textiles. Paul, you will continue to work your magic in fixtures and fittings turning the bolts that hold us together, again there was laughter around the table. Whatever you need you just need to ask. We will grow; we will survive and in memory of my late wife who helped set up this company in our small flat, dreaming of one day having a business we can be proud of, we will continue. The room erupted and Fran sat back, watching in awe as colleagues shook his hand and the positivity flowed in the room. He had not mentioned Sarah Mackenzie for years, why now....to further hurt her or to inject trust back into the company....she hoped it was the latter It was hard to believe that this was the same man, that had been so hurtful an hour previous but maybe it was understandable, that newspaper article had been so damming. His voice cut through her thoughts "Fran, Hazel are you coming?"

Fran stood and walked towards him, but deep in conversation with Hazel, his secretary, he had forgotten her and feeling exhausted, she sat, watching the goings on around her. The day continued in the same vein, and somehow Fran find the energy to carry on. She found herself in the midst of planning, hearing names, telephoning companies and actioning strategies that would grow and promote their assets. Sanjet was bringing in a colleague from California to work with him. She was well known and had a good business head on her shoulders. Sarah Burford had jumped at the chance. Richard argued about her remuneration but in the end it was agreed, and she would arrive in the next month.

By Wednesday afternoon they were exhausted, and Fran suggested an early dinner before they all went home. "Sorry Fran, Sanjet and I are meeting Paul, he has some questions." Seeing her expression he continued, "you are very welcome to join but don't you need to get back?"

She looked at him sadly "Richard, I thought we were driving back together, to pick up Emily?" But he wasn't listening and had continued walking on with Sanjet, lost in thought and conversation, focussed on more important things. As the lift dinged, he turned back and saluted her as he stepped in.

Alone in his office, Fran wearily picked up her bag, put on her coat and walked out, saying goodbye to Hazel as she left.

With unwavering certainty, she drove with determination down the motorway and like the company, she knew which way she was heading. With her foot hitting the accelerator she drove towards Robbie and her future.

CHAPTER 18

INEVITABLE EXPOSURE

1995

Fran's arrival at 'The Hollies' was later than expected. It was dark and the night air, still.

There was a layer of snow on the ground and more hung in the air. She could smell it. Due to the weather there had been a back-up of traffic on the motorway and given the conditions she knew she should have stayed on another night. Her journey had been fraught with problems but her determination to see Robbie and her daughter far outweighed the issues that were occurring in front of her.

The Hollies was a series of cottages set in a cul-de-sac. Robbie lived at number 3, set back, and left of the large beech tree. She parked her car on the road and walked up the pathway, her shoes crunching on the pavement, leaving footprints in the snow. She was not only freezing but starving and hoped that Robbie had something warm for her to eat. As she approached his cottage, she stopped and stood under the beech tree, looking at his door. Her head told her to walk in, pick up Emily, thank Robbie and go home, but her heart told her to stay. She didn't intend for anything untoward to happen and to stay longer would certainly give out a different message. As she stepped from the shelter of the tree, the door of number 3 opened and light spilled onto the street. Fran ducked back into the shadow of the tree and watched as Robbie, looked up the street. Checking his watch, he wrapped his arms around his body and stamped warmth into his feet. With another look from left to right, he took himself back into the warmth. From her hiding place, she looked at his tall stature as he retreated and memories of old flooded back. Her breath came quickly and the cold vapours leaving her mouth evaporated into the air. "Fran Taylor, what are you playing at?" she reprimanded herself. "Enough!" She stomped up the steps and knocked on the door.

The warmth of the house made her skin itch and her feet ache, but it was so much better than being outside where it had started to snow again. "Sorry, Robbie, for being so late. Traffic was at a standstill, weather was terrible."

"It's not much better now, and it's perfectly alright," he said, pouring her a red wine and offering it to her. "Yes please", she said, gratefully.

"Look, Bean, the snow is really setting in and Emily is already asleep. Why don't you sleep over and leave first thing in the morning?" Seeing her expression, he added "Don't look so shocked. I do have a spare room, you know. Emily doesn't take up much room. You can share."

Fran got up and walked over to the window. Snow was drifting into piles; the roads would be treacherous. "Thanks Robbie. I might just do that. I don't suppose you have a packet of soup I could have? I am absolutely starving."

"I can do better than that. I wasn't sure whether you would both be coming so I made a big batch of vegetable soup. I hope that will do." He disappeared into the kitchen and Fran kicked off her shoes and warmed herself by the open fire. Whether it was the red wine or the hypnotising flicker of the flames, Fran felt more relaxed than she had done in weeks and her eyes started to close. The sound of dishes clashing together as they were lowered onto the table woke her with a start. "Oh God! Sorry, Robbie, I am exhausted."

"Too exhausted to eat?"

Fran sat up and laughing replied, "Absolutely not! That smells amazing." The soup was thick and full of vegetables and beside it there were chunks of thick buttered bread. It was heaven and Fran ate hungrily. He poured her another glass of wine and then joined her. Sitting in silence, with only the sound of the spoon against the bowl, they sat companionably, sipping wine, and staring into the flames. When Fran had finished, he took the dishes out to the kitchen. When he walked back in, he looked at the woman sitting on the couch. Her tousled curls and pale face. "Are you ok Fran? You look sort of sad or is it just exhaustion?" "A bit of both really," she replied.

"I thought Richard was coming with you tonight?"

"Yeh, well, he had other plans that don't really figure me or Emily in anymore. Actually that isn't really true. He has plans for the company, big plans. There just isn't time for family. We really have different ideas about life in general actually and he will need to focus on Mackenzie Taylor if we are to save it. It's just I am not sure whether it's what I want anymore!"

"Does he know that?"

"He has a pretty good idea!"

"Oh my poor Bean, life can be so cruel." Whether it was her exhaustion or the wine, she started to cry, large tears pouring down her cheeks. "Richard blames you. God knows why."

"And what do you feel?"

"It's not your fault that share prices dropped; it's not your fault that clients want a cheaper product."

"Bean, that is not what I meant. How do you feel?" He had moved closer, sitting on the couch next to her. She could hear his breathing and felt his warmth. It all seemed so real.

"I don't ...." Before she had finished the sentence, his lips brushed hers and his strong arms held her. Fran didn't resist. It felt so good to be actually wanted and this was so beautiful, so natural. Hungrily she kissed him back and his hands moved to the curve in her back pressing her closer until they were one. After a few minutes, he pulled away and stood up. He combed through his hair nervously. "Sorry Fran, I didn't mean for that to happen, but I love you. I don't want to hide behind our daughter anymore. I have always loved you and ....and I know this is wrong, but I can't watch from the side-lines anymore." He watched helplessly as she stood and walked over to the window, staring out at the white blanket of fresh snow. Then she pulled the heavy curtains across, shutting out the world beyond. She turned and stared at him, without any guilt, wanting more. Uneasy, he combed through his hair nervously. "Fran? Say something for Christ's sake."

There was a slight smile on her face. "I love you too." She walked into his arms and five years of pain fell away effortlessly. There was no awkwardness in their love making. Familiar with each other's bodies and safe in each other's arms they lay comfortably in front of the fire. Fran felt as if she had come home and finally, she fell asleep.

When she woke, she had no guilt. For the first time in many months, she felt happy. She could hear Robbie, talking to Emily in the kitchen, about making a snowman and it all felt so natural. She laid under the blanket, naked and whole, how could this be wrong?

"Mummy! Wake up mummy! Where is daddy?" Her daughter was standing next to the couch and suddenly her resolve left her. Her daddy; Richard. Oh my god what had she done.

Fran reached over for her mobile where she found three messages.....

"Fran it's Richard, the weather is dreadful out there, let me know when you get home."

"Fran are you ok, can you give me a call when you get home."

"Look I know you are cross, but I am worried. I am on my way home".

Fran read the messages, and reading the last one, jumped off the couch and threw on her clothes. "Come on Emily, time to go".

With any luck she would get home before Richard did. She said goodbye to Robbie and got into her car. Robbie looked in the window, saying goodbye to Emily, and then put his head in through the driver's window.

"Fran?"

"Yes Robbie, I know, we will talk but I have to go."

"I don't want to lose you again…"

Fran turned on the ignition and smiled, "Robbie, you won't!"

CHAPTER 19

DECISIONS TO MAKE

1995

Fran looked at her watch, one o'clock. she rolled over and nuzzled at Robbie's arm. Wake up, sleepy head, I have to go soon, and I haven't finished with you yet.... she giggled and stretched her naked body against his. Groaning, Robbie pushed himself up on his elbow "You insatiable wench, can't a man get some sleep?"

"Absolutely but definitely not on my time," Fran laughed. He kissed her tenderly and shifting his weight rolled on top of her loving her all over again. The pleasure in feeling her smooth skin under his, aroused him and their passion climaxed until they cried out in absolute exhilaration. This, Fran thought, justified everything, the last two months of just being loved, and as they lay panting on the bed, she knew she wanted more. They had talked about Fran leaving Richard but there was never the right moment and of course there was Emily.

Emily! Sitting up and checking the time, Fran leapt out of bed, it was cold, and she hurriedly jumped under the warm shower. Today Emily was at kindergarten, and pick up was at 2.30, she didn't have much time! Tonight, she had a meeting at the local primary school for Emily's enrolment and needed to get Emily fed, bathed and up to her father's by 6pm. With a sinking heart, she remembered that Richard was travelling back tonight so he could attend; let's hope, she thought, that it would be more successful than the last time he was home. Either he talked incessantly about having another baby, for he felt that was what they needed to get back on track or he talked about work. The act of love making was thankfully few and far between, as he often came back exhausted. He also had very little time for a four-year-old that had turned into a monster, although he had plenty of time for the many phone calls that he took. Rarely did he actually ask how she was, unless it was about textiles, trade and business and rarely did they go out, unless it was for a business dinner.

"Do you want tea or coffee Fran" Robbie yelled – "Neither thanks, I have got to go!"

She came out of the bathroom, "Have you seen my other shoe?"

"What this?" He held it up high, dancing around as Fran attempted to get it back...." Robbie, seriously I have got to go"

He relinquished the shoe and kissed her on the nose.... "Will you talk with Richard tonight; we need to do something? I can't keep going on like this Bean...."

"I will, Robbie, but I need to pick the right moment.... I love you; you know that don't you?"

He kissed her "Yes but I want all of you".

She wanted all of him too but didn't know if she had the courage to actually make it happen. She slammed the car door and drove off.

There was a knock at the door, Richard looked up, "Come" he shouted, annoyed at another interruption. An attractive tall blonde walked into his office, confident and sassy. A long slim hand was offered, and a soft American voice spoke "Mr. Taylor?"

"Yes, can I help you?" She removed her hand before speaking, "My name is Sarah Burford, I believe you are expecting me!" It was more of a statement than a question.

"Ah Yes, Sarah Burford. I believe you are late!"

"Late? – I have only just got here." Richard saw the laughter in her eyes and smile, which opened her lips.

"Exactly, weren't you meant to arrive in January" He made a show of looking through his calendar "We are now in the middle of February!" Laughing, Sarah took the proffered hand and shook it warmly, "You got me there! "Taking a seat, Richard couldn't help noticing her long legs as she slowly crossed one across the other.

"Unfortunately, Immigration doesn't give a fig about Mackenzie Taylor, however I do." This time he smiled a genuine smile and she noticed for the first time, a good-looking man sitting in front of her. He turned and picked up the phone "Hazel can you find Sanjet for me and tell him to come to my office please!"

Looking at her surroundings, she saw the expected trimmings of an executive life, a photo on his desk of a beautiful woman, probably his wife, and one of a little girl, who looked oddly familiar. "She's lovely!"

"That's my wife, she is Head of Organic Textile Design, she works mostly from home but travels up each week- you will meet her Wednesday and that", indicating the other photo, "is my daughter."

"Pretty girl! It must be hard, running a household with the added responsibility of running a department, I am not sure I could do it."

Richard got up from his desk, for some reason, of late, he felt uncomfortable talking about Fran. Over the last month they had become more distant than ever. He had tried to be home at the weekends, but Mackenzie Taylor was getting a good reputation and it was growing fast. There was justification that he needed to be here at the helm and Fran seemed to understand although she had been awfully distracted lately. He wandered over to the coffee percolator and looked up...

"Coffee?"

"Yes, black please". The silence was interrupted by the appearance of Sanjet who apologised profusely for keeping them waiting. Sarah jumped out of her chair "Wow it's so good to see you again, Sanjet, how are you? "She enveloped him in a hug... "Sarah Burford, at last...., we have so much to talk about but first, what took you so long?"

With the niceties over, Sarah and Sanjet left with an offer to come to dinner once Sarah had been shown around. Richard had been due to go home that night, something to do with a new school but he told himself that business had to come first, it was critical to get this right and Fran would just have to understand.

Wearily he picked up the phone "Fran, it's me.... Yes, I know but something has come up.

No sorry, it can't be helped, Sarah Burford has arrived, and I have to do the right thing and take her out to dinner, it's her first night and we have to keep her happy and engaged............

No, she is not more important than Emily but isn't Mary going too? She will be much more helpful than me!

Sanjet? No, he is not available ...... Look it can't be helped, you know how it is.

Sorry Fran........Fran?......Francesca!" She had hung up on him again. Richard stared at the receiver then slammed it down hard. They needed to talk and sort things out but when?

Richard sat looking at Fran's picture. He didn't know why he had just lied to her either, of course Sanjet could have easily taken Sarah out for dinner alone but she interested him, and he wanted to find out more.

He chose a restaurant near to his London flat, a lovely little bistro that he often frequented and sitting in a booth Richard discussed his plans for the company. He found Sarah attentive and bright with her ideas refreshing and coupled with Sanjet's enthusiasm, he left feeling more positive than he had for months.

"Sarah, it's been an absolute pleasure. I am very much looking forward to working with you."

"Thanks Richard, likewise." She hailed a taxi and as she got in, smiled up at them both; her beautiful smile lit up her face, and her blue eyes, mesmerising. As the taxi sped off in the direction of her hotel, Richard turned to Sanjet, "she will do well Sanjet, I am certain of it! "They walked companionably, talking about the future, until Sanjet caught his bus home. Saying goodbye and shaking his hand warmly he carried on walking, god it felt good to feel so excited again. Reaching his apartment, he ran up the stairs two at a time, feeling energised, he could feel that a change was in the air and to celebrate he poured himself a brandy. Draining his glass, he poured another, relaxing for the first time in a long time - eventually he made to get ready for bed; he was tired, and the brandy had made him sleepy. The sheets felt cold, and he cuddled up, missing the company and warmth of another person and just as his eyes closed the phone rang.

"Richard Taylor..........," he yawned, "sorry, how can I help you?"

"Hi Richard, it's me, Fran."

"Hi, are you ok, it's pretty late......is Emily alright?"

"We are both ok and Emily is asleep. In case you are interested she has been enrolled in the local school for September."

"Yeh of course......and?"

"And what?"

"Fran, it's late, you didn't just phone me to tell me that, what's up?"

"And .... well ...we need to talk. Richard, we can't pretend that all is well, yet we are doing nothing about it. I need a break, from Mackenzie Taylor, from everything. I am really tired and all we do is talk shop. Perhaps I could find my interest again, if I didn't work there, as it is........"

Richard interrupted her, "I see! Do you want to think about this Fran, it is rather a sudden decision, don't you think? And It's late, let's sleep on it"

Fran could hear the anger in his voice or was it disappointment she wasn't sure but either ways knew she needed to carry on.......

"Richard that's just it I have thought about this a lot ...... Gisela can take over from me or maybe this new Sarah that you talk so highly of; I can finish the last order, which should take me through to end of March and then handover. What do you think?

"I don't think! No Fran! I agree it's been incredibly tiring, but I think there is light at the end of the tunnel, don't you agree? Let's talk tomorrow when you get here. I am sure you will change your mind once you hear the new plans we have been talking about. For once I feel really energised and excited; I came away from dinner tonight brimming with ideas, well Sarah's ideas, I can't wait to share them with you. Oh and before I forget, I have been meaning to tell you... good news Suri Lo's stocks have dropped incredibly due to her husband's shaky deals, and some companies have lost faith in her and I think, I..... we, can win them back. So, don't you see we must stick together at this stage., show a united front as they say."

Fran felt, exasperated. Once again, he hadn't listened to her needs, it had been all about the Company and what Richard Taylor wanted!

"I hear what you are saying Richard, but I have made up my mind. What time are you free tomorrow, I have the Jameson order to go through with you and. one or two other things to discuss. Just give me a time and I will pop up to your office."

"I will check my diary and let you know, okay? By the way make yourself free about 10 o'clock as you have a meeting with Sarah. Goodnight Fran. Love you." And without waiting for her reply, the phone hung up.

"Yes Richard, whatever 'you bloody say. What Richard Taylor wants, Richard Taylor gets!" but her sarcasm was wasted, he had already gone.

Richard lay there wide awake thumping the mattress in frustration and once again sleep was void.

Fran woke up the next morning with absolute dread. She skipped breakfast feeling quite sick putting it down to nerves and downed a black coffee which scolded her mouth. She had dressed carefully choosing a navy suit and crisp white blouse. She piled her red curls up on top of her head fastening them with a matching blue ribbon and added a red pair of kitten heals to finish it off. For some reason she felt that she needed the power suit to aid her with her day, maybe a one up on this Sarah that Richard raved about. Irritated she looked in the long mirror in the hallway and admitted out loud to no one in particular that she looked smart, "Not bad, Fran, not bad. You tell him to stick his job". Fran laughed at herself and then patted the skin around her eyes, she looked tired and her face gaunt.

Her thoughts were interrupted by the doorbell and ran through to the front door it would be Robbie

"She is in the kitchen playing with her food, refusing to eat. Mum popped in but even she can't get her to eat her eggy soldiers. Please find my angel for me by the time I get home, she has already had a tantrum, little monster."

Robbie whistled... "Wow, you look all grown up and everything!" And grabbing her around the waste tried to kiss her..." No Robbie, not here, mum might see. Robbie!"

Reluctantly he let go and blowing her a kiss sauntered through to the kitchen.... Fran watched him go, this was madness.

Walking through the glass doors at Mackenzie Taylor, Fran was reminded of how she felt when she started with the company; how things had changed. She had been very much part of the company's growth and with it her own reputation had excelled, but somehow now she felt suffocated, and her creative juices were stifled. The demands continued to be high, and she just wasn't prepared to do it anymore.

Staff greeted her as she walked up to the 5th floor, always using the stairs, and walking through each floor, greeting the staff. Keen eager faces, which once was hers, smiled up at her as they called out.....she knew she would miss them all.

"Good morning Mrs. Taylor, Richard is waiting for you"

"Thank you, Hazel, how are you?"

"I am well thank you and how is Emily.?"

Fran pulled a face, "A monster!" They laughed as they walked into the boardroom together.

Hazel was the sort of person that could put a person at ease but somehow still managing to keep the cool exterior of a professional.

"Good morning Mr. Taylor, can I get you and Mrs. Taylor a coffee?"

"No thank you Hazel, we are fine, but can you fill up Old Trustee and bring the necessaries."

"Of course Sir". She shared a smile with Fran at the thought of Old Trustee and left the office. Old Trustee, a percolator which he had bought years ago, was now so old, that it was difficult to get supplies, but Richard refused to let it go, preferring the smell of coffee permeating his office and preferable to the newer models coming out. As Hazel turned it on, it spluttered to life, gurgling, and hissing but it was not long before the rich aroma of the coffee beans filled the room. Only Richard and Hazel could make it work and many a meeting had been held with it chugging and gurgling in the background; Richard, preferred it that way.

With Hazel gone, he looked up and smiled at Fran, coming into the room. "You look lovely, is it new?", indicating the dress. He got up to make the coffee and Fran watched him, his lithe body, well-toned in an expensive suit, sauntered towards the machine. "Do you want one?"

"No thanks. I have had this suit for a while".

"It looks nice, I haven't noticed it before."

No, you haven't noticed me for some time Richard, Fran thought to herself.

They sat down as they always had across the desk from each other, Fran had the Jameson file open, discussing the finalities of the account, intently pouring over the swatches of agreed colours, they were interrupted by a soft drawl as Sarah walked in.

"Hi, you must be Fran!" and as Fran turned, she saw a tall well-groomed attractive woman stretching out her hand. She stood and shook the proffered hand "Francesca Taylor". She had no idea why she used her fall name and why this woman made her feel uneasy but there was something about her that made alarm bells ring. Although Sarah was smiling the smile did not actually reach her eyes, giving the look of a tiger on the hunt and her next comment made the hairs on the back of her neck quiver; "So what are we working on..." her long fingers turned a page of the portfolio sitting on the desk. "I am working on finalising a clients request" Fran slapped the folder closed and stood. Turning to Richard, and seeing his quizzical face, "I will be back at

10am for our meeting." She nodded at Sarah dismissively and walked straight backed out of the room.

Her meeting with Sarah went well and although she found Sarah knowledgeable, she still felt uncomfortable, but couldn't put her finger on why. Yet both Sanjet and Richard hung off every word that she said. There was no doubt in her mind that Sarah could easily take over from her when she left the business, it was just convincing Richard, that it was the right thing to do

Fran felt tired, mentally, and physically, her body ached all over. She put it down to stress as she desperately needed to talk with Richard. She knew a decision had to be made; her head ached with the accountability of thoughts that rushed constantly through her mind, knowing that inevitably someone would get hurt. This inner turmoil went unnoticed by others as she went about her business and greeted people in her normal friendly but professional manner. However, standing after a rather long lunch meeting, Fran had felt dizzy, she had tried to steady herself, but her head pounded, and her eyes could not focus. Holding onto the edge of the table she heard but did not see someone say her name and before she knew it she had fainted, crashing to the floor.

Somewhere overhead muffled voices spoke to her, "Mrs. Taylor, just breath" but all she wanted was sleep. She felt the sting in her arm, of a needle or something but to open her eyes took too much effort.

CHAPTER 20

FIGHTING GHOSTS

2019

"123, lift" – different voices, a little clearer but still so far away.

Another voice.........was that hers' she couldn't make sense of it all.

"No please don't make me go!"

"Fran, hold my hand, it. that's I am so sorry."

"She's fighting this let's give her another 10 mls. Keep still love."

"It's ok Fran, I am here, I've got you."

"She's out! Sleep tight missy."

"Take good care of her."

"Of course! See you at the hospital."

They were gone. The house seemed so quiet, and he stood letting out the breath that he had been holding. He ruffled the fur on Rupert's head, looking down into his worried eyes and said reassuringly "She be home soon boy". Grabbing his keys, he walked out of the house and jumping in the car, drove to the hospital.

It was morning before Fran woke, her head hurt and her mouth dry. As she moved to sit up, she realised that her arm was attached to a pump, and her chest was covered with wires leading to a monitor. "Dam, it must have been a bad one!"

"Like a truck has hit me, what happened?"

"You had another large fit my dear" The nurse checked her observation chart and then went to the door, "We were told when you came in that you seem to be having quite a few lately. "Good morning doctor".

"Good morning, and good morning to you Mrs. Taylor. Let us have a look at you shall we! That's a lovely bruise on your forehead"

Fran felt hands pulling and pushing her, feeling like some sort of puppet under a master puppeteer. All the time her mind kept drifting into repressed memories which now refused to stay buried. She felt as if she was falling again, but something, someone was calling her...................

"Fran.....Francesca?"

She heard the questions but drowning in thought she wasn't sure that she wanted to surface, but the voices came again, crossing her sensitivities. She just wanted to sleep. Why won't they let me sleep? Just leave me alone and go away, but the voices were relentless. Reluctantly, and with a deep intake of breath, she exasperatingly replied with an ungracious "What!" She wasn't quite sure whether she was ready to share her returning memories; the pain it would cause would open an unanswered void of discretions bringing the wall, that had protected her, for so many years, down.

Fran turned and looked at his handsome face. He had grown grey at the temples, but his smile was the same and his eyes still bright. She had put him through so much, but he had stayed, always there and always by her side. He absently stroked her hand, worry creasing his brow as he searched her face for answers.

Fran noted the lines etched around his eyes and deepening round his mouth. The tireless grind of his day had aged him. but still so handsome, turning many a head. She lifted a shaky finger up to his face tracing around his cheek and he caught her fingers in his, kissing them. Tears cascaded down her own cheeks....

"What is it Fran, can you talk to me?" .... "Please!"

She took a deep breath and he saw the difficulty she was having. Breathlessly and with great effort her words tumbled out, falling over each other....

"It's just that my memories are coming back, and I keep getting lost in the past! I am trying to unlock them but just as I do, I get confused and become trapped somewhere in between. Sometimes I just don't want to leave them, the reality of now just hurts too much.......like a time warp.

"I think it's time Fran. We always said that we would see Caris if this happened. You know she can help you don't you! Do you think you are ready?"

The tears now came unchecked, and Fran fell back on the pillows, pale and distraught, vulnerability showing. She shook her head it was all too hard. "I can't, I'm sorry, it hurts too much, please leave it alone!" Her raised voice brought the duty nurse into the room.....

"Now what's all this, you know you shouldn't upset yourself like this, we don't want another episode, do we?" Efficiently she bustled over to the Intravenous drip attached to Fran's arm and checking it, increased the medication into the chamber. "This will help my dear, what you need is rest". Patting Fran's arm, she smiled sweetly and bustled out of the room to carry on with her days work.

He stayed with her until she slept and then quietly left her room.

He was so tired; the fits were getting worse and were happening haphazardly to a point where the triggers were unrecognisable. Perhaps fighting the demons that had been locked away for so many years and the confusion of jumbled thoughts were accelerating brainwaves into panic. She had said clearly no to ringing Caris, but he couldn't leave it. If he were ever to get Fran back, he had to try something....

Picking up his mobile, he hesitated, remembering the disaster of the last time they had met with her. Renowned for trauma psychology, her methods rather unconventional, had been too much for Fran and the mental turmoil had resulted in a complete shutdown of emotions. Had she continued treatment she may have got through it, but she had refused to go back and no amount of convincing would change her mind. With a shake of his head, he remembered that Caris had said it would get worse before it got better; it couldn't be any worse, surely?

He picked up his mobile and tapped in Caris's number......no answer... she had said ring anytime. He tried again......

"You have reached Caris Goodman, thank you for calling., I am not available at present, but please leave your number and a short message and I will get back to you."

Leaving a brief message he walked away from the hospital, he shivered, it had got colder, and he didn't have his jacket. He turned down the passage that led to the car park and with cold hands fumbled for his keys, which dropped to the ground. Cursing, he fished them out of a small patch of grass growing at the end of the paving. A small but resilient clump of buttercups bobbed in the breeze and bowed their heads as the keys were retrieved. He smiled at their pretty yellow bonnets and not for the first time marvelled at their strength against the adversity's thrown at them. Fran had always loved them, delicately picking their dainty stems, and holding them under her chin, eyes dancing she would announce, lifting her head and showing the yellow reflection under her chin, that she loved butter. The memory made him smile. Looking back at the hospital, he hoped with all his heart that Fran would have the strength, like these buttercups to weather the storm and remain standing, and with all hope pinned on Caris, he drove away, sending a silent prayer to his Fran.

Caris Goodman, kicked off her shoes and finally sat on her couch. Her workload was insane at the moment and her days long. She dug into her briefcase and pulled out a file and with a sigh, opened it. Reading the contents, she traced down the page as she took in the original narrative and then slammed it shut. She had failed to crack this one. Getting up, she poured herself a drink, and started to pace her sitting room. The case had been so delicate and just as she had got close, it had all gone so very wrong. She shook her head again; her failure would haunt her; it had never left, and now she had been asked to revisit.

She remembered the introduction to the patient when the Head of Psychology singled her out to manage it; she had been young, ambitious and had shown a lot of promise in trauma psychology. Professor Kendall had given her Francesca's file and together they had poured over the details, so far written.

Francesca Taylor
DOB March 12th, 1967
Female
Age 29 years

The personal data went on and on; weight, height etc, painting a picture of a stranger, who although had a name, meant very little to Caris. As the page turned, the stranger became a person, a pretty face stared out of the photograph. Titian curls wrapped around a doll like face, green eyes twinkling with humour and a smile so wide, inviting you to laugh with her. Then another picture, quite different from the first. Damaged! Bloody! The eyes closed and the body hooked up to machines. A red curl sticking out from a bandaged head, arms cast and leg in traction. The police report read, that on January 15th, 1996, a female was admitted to St Thomas hospital. Her white sedan had hit a truck on M25 head on. There was one survivor. A female child and a male were found dead at arrival to the scene. The female was found with multiple contusions and fractures. Evidence of progressive internal bleeding have been recorded. The female was heavily pregnant and unconscious when the paramedics arrived. She was stabilised but critical.

Details about the car, road conditions and trajectory of skids marks etc blurred and Caris turned back to the picture of a very much alive Francesca. Looking questionably at Prof Kendall, she remembered remarking that it was two years past the accident and what was Francesca's status now? She could hear the answer as if it were yesterday...

"Caris, this is a very sad and difficult case. She has no recollection of the loss of her family, and therefore an extremely sensitive. Francesca had Retrograde Amnesia; memories locked away before the trauma of the accident. Although she is now awake, it has taken a long 18 months for her to come back to us. On waking she had remembered her name but little else, and gradually with help from the team, and her parents, certain areas of her life were returning. She still has no recollection of the accident, which, I suppose is a good thing but has no idea of the considerable losses in her life. The fear is that when she remembers it will be so traumatic, that it will set her back to the cationic state that she was in prior."

"What about her injuries?"

"She has multiple lacerated scars running the length of her face and remains with a traumatic brain injury due to a skull fracture which depressed has caused immense pressure on the brain. She is sensitive to light and complains of headaches, however there is no evidence of epidural bleeding, but it is still monitored. Limbs, fractured are completely healed, but when walking there is a pronounced limp."

Turning the page, another photograph; the same face, but eyes dull and worried, dreadful scarring pulling her mouth down and that beautiful hair hanging limp. The smile gone, her face was aged but it was the eyes that held Caris's attention, haunted and lost, full of pain and holding an element of suspicion.

"What is it you need from me?"

"She has moved home with her parents, Mary and Joe. Lovely caring couple but this has taken its toll on them too. Last week, although all memorabilia of concern had been removed, Fran had wandered into her parent's room and was found, sitting on the bed, staring at a photograph of a little girl, standing in a field, hands outstretched, laughing"

Caris rummaged through the file and found, a copy of the photograph; on the back, two words "The Buttercup". Mary remembers taking the photograph; it was June 1995. She told me that Fran, had often, as a child done the same thing, hands outstretched and head up with wild red curls flying as she swirled, her little face tipped to the sun.

The image of the child was a happy one. She was dressed in a bright yellow dress and her hair, hung down with red curls framing her little face.

"Mary had said that this had reminded her of a buttercup in all that yellow and had written it on the back of the photograph.

When Mary had asked Fran what she was doing, Fran had held out the photograph and asked if it was her as a child and Mary had said yes, although she knew that it wasn't. Two days later, Fran had come downstairs with the same photo clenched in her hand. Her face contorted, and pale, a tremor running through her hands as she held it out. "But mum, this photo is in colour. Who is it?" When Mary didn't answer, Fran had become agitated asking the same question again and again, resulting in hysteria and hospitalisation. Unfortunately, Caris, Fran hasn't spoken since, do you think you can unlock her mind and get her to talk. We may actually find out what happened to her"?

Caris remembered the feeling of excitement and fear that ran through her, this was what all those years of training had been for.

"She has Post Traumatic Stress Disorder, with a capital P and with her closure of thought, I am going to have to be careful. Does she recognise herself in the mirror?"

"We are unsure, she touches the scars but does nothing about hiding them and hasn't asked about how they got there."

Caris let out a long breath. Professor Kendall continued. "There is one other detail you should know about. Dr Robbie Harvey is her, well her, very good friend. He is very closely involved with this case. Too closely involved for our liking. This is something that everyone is very tight lipped about and we have left well alone..... for now anyway."

"Dr Robbie? Consultant at......"

"Yes, so tread carefully. Francesca used to be in charge of Organic Textiles, at Mackenzie Taylor, her husband's company. She will often be found with swatches of materials, which Mary has brought in, of different colours, holding them to the light, mix and matching. This may be a way of getting close to her, breaking the seal of silence. I trust I can leave this with you?"

Trust.......she had been trusted to care for this woman, crack the case and move forward. She cursed herself as she had done all those years ago; her stupid ambition getting in the way of reality. And now, now he wanted her to try again.

Caris poured herself another drink, she wasn't sure if she had the energy to reopen this again.

Two years of getting close and then.......she slammed her glass down and pushed her hands into her eyes to stop the tears. She had been told that her breakthrough had been incredible and that the setback, shouldn't be taken personally, but she had and did.........

Could she go through this again so many years later? Why now!

That last visit, that awful last visit when she had pushed too hard, when Fran had seen them together. One stupid mistake! That scream of anguish and the massive fit that had seen her back in hospital and inevitably refusing ever to see or speak to her again. Ended the case for her.

Her colleague, who had taken over from her, had reported that Fran's obsession of everything being uniformly the same and familiar had actually helped and after a long period of time had returned unbelievably to her home. Furthermore, eventually she has returned to work, of sorts. The firm was now run by a corporate, with the boutique business become rather more industrial than before and knowing of the tragic events, had offered Fran a seat on the board and minimal designing stress. Caris was pleased that Fran had managed to get a life back, well of sorts and so had she, so why now?

She listened to the recorded message and the awkward voice of Dr Robbie Harvey.

"Caris, hope all is well! Umm …long time no see. Do you think you could call? You have my number, or find me at the hospital, yes I am still there…. I' m always there. It just that, well its Fran and"

The call hung up and then a second message……

"Sorry Caris this is…. this is ……shit! This is so hard. You see Fran is in hospital, she has had a series of grand mals over the last few months, and the last was horrendous…..she tells me that she is getting her memories back, that they are tumbling out and she s doesn't know what to do….. we need you Caris……"

And a third message……

"I need you Caris…. thank you." She heard it, "I need you." It was obvious Fran didn't, but he needed her and that was all she'd waited to hear.

Caris felt drained as she stood up, her legs felt strangely weak, and she sunk down on the couch again. Tears poured down her cheeks… it shouldn't have happened, professional distance and all that. Could she face him, or more importantly could she face Fran? A lot of years had gone by, her life had changed, and I am sure so had theirs. With that she took herself off to bed, where sleep eluded her and darkened thoughts of that bloody night troubled her, fighting ghosts that had come back to haunt her.

CHAPTER 21

THE BREAKTHROUGH

2019

"Have you ever seen a buttercup standing proud and tall in a field amongst the weeds and tufts of grass, it's delicate petals bright yellow, smiling up at the sun and swaying ever so slightly in the summer breeze.........."

"Yes..........Francesca.? Caris prompted her but was conscious that if she said too much it would shut her down again. This was their third session. Three hours of an exhaustingly silent battle and then suddenly Francesca had turned her head; she had been looking out of the window and then walking towards Caris, sat down on the bright green couch, and started to talk.

"They are stronger than you think. It doesn't matter what is thrown at them, they bounce up again." She stopped and stared ahead; silence hung heavily. Caris held her breath, was this the breakthrough? Years of pent-up pain, anguish, even truths trickled ever so slowly into the room. Francesca turned her head, her titian curls hanging over her face, hiding expression and looked out of the window again. Not looking back at Caris, she went on "I see her all the time arms held out wide, twirling round and round, her laugh ringing in my ears, but then I lose the image as if rain washes the picture from the canvas."

Caris thought before she spoke but asked "Who do you think it is?

"Well that's just it, I don't know. Sometimes I think it is me but more often a little girl, but I don't think I know who she is."

"What does she look like........can you see her face?" Be careful Caris, be careful, this was more than Fran had ever said before.

"I think so, but I can't tell you what she looks like. I can see her, but I cannot see her features, it's like they aren't there"

She spoke plainly, there was no sign of the emotional outbursts that had happened previously. In fact she was calm, too calm.

"That's really good Francesca, do you see anything else?.......Take your time!".

Francesca wiped her hand across her face and remained quiet, she looked exhausted. Her inner turmoil palpable. It strangled her like a vice, forbidding words and mustering a fear, which locked all her memories, good and bad, inside of her.

"Perhaps you could have a go at drawing what you see?"

There was no answer. Caris then remembered there was a trigger, just before the fitting started but she couldn't for the life of her remember what it was, it had after all been 19 years. She walked over to her notes and waited and watched. Francesca's fragility seemed to sink into the vibrant green of the couch, making her look paler than ever. Her eyes cold and down cast, she stared at the multicoloured rug that adorned the wooden floorboards and said nothing.

The room was painted a light green with white furnishings, which were covered with inside house plants. There was the obligatory fish tank with its small inhabitants and the gentle hum of the pump adding to the serenity. The quintessential psych room: a place that Caris found her own comfort within. She stood from her chair and walked to the bookcase ladened with books and pulled from the shelf a large leather-bound volume. It was old and tatty, she held it close before opening it reverently. "My father gave me this book Francesca, just before I started university." There was no response and she carried on, "It contains portraits of unknown figures, abstract in appearance." She walked over to Francesca, careful to keep her distance.....

"In fact this portrait is titled **The Unknown Woman.** When you first look at the picture, it seems there is a series of eclectic shapes which form the face, but when you look deeply into her eyes, you see her beauty exudes from the page, do you see it Francesca?" Still no movement. "I love this book, it reminds me of my father and the weird way he looked at life, I truly miss him........... Maybe if you look hard enough, you might find something more than just the shape of the little girl instead you might see what she is made of. Do you see?"

Francesca shifted in her seat as the sound of a knock was heard on the door.

Caris looked at the clock, it had been more than an hour and he was here.

"Hang on. Just a sec"

Afterwards, reflecting on the session she felt that there had been a definite breakthrough, not huge, but considerable in content. Caris, exhausted sank into the couch. He had been so happy to hear of the progress made and nurtured Francesca as if she was a fragile doll. He had smiled at Caris as he left the room, an apologetic smile for a mistake that still hovered over them; of a different time, when he had needed her, and she had relented. Still good looking, there were worry lines that claimed his face and tiredness that haunted his eyes.

Nineteen years later, the meeting of emotions entered her thoughts but then she was a fresh intern at St Luke's, 25 years old and keen to make an impression and he, the charming Chief of medicine. Now at 44, she had her own private practice, was well thought of in her chosen profession and definitely did not need this complication in her life. However, she knew that she could and would rise above her own feelings to help unlock Fran's ghosts and only hoped that hers' would stay buried.

Yawning she stood, walked over to the door, switched off the light and left.

CHAPTER 22

DÉJÀ VU –
THE ANGER WITHIN

1995

"Thank you, Dr Eaves. Goodness, that is a turn up......I'm in shock, actually but not too much to worry about is there?"

"Well I didn't say that Mr. Taylor. your wife was extremely dehydrated and because she is not eating well and working too hard, this caused a bit of a hiccup. This, I must add, is not good for her pregnancy, particularly as her blood pressure is dangerously high. Has she been overly stressed lately?"

"She did say that she had felt tired and stressed. Actually she hasn't been herself at all, but..."

"That is my point, given her blood pressure, she needs to relax, stop, and rest, or she may have difficulties. My estimation is that she is about 8 weeks and the first trimester can be tricky. Were you trying for a baby, given your busy lifestyle?"

"We have been trying for ages; it will be quite a shock for her unless she already knows. Actually come to think of it she did want to speak to me today...perhaps it was.....but we just didn't find the time."

The doctor smiled at Richard's flustered pattern of speech. He had been delivering this type of for 30 years, and he had never got tired of the impact, good or bad. He patted Richard on the arm. "These things happen, go to her now and look after her." Fran Dr Eaves stood, indicating that the meeting was over. Richard shook his hand and made his way to the door. "Thank you, doctor, I still can't quite believe it. I am very happy about it, and so will Fran be."

Dr Eaves replied, with a little chuckle, "I suggest you break it to her gently, remember that blood pressure, and Mr. Taylor, remember that your wife needs to rest."

Walking up to the ward, where Fran lay resting in bed, although excited, something niggled at him and the more he thought about it, whatever it was, the more it eluded him. He had desperately wanted another child, and although he loved Emily, as if she was his own, this baby would be theirs and perhaps mend their lost relationship. It had confused him that Fran had put barriers up, but she probably had her reasons; He was sure this news would change her perspective on things. He saw the double doors looming up and his step lightened, a new baby would balance out the issues and life would go on.......happily ever after.

Putting his doubts out of his mind he pushed through the doors. He found Fran, her face pale and her eyes closed with her titan curls spilled over the white pillow and her slim figure curled on its side. She stirred as he sat down and turned her head to look at him, her green eyes staring at the concern on Richard's face. He smiled at her and picked up her hand bringing it up to his lips and kissed her fingers. It was a gesture she was unused to and pulled her hand back. "What is it, what's wrong with me?" Her voice had a tremor and she looked frightened. Richard started to comfort her, but she could see there was something else.... "What is it Richard?" She had risen from the pillow and was sitting upright, her colour, now even paler than before .... "Oh god, sorry, I feel really sick". Her head flopped down onto the pillow again and breathing heavily vomited into the receptacle that had been left on the locker next to her bed.

When her nausea settled, she apologised but asked again "What the hell is wrong with me, I feel like crap?."

"There is nothing wrong, Fran. It's just that......." He grabbed her hands "We are going to have a baby; can you believe it?"

The silence went on far too long… "Fran?"

Her voice sounded strained when she answered, "Are you sure but how?"

"I don't think I need to tell you how and yes, you are about 8 weeks". There was no exuberance, in fact there was nothing. "I expect you are in shock, but it's a good shock isn't it?" This wasn't going well.

"Yes, yes…Sorry. I wasn't expecting it ...."

The vomiting started again, and her words lost.

Between bouts of exhausting nausea, she asked him to go. She told him she was sorry, it wasn't that she didn't want a baby, but she felt so ill, and Richard felt helpless, watching her suffer. Fran lay exhausted, head resting on the pillow and Richard, kissed her on her forehead and stood looking down at his wife.

"I will be back tomorrow, sleep now. I have let your mother know, and she has Emily. I have to go back to the office and have a meeting tomorrow morning, so I will see you after lunch. I Love you Fran." He waited for a reply but there was none, he looked down at her as he stood, but her eyes remained closed, her skin deathly pale and so he left, not feeling the exuberance he thought he would be feeling.

She watched him leave, feeling nothing. Pregnant, 8 weeks...the words bounced backwards and forwards through her head. Pregnant, 8 weeks and she knew, she bloody well knew. Pregnant 8 weeks and not Richard's. Oh my god, not Richard's. She was reliving history but this time, it was so much more complicated. Fran Taylor you have done it again. She threw her face into the pillow and sobbed. Now what!

161

A few days later Fran was allowed home with the promise that she would relax, not work, and look after herself. She had asked Robbie to come and see her and the conversation that she had with him, regarding the pregnancy had been difficult and had not gone well. It had started tentatively but calmly, in fact with very little emotion on her part. Predictably Robbie had been jubilant and scooped her up into his arms excited at the prospect that finally they would be together and with another child to love; he could not have been happier. His plans for their future that had been on hold for so long, now were assumed with the assumption that Fran would now leave Richard. His euphoria was short lived and was soon deflated. Fran had listened quietly to Robbie's dreams and life ahead and knew that she too should have been excited about their new life together but how could she hurt Richard, when he too had been so excited about the baby. Her mind in a turmoil, she had stood and walking over to the window. She badly needed solitude, a time alone with her own thoughts and she was so dreadfully tired.

"Robbie, I love you, you know I do, but I need to get used to the idea of having another baby first. I cannot suddenly leave Richard; He of course thinks the baby is his and perhaps it is! You didn't see the excitement on his face when he told me our news........" Robbie interrupted and was so angry, that the ferocity shocked Fran. "You know the baby isn't Richard's, don't you! You are 8 weeks, aren't you?"

Fran nodded miserably. "8 weeks ago Richard was away at the expo, remember you were meant to go too, but you made an excuse and Fran we were together, weren't we! The whole time..........Since then he has hardly been home..........You know that I am the father of our baby, the same as I am the father of Emily and not her Uncle!"

"Robbie, please stop!" Tears poured down Fran's cheeks. "I know the baby is yours it's just ....I need time Robbie. It's is a big decision and I just need... Where are you going?"

He had stood up and walked to the door, with his back to her and quietly spoke,

"Francesca I have waited long enough; you have had all the time you need!"

He opened the door and stormed out, leaving Fran tearful and confused.

Tears cascaded down her pale cheeks, Mary would be back soon with Emily, she too was excited about the new baby and would want to hug and chatter. Fran buried her head in a cushion and cried until her eyes closed and she fell into a restless sleep.

"Congratulations Boss." Sarah's slow American drawl, which came across so effortlessly, was spoken as she leant over to Richard and planted a kiss on his cheek. Awkwardly he rubbed his cheek as he spoke, that gesture had been far too familiar for his liking. He indicated for her to take the opposite seat. "Yes, well, thank you Sarah, it has come as a bit of a shock for both of us and with Francesca not feeling so well, she will need to rest. Look, I know you have been insanely busy of late, but I wonder if you would be able to close the Jameson deal and oversee her workload, just until she returns?" Getting up from his desk he wandered over to the bookcase, he felt distracted by Sarah, as he always did. Her long legs crossed over and her piercing blue eyes, opened wide, looking at him, but it was her smile that jolted his senses, lips just a touch open, sort of asking a question, taunting him.

Her voice interrupted his thoughts.

"Yes, sure I can. May I go into her office and have a look at her portfolios, if they are here? Weren't you looking at the Jameson file the other day?

"Yes, luckily, she brought it up to London with her and it's still in her office. It's near completion and I am sure if you give her a call, she can give you any assistance that you might need. Come on I will show you. Luckily for you, Fran is very organised and anything outstanding is usually easily found."

She followed Richard out of his office down the plush corridor to Fran's office, smaller but equally as impressive. As Richard walked, she watched as he acknowledged staff his smile and pleasant confidence around people was endearing. Sarah noted his long back with broad shoulders, showed an athletic body, Fran was one lucky lady!

Sarah sighed, it seemed cruel to her that some woman had it all, a great husband, a career, and a child. She wanted that too and what she wanted she normally got. Eventually, she knew that Richard would want her because, she smiled, they always did.

As she rounded the corner into Fran's office, Richard held open the door, she looked up at him, holding his gaze, just that little bit longer before gliding smoothly under the arch of his arm. A shiver went through her as he smiled down at her.

"I think it's all here, Hazel can help you, if you need anything and I'm just a call away, ok?"

"Okay boss!" She saluted him, an American GI, two finger to the head kind of salute and he laughed as he shut the door. She watched through the window as he walked down the corridor and then closed the venetian blinds, smiling to herself, Richard might just take a little time, but she was prepared to wait.

Alone in the office, Sarah sat in Fran's chair and leaning back put her long legs on her desk. She stared at the photo of Fran cuddling Emily, once again the child so like her mother, reminded her of someone else but annoyingly, once again she couldn't remember who. Her foot knocked the photo flat, and she swung her legs down.

Opening up the Jameson portfolio, she marvelled at the intricacies of Fran's work. Page after page were linked together with colour and materials. Flicking through, Sarah fingered the different textures of the swatches attached. Fran sure knew her stuff. The hues and textures complimented each other, and Sarah could see why Fran was in demand. She was good, really good!

Pushing the file aside, she opened up the computer and could see similar projects neatly filed and likewise the walls of her office were covered with drawings, swatches of material and colour charts. Sarah looked at everything carefully. Returning to the desk she saw Fran's diary and picking up tentatively Sarah opened the diary, which, seemed rather invasive, but she had a job to do...

Appointments neatly scrawled, always accompanied by a phone number, scattered the pages. Each month was categorised with Wednesday predominantly marked being her London day.

Sarah noticed all pages had been managed with the same meticulous organisation, with several entries stating Richard's movements for when he was away at conferences or when there were meetings keeping him from going home. On each of these entries the corner of the page was coloured in blue, with letter R printed, obviously an indication of her husband's events.

There was nothing more eventful and finding the date for the Jameson meeting she closed the book.

Next, she opened the desk drawer and apart from the normal paraphernalia found in an office desk, there was nothing much of interest but as she closed the drawer, something caught at the back preventing closure. Kneeling, Sarah pulled the drawer out and reached through to the back. An envelope had got caught and pulling it free, released it and shut the drawer.

She knew it was wrong, an invasion of privacy, but opened the envelope anyway. Inside the envelope she found a few photos, mostly of Emily, in various cute poses but as she turned over the last photo, a very familiar face looked out at her. Sarah held her breath and looked closer, asking herself why Dr Robbie Harvey was holding Fran and Richard's little girl. She checked through the other photos again but there was only one of Robbie with that boyish grin and those blue eyes laughing up at the little girl he held in his arms.

Sarah suddenly snatched up the framed photo on the desk and compared the two. A slow smile spread across her face, there it was, the same smile and eyes, the little girl who was the image of her mother but also undoubtedly her father, Dr Robbie Harvey. Robbie's baby, Robbie from Australia, her Robbie!

As anger bubbled to the service, she stuffed the photos in her bag and walked out of the office. She needed to think but one thing for sure, Francesca Taylor would not have it all.

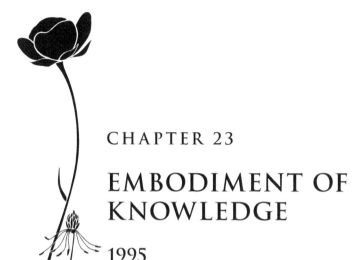

CHAPTER 23

EMBODIMENT OF KNOWLEDGE

1995

After several calls to Francesca, Sarah finally closed the Jameson deal. She had been extremely thorough and had taken pains to make any changes with Fran's approval. Along the way, somehow the two woman had become more than co-workers and a friendship began to form. Sarah had consciously empowered Fran, and became the student, Fran, the trainer. Although Sarah had enough experience to manage the account, she manipulated the situation otherwise and in the short period of 5 weeks, the daily phone call, often ended up in girlish chatter and laughter.

Fran now 15 weeks pregnant, and feeling a little stronger, made the journey to London to celebrate the win of this exclusive deal. Calling staff into the boardroom, Richard enthused about the company's growth, and thanked both his wife and Sarah for their hard work in closing such a lucrative deal. He happily recognised their growing friendship and mentally noted that Fran may have possibly been right. He could see that the break had down her good. Richard watched as she circulated around the room, smiling, and laughing, relief that the Jameson deal was sealed.

He excused himself from an overzealous graduate, patted Sanjet on the back as he walked past, and excused himself, he had calls to make.

Francesca watched him leave, his straight back and slightly jaunty walk striding towards his office. She seen this a thousand times, but today was different, perhaps more poignant than before. With a sigh she turned back into the dispelling throng of staff, a bright but false smile on her face, acknowledging everyone that walked past. A deep knot had formed in her stomach and she knew it was now or never.

Looking back, Francesca remembered that day as being the turning point in her life, with the significance of her actions so very damaging.

As the boardroom cleared, Francesca and Sarah found themselves alone...

Turning to Sarah, who was clearing away the remains of food platters, Fran spoke, surprised at how shaky her voice was. "Sarah, you did a fantastic job, but I need to ask you something important. Did you enjoy doing it?"

"Sure, I got a real kick out of it, but you did all the hard work!" Fran smiled but with urgency carried on speaking.

"That is good to hear......look, before Richard comes back, I need to ask you something. Would you take over from me?"

"What, whilst you are on maternity leave? Yes of course I can. I can certainly help out anyway?"

"No, not quite, I mean ...take over permanently. I just don't want to do this anymore!"

Sarah looked at Fran's troubled face and waited. "You would be blind not to see that things have been strained between Richard and myself, and actually have been for a long time......"

"But Fran, what about the baby?" Sarah moved closer to Fran and could see that there was more she had to say; she seemed to be having an internal battle and to her horror Fran's eyes were filled with tears. Sarah took hold of Fran's hands and gave them a squeeze. "Fran it's understandable, you are probably exhausted, I will help where I can."

"No you don't understand, please, just listen .... I am leaving Mackenzie Taylor, and whether you take my place or not the Jameson account was my last hoorah! I can't do this anymore. I ... I just can't!"

Fran broke off as turning she saw her husband walking their way with that satisfied look on his face. Turning back, Sarah could see the pallor of Fran's face, the over bright eyes, and the determined line of her mouth.... "I can't do this!" Her hands indicated the gap between her and Richard and her eyes beseeched Sarah to understand.

Sarah understood only too well, she would need to play this game carefully.

"Fantastic result ladies, well done. Client is happy which makes me happy, time to celebrate".

Sarah, sitting on the edge of her desk, smiled broadly. "We make a great team don't we Fran!"

"Exactly, we need to see more of this collaboration but enough of work now. Let's get a meal and make a night of it, you both deserve it".

"Not for me, I am heading home, I am absolutely exhausted" and seeing Richard's expression, she added, "Sorry Richard, I am really tired, it's been a big day but by all means stay and celebrate with Sarah, it wouldn't have happened without her." Richard moved toward Fran concerned, "Are you feeling alright? You aren't faint again are you?"

"No, just tired". Sarah noticed how Fran had manoeuvred herself behind her desk, and had sat down, making hard for any intimacy between them. This she noted was not a happy marriage.

"Don't worry Fran, I will look after him, we won't stay out late, we have any early start tomorrow."

Picking up her bag, Fran smiled at Sarah, "thank you and enjoy". She walked past Richard and kissed his cheek, "Are you home this weekend? Emily was asking for you, yesterday."

"Yes, definitely. Is she okay?"

"Yes, she is fine. I have had to leave her with Robbie tonight, as mum has a parent meeting, so I don't want to be too late back."

With that, she smiled at Sarah and left.

Richard turned to Hazel as he and Sarah left the office, "we won't be back today, so if you can take down any messages please. I doubt there is anything that needs urgent attention. Thank you Hazel.".

Hazel smiled "Goodbye Sir." She had seen her fair share of drama during her years at Mackenzie Taylor and as she watched them leave, her gut told her that there was trouble ahead. She had to admit to herself, that they made a handsome couple... strong and good looking and she had been aware of an obvious distance between Richard and Francesca for some months now, even before the surprising news of the pregnancy. She also had strong misgivings about Sarah, she didn't know why, and she had certainly given her no cause, but she just did not trust her. She chastised herself silently, it was probably nothing, just an innocent dinner and she wouldn't presume anything else, but that feeling just wouldn't leave.... Sighing she got back to the pile of letters to be typed up and head down she started to work.

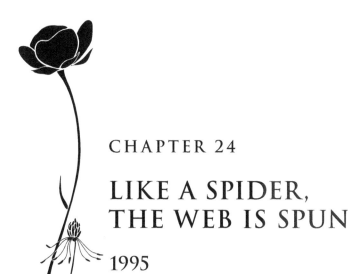

CHAPTER 24

LIKE A SPIDER, THE WEB IS SPUN

1995

They walked from the office, Richard deep in thought, and Sarah quietly walking beside him. The silence was companionable, and Sarah felt comfortable in his presence. The thought occurred to her that at some point she would need to discuss Fran's request but maybe not tonight. He turned to talk to her as she turned to him and both stumbled over their words

"Where are we going to......." interrupted by Richard "I thought we would go to the Italian...is that okay? They laughed and both said sorry, which made them laugh again.

Tension broken, they turned into the "The Little Italian" on the corner of a Grosvenor Street. It had the old-world charm of a past gone by and was deceptive in size going back much further than first thought. Tables and chairs were squeezed in at all angles and a long bar ran the entire length. The kitchen took up half the space and was open to public view with its huge pizza oven in its terracotta glaze taking precedence in the middle. The other half was a bar which housed exclusive wines with some expensive labels.

"Man this is mint, I love it" Sarah, turned her face up to Richard, her blue eyes wide and sparkling.

"I knew you would. Funnily, Fran always had a problem with the atmosphere here, she told me it was "pokey!"

"No! Really....what's that all about?

Richard shrugged his shoulders and was just about to speak when a loud Italian voice boomed from the recesses of the restaurant. "Richard, how are you? Long-time no see. Too much work heh? Oh and so beautiful - Bellissima....Quetta Bellessa ha in nome (does this beauty have a name)"

"Mi chi amo Sarah. Hai un bellissimo ristorante.... Grazie per avermi fatto sentire cosi benvenuto e per il complimento"

They both looked at Sarah in amazement and she continued......" e per favoure, il tuo nome?

"Ah, Mia principessa, sono onorato di averti visitato. Il mio nome e Chris.... buon divertimento."

Chris turned to Richard, and nudged him, laughing. "Richard, she is a bright one.... Come.... now you sit and we will give you delight on a plate." With a great belly laugh he called to the kitchen in fast rapid Italian...

"That was impressive, where did you learn Italian?"

"My father knew some very interesting men and in order to learn secrets, you learn the lingo - they don't know that an innocent child, reading a book, is listening to everything said and it grew from there"

"I think I need to watch you. Secrets hey?"

"My life was very different then."

"And........?"

"And now, Richard, I am hungry.... let's eat".

Richard looked at Sarah, with a newfound interest and laughing, picked up the menu to study it, although he knew exactly what he would order. With her blonde head bent, examining the menu, he took the time to look at her. Chris was right, she was a beautiful princess with her long legs, good body and an intelligence that shone through her eyes. He sighed, and she looked up at him and smiled. He knew he would have to be careful here.

The meal was beautiful, and the conversation flowed, as did the wine. As the restaurant filled, they bent their heads lower to talk, so that they could enjoy their discussions without interruption from the noise that filled the surrounding areas. Both were acutely aware of their forbidden chemistry and each strove to ignore it.

Richard for the first time in months felt relaxed realising how much he was enjoying Sarah's company and the ease in which she mingled business and pleasure. It had been a long time since Fran and he had talked in this way, in fact he had to admit that it was a long time since they had done anything together, and there it was again, that nagging thought about her pregnancy. He had counted back the weeks, but then doctors were not always spot on with the dates, but if it was, as she said, now 15 weeks, he had not been home. He had been away that week, at a conference..........

"Richard?" Sarah soft Californian accent cut through the turmoil of thoughts. "Richard, are you okay, you seem miles away suddenly."

"Sorry, so sorry, I was just thinking how much I was enjoying this..." Whether it was the wine, which he justified after as being the case, or just the company he relaxed further and suddenly he felt he needed to share far more than he would have normally, opening up and letting all guards down.

"Sarah, can you remember the dates of the conference, the last one?"

She confirmed his suspicions. "What's up Richard, you look concerned, is there anything I can do to help?"

"I shouldn't be talking about personal issues, it's just there is no one else to talk to, and I have to say…" he paused and looked directly at her … No, sorry, let's leave it there, sorry."

Sarah didn't probe further. Richard obviously needed to talk, and her female intuition told her, that eventually, he would spill, and she would wait just like a spider in its web, and she began to weave and pull her prey into it. It was, she thought without considerable effort, he was already succumbing to her charms. She looked up at him, grabbed his hands and stared into his worried eyes… "Hey, that's okay honey. I am always here if you need to unburden. You and me, well, we're the same and I am here for you. You know that don't you?"

The mood had changed and with meals completed, they stood to leave. The rotund figure of Chris, who considering his size, seemed light on his feet, swirled around towards them

"Princess were you going, huh? You want some desert, yes?"

Emphatically, in unison, they both said "no!" And then made their excuses of being too full, but Chris wasn't having it,

"Then my best brandy for my best customer and his princess, yes?" And laughing they both sat down again and said "yes". Apologetically Richard shook his head, "I don't think we have a choice, my princess!"

She laughed, and he watched as her hair tumbled off her shoulders, a sheaf of golden silk. Her eyes twinkled and her mouth wide, smiled "I don't think so, but truthfully, I am so full, and I have to say just a little tipsy, not sure I can handle another drink and get home safely."

"I have a spare bed, if you need." Seeing her expression, he continued, "please don't feel too uncomfortable staying at my place, we have an early start tomorrow, it might be for the best, I am sure you can find something of Fran's to wear, she won't mind, and I think you are of similar size, but what would I know."

"Not uncomfortable at all, that would be grand. I have slept in worse," she giggled, and he liked the sound of her, he liked a lot of her. "You know," she continued, "It's been a long time since anyone called me princess. The last person to say it was my daddy. Well actually he wasn't my daddy, he was my step-father, but he preferred me to call him daddy, it made him feel good." He watched her screw up her nose as she thought back and shrugging her shoulders, knocked back a huge swig of brandy, it's golden depths loosening inhibition in both.

"Tell me about your family in LA, Sarah. You seemed to have had an interesting life so far."

Sarah looked at him, her blue eyes darkening, "I think not!"

Richard was taken aback by the change in her voice, it had a coldness to it and as quick as her smile disappeared, it suddenly appearing again.

'Why don't you tell me about life in South Africa, I can detect an accent and how did Mackenzie Taylor come about?" Subject changed, Sarah became composed again and after the second brandy they left the restaurant, saying their farewells and promising to return. As they stepped into the cold night air, they felt a sudden rush of adrenalin, and Sarah swayed into Richard as they stepped off the curb. "Steady" and he grabbed her to prevent her falling. "Oops, sorry Richard," and promptly did it again... "Oops, the brandy has gone straight to my head, I may need a hand here." They laughed as he grabbed her around the waste and pulled her into him. He had to admit they fitted together well, and he liked it. She looked up at him, at the precise moment he looked down and she smiled, that secret smile of knowing. "Sorry boss." They walked the short walk to Richard's apartment in silence;

both knew that the sexual tension was building and at that moment neither cared.

"Nearly there, said the spider to the fly, just a few more steps and then you will be mine, don't hurry now, take a breath, don't think, just act, all in good time......."

Once in the apartment, coffee was offered, and saying yes, Sarah kicked off her shoes.

"This is a great apartment Richard. Have you had it long?"

Sarah was wandering around but although there were a few photos here and there, it was relatively stark and very masculine. She noticed it was immaculately furnished but it didn't feel like home at all. She picked up a photo and studied it. It was of smiling faces, Richard, Francesca, and Emily, seemingly at the seaside with hair blowing across their faces. Another of Emily in a party dress, and then a larger one of Fran, decked out in some expensive label, her hair piled on her head and dramatically made up. She was slim and in control and beautiful.

"That was at the Industry Awards Night last year. Fran hated that sort of thing, she also despised dressing up and wearing gunk on her face, as she put it. It actually was a great night."

"She looks beautiful." On closer inspection, Sarah could see uncertainty in Fran's expression, and wondered what had been wrong. Although smiling, it didn't reach her eyes and there was a vulnerability about the way she posed as if she had been told to do it. Sarah knew that feeling and moved on to the next photo. "Emily looks like her, same hair and expression. She sure is her spitting image, missed your genes completely."

"Well actually I am not Emily's biological father, but I have been her daddy from birth, and she knows no different. To her I am just daddy."

Sarah rose a quizzical eyebrow and suddenly Richard found himself spilling out the whole story... "So you see, Emily knows no difference, I even helped deliver her."

"Wow that is a huge responsibility! Does her real daddy know, or see her?"

Here she felt, rather than saw, hesitation. "Sorry, Richard, that was too intrusive, I didn't mean to..." Richard interrupted, "Don't.... it's okay. It's complicated. Emily's father, Robbie, didn't know Fran was pregnant when he left to go back to Australia and when he did find out he was already caught up in another relationship and by all events, a crazy one. As time went on their lives went in different directions. It was hard for Fran at first, and I suppose selfishly, not wanting to lose my best worker, and being a friend, I stepped in and helped. Eventually our feelings, well my feelings changed, and it seemed the best thing to get married and we did. Until recently we had a happy marriage but...but now with the pressure of work ..."

Sarah could see that Richard was struggling but couldn't stop probing and interrupted him mid flow, "And does Robbie, I mean the father, see Emily now that he knows...I mean Australia is a heck of a long way from London, that must make it easier on you?"

"Ahh, yes, well that's where it becomes interesting. He moved back to England when Emily was one. Actually on her first birthday. He is very much part of her life and Francesca's. Oh yes, Uncle Robbie, is very much part of our daughter's life". The hint of sarcasm and anger was not missed by Sarah. "Uncle Robbie?"

"Well there can't be two fathers can there!" There was an element of anger entering the conversation, and she decided to lighten the conversation. "You are a Bonafede knight in shining armour, hey Sir Richard." She stooped into a low bow but lost balance and toppled forward. As she fell, two strong arms caught her and pulled her up before she hit the floor. "Woah, that was embarrassing, sorry Richard! Where is that coffee? I think I need to sober up!" Richard righted her, laughing, but didn't drop his hands. She was tall, even with her shoes off but he was still taller and could look down at her pretty face. Her words were slightly slurred, and he felt her hands tighten on his shoulders to keep balance. Her blue eyes were hypnotic, and he remained staring into them, and she smiled up at him. The chemistry between them increased and suddenly Sarah found herself, disentangling herself from Richard's grasp.

"Um, I think I had better call a cab."

"Really, why?"

"Why? I don't know about you, but that drink has gone to my head, and I am feeling things that I shouldn't be feeling... and, and you're my boss!"

"What if I said, I didn't want you to go home. That I didn't want to end this night in that way and go to yet another cold bed? A long night just wondering what could have been with you in my arms...I know you feel the same...or am I wrong? And if I am..." Richard ran his hands through his hair, had he made a mistake?

"Sorry Sarah, say something, anything..."

She didn't reply, she had walked across to the hall table to find her bag and had stopped midway, her back to him. He couldn't see the smile or the shrewd calculating eyes......her thoughts laughing silently at the revelation that Robbie Harvey, her Robbie, was once again in her sights. One way or another she would find him and hurt him, the way he had hurt her, but for now...why not have some fun......this was far too easy.

"Just like that the web was spun and now it's time to have my fun, spin you left and spin you right, spider morsel for me tonight"

Not turning, she spoke, slowly and deliberately, "And what about Francesca and the baby?"

She hadn't heard him walk up behind her and jumped as he spoke. "You would have to be blind, not to see how distant we have become... she even wants a break from working. Now that the Jameson deal is completed, she has made it clear she wants out."

"Yes, I know, but it cannot be easy with a 4 year old and the difficulty of being pregnant."

Sarah had turned and walked towards the couch. Sitting she was aware that the initial urgency from Richard was waning and she somehow needed to get it back. Ripping her clothes off was not ideal, not in this environment anyway, no, she had to pull him back into her web subtly, without obvious ploy. She patted the seat next to her and he sat, staring past her.

Picking up his hands in hers, she looked kindly into his eyes, her own eyes brimming with tears... "I just don't want to make things worse. Fran and I have become quite close, and, as much I want you, Richard, I couldn't do this to her, could I!" Her hands stroked his and tears poured down her cheeks. Releasing his hand, he reached into his pocket for a hanky and handed it to her. Sarah took it gratefully, noting that his hand was now resting on her bare leg and had difficulty paying attention when he spoke.

"She told you then, that she was unhappy?"

Sarah nodded with a sniff and gulp. "She asked me to take over from her, she doesn't want any part of the business Richard, I am sorry but that is what she said. Maybe once the baby arrives...she said it had taken a while to get pregnant, perhaps she wants to enjoy it without the stress of work."

"Hmmm, yes it had. It is quite a miracle that it happened at all...and I keep thinking...how!"

"Richard! I think you know how," Sarah laughed but seeing his face she realised he was serious.

"Sarah, if the dates are correct, I wasn't with her, I was away...I keep saying to myself that doctors can get it wrong but..."

Sarah moved closer to him, with their knees touching, his hand sliding higher up her thigh. With her free hand she stroked his arm and looked up at him feigning innocence "I am sure you are wrong, Richard. Come now, it's been a big week for you, and you must be tired". The weight of his hand on her thigh was teasing and she could feel the heat rising in her body. "How about I get us a night cap before bed?" As she went to stand, he pushed her down, levering his weight on to her. His hand slid between her thighs and caressed the soft flesh. He needed her, he needed this.

"Richard, please! I don't want you to regret this tomorrow." Her dress had ridden up and she made a feeble effort to pull it down, but his mouth was now kissing the tops of her breasts as they peeped from her dress.

"Please Sarah, I need you!"

She squirmed from under him, pushing him off. Her face hot and her hair dishevelled, she pulled her dress down and stood staring at him. His was obviously aroused and sat up looking into her face quizzically. He just couldn't read her, he thought it was what she wanted. "God I am so sorry". He lowered his head into his hands, and to her amusement he started to cry. She had the upper hand.

Dropping to her knees, she caressed his head against her breasts....and crooned gentle loving words to him until he pulled away and looked again into her eyes. Those brilliant pools of azure blue. "I'm sorry Sarah, I misread the situation, and the alcohol didn't help..."

"Nothing to be sorry about. I just needed to be sure ...."

"Sure? Sure about what!"

Honestly men were so stupid! "Sure whether you wanted this!" She stood up in front of him, and slipped one, and then the other spaghetti strap of her slim shoulder. The dress slipped to the floor. Richard was mesmerised, he looked at her long limbs and long torso, her beautiful, tanned skin and the main of long blonde hair, shaken free and hanging in coils around her shoulders. Undoing her bra, her voluptuous breasts were then set free with her nipples erect.

"Oh my god, Sarah, you are beautiful"

Still she said nothing but continued to stare at him whilst her last piece of clothing was removed, and with her naked body in front of him she held out her hand and pulled him up towards her.

"The question is Richard, are **you** sure?"

There were no words as he pulled her towards the bedroom and closed the door.

> *Nearly there, said the spider to the fly,*
> *just a few more steps and then you will be mine,*
> *don't hurry now, take a breath,*
> *don't think, just act, all in good time.......*

> *And just like that my web was spun*
> *and now it's time to have my fun,*
> *spin you left and spin you right,*
> *spider morsel for me tonight*

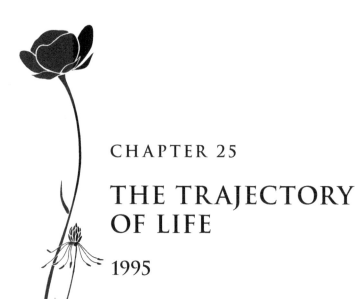

CHAPTER 25

THE TRAJECTORY
OF LIFE

1995

Sarah laid quite still looking up at the ceiling. If Richard could hear the cogs and wheels of thought turning and whirring through her head, he would surely awake, but he slept on. She looked down at him. Their love making that night had been almost desperate on his part and very passionate. She mused at how giving her body had been, and how accommodating she was to his needs. Actually, she had quite enjoyed herself..... but now, it was time to think, to plan the next chapter.

How fortunate she had been, not only had she managed to get her boss eating out of her hand, who undoubtedly would want more, they always did; but by some amazing twist of fate, she had found Robbie. She now knew how he fitted into the picture but there was more to his story, she was sure of it; she would find out, and not only that ruin him! Oh yes, the great Dr Harvey, father to Emily, loving Uncle Robbie and perhaps rekindled lover to Francesca, would get his comeuppance, there was no hiding now.

Of course, back then, she had been someone else, living in Australia; then she had had the perfect lifestyle and the perfect man. Had she not been enough for him, did she not give her all to him, comfort him, love him unconditionally? It was never enough; there had always been the shadow of Francesca, lurking in the recesses of his thoughts. She admitted to herself, that he had always been honest with her and she knew and had discussed the baby, Robbie's baby but until now had not linked his story with this one, Richard, Francesca and Robbie, what a ménage a tuoi!

It all seemed so long ago but not forgotten. She had been a student and an assistant, then a wife! Robbie's wife......

Richard groaned in his sleep, and she held her breath, but he nestled back into his pillow and settled again.

Her mind drifted back through the years, matching her different aliases to situations and companies she had worked for; there were many. She always seemed to be searching but never found that she was satisfied. There had been affairs along the way, but always to the gentleman's detriment and always for her gain. None had ever lived up to Robbie but all had served a purpose. She found that men ate out of her hand, they always had, from a very young age. She had been useful too, satisfying her father's connections. He had called her his little princess and showered her with love, that was until she displeased him. She had listened to, and watched his business customers, gaining much needed information by any means and encouraged by her father gave him what he wanted. Her conquests, heartbroken, wanted more but her cold heart, used, abused and threw away, when the subject outlived the requirement. Often without thought marriages were torn apart, to get what she wanted, what her father wanted. He had a saying, which he would say when stroking her hair... "This girls' got to do what a girl got to do" and she did whatever pleased him. It was only lucky that her insatiable appetite for sex was never satisfied.

Her father relied heavily on her talents, as he put it, often getting her out of trouble as fast as he got her into it. He was none too pleased when she left for Australia and not surprised when she needed to return. His daughter like him, lied to survive and like him was good at it.

Her mother had died in a car accident years before and her father now also dead had left her very rich and the heiress of Brookes Shipping. She was protected by many, and all over the world had connections that she could rely on; one phone call would see her out of trouble leaving all messes cleared up. She felt free to do what she wanted, when she wanted and she loved the games she played with the smell of the hunt exciting her.

Laughing to herself she mentally ticked off the various aliases used; Sarah, or was it sweet May, Nikki, Cassandra, or maybe Vanessa, but she never used her actual name, that name went to the grave when her real father died, for that was the little girl that was loved by all and one without a past.

She had to admit that she was clever, very educated and had a plethora of qualifications which some would say was a dangerous cocktail. Beautiful, eloquent and intelligent gave her the popularity that was required and added to that she could speak many languages, always helpful. Now was no different, she would bide her time and when the time was right she would strike! Sarah's adrenalin was pumping, her mind was whirling as she schemed, malice running through her veins. Fran's pregnancy was the key. Richard was right he had been at a conference, and although there was a possibility that the doctor could have the dates wrong, Fran did not. With Richard up in London and away so much, Sarah was certain that Richard was not the father, and she was fairly certain that Robbie featured heavily in the picture. "Fran you are a naughty girl!!" Sarah suppressed a laugh as Richard turned over onto his side. "mind you I don't blame you."

She mulled over the last conversation she had had with Fran and was sure that there was more that Fran had wanted to say before being interrupted by Richard.

Over coffee, good friends would talk. Fran would eventually confide and trust her with this precious information, she knew she would; this would be easy.

She imagined the following conversation.....

"Fran my friend, sorry, nothing against you, but my dear you have my man, and I would like him back please....in the meantime let me mess with your husband's head." Sarah snuggled into Richard's back, laughing to herself, her naked body entwined with his, it had been an eventful night. "You my dear Richard, are mine and there is no escape!"

Her thoughts had excited her and she wasnt going to go back to sleep now. She couldn't help but think of Robbie and the steamy nights that they had once had. His beautiful eyes, tight butt and long body sent shivers of delight up her spine and the hair on her arms stood erect, now that was a man. "Vanessa Brookes come out come out wherever you are!" Smiling she rubbed her body against the sleeping Richard, she took what she wanted and there was no refusal.

They made love again, that morning, with Richard holding her tight. Once again, she wound her long legs around him, thrusting her hips forward and arching her back.... her sexual prowess was insatiable, and they climaxed more than once. It had been a long time since he had felt so free and exhilarated, he could not get enough!

Eventually, they showered and dressed, leaving little time to get to work. Sarah had borrowed a navy-blue number from Fran's wardrobe, but chose to come through into the bedroom with only Fran's lacy underwear on. Richard looking up stared with open mouth, he had never seen Fran wearing these before and he had difficulty concentrating. Sarah straddled his leg, and he groaned, whilst she tied his tie for him. Then donning the dress, which was much shorter on her, they left the apartment in search for coffee and breakfast. Once out of the appartment, professional distance prevailed but their eyes told of a multitude of sins......it was going to be a good day.

Arriving at the office, they were greeted by Hazel who gave them both their messages. Something felt different; and she was sure that Sarah was wearing Fran's dress? She had seen one just like it anyway.

Although Sarah and Richard, had often came into work together previously, today, there was a something, she couldn't put her finger on.

It was only when Sarah spoke to Richard, that she saw the betrayal, the exchanged looks between them, that confirmed her worst fears.

"Richard, before you go in your office, your wife, Francesca has phoned twice this morning, she needs to speak to you urgently and your 9 am meeting is delayed, due to traffic."

"Thank you Hazel, put her through to my office."

Hazel sighed, the looks had not escaped her, nor the secret smile but it was none of her business, none at all.

The phone rang, "Mackenzie Taylor how can I help you? No problem, I will put you through" and with that her day continued with work piling up and her thoughts pushed to the back of her mind.

"Hi Francesca, are you ok?"

"I went to hospital last night, I tried ringing, but your phone went to message bank"

"Oh my god, the baby? Are you alright.....is it.........," she interrupted him.

"I phoned Robbie; he took me."

"Of course, he did" Richard said rather tersely

Fran continued, she sounded tired. "Don't be like that, you weren't here! There was some bleeding, but we are fine"

"Thank God? I will cancel my meetings and come home tonight."

"There is no need, I am staying at mum's tonight. I am so tired; I won't be much company. Robbie will check on me tomorrow with Dr hat on. Just thought you should know"

"Oh, I see! Well, if you are sure, I will see you Friday night as usual?"

"You see what?"

"It's nothing!"

"Richard!!"

"Well, it seems that Robbie is always around when I am not, he practically brings up our daughter and....,"

"And you are never around. You seem to have forgotten it is his daughter!"

Fran knew she was being cruel but this seemed the norm lately.

There was a pause, Richard took a deep breath "Fran we need to talk, this isn't us, is it!. I will see you Friday then but only if you are sure."

"Yes Richard, I am. See you Friday." The phone clicked dead.

Francesca stared absently down the hall. The light was streaming in from the kitchen window, giving an ethereal feel to her surroundings; She had to tell him the truth! The stress of living a lie, gnawed at her and she owed it to both Richard and Robbie. The baby, this precious being was not Richard's and she knew she was no longer in love with what he had become. Maybe she never had been, not truthfully! Fran knew without a doubt that she had never stopped loving Robbie and the truth could wait no longer.

Richard stared at the receiver, his happy bubble burst and guilt of his actions manifested into something he didn't want to see. This affair would need to stop, but how? He now knew he needed Sarah, or rather he needed that sexual excitement that electrically charged them the night before! He argued that he couldn't do this to Fran and would have to talk to Sarah before it went too far, but, he knew like a drug, he was hooked and needed more.

"Christ, what a fucking mess!" Slamming his fists on to his desk, He remembered the way she touched him, the way her legs, powerful and strong, wrapped around him. She had been masterful and he vulnerable as if he was her prey that she devoured. Once was not enough, and he knew it!.... His head dropped into his hands, a broken man and so absorbed in thought that he didn't see the blue eyes staring through the double glass doors to his office, the way they narrowed and the crease in her brow. Like a feline ready to pounce, she turned and walked towards Hazel and purred, that there was an issue with the delivery on ground floor and could she be a dear and sort it. Hazel stared at her, puzzled as to why she was required to sort an issue on ground floor; she had a lot of work to do for Mr.Taylor and, it wasn't her job. Nevertheless she would call downstairs to sort out. "Of course, no problem at all Sarah". She was rewarded with a dazzling smile, which Hazel noted, did not reach her eyes and went to pick up the phone. She was therefore surprised when Sarah's cold hand, with her red manicured nails, pressed down the receiver buttons, disengaging the call. "Hazel as asked, will you please go to the ground floor and sort out the delivery of materials. Lorraine is off sick today and Patel is sending them incorrectly into the warehouse". Seeing the frustration on Hazel's face, Sarah continued, her voice sickly sweet. "We must all do our part when the troupes are down, don't you think sweetie?"

"But, Ms Burford, it isn't my role and I have contracts to complete..... Mrs. Taylor often supervises the warehouse herself, she loved that it........". Hazel was cut off mid-sentence. There was a noticeable chill in the air as Sarah slipped off the edge of the desk and tersely retorted, "I am not Francesca and when I want something done, I expect that it completed, so please report downstairs and assist Patel......thank you!"

Sarah turned on her heel and stormed up the corridor and went back to her office. She watched as Hazel walked past, her chin jutting out, hitting the button next to the lift with decided force. Sarah moved quickly returning to Hazel's desk, and lifted the phone off the receiver, the engaged tone sounded. She estimated that she had an hour at the most......

Her fingers moved to undo the zip that ran down the front of the dress, opening up just enough to show significant cleavage. She pulled the tie from her hair and let the length fall past her shoulders; the dress was shorter than when Fran wore it, and it showed her long muscular tanned legs in her high heeled shoes. She glanced at her reflection and nodded. She knew how to get what she wanted that was for sure.

Opening the glass door quietly, she noted that Richard had turned his back to the door and was leaning back in his chair. He didn't seem to hear her approaching, which gave her the advantage. Walking around to him, his eyes were closed, and hands laid limply by his side....." Richard, you ok hun?" He opened his eyes, looking at the vision bending over him, those bloody baby blue eyes, wide with concern. His eyes undressed her seeing an endowment of cleavage clearly showing and he reached up taking hold of the zip that dangled before him. She was so beautiful, and as her mouth closed on his, he pulled the zip further down, lace and breast spilling out into welcoming hands. At that moment, in his aroused state, he didn't care about consequences, he cared about Sarah, only Sarah. Her left leg, long and tanned, lifted and straddled his lap and his hands moved her dress up to cup her buttocks, the lace and silk soft and delicious. Groaning, his hands worked fast and once again their passion engulfed them. Her eyes bore into his, changing from soft baby blue to an ice glacier that burned into his soul.

There were no words, there was no need, she had him exactly where she had intended. When his sobs racked his chest and dripped onto her, only then did she speak, telling him that she loved him, that she wanted him and that she was there for him and when he dragged her down onto the floor, she submitted with a vulnerability that gave him strength to take her again.

They lay panting on the floor, all energy spent…. "I am so sorry Sarah, that wasn't meant to happen!"

There was silence and that awkward moment as one person disengages with the other. He watched as Sarah stood with as much dignity as she could muster, straightening her dress and other clothing. She ran her hand through her dishevelled hair and looked down at her lover, still prone on he floor, "Do you regret it?" she said, shakily, looking vulnerable and uncertain. "If so, I am sorry too," and bursting into tears, she left his office.

Walking into her office, she smiled. Tears always worked and slamming the door gave the final cherry on the cake. Now she would wait. Brushing her hair back up into the tie, she blew her nose and was just in time to see Hazel return to her desk, her disgruntled expression turning to surprise at the phone not set in the cradle.

Drumming her well-manicured nails onto her desk, Sarah counted "1,2,3,4,5,6 "- she didn't get to 10 before Richard knocked on her door.

Hazel watched as Richard's dishevelled appearance came down the corridor. He looked harassed and in fact quite awful. He didn't stop and chat, as he usually did, with no mention of her absence, which surely, he had noticed. She would, she told herself, definitely report this to him later. Instead, she watched as he proceeded to go into Sarah's office.

This she would report to her husband later, something was wrong very wrong, and that scheming demon was behind it

CHAPTER 26

TRANSITIONAL THOUGHTS

2019

Francesca sat still. She felt enveloped in the green couch, Caris words drumming in her head and anxiety twisted through her body. She wanted to sink into oblivion, disappearing from view, and just as she fell, reality pulled her back. There was no escape. Her body felt warm, slightly sensual and aroused, and yet it was not through pleasure. The hypnotic, words trying to pull information out of her, information that was buried deep; she was, sinking, sinking into the green couch.

She was there again, the little girl, arms out wide but this time she heard laughter, as if a small child was giggling. The sound like a babbling brook made her smile and she held out her hands to hold her, but then her hands were slapped away and the sound of crying, pitiful crying reached her. "Mummy!" The voice screamed "Mummy!"

There was more screaming and crying. It wouldn't stop but then another voice... "Francesca come back, Francesca!" The screaming and crying continued.....and then nothing. She was falling forward; the screaming was still there but the child who was crying had gone. Yellow buttercups fell from the sky and landed on the green grass where she lay.

"Francesca, wake up now. It's ok, you are quite safe!"

Caris leant over the shaking, screaming form. "Francesca, come back!"

Her closed eyes, shut so tightly, flew open and stared into Caris's face not seeing... "You had them both......you had it all and you left me with nothing!" Fran's hands reached up and gripped Caris's throat, and then she went lifeless and there was nothing. Caris looked at Fran's body curled up in a ball moaning, rocking backwards and forwards, until the rocking became rigid, her eyes cationic.

Caris had seen this happen before and waited. Either her rigidity would turn into a fit and she would phone an ambulance or slowly she would come out of wherever Fran had gone to in her cationic state; that deep secretive place that held the key that could unlock so much of her life. Caris hoped the latter. Something had to unlock the Pandora's box that bound Francesca to secrecy, and she had seen and heard more in the last few sessions than she had previously.

As Fran came back to reality, tears poured down her face.

"There you are Francesca how do you feel?"

There was no answer.

"You did well today, you really began to open up, I am so proud of you. At your next visit we will try again, yes?"

Fran raised her head slowly and replied, "I can't, she won't let me!"

Later the same day, standing in her kitchen, Francesca, watch as he walked from the car. He looked tired, he had had another mad dash from work to pick her up and yet by the time he had reached her, she was sitting drinking tea. There was no point apologising, it was out of her control and anyway, she reasoned, she didn't ask him to come. She watched as he stooped and picked a weed out of the pavers leading up to the front door. Standing, he held his briefcase in one hand and in the other a limp bunch of green stems, their yellow heads bowing as life left them. Francesca's eyes homed in on the yellow bonnets and her cup dropped out of her hand and smashed to the floor. The fit followed shortly after that and he found her unconscious on the floor.

CHAPTER 27

HISTORY REPEATS ITSELF

1995

And just like that her marriage was over. She leant against Robbie's lean body, exhausted. His arms wound about her, holding her tight, as she cried. She was angry, yet her tears were full of pain and sadness. Accusations had come and now gone; the afternoon, had been a heated discussion which petered out into despairing silence.

The discussion with Richard wasn't what she had expected, in fact her carefully planned conversation in which she had practiced executing every word and every explanation, was anything but planned - it had been a right mess!

She had decided to be as honest as she could be about everything. Her mother's words echoing in her head – "Honesty is the best way to go, just say it how it is, and you will be right. It will all wash out in the end."

And so, she had listed everything down in an order that made sense to her.

The list started with that feeling of neglect; with work seemingly more important to him than her and Emily and then how she herself was feeling about Makenzie Taylor, her disinterest in the company, with its growth, which was good and what they had wanted, but which had added pressure that dulled her senses leaving her without any passion or individuality. She wanted him to realise that her creativity was no longer an enjoyment but rather a task but with his competitive streak, that was insatiable, would he understand. She acquiesced that competitiveness in the business was necessary, but this had become their only conversation and it was their different needs that had put distance between them and started the rot within but here she began to hesitate; the personal side of things were far more difficult to put into words.

Richard's desire to have a child of his own and his belief that it would fix their failing marriage had worn her down and making love, became equally as competitive and like his company, had a drive that was personally driven without much thought of her needs; almost automatic, without feeling.

Fran thought that she would tell him that she had loved him and still did to a certain degree, and that their life together had saved her, but the simple fact was that she had never stopped loving Robbie. She would tell him that she had tried really hard to ignore her feelings but seeing Robbie with Emily had brought them closer. He never made her feel unheard as Richard had and was always there to lean on whereas Richard never was. Mixed with her frustrations of work and at home, it seemed so natural to be together and at the time never wrong…………..

She knew all of this would deeply hurt Richard but living this lie put stress on her and the baby, Robbie's baby. It could wait no longer and tonight they would talk. She had planned for Robbie to take Emily home with him, nothing unusual in that, giving her the time to speak to Richard, alone and unhindered. Richard would be home by 6pm and she would be ready.

Richard too was struggling with his own demons and felt that he needed to tell Fran the truth about himself and Sarah. It didn't rest easy with him and he could not lie any longer. This duplicity would hurt her, he knew it but continuing the lie would be so much worse and if there was any chance of saving his marriage he needed to come clean.

In fact, oddly enough, Sarah, had insisted that he did and then she simply got up and left.

He had watched as she got out of the bed, naked and beautiful, slipping on her dress and turning to blow him a kiss. She never said another word, just walked out of the apartment flicking her long blonde hair behind her.

It had been Friday afternoon, after lunch. Normally he would be trying to get his work done so he didn't miss the 5pm train but instead they were together in the apartment. They had made love, ferociously with a passion that surpassed previous liaisons. Sarah's eyes had bored into him as she pushed him down and straddled his body. He had groaned in pleasure as she took control and pulling off her dress, revealing her naked body.

Much later, sitting on the side of the bed, he put his head in his hands. She had come behind him, wrapping her arms about his chest leaning her breasts against his back. "What is it Richard?" Sarah had almost purred.

"I have to......I need to talk with Fran. I cannot carry on with ...... with!" His words floundered and her body pressed harder against him. Although he desired Sarah, he had the baby and of course Fran to think of and they deserved to know the truth.

"I am so sorry Sarah this will have to stop; it should never have happened!"

She said she understood, and she didn't want to get in the way of his marriage. That these things happen...... she had stroked his back and kissed his neck, speaking in that soft accent of hers. He leant back into her....

"Hun, you look awful, this is eating you up, and you have the baby to think of. It hurts, man it hurts a lot, but I understand." and then she had got up and left.

The words had gone round and round in his head. "These things happen!".

Richard sat on the train, looking out of the window at the same houses and the same gardens…… "Is this - what I want?" Words drummed in his head, until he realised he had shouted them out and passengers were looking his way. He put his head back into the newspaper he was reading, and he realised he was asking himself, if going home to a woman who barely registered him, to a child that wasn't his; to an unborn baby that possibly wasn't his, was what he wanted. Or was it Sarah? To the excitement of a new relationship which held so much promise…. Her words again ruminated around and around………………

"You have the baby to think of."

Stepping off the train the decision was made with a determination to do the right thing. Richard Taylor had always done the right thing and he would again.

Richard had arrived home early on Friday at 3pm instead of his normal 6pm and had found Robbie and Fran drinking coffee on the patio. Emily was showing them a picture she had drawn. It was, as Richard watched from the kitchen, a picture of the quintessential family; the only thing missing was himself. It hurt him to see how attentive Emily was to Robbie and how Fran looked so relaxed. As he stood back he noticed how alike Emily and Robbie was now that she was older. However, it was when Fran throw her head back in laughter at something that Robbie said and the affectionate way Robbie touched her hand, that reality hit home. That ticking time bomb that for so long had laid dormant inside his head, now exploded and repressed thoughts, infused his thinking. He could feel anger and pain surging through his body and his determination to save his failing marriage faltered. For his duplicity was matched with her own.

Leaving the kitchen, he withdrew into the hallway standing unseen in the shadows. From his position he could only see part of Robbie's face but there was no mistaking Fran's smile, the one that lit up her eyes. Her titian curls slightly blowing in the breeze blew into her face as she leaned over to say something, brushing them away she laughed as Robbie's fingers lightly tucked the stray curl behind her ear. It was act so simple but so tender that there was no mistaking the chemistry between them.

Emily, oblivious to the serenity was running about the garden, arms out like an aeroplane, she turned and called out, interrupting the moment; "Come on Uncle Robbie, come and fly with me" and with one long stride he jumped down the patio steps and raced over to a squealing Emily, who he scooped up and swung her around with her arms out wide as if flying through the air and her hair so like Frans' streaming out behind her. Her giggles and screams permeated the air, along with the aeroplane noises that Robbie was making.

Richard could not remember the last time he had played with Emily like this, in fact he couldn't remember ever feeling so free. Yes, she called him daddy but had work absorbed him that much that he no longer had time for his family? Had he, in his neglect, pushed Fran into Robbie's ready and waiting arms?

Desperately running his hands through his hair, he argued that he had done all this for them, how then, had it gone so wrong. He had worked hard for their future, their lifestyle, for Fran and Emily's happiness.

He recalled again Sarah's words – "These things happen!" and "You have a new baby to think of!. Did she have the hindsight to warn him, did she know what was happening right before his eyes. Sarah and Fran had formed a friendship, did Fran share with her the one thing that he was now certain about. He had probably lost her as well.

With pieces falling into place and his life unravelled before him, he walked slowly through to the kitchen, with his family oblivious to his presence and the turmoil within.

"Daddy!" screeched the small child being catapulted through the air, "I am an aeroplane, daddy can you see me, Daaaddy?"

The aeroplane stopped to a sudden halt. The pilot laid still in the air, confused as to why her flight was cancelled. She kicked her small legs and bucked her body to kick start the motor but the motor in slow motion was lowering her to the ground and then, denied flight, she whined…. "Do it again, Uncle Robbie, please!"

"Run along Emily, Daddy is home" and seeing her pained expression, he chuckled, "You're making my arms ache muffin."

Skipping off towards the house, she called out again "Daddy did you see me? I was flying an aeroplane and Uncle Robbie was the engine, did you see me?

Richard tore his eyes away from Fran whose eyes were filled with tears, which alone gave away the guilt that she was feeling. It wasn't as if Richard hadn't seen Robbie and Emily play before, but both knew this was different and he had seen more than a noisy child and uncle playing in the garden.

"You looked fantastic, my angel, just like a real pilot".

"I am going to Uncle Robbie's tonight, daddy because mummy said she would be busy, do you want to come too, we could play a game."

"Well not tonight Emily, mummy and Uncle Robbie are good at playing games, aren't they"?

"Oh yes!" She stood in her innocence, twirling her hair around her small chubby finger. Richard knelt down to speak with her hugging her tightly too him. "But daddy, we can teach you the games, can't we mummy?"

"I think daddy already knows them he just can't remember how to play. Now you go with Uncle Robbie and I will see you later okay."

"Okay mummy."

"Emily, I love you!"

"I love you too mummy. Come on Uncle Robbie. What are you standing down there for?"

Robbie had remained at the bottom of the steps, not taking his eyes of Fran. "Coming muffin, get your bag."

As Emily skipped off, he turned to Richard, "She keeps me on my toes."

"Someone has to Robbie, or maybe it is my wife that does that."

"Richard! Not now and not here! Robbie, take Emily and please leave!"

"Fran......I..."

"Leave Robbie, please"! Fran had gone ashen with tears spilling down her face. Sinking into the chair her head went in her hands and she muttered, "Don't let Emily see this." She indicated the stand-off that was happening "Richard and I need to talk".

"Do you need me to stay, I could ring Mary"?

In unison Richard and Fran, shouted "No!" and reluctantly Robbie nodded and went into the house, to collect Emily.

There was silence on the patio, until the front door slammed shut. Richard was standing leaning on the fence that surrounded the little patio, his back to Fran and head bowed. "How long Fran"?

Fran sat, her titian curls brighter than ever against her pale face. Her eyes cast down looking into her hands that were clasped in her lap. No words could repair the look of devastation she had seen in her husband's eyes. No amount of planning could prepare her for the guilt that she felt.....

"How long have you and Robbie been together"?

"Not long!"

"But long enough to make a baby"? Fran's eyes shot up and met Richard's rigid back. No more lies, she was too tired anyway and the strain on the day was making her feel ill. Reluctantly she replied in almost a whisper "Yes."

There was silence...... "Richard?"

He turned slowly, his face drawn, "I suppose you could say that I haven't been here for you and that you felt neglected. You could tell me that Robbie was here to listen to your problems, and I wasn't. That I have always known that I was the next best thing and that you never returned the love that I felt for you and you had never stopped loving Robbie... Am I close"?

"I did...I do love you Richard, there were times when you were so tied up with work that you didn't hear what I was saying, and you just wouldn't listen to me and you didn't notice how unhappy I was. I felt so lonely all the time and ......"

"And Robbie was there to warm your bed............" This said rather tersely. "It didn't matter that I did this all for you and Emily. That the long hours I put in was so we could have a better life".

"No Richard, for years you have worked with an insatiable appetite for the glory of you. You were not content to build the business to boutique standards you wanted to crush Suri Lo and any other of your nemesis, and you tried to take me with you. I tried to tell you that it was crushing my individuality and my passion, but you were too busy to listen. You might not be aware, but I have asked Sarah to take over from me; she is more the business woman than I and seems happy to do so. I am sure she is more your equal than me."

On the mention of Sarah, Richard's neck flushed red; it did not go unnoticed by Fran. She had always known when Richard was not entirely truthful with a business associate as a red snake of embarrassment would climb up from his shirt collar to his ears and the very same was happening now.

"Yes she mentioned it when we were together the other night."

The blush crept higher, and his eyes became shifty..... "We discussed the possibility, but dam it Fran, you and I hadn't had the chance to discuss anything and now this!" In frustration he slammed his fist into the door. Fran jumped and looked away.

"Why Fran, wasn't I good enough for you?"

"Please Richard, you need to understand…"

"Understand what? That history has repeated itself, that you are once again having Robbie's baby. Well at least they will both look alike! Let's just hope he doesn't run back to Australia and leave you stranded because I won't be here this time to bail you out!"

"Richard, please, please don't say that. Emily loves you and…"

"And what? How are you going to explain this to her, that Uncle Robbie is in fact her daddy and I am …. What am I to her Fran?"

"Stop it! You are her daddy and always will be. You can come and see her the same as you do now on Friday through to Sunday, nothing will change."

"Everything will change, you have seen to that, you and Robbie."

"I didn't mean for it to happen, truthfully. I don't think I ever stopped loving him you see, and, well, he never stopped loving me. Neither of us wanted to hurt you and we still want you to be part of Emily's life….."

Richard stared at his wife with disbelief, he couldn't speak and turned to walk into the house…..stopping, he turned towards her, "Does anyone else know of this façade; Mary, Joe……Sarah"?

"Mum asked me why I was so unhappy, and I suppose she guessed – I don't think she has told Dad and, no I didn't tell Sarah, why would I"?

On the mention of Sarah's name, Richard once again reddened. "I presumed as friends you would have confided in her, although she said nothing at dinner."

"Dinner?"

"Yes dinner! You are in no position to quiz me about my movements Fran. You were also invited, were you not, but once again, declined. We went to dinner, we discussed work and then we had a few drinks!"

"And then you went back to the apartment and slept with her in our bed!" Fran retorted.

"I also needed someone to talk to, I also had a wife that never wanted to listen and had no interest in my successes and the business. Sarah is a wonderful listener and contributes far more than you have ever done."

He saw the hurt in Fran's eyes', but he was angry and in pain. "And yes I slept with her, she is a wonderful lover and Fran, she was there for me!"

Richard turned and slammed into the house. She heard the front door open, and his car leave. It was over and all that could be said had been said.

She got out of the chair and pulled her cardigan around her, it had got cold, and she walked slowly inside. Picking up the phone she dialled Robbie's number ….

"Hello Bean, are you okay?" His voice, his lovely gentle voice brought tears to her eyes.

"Can you come, please?"

"I am going to drop Emily off at Mary's and I will come straight over. Everything will be okay just give it time. I love you Bean, I really do!"

The receiver clicked and she held the phone close to her heart. Fran had heard those words before, and she prayed with every fibre of her body that this time he meant it.

CHAPTER 28

RESPONSIVE VISIONS

2019

"During our last session, Francesca, you had a vision, do you remember anything about it"?

Fran looked at Caris strangely but said nothing.

"You called out several times, I wonder if you can recall the words"?

Fran shut her eyes as if to remember but remained silent and Caris tried again.

It was something like……. *"You had them both……you had it all and you left me with nothing!* – Does that mean anything to you at all"?

She watched for a reaction, but still nothing. She didn't want to push her but felt that they were so near that a little shove in the right direction wouldn't hurt.

"We could try again, with the hypnosis and maybe…….." she was interrupted……

"STOP!" Fran was standing and pacing the floor, "Just stop, please!" Her hands had covered her ears. "All of this noise, I cannot think!" She began to pound her head with an open hand. "I can hear the words, but I can't get them out and you….you keep talking at me".

The clock ticked and the fish tank hummed, the silence was deafening; Caris moved to her desk and started looking through a book, pretending to ignore Fran's pained expression. Flopping down onto the couch Fran began to pluck at the blanket that had been placed over the arm. The anxious worry creasing Fran's face told Caris that she was watching the person in front of her unravel. There were no words but from time to time, Fran would moan as she began to rock backwards and forwards.

As time ticked on, the silence became deafening until Caris heard a quiet tremulous voice. Lifting her head, she watched as Fran, with difficulty began to speak……

"I……I wanted to die too…but I wasn't that lucky!" Fran was talking to her hands, in a low whisper. She continued to repeat it with each time getting more manic and louder.

Caris stood and made two coffees, passing one to Fran, who took it and said, in a normal but distracted manner, thank you. She passed her a tissue, and Fran wiped her eyes, again she said thank you.

The muttering continued but the words made no sense. It was as though there were several conversations happening with Fran amid the discussion.

Moving back to her desk, Caris continued to flick through the pages in her book. Without looking up she spoke to Fran – "It seems, Francesca, that your memories are finding their way back. How do you feel about that?"

No answer! Caris continued. "I am here to help you get through this; is that okay with you"?

No answer! She watched Fran's hands continually stroke the blanket –
"It's nice isn't it, I got it at the market, it is very warm in the winter.
Do you like it"?

Fran stopped stroking it and picked it up, examining the material with
interest……..

"It isn't pure wool, it's synthetic and will not last as long, but it is soft
and yes, I like it, wash it carefully and it will keep its shape".

"Thank you Fran, I will."

"The colour is interesting; it reminds me of something, but I can't
bloody well remember".

"Take your time!"

Caris looked across at the blanket. She has liked it instantly when she
saw it hanging up in the market. The bright colours brightened up
her day and it made her feel happy. It was blue, with a yellow splash of
colour that ran through it, and as it lay on the green couch the blend
was beautiful. …perhaps it would evoke more memories.

"Anything Francesca?".

"Not really, but I like it".

"I am glad that you do.. Tell me do you still feel that you want to die?"

"What sort of question is that?"

"Just wondered."

Fran finished her coffee, she stood and put the cup in the sink. Turning
she looked at Caris, who was sitting at her desk. Fran's face was anxious
and held the oddest expression in her green eyes, which stared across at
Caris, her chin determined.

"Are you alright Francesca"? Caris got up from her desk and walked around to the front, perching on the edge. She didn't want to get too close, preferring to give her the space she needed. "You are swaying come and sit down". Fran lifted a hand as is to stop her.

"I know what you are doing to me, but it won't work. I am not ready to give them to you, they are mine to keep, and you are meddling in my business".

Caris remained where she was, silently watching the transformation of one who had been scared and emotional to one whose face was filled with malice.

Suddenly Fran walked towards the desk with purpose, she moved so quickly, even with a pronounced limp, that Caris was taken aback…

"But you would know about meddling, wouldn't you Sarah! You have done it before!

I thought you were my friend, but you cheated me out of both of them. What was it you said, I normally get what I want, and you did, you bitch! You took everything!"

Her hand lashed out and grabbed Caris's arm, twisting it with more strength than she seemed capable of, her green eyes full of anger.

"Francesca, I am not Sarah, let me go!"

Fran's voice became child-like, speaking in a sing song manner. The sinister sound sent shivers up Caris's back as the voice continued. "Maybe it's Vanessa or is it Claire we don't know…we don't know and today it might be Caris." The hand tightened, her grip beginning to hurt. "Did you sleep with him Sarah?"

"Who? I don't know what you are talking about Francesca!" Caris tried to remove the fingers bruising her arm but it was held in a vice like grip.

"You were with him, I saw you, when you thought I was sleeping. I don't blame you, I was, and I am pretty much useless, but I saw you Sarah, he had his hands on your face and you kissed him. You do remember that Sarah, don't you!" It wasn't a question but rather a statement.

Caris began to panic, the pressure on her twisted arm had gotten worse and Fran had now pushed her weight onto her, pushing Caris's body down onto the desk. Her mind was racing, Fran couldn't have seen them together, it was nothing really, just a kiss….. just a bloody kiss. Christ she could get struck off if found out. She tried again…. "Fran let go of my arm, I want to help you….. Fran, please get off, you are hurting me!" She was interrupted by the child like voice above her.

"You know Sarah, it's been bothering me quite a bit lately and I wondered why he was so insistent that I saw you. YOU of all people! I thought that he would have learnt his lesson but there he was kissing you, holding you and all the time I couldn't move, I couldn't stop you!"

"Francesca, stop! My name is Caris Goodman, I am your psychologist. I am not Sarah! So please let go right now!" The pain in her arm was now alarming her and she began to fight back. The voice continued…..

"You had them both……you had it all and you left me with nothing and now it is time to pay. I can't let you leave the room, can I?"

Caris, now terrified, managed to get her other hand free and grabbed Sarah's hand trying to prize the fingers away, but Fran's grip was like a vice and slammed Caris into the desk……

From the corner of her eye she saw the door open, and a male voice from a distance shout "FRAN! NO! STOP!"

All of a sudden the grip was released and Caris fell forward relieved of the weight of Fran's body. She gasped for breath and started to cry as Robbie helped her up holding her tight before placing her into her office chair. Her colour was pale, and her upper arm showed vivid red finger marks which were beginning to turn purple.

Francesca was by now sitting on the couch with the blanket wrapped about her shoulders. Her catatonic eyes staring ahead, non-seeing. The corner of the blanket was in her hand, as she rubbed it across her face and Robbie could see that she was no longer a risk to anyone. He picked up the phone and dialled for an ambulance, Francesca needed admission.

Once done, he turned back to speak with Caris.

"How are you feeling Caris? I am so very sorry! Are you able tell me what the hell happened?"

Although shaken, Caris gave him a run-down of the incident that had occurred.. "I think I pushed her too far, she thought I was Sarah… Who the hell is Sarah?"

Robbie looked at the chaos that lay around him and wondered how much more he could endure. He sat down heavily in a chair as if all the energy had left him. "Sarah or should I say Vanessa, was my wife when I lived in Australia years ago."

Seeing Caris's confusion he continued………

"After Vanessa and I were divorced I came back to England to look for Fran and my daughter Emily. However, by the time I returned, Fran had married Richard, and Emily in all sense and purpose was Richard's daughter.

I got a position at the local hospital and eventually became part of Emily's life as her Uncle Robbie and cared for her when Fran worked. It was a good arrangement and her family accepted me into their lives again. The trouble was Fran and I still loved each other and eventually we became pregnant again. To cut a long story short, Fran left Richard and came to live with me."

"But where does this Sarah fit in?"

On the rebound, Richard and his co-worker Sarah Burford, had an affair. Sarah was in fact Vanessa, but at the time I didn't know that, and didn't find out until much later. When Sarah found out that I was not only here, but also part of the triangle, she manipulated the situation to her benefit! From there it got nasty and complicated."

"You still haven't explained how Fran was mixed up with Sarah, and why she was so angry with her. I mean she had left Richard hadn't she? Then why would she say Sarah took both of you?"

"We would see Richard when he picked up Emily on a Friday and for Emily's sake it was always cordial. On one occasion, with Fran heavily pregnant, he told her that he was worried about Mackenzie Taylor, that profits had been put into overseas investments and not ploughed back into the company. These investments had not had a good return and with the textile market also suffering, they were in trouble.

Fran did some digging, she phoned her contacts and looked things up on the computer. Eventually, she found that the investment had been put into a company in LA….. Brookes Shipping Company. Brookes was Sarah or should I say Vanessa's father's company. It got nasty and even more complicated…."

There was a knock on the door, interrupting the discussion and Robbie stood up to open it, and let two paramedics in.

"Good evening Dr Harvey, not a good night eh"?

"No Pete, sorry and all that, but she has had a bad turn. and it isn't safe to transport her whilst I am driving. Unfortunately she had an incident with Dr Goodman here who has had an injury to her arm. I don't think it's broken but it may be dislocated.."

"Quite understand sir. This is my new partner Erica. Erica meet Mrs. Taylor, Fran to her friends.... Ay Fran. Erica will check out Dr Goodman whilst Fran and I have a nice chat."

"I will meet you at the hospital Pete, she will need some sedation as she may get agitated, she hates going there but I am afraid there is no other choice."

"Right, no problem – we will just do some checks on her before we leave. Erica, how is Dr Goodman?"

"I think you'll live Dr Goodman, now, let's put this sling on. There now, that should make it feel a bit better. A couple of Panadol and a good night's sleep will see you right as rain, but if it is no better tomorrow pop in an get an Xray. Ok my love!"

"Right Fran let's roll up this sleave." This done, Pete put a blood pressure cuff on.

"Let's look into those beautiful eyes of yours, he shone a pen torch and her pupils reacted, "That's it... well look at that your blood pressure is fine; Let's go for a little ride together hey!" Fran had not spoken since that attack and did not react to the prodding and pushing that was being done to her, instead she sat on the couch stony faced, her hands gripping the blanket.

The rocking was small to start with and went unnoticed until the tremors got bigger and within minutes her body arched stiffly as she fell to the floor, her awkward movements, flailing limbs and great spasms threw her out of control. A vaccine was given, then another, until finally it stopped and the person before them lay unconscious, in a pool of sweat and urine.

"That was a bad one, and she is not coming round, best we take her, blue light all the way. See you there Doc!"

"I will follow you there".

As they lifted her onto the gurney and went to leave, Caris called after them "Can you wait a minute"? She took the blanket from the couch and wrapped it around the sleeping Fran. She leant over her, whispering, "Take it with you, and remember that it reminds you of the blue sky and the buttercups!"

Robbie smiled at Caris and then left, following the paramedics out of the door.

And with that she was left alone to clear up her office. Her arm throbbed and she suddenly felt very tired. She stood amongst the books that had fallen to the floor, the water that had been knocked over and the urine stain that was seeping into her rug and wondered again why she had re visited this difficult case.

She desperately wanted to know the conclusion to Robbie's story and hoped that there would be time enough to fathom out this mystery. If she could only find the key that unlocked the pain that had haunted Francesca for so many years, she was sure they would find the real Francesca again.

One could only hope.

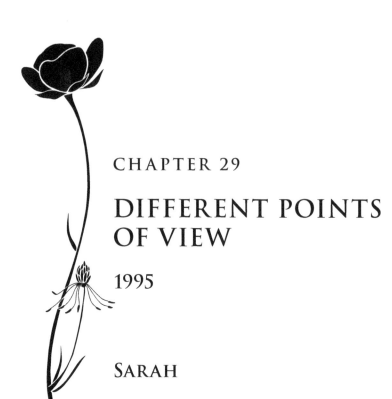

CHAPTER 29

DIFFERENT POINTS OF VIEW

1995

SARAH

"Stop worrying Richard, the investment is a sure thing." Sarah was sitting opposite watching as he poured over the monthly figures. "You needed the capital, and I found the backer. We looked over it carefully together, and you know there is always a lull before profits pick up."

Richard wasn't listening, he scratched his head, and looked again at the spread sheets that had been presented to him that morning. "It doesn't make sense, even before the investment, we were doing better than this and October is normally our better month due to the textile expo. However, this…." He stabbed the document in front of him with his finger…"Is showing a decline! The only department that is showing any growth is Organics, which is yours. If we continue like this there will need to be some labour cuts and I have never had to do that before."

Sarah yawned and stood up. "Richard, you are becoming quite obsessed. Brookes Shipping has invested a shit load of funds into Mackenzie Taylor, and they are not expecting a return any day soon. You have to admit, with the textile industry suffering this year, no one is making any money and we are lucky to still be afloat. Quadrant closed its doors last month and Suri Lo, I spoke to her last week by the way, says that the bank is foreclosing on her. Come on babe, you were up all night worrying and all you can talk about is money or lack of. We are doing okay, really."

"I will need to talk to Fran, this week when I go home, she still has shares, and it might be time to give her the heads up."

Sarah's, eyes narrowed, she hated when he spoke of Fran as it was always said with such regret. Over the last two months the excitement was somewhat stale between Richard and herself and although they still had great sexual chemistry something had soured and she, for one, was getting bored.

'Perhaps, I should come with you don't you think? I mean it's been 2 months since you split and she and Robbie, are playing happy families now. Maybe if we explained the investment together, it might be easier."

"No Sarah, it is too early. Besides this pregnancy has been very difficult and she is not doing too well. Your appearance will not help I can assure you and I don't want to add further stress at this time."

"You seem to be forgetting that it was Fran, who upset you. Do not underestimate the cunning of her and that she is pregnant with *his* child".

"I haven't forgotten but for Emily's sake we have to keep things pleasant." He sighed…

"We have actually spoken since I walked out. Amazingly we managed to speak without any cross words rather an agreement of how to move on. It doesn't matter how you look at it, we were equally to blame, and she readily admits it. I was so wrapped up in the business that I forgot her needs and, although I loathe to say it, Robbie was there. They always had good chemistry between them and that feeling just reignited, particularly after he met his daughter and was still part of her life. Sadly, as I have said before, Fran never really felt the same about me, but I had hoped in time our family would grow and love would come but ………." He was interrupted rudely by Sarah," Yardi yardi ya! Boring! I have heard all this before, several times! Your relationship is not with Fran but with me now! Don't make the same mistake twice!"

"Sarah I didn't mean it like that……"!

"So take me with you, I would like to meet Emily!"

"Not this time, I am sorry, but I am adamant about this. We just need to give Fran the space."

Sarah picked up her files and slammed out of the office. Things were not progressing well. She still hadn't gone back to Little Stockton and she still hadn't confronted Robbie and the chance to do so was getting slimmer.

She stormed past Hazel and then stopped. She had tried, for appearances sake to like her but she didn't trust her. If it was not for the fact that Richard respected her, she would have been gone or moved long ago. Sarah had the feeling that her dislike was reciprocated..... Hazel was from a different era; a time when Richard had married the young bright Mackenzie with stars in her eyes but who had also wept at her funeral. Richard has always said that Hazel was part of his family, holding the business together whilst he grieved. She was there when beautiful Fran, would rush breathlessly up the corridor, always stopping to have a word with her before entering a meeting, looking back and rolling her eyes with that beautiful smile on her face and when Fran and Richard played happy families. Although nothing was ever said, Sarah could tell that Hazel watched her and probably reported her private opinions back to him. Hazel was in her way and people like that usually didn't last long.

"Hazel, were those documents completed that I left?"

"Yes Sarah, they have been left for signing on your desk."

"Good thank you. By the way, I think it is high time that old coffee machine is removed from Richard's office, don't you? I think he needs something a little more modern, don't you agree? It is very hard to concentrate with that thing clunking in the background. Old relics should be put to pasture, can you see to it Hazel!"

Hazel hesitated, Richard loved that old machine, it reminded him of humble beginnings and staying the course.

"Did Richard ask you to tell me because......."

"Because what!. If I ask you to do something, I expect there to be no argument. Please remove it and buy something more appropriate and when you have bring me the invoice."

"But Sarah, Richard said that there was to be no unnecessary expenditure. Besides he loves that coffee machine, it reminds him....."

"Hazel, when I want something done, I expect that it is done. Richard doesn't know what he wants at present. He has a lot of worries and I am here to take the worry away, do you understand?"

"Perhaps we should ask Richard what he wants first, I don't want to get in trouble with him...."

"It would be far worse to go against my request Hazel, just do it".

Sarah swept past the desk and entered her office.

"Hazel" she yelled "Hazel!"

Hazel got up from her desk, she was used to Sarah's tantrums and her controlling attitude. The aches and pain of age was settling in and as she stood, she rubbed her back. Her husband had told her to retire but she felt a sense of duty to Richard and had not. Perhaps now was the time, she didn't like the way the company was going, and she too could see an issue with the downtrend of figures. She had also done some digging of her own and was not sure that the investment company was all it was cracked up to be. But who was she to have an opinion.

"Yes Sarah, is there a problem"?

"There is a letter missing from this pile, a particularly important letter. Where is it"?

"I have typed everything that you gave me but if you mean the letter to Brookes, Richard asked me for it this morning. It is typed, but he has asked that anything to Brookes gets signed by himself."

Hazel looked on and waited instruction. When there was none, she turned to leave. Sarah sat upright staring at the remaining letters and just as Hazel opened the door she spoke. Her voice was icy cold. "I will speak to Richard but Hazel, be warned that I don't like people going against my decisions, it doesn't not end positively."

Hazel took a deep breath and turned slowly. "That sounds like a threat to me. I have seen things and kept things to myself for years. I have worked tirelessly for the good of this company and I am not about to change my work ethic now. Richard is my boss, and I take orders from him and if he says jump I jump. Good morning to you Ms Burford."

Sarah watched as she stomped off back to her desk.

Eyes narrowed she spoke softly to herself "And if I say go you will go"!

ROBBIE:-

Sitting on the back porch, he reflected that it had been a difficult two months and not at all how he thought it would pan out. Working at the hospital was hard enough but coming home to a distant Fran, well that was harder. Emily had started school in the September and went from a happy imaginative child to a difficult sulky child. She wasn't making friends easily, which was strange as she had always been sociable, and she had made it quite clear that she didn't understand why Uncle Robbie was around all the time and that the new baby coming was his. She was used to her daddy coming home at the weekend and that hadn't changed but the fact that he took her away from her home had and she didn't like it. Both Fran and Robbie had spoken to her and it had been decided that the status quo would not change; Richard was her daddy; there was no need to hurt her further.

The end of her marriage had hurt Fran, particularly because her duplicity was matched by his own sordid affair with Sarah. Robbie just didn't understand the anger within her, but she refused to speak about it.

He made himself scarce when Richard came to pick up Emily, but he would watch from the upstairs window, as Fran waved off Emily and Richard would lean down and peck her on the cheek. Often Fran could be found crying after such a visit and it seemed impossible to comfort her.

Robbie had asked her if she still loved him, and she always replied yes, but the warmth had disappeared, and the excitement of their forbidden love had died.

Emily had known it was Friday because school had finished but Richard has not turned up. "Where is daddy"? She had demanded. Fran wearily stated that he wasn't coming as he had a work function but would be here in the morning. There followed a tantrum of monumental proportion, until Robbie had picked her up and put her in her room. "I hate you Uncle Robbie" she screamed behind the closed door, "I want my daddy!"

Robbie walked down the stairs feeling rather dejected. It was bad enough that Fran had refused to leave their home and live with him, saying that it would be too disturbing for Emily but after he had moved in to support Fran, Emily had turned on him. Mary had said to give it time but two months down the track, it had not got better, if anything it had got worse. Both Joe and Mary had been shocked at the turn of events but didn't hold grudges and had come round eventually. Tom and Nancy had said as long as Fran was happy it was alright with them. Robbie supposed that he had been lucky as all in all Fran's family accepted the new arrangement. However, what didn't help Fran's state of mind was when Mary, who kept in touch with Richard, reported back that things were not going well with the company. She said he looked grey and years older. This of course added to Fran's stress and her depression deepened, which ultimately affected her health.

It was a complete surprise to Robbie whilst drinking his morning coffee that Richard strolled through the back gate and up the steps onto the patio to the greet him……

"Good morning Robbie," Richard's voice shook him out of his contemplation "Enjoying your morning coffee I see".

Steadying his hand and placing his cup on the table, he looked up as Richard plonked himself down opposite.

Robbie looked across at Richard. He looked his normal suave self, comfortable at what was, after all, his table, and openly relaxed. HIs long legs crossed, he smiled across at Robbie, fully aware of his impact. Robbie stood, feeling that his height was called for, "Can I get you one Richard? The pot has just brewed".

"That would be great…. Is Fran around, it seems awfully quiet around here."

"Fran had a bad night and has only just got up. I am afraid that Emily has been rather difficult of late and we took the brunt of it last night!"

"What was the problem?"

"On this occasion, you were!"

"Really"? Richard looked rather quizzically at Robbie. "That's not like her, what's up?"

"Emily realised that it was Friday because school had finished for the week and you were not here. Fran let her know that you would be coming today but she had a tantrum and was not easily pacified. Apparently, it was my fault but then everything is these days". Regretting this statement instantly, Robbie, shrugged, "You know how it is."

"Oh, I see...... big bad Uncle Robbie. I expect it is quite hard for her to understand.... the change I mean."

"It is!" Not wanting to discuss further, Robbie excused himself and went inside to make the coffee. Pouring the milk into the cup, he was puzzled by the change of attitude. Richard was being more than just friendly, he seemed supportive and more like his old self. Something wasn't right that was for sure.

"Here." Robbie passed the coffee cup over to Richard. They sat sipping their coffee without further conversation. Robbie finished his coffee and put the cup down on the table and spoke, "Richard if you don't mind me asking, why this change of heart, I mean normally there is a near Mexican stand-off and now these pleasantries. Why the change has something happened?"

"No,...... well yes. Actually I am rather worried about Fran... yeh yeh, I know, not my problem, but she doesn't look well at all and I wonder, as you're a doctor, perhaps there is something I need to know about.........I mean there is Emily to think about."

"You are absolutely right! I am a doctor but incidentally, not her doctor and therefore cannot tell you anything Richard, and there is such a thing as patient confidentiality. So, I am afraid that it is up to Fran to tell you. Have you asked her?"

"I tried but she just shrugs it off and I am worried, she is just not herself!"

"Worried about what?" Fran had stepped on to the patio, cup of tea in hand. Both guilty faces looked up at her saying nothing. Her eyes a vivid green narrowed at their expressions……. "Ask me what?" her question contained an icy and rather irritable tone.

"About this?" She pointed to her small-rounded tummy, "Or this?" Pointing to her head. "If it is about the baby, my blood-work has come back fine and the ultra -sound shows a healthy viable baby…" She smiled, but the action did not reach her eyes as she continued to stare at them, her green eyes overly bright. Richard looked away, feeling awkward and uncomfortable. "Sorry Richard… but you did ask. Or maybe you both feel that I am mentally unstable and unable to make decisions. Perhaps that's it! Well I can assure you I *am* mentally stable, and I am absolutely bloody well fine!" She turned on her heel and slammed into the kitchen.

They looked at each other both acknowledging that something was far from alright. Robbie sighed "Her depression is getting worse, and she seems obsessed with the slightest of things, I dare not look the wrong way these days, have you seen her like this before, maybe through her first pregnancy?"

Richard rubbed his fingers across a rueful smile…."No nothing like this, there were other areas of concern but not like this."

"Look I won't keep you." He could see Fran and Emily heading towards them, "but keep an eye on her, she still means the world to me". As he stood he looked at Robbie, "You know, she never stopped loving you and I was never quite enough. I tried to fill the gap, but it was always you, Robbie." His sadness was patently obvious, and Robbie understood his pain…. "I had thought to bring Sarah with me, one of these days, to show Fran that I, too am happy, what do you think"?'

"Perhaps, but maybe leave it for now. Just whilst she sorts herself out."

"Yes you may be right, thanks."

A bright button face threw itself onto Richard's leg… "Darling how are you, I am so sorry I missed you yesterday but looking at your sleepy face, I don't think you have had breakfast to wake you up…. Am I right?" The bright titian curls bobbed up and down as she clung tightly. "Then I think a trip the Blue Café is in order…. Waffles are calling us". With that he lifted his daughter high into his arms and with a salute to Robbie, he marched down the path to the gate.

"1 2 3 4 we are heading out the door"!

"Again, Daddy again…….1 2 3 4 we are heading out the door"!

With squeals of laughter, they left, leaving Robbie staring after them… shaking his head he went inside to find Fran. Life wasn't meant to be easy, but this was bloody hard.

FRAN:-

From the moment life's pathway changed, something felt wrong. Richard had gone and Robbie had arrived and that was what she had wanted, wasn't it? So why did she feel so out of sorts. She felt cross all the time with everything and everyone.

Robbie just annoyed her! She didn't know why, but he did. He had bent over backwards for her, and was always there, with his gentle voice of reason and his boy like smile but try as she might, having him around all the time was claustrophobic and the freedom that she thought she would have, wasn't there. She had always said Richard was never around, but here was Robbie, always ready to help and still it didn't feel right! She had asked herself why, over and over, but no answer would come. Maybe it was her hormones gone haywire.

She didn't feel well either which didn't help things. Her nausea was awful, much worse than before and the only thing that helped this whole situation was her obsession with routine. Emily's behaviour had become intolerable with poor Robbie copping most of it but even when she thought that this was possibly the reason, she knew that it wasn't ….

She find herself saying "Pull yourself together" and "smile you wanted this" but nothing helped.

Fran had spoken to her mother, Mary, but practical as ever she smiled patted her on the hand and said, "Well Fran, you're just out of sorts because all that you knew has changed and it's a bit of a shock to the system, but you made your bed, and you must lay in it".

Fran patted her stomach "Well little one, my bed has been well and truly laid". She picked up her cup of tea and walked out to sit on the patio to wait for Richard. She had got up late due to Emily's upset the night before. Once again Richard had let her down; not coming on Friday as promised with dour consequences. Luckily Emily was still asleep which gave her time to shower and have a bit of time to herself. She hoped that Richard wouldn't turn up too early but opening the back door she saw them sitting together, and unbelievably talking; talking about her! In itself the conversation wasn't too damming but the fact that they were in the same place, together, sipping coffee seemed contrived and she didn't like it.

"I tried but she just shrugs it off and I am worried, she is just not herself"!

Robbie's words hung in the air and hovered over her. Her annoyance was evident and spilled over with contempt disrupting the conversation.

"Worried about what"? She saw the guilt written over their faces. Her temper was rising, and she knew she needed to keep it under control. More icily but calmly she added, "Ask me what? About this"? Fran pointed to her small-rounded tummy, "Or this"? pointing to her head. "If it is about the baby, my blood-work has come back fine and the ultra -sound shows a healthy viable baby…" She watched as Richard looked away. "Sorry Richard… but you did ask. Or maybe you both feel that I am mentally unstable and unable to make decisions. Perhaps that's it! Well I can assure you I *am* mentally stable, and I am absolutely fine!" Turning on her heel she slammed into the kitchen. How dare they talk about her behind her back. Who the hell did they think they were!

She stomped up the stairs to wake Emily. The little girl so like her mother looked up. Her bag already packed by Fran the night before, was by the door but she had dressed herself and was smiling proudly at the bag of toys she had put together, "Is my daddy here?" She demanded. Looking at her daughter's choice of clothes; a mix matched assortment of colours Fran chuckled to herself, she didn't feel it appropriate to change the outfit but instead dropped to her knees and throw her arms round the little girl loving her free spirit and individuality.

"Love you Buttercup"

"Love you too mummy but I am very hungry - please tell me daddy is here! He can take me out for breakfast!"

"Oh can he, you presumptuous terror.... as a matter of fact he is, come on."

She watched her child's departure from the safety of the kitchen. It always upset her seeing her leave knowing that her family was fragmented because of her. The guilt she felt riddled her with fear and she now knew why she was so angry. She wasn't angry with Richard for neglecting her or with Robbie who loved her. It wasn't the new life who grew inside her or Emily who could be difficult in this phase of her life. It was herself that made her so angry and so resentful. She had let Emily down and hurt Richard. She had ignored his needs as a wife, shut him out, forgetting he had saved her all those years ago. She had turned to Robbie because of love; because of history and for her own selfish need for attention. She had never loved Richard in the same way that she loved Robbie and for that she hated herself. Richard had taken on the responsibility of Emily and there was no doubt that he loved her and she him; her squeals of laughter that reached her was testament to it, but it hadn't been enough. Her eyes filled with tears, reminiscent of what should have been but wasn't and never could be. Looking out the window she saw Robbie's hunched figure leaning on the patio fence. Although she could not see his face, she could tell that he was unhappy.

She watched as he shook his head as if to shake some sort of sense into their muddled lives and then he turned just as she came to meet him.

Meeting in the doorway, he stood tall and handsome. His face was pale, and she noted his eyes and end of his nose red. She couldn't ignore the pain she had caused and went to him. Automatically he enveloped her into his strong arms, his warmth, comforting and his smell, undeniably provocative. "I'm sorry" she mumbled, muffled into his jumper. "I'm so sorry, it wasn't you, it was......." He pulled away and looked down at her, those green eyes pleading with him. He stared at her for what seemed an eternity, "Ssh, it's okay Bean, you had to work through it didn't you. You had to work it out." She nodded and as she went to speak, he put his finger to her lips. "No, I don't want to know. You had your reasons and I think you have punished yourself enough, haven't you? As long as we are okay, you, me and Emily. We are okay aren't we"? She heard his vulnerability and saw the intensity in his eyes as he waited for her answer.

"You are forgetting something". He looked warily at her as she continued to speak. "You, me, Emily and baby Bean and yes, we are alright, if you will have us?"

He bent his head and their lips met, sealing the answer with a kiss. Words not spoken, they walked inside and for the first time in weeks found their unconditional love.

CHAPTER 30

HOUSE OF CARDS
BEGINS TO TUMBLE

1995

Fran paced the floor, and waited. It had been the phone call that had set her heart racing causing an uneasiness within.

"Mrs. Taylor, Francesca, I need to speak with you, urgently. I wouldn't normally bother you but I think you need to see something."

"Hazel whatever is it, you sound awful"?

"I can't talk here, can we meet or perhaps if you don't mind, could I come to you, if that is okay".

"Of course it's okay, when we're you thinking of coming"?

"Now" the phone had clicked and the tone sounded. Something was very wrong.

Fran, now 6 months pregnant, knew it would take at least an hour for Hazel to arrive but try as she might she could not rest. It was the urgency of the call that had scared her. Hazel, so calm normally, was definitely not herself, with her feathers very ruffled.

The baby moved and gave a sharp kick as Fran's anxiety increased and she sat down to wait. "Sorry little Bean" she crooned stroking her protruding belly but no sooner had she sat down, up she stood again.

The little blue Fiat drove up the driveway and the small stout neat body of Hazel, jumped out, walked up the driveway purposely and rapped on the door.

Fran opened it and greeted her old friend, "Hazel, it's been too long, how lovely to see you."

"You're looking well Francesca, pregnancy suits you." Fran couldn't help noticing a coldness to the greeting and although the sentiment was there, it didn't quite have the warmth of before.

"Please come in, would you like tea or coffee?"

"No that's quite alright, I don't really have the time." There it was again, a formality that was never there before. As they walked through to the kitchen, Fran called over her shoulder, "well if you don't mind, I need a coffee, your phone call has unnerved me a little Hazel. Let's sit at the table and chat. What's this all about?"

"And so it should! I am unnerved myself and out of my mind with worry!"

"Hazel I hate to state the obvious, but have you spoken with Richard...?" Fran watched as Hazel shook her head, looking dejected. "There is no point Fran. Richard hasn't been himself lately, very distracted and he looks dreadful but then I don't need to tell you, I am sure you would have noticed. You have seen him lately haven't you?"

"Of course I have seen him!" Fran said with slight annoyance. She thought back; Ricahrd had seemed rather vague and distracted, but then so had she been. Emily had lost her bunny, a soft and rather repulsive toy, that she loved. Emily refused to go with Richard until it has been found. Having eventually found it, Richard said he needed to go. There

228

wasn't much time for pleasantries and she admitted to herself that she hadn't noticed his appearance. "He was here Friday but he didn't stay long."

"Well I can tell you that he isn't himself! It's the business, it's in trouble!"

"That's a rather sweeping statement Hazel. Have you proof? If you can't talk to Richard, perhaps Sarah can....."

Hazel interupted... "Huh! Sarah! I wouldn't speak to her if my life depended on it. She is the problem or at least part of it. She is so controlling and the decisions made are so controversial to how we have run the business before".

Fran's stifled a smile at the comment and the inclusion of "We", but then, Hazel had been there from the start and was and should be very much part of the business. She turned away and made two coffees. "Unfortunately, Hazel, growth is part of change and I am sure that they have it hand. I believe the textile industry is not doing well in general, maybe that's what you are seeing. "Turning back Fran could see Hazel's expression and hurridly carried on." It is great to see you taking an interest Hazel but Richard will manage he always does, and you must remember the rocky times that the company has gone through before. There must be someone that you can talk to? Richard has always had time for you in the past, you are part of the family."

"I can't, I have been moved"!

Fran nearly spilled the coffee and carefully put them down before sitting.

"What! Why? How has this happened and where have you been moved to?"

To Fran's dismay, Hazel started to cry. "Please Hazel, please don't," she stood, gave her a tissue and put her arm around Hazel's shoulders.

"Oh I'm sorry, my husband told me not to bother you with being pregnant an all. He said you wouldn't be interested seeing as you had walked out and left him......sorry, I wasn't meant to say that...It's none of my business after all but ......".

"It's ok. Now drink your coffee and take a deep breath and tell me what has been going on."

For the next couple of hours Hazel spoke of her treatment from Sarah and how she had plotted to get rid of her. There were several incidents but the one that turned the trust was removal of the old coffee machine. This surprised Fran; Richard loved that machine, it reminded him of humble beginnings. He made it known that he despised the silent new creations and had never liked the coffee from them, but Fran remained silent on this seeing the anguish on Hazel's face.

As she spoke, Fran's blood began to boil as she listen to Hazel's encounter. Under instruction Sarah had told her to remove the old coffee machine from Richard's office. She had been told that it had broken and he no longer wished for it take up the room. She had been given commercial credit to order and purchase a new machine. Hazel had argued but eventually did as she was told. Richard had of course been furious and even when Hazel had explained the situation, she could see he didn't believe her. Hazel later found out that the commercial credit receipt had been destroyed and with no paper trail as evidence, she had no back up. From then on a series of events occurred until Hazel faced Richard. She told him of Sarah's deceit and how she had been treated. She also tried to tell him that she felt that something underhand was happening with the business and that it was her belief that Sarah was behind it. Richard had stopped her. He told her that it was obvious to him that his separation from Fran had upset her and in doing so, her clash with Sarah had become more and more apparent. Both he and Sarah had thought it might be better if Hazel had a change of scenery and felt a move to Dispatch may assist the situation. He was very grateful for all she had done, in particular how she had kept him sane after Mackenzie's death but that he thought, well they both thought, perhaps it would be less stressful and quieter particularly as she was nearing retirement.

Fran comforted her distraught friend and was disgusted at her treatment. She agreed it was obvious that Sarah had influenced the decision and for whatever reason, Richard seemed oblivious to the pain he was causing. She would speak with him Friday, reminding him that Hazel was part of the family.

Throughout the revealing disclosure it had been difficult to keep Hazel on track, but eventually the crux of the matter was revealed. Fran listened with open mouthed disbelief as Hazel spoke; each word worsening the situation. Apparently, Richard, under Sarah's business advice, had sort an investor. The company had not had a profitable year and Sarah had persuaded Richard to look beyond the textile Industry and the banks. She had told him that with the instability of Textile at present no bank would touch them and as all textile companies were in the same boat and with many of them closing, an overseas investor would bring the capital that was needed. She had floated the business and Brookes Shipping had invested. The staff had been spoken to as many were concerned that Mackenzie Taylor would downsize or worse shutdown.

At first there was relief that they had remained solvent but after several months, the profit margin significantly dropped and had continued to do so. Correspondence to and from Brookes Shipping disappeared from her desk, before Hazel had a chance to open it, however, one morning Richard had come in early and on passing her desk took the mail, unopened, into his office. When Hazel arrived at work, she was met by a shrieking Sarah who excused her of hiding mail from her and on hearing the mayhem, Richard had come out to see Hazel, white faced, yelling right back at Sarah, which sealed her fate. Hazel never understood how Sarah got away with her deception but knew that she was clever enough to explain herself out of it.

As Hazel finished, Fran stood and went to the fridge, "I think you need more than coffee"!

She poured Hazel a large glass of wine and set it down in front of her.

"Is there anything else, you poor thing"?

"I'm afraid there is Francesca!" Hazel took a large gulp of wine and continued. "After I had been moved to Dispatch, I found I had time on my hands and did some investigation. No one in the Industry knew of Brookes Shipping and my Larry, our youngest son, who works on the stock market, well he hadn't heard of them either! That just didn't seem right as all investors are right up there aren't they? Anyway to cut a long story short, we did some more digging and you will never guess what was found...?" Hazel paused and took another gulp of her wine....

"Hazel?"

"Brookes Shipping belongs to Vanessa Brookes. It is a shipping company in LA. It is not an investment company, but rather a private corporate, with some shady history!" Seeing the confusion on Fran's face, Hazel continued, "Francesca, where do you think Mackenzie Taylor's profits have gone to?"

"So you think Sarah is working with this Vanessa Brookes?"

"Exactly!"

"The question is, who is this Vanessa Brookes and why is her company not on the stock market? How the hell do we tell Richard?"

With both of them so deep in conversation, neither had heard Robbie come home and both their heads turned as he spoke......

"Who wants to know about Vanessa Brookes?" He walked through the door and stood behind Fran, his hands placed on her shoulders.

"It's nothing Robbie, I will tell you all about it later. You remember Hazel, from the office don't you?"

"Yes of course, hello again." Robbie turned away and put the kettle on to make himself a cup of coffee. "Seriously," he said why *are* you talking about Vanessa Brookes?"

"Robbie, I told you I will explain it all later! Why the interest?"

"Well Vanessa Brookes, if the same person, is my ex-wife!"

The kettle boiled, it's whistle shrilling through the air. Coffee made, he turned around to see two shocked faces, mouths open, concern in their eyes.

Later Fran, said goodbye to Hazel and promised she would investigate further and speak with Richard.

Once she had gone, Robbie mulled over the information given to him. His distress was obvious and added to Fran's concerns. He had stood and was now pacing the floor...

"Don't you see if this *is* Vanessa she has come back for me, she always said that she would"?

"But darling, how would she know you were here, after all it has been 5 years now?"

"It wouldn't have taken her long to figure it out Fran, but what I don't understand is why has she waited this long?"

"Exactly!"

Fran now tired from the day's excitement, was laying on their bed, trying to rest. "Robbie, this is silly. If this is your Vanessa, how would she know that you had anything to do with Mackenzie Taylor and come to think of it, if Sarah and Vanessa, are trying to ruin Richard, how is that getting back at you. The sensible thing is to talk with Richard and give him the heads up."

"You don't know her; she will go to any lengths to destroy people that get in her way. She knows that you were, are, part of Mackenzie Taylor and that I am your boyfriend.

I am absolutely certain that she knows by now that I am the daddy of this baby and then there is Emily to think of. That is all the ammunition she needs. Quite frankly Fran, in her twisted mind, you have got everything that she hasn't, and you will need to take extra care!"

"I think that is a little melodramatic Robbie. Now if you don't mind I feel bloody awful and I need some sleep!"

"Yes sorry Fran, get some rest, you must be exhausted after the day and I will go and watch a bit of TV. I am not the slightest bit tired, and you are right I will need to think this through."

He looked over lovingly at Fran, but she was already fast asleep and tiptoeing out of the room, he hoped with all his heart that he had got it wrong.

CHAPTER 31

DOUBLE JEOPARDY
1995

Having moved Hazel from her front desk position, Sarah was able to intercept mail before it reached Stephanie, the new receptionist that she had hired. Her instruction to Hugh, the young boy who wheeled the mail trolley around the building, was to leave mail marked Brookes Shipping on her desk as it was highly confidential. It was duly done, with Hugh none the wiser. Unlike Hazel, Stephanie, was young, pretty, and useless. Never in the office before 9am, her official start time, and capable of answering a phone and not a lot else. Richard was not happy. Sarah recalled the conversation and smiled to herself.

"I don't know how you convinced me that Hazel needed to have less stress in her life. I know you didn't trust her, but she was more than capable and was always at work before you and I. There is never any coffee and once again there is no paper in the paper copier and that's not all.............."! Sarah opened her eyes wide and smiled sweetly whilst interrupting Richard, simpering out her words like honey dripping from a knife.

"I know Richard, but she was going to leave anyway. She told me or rather yelled at me that it was time for her to retire. I thought I was doing her favour moving her to a less stressful role to finish her days.

If you want paper, it is kept behind this desk, I will remind Stephanie that the paper copier must be filled before she leaves, okay?

I will get your coffee when I get mine on the way to work; you don't like that coffee anyway". She indicated the new percolator, that sat unused behind him. Her blue eyes suddenly filled with tears; it was far too easy to play the victim. "Gees! I was only trying to help. Hazel had started to make mistakes and I felt awful picking her up on things. I know you felt loyal to her, honey, but we have a business to run. I am sorry if I made the wrong call.." She dabbed under her eyes with her finger, sniffing slightly; she knew exactly how to make him see it her way.

He looked into her beautiful eyes, filled with tears and the dejected way she stood.

"I am not good with change, you know that, and Hazel has been with me for so long, she is part of the furniture, more like family really...." He was interrupted by the now crying Sarah, "Oh for goodness sake Richard, please don't tell me that again! I know that you and Hazel, and Hazel and Fran go back a long way. I know because you have told me before, several times! I was only doing my job and trying to help, but these days it seems that I do nothing right!" Tears now freely flowing she took the offered tissue and blowing her nose sunk into the chair opposite, sniffing, and gulping as Richard continued to speak.

"It's just that I felt awful speaking with her after all she had done for me. You didn't see the way she looked! I felt like I had let her down and now I hardly see her and to be truthful I miss her. That Sharon is useless! Where the hell did you find her from?

"It is not Sharon, it is Stephanie, as you very well know. She came highly recommended. She has a lot to learn but she is trying really hard and is still quite new. It wouldn't hurt to be a bit more pleasant". Sarah was now sobbing in between blowing her nose.

"I'm sorry Richard but I have had it, I cannot do this anymore, I think I need to go home!"

"Sarah! This is not like you, please don't cry!" He went to stand but sat as Sarah stood and advanced towards him, her eyes blazing and looking furious.

"You hardly speak to me these days, and you are always so tired. If I look at you the wrong way, you snap my head off. We haven't had a long lunch for weeks and frankly I have had enough!"

Again, he stood but she had put her arm out as if to stop him coming close. Quietly and calmy Richard sat again and spoke...

"I am sorry that you feel this way, but work has preoccupied me lately. The business is not doing very well, and these ledgers are not making much sense. The figures are all over the place, and I can't find out where it has gone wrong. Our outgoings are more than our revenue and it is not adding up. We will have to close the doors if it doesn't right itself soon! If I have to look at another spread sheet today, I will go mad!" She watched as he slumped back in his chair, his face grey with concern.

"I can look at the spread sheet, if you like, I have some free time today. Please let me help! You know, a different perspective and all that, unless you don't think I am up to it."?

"Of course you are, don't be silly. it's just that….."

"It's just that…. what Richard"? She had walked behind him and put her arms around his shoulders, her head close to his ear. He could smell her perfume and her touch aroused him just as she knew it would. This was easy, he like many others, was putty in her hands.

"Thank you Sarah, that is good of you. Please by all means take a look and then maybe we could go through them together later!"

Over his shoulder, she flicked the pages of his desk diary, and with one long finger nail she tapped the page. "Looks like you have a couple of long meetings today, you won't have much time." Checking his diary, he moaned and ran his free hand through his hair. Seeing his stress, she pounced, "Whilst you are in the meetings, I could work my magic and see what's going on, what do you think? Sarah saw the frown marks on Richard's forehead ease slightly and hurriedly added "Just a suggestion!" He looked up, her eyes meeting his. "That would be great, thank you Sarah. No more talk about leaving hey. What would I do without you?"

"Be very lonely in bed!" Tears dried up she laughed as she swung his chair around and planted a kiss on his lips. His arms pulled her down onto him and she continued to kiss him passionately before being interrupted by a knock on the door.

"What!" They both shouted. The door opened and Stephanie walked in as Sarah detangled herself and jumped up. She didn't miss the smirk that was on Stephanie's face as she spoke, "Mr. Abbot is here to see you Mr. Taylor."

"Good, um very good!" Straightening his tie, he busily shuffled papers together that were on his desk. "Sarah, here is the paperwork that we were discussing. We will convene later today and go through it. Thank you."

Sarah picked up the paper and sauntered out of the office. Noticing that Stephanie was standing awkwardly, waiting instruction, he sighed. "Well show him in then Sharon. Oh, and please bring in coffee and morning tea in about 40 minutes". He knew it wouldn't get done, and that he would have to remind her. He missed Hazel in more ways than one.

On Friday, Richard arrived to find both Fran and Robbie waiting for him. Fran had to admit that he did look extremely tired, and his skin was pale and waxy under the light. "Where is my little munchkin?" Looking around not only did he not see her smiling face under a mass of red curls, but he didn't hear the screams of "Daddy" either.

"She isn't here, she is at my mum's!"

"Did you forget it was Friday, Fran? Gees I have a lot of work to do tonight, I really can't be late back!"

Robbie got up and walked to the fridge, he took out two beers and offered one to Richard, who shook his head. "No that's alright Robbie, but thanks anyway." Richard looked at his watch and then at the door; he seemed nervous and obviously uncomfortable.

"I think Richard, you may need it, please come and sit down, Fran and I need to talk to you." The gravity of his voice was enough for Richard to sit with a raised eyebrow and a look of concern.

"You are ok aren't you Fran, is Emily ok?"

"Yes she is fine, it's just that......"

"Oh shit! The baby, are you unwell? What can I do to help?"

"Richard please slow down we are both ok and so is Emily as is the baby. We sent Emily to mum's because I, I mean we, needed to talk to you about Mackenzie Taylor."

Richard, giving a quizzical look, sat down, and picked up the bottle that had been placed on the table. He turned the top of the bottle and took a swig of beer.

"You have my attention, but truthfully and I don't wish to be rude, but what has it to do with you, Robbie. You might have got my wife, but you haven't got my company!"

"Richard! Please don't! Robbie has a reason to be here, so just listen. We think something untoward is happening within the company, which you need to be aware of." Richard took another swig of his beer. "Go on, I am listening". His voice was harsh, and filled with tension, the bottle he was holding slammed down onto the table.

"I know that I chose to pull away from Mackenzie Taylor, but the last time I looked I still owned shares and was part of the Executive Committee, am I right?"

"Yes you are but ……"

"And as far as I know I still have a vested interest in the business and always will have unless I release or sell the shares…… which, I have no intention of doing!"

"Well that is a relief and yes that is the case."

"So, can you tell me why you floated the company, without discussing it with me?" Richard paused, his eyes met Fran's and then looked away. Turning his head back he spoke but it was with resignation in his voice.

"I didn't think you would be interested and Sarah……" Richard was interrupted again by the icy tone in Fran's voice, "Sarah, well I will get to her in a minute. So, I am led to believe you have an investor, Brookes Shipping. In fact, an investor that has invested heavily in the business, is that correct?"

"You seem to have your facts right, so why the inquisition? For Christ's sake I don't need this at the moment!" Richard stood and putting his jacket back on, made to leave. "When will Emily be home, or shall I pick her up from Mary's?"

Robbie also stood, "I think you need to hear what Fran has to say, in fact I insist! Emily will not be home until this is over, so I suggest you sit down, and listen! It isn't easy for Fran either!"

"What! How dare you! I will not stand for……."

"Richard, shut up. Just for once be quiet and listen to what I have to say."

Richard reluctantly sat down. He took another swig from the second bottle of beer placed in front of him and turned to Fran, gesturing for her to carry on.

"Are you telling me that in the 3 months since I have been gone, the business has got into such dire straits, that you needed an investor, and you didn't think I would be interested! How the bloody hell did you get in such a mess Richard?"

Running his hands through his hair, he tried to explain that he had become increasingly concerned at the decrease in profit margins. It had happened suddenly, and as many businesses had already closed, he had begun to panic. On top of that clients had become careful with their money. The textile industry was in an ever decreasing spiral and the custom-made quality that had always commanded customer attention now appeared too expensive. The "Do it yourself" trend was becoming more and more popular, as had the copy-cat ideas cheaply imported from Asia. Suri Lo's company has gone bankrupt, and she had disappeared out of London leaving debt behind her, which had tainted the independent backers. He had a suspicion that a lot of the copies were coming from her adjacent company in Singapore. This quantity not quality, was all the public seemed to want, with only the Organic branch doing well.

Fran sneered "Surprising that! but was stopped from anything further, as Richard looked at her abruptly, his face tense and his lips drawn in a thin line.

"Sorry, carry on" and on seeing hesitation on Richard's part, she added, "please."

Richard took another swig of beer, he looked from Robbie to Fran, anxiety filling his eyes, his brow furrowed, and shoulders slumped. He spoke, almost to himself, mumbling his loss, making it difficult to decipher. Fran strained to hear the words but refrained from speech as Richard continued.

"I was desperate not to lose the company. Mackenzie Taylor has been my life and I owed it to not only to the memory of Mackenzie but also what we, together, had done, Fran! I still don't understand exactly what has happened but as I said Sarah is looking over the figures at present." Hanging his head, his eyes filled with tears and although surreptitiously wiped away, it had been seen. No one spoke and the atmospheric charge that hung in folds around them brought a chill into the room as he continued. "I became increasingly worried about the staff who had stuck by us. They never complained, implemented change when given the challenge and did every dam thing we asked of them. The last straw was when I withdrew from the apprenticeship program. That injection of positive excitement and creativity was gone and those left behind, began to struggle, ultimately putting more and more pressure on to Sarah and myself." Seeing Fran's expression and watching the look she gave to Robbie, he continued, louder and more assertively. "Yes, Sarah! Say what you want about her, but she didn't leave. She could have done, as she was well sought after, but she stayed by my side. Often working into the night to get orders completed. One desperate night, when both of us could have thrown the towel in, she suggested an investor to boost funds and I was so busy with the failing business, that I agreed for her to investigate. Before I knew it, she had found a willing investor in LA and the deal was done. It gave me the breather I needed. We told the staff, to their relief and I started to look around for business opportunities with the injection of considerable funds. A month later, however, the roller coaster started again; the outgoings increased, and the revenue decreased it just didn't make sense and it seemed that collapse was imminent!"

"And Richard, you didn't think to tell me?"

He shook his head. "Do you really think I wanted this? To have some stranger dictating the terms. I have poured over the figures day after day but can make no sense of it. You asked why I didn't involve you, Fran, why do you think? You made it quite clear that you wanted out, why, then, would I face you with this mess, especially in your condition? I mean I had new client meetings set up with some fairly exciting lucrative deals on the table, but even with this influx of business, nothing added up. Sarah has been pouring over the books over the last few days and I have my fingers crossed that she can find the problem, she is good like that, I suppose that is why she has always been a success. She feels that there are a couple of glitches that will hopefully keep us out of the drink and if so we can recover some of the lost funds. Here's hoping!" He rose his bottle up and then took a swig giving a week smile.

"Sorry to say that is the whole sorry story in a nutshell and said nut has now pulled you up to speed."

Robbie leant over and offered another beer which Richard, rather absent mindedly opened and was now drinking. Fran noticed a slight slur to his words; he probably hadn't eaten and unlike Robbie, was not a great beer drinker and the now three bottles had gone down far too quickly. This was not going to be easy.

Looking at her husband she felt a sudden rush of sympathy for the man who had built up Mackenzie Taylor and who now seemed to be watching it fall away. Fran took a deep breath and reluctantly spoke, breaking the uncomfortable silence, "Unfortunately, Richard, that is not the end of it, there is much more."

Richard looked up from his beer, his eyes darkened and hooded. "Oh and pray tell me something that I don't already know!" The words caustically spat out with venom were sarcastically threatening.

"How much do you know about the investment company, Brookes Shipping?"

There was no reply, Richard's eyes held hers. "My guess is you don't know much!"

"Now hold on, Fran….." Fran interrupted his blustering attempt to speak. "I have done my own investigating and you see, Richard, there is no such investment company! Brookes Shipping does exist, but it is a private family business and does not invest! It isn't even floated on the Stock Exchange, therefore with no license to invest under that name, so I repeat my question, how much do you know?"

There was silence and she continued, "After looking through the paperwork, the only Brookes that is relevant and mentioned, is a Vanessa Brookes. Does that ring any bells?" She pulled out a contract and laid it on the table in front of Richard. "You see this is her signature written here!" She pointed to the signature sprawled across the dotted line, "witnessed by one Sarah Burford, here. So obviously Sarah, knows Vanessa well enough to have witnessed this business document!"

"Well, yes. Sarah knew of a company in LA who would assist us. I don't see how this is a problem. This is nonsense and…"

"And, Richard, you are the main share- holder and director of Mackenzie Taylor. Did you not question that Sarah, signed as the Director of Mackenzie Taylor, with no countersign from yourself, or in fact me? Did it not occur to you that anyone could have signed this form without endorsement from you and that in fact this whole business deal is a façade? Richard wake up! If Mackenzie Taylor cannot meet their obligations to Brookes Shipping, then one Vanessa Brookes will take ownership and I have a sneaky suspicion that Sarah is aware of this. How else would the company be failing so spectacularly in such a short spell of time. You told us today, that you were worried about the textile environment; of people losing jobs but at that point, Mackenzie Taylor was surviving, be it under difficult circumstances. We had been there before and tightening our belts is not a new phenomenon but to lose the company out from under your nose, well that is something else!"

Fran was breathing heavily and took the seat opposite Richard. She grabbed his hands, we......" she indicated all three of them, "need to stop her before it is too late and you lose everything!"

Richard pulled his hands from Fran's and stood up, the chair slamming behind him. He grabbed the contract and stared at the signatures again. "Where the hell did you get this from and who have you been speaking to?" He leered over Fran, his voice cold and loud. Robbie interjected and put a hand on Richard's shoulder, "Calm down mate." Before Robbie knew it, Richard had punched him across the jaw, and he fell to the floor.

"Richard!" Fran jumped up and knelt over Robbie, who had sat up and was rubbing his chin. "What the hell are you doing? Who the hell are you?" She helped Robbie up "We are trying to help you!"

"Who have you been talking to and what rubbish is this?" He threw the contract at Fran and sat heavily down. "Of course I know of Vanessa Brookes, she *is* Brookes Shipping and as I said before, it all happened very quickly! If it hadn't been for Sarah, we would have lost the investment. Unlike you Fran, Sarah stuck around to prevent the ship from sinking and I personally, cannot thank her enough but I ask again, what the fuck, has it got to do with him?" He jerked his thumb towards Robbie who was rubbing his chin. Slowly Robbie got up and walked over, leaning his hands, palm down on the table he turned his head to Richard. He spoke slowly and menacingly quietly, "Because, whether you like it or not, I believe Vanessa Brookes, to be my crazy ex-wife and it doesn't take an idiot to see that this scam is to get to me by any means and if it means destroying those around me then she would do that without compulsion!" Seeing the lack of comprehension Robbie continued, "It may seem far-fetched, but the coincidences are far too many for my liking. I know her and she is capable of anything. This company means nothing to her, a whimsical toy to be broken, but it's destruction will act as a warning for anyone who messes with her intentions. I warn you to take heed now, she will not stop until she gets me back, and anyone, I mean anyone getting in her way will go down too. This means Fran, Emily anyone or anything. If losing the company hurts you and in turn hurts your family, then that is what she will do! Do you understand now?,"

"Do you think Sarah is aware of this Richard? Do you think she is working with this Vanessa?" Fran's tentative voice cut through the explosive silence.

"I don't know, I mean I don't think she would do that to me. She wouldn't want to hurt you, Fran, or Emily. She has been asking to come and meet with you and set the record straight. I mean you have Robbie, and we should make amends so that Emily feels secure, but I told her no; that you were not ready! Shit, what a mess! Robbie this seems ...."

"Stupid, yes I know and look mate, I could be completely wrong, but I don't think I am. I would like to suggest if that is okay with both of you?"

Richard lifted his hand as if surrendering and Robbie, feigned a swift duck away from it. Shaking his head Richard seemed genuinely upset at his previous behaviour, "Sorry about earlier, this has been a bit of a shock. Robbie, please, at this point I will listen to anything."

"I suggest that this conversation stays hush hush. Do not talk about it with Sarah, or anyone. Fran, invite Richard and Sarah to dinner next week. At the dinner we talk about the investment company and how it is doing. Let's see how this develops and we go from there, agreed?"

Both Richard and Fran spoke at once agreeing to the suggestion interrupted by Richard's phone.

"Hello? Hello Sarah, you did? That is fantastic news...just leaving now and will call later, bye for now."

Beaming Richard turned around to see Robbie and Fran looking quizzically at him. "Sarah has worked on the reports all day and she feels she has found a considerable error, which will make a hell of a difference to the bank balance. Now that is someone, who is on our side. Right I am off to get Emily, unless you have anything else you want to throw at me? No, good!"

With the door closed, Fran sunk into the chair and Robbie put the kettle on. Neither spoke, and sipping their coffee, Robbie put his hand on Fran's – this would be a battle that he had to win, for the sake of their family, bugger the company.

CHAPTER 32

DECEPTION PERSONIFIED

1995

Sarah took her time getting ready for dinner, brushing her hair until it shone, leaving it lose, with it hanging straight down her back. It was held off her face with a black velvet band giving her a girlish look. Her makeup although subtle, enhanced her blue eyes with just amount of blusher highlighting her high cheek bones. She looked into her wardrobe for something that wasn't too riské. The outfit needed to have that feminine flair that would catch the eye but also one that would hug her figure, enhancing the contours of her body. She had chosen a little black number which had the right amount of suggestion, showing off her long legs but modest enough not to be openly sexy; coupled with her black heels and with an application of a Mary Quant pink lipstick, she was ready. She smiled at the reflection looking back at her from the mirror and blowing a kiss she laughed as she said, "Robbie, I am coming right for ya!" Smiling, she walked out of the bedroom and down to a waiting Richard.

"Wow, you look beautiful who are you trying to impress?"

"You silly".

She wound her arms around his neck and kissed him lightly on the lips. She noted with pleasure how his hands travelled down to her bottom, resting there, giving her cheeks a gentle but provocative squeeze.

"Hey, you will mess up my dress, cut it out," she retorted, laughing.

"Can't help it, you look irresistible darling, but you do realise we may be sitting around a kitchen table, with a pregnant Fran, who will undoubtedly dress for comfort. You don't want to outshine the hostess, now do you, or do you?"

"Yes Richard, that is exactly what I want to do!" She laughed again and did a twirl.

He caught her in his arms and kissed her again. Things hadn't been that good lately and Sarah has taken the brunt of his moods. He was cross with himself, but he would make it up to her somehow and tonight would be the start he told himself and hugged her closer to him. Her lithe body fitted in his arms so well, but why then did he suddenly have a flash back to a time gone by, with Fran heavily pregnant wearing a pair of his old track pants, crying into shoulder because she couldn't fit a dress she had wanted to wear. He remembered telling her how beautiful she was and that he loved her, even though she was the size of a whale. She had laughed, throwing back her titian curls, her green eyes sparkling. He remembered that he didn't think he had ever seen anything so beautiful but that was then and now was now. Sarah's words cut into his memories and ashamedly he realised he had spoken out loud.

"Thank you Richard, I love you too, now come on or we will be late."

He hoped with all his heart that this meeting would not end in tears, with neither lady getting hurt. Please god, he thought to himself as he helped Sarah into her coat, that this was not a mistake and some sort of truce would clarify the future and make going forward easier. He shrugged into his coat and they left the warmth of the house walking into the cold night air, cuddled up close to keep out the damp as they walked to the car.

Fran was also getting ready she had tried on several dresses, but nothing fitted, and everything felt uncomfortable. Sighing, she opted for a pair of black leggings and a pretty smock. Truth be known, it didn't matter what she wore as Robbie thought her beautiful in whatever she had on. In fact, she could wear a paper bag over her head, and he would find a way to tell her how lovely she looked. She loved that about him, he was so unpretentious and caring. Applying her make-up, she looked into the mirror searching her face for answers.

Richard had been attentive and loving when she had been pregnant with Emily and even though he knew that the baby was not his, he had been, was, a fantastic father. Fran wasn't quite sure when the relationship had changed and had often asked herself why it had never been enough. She knew of course that the love she had for Robbie was undeniable and had always been there hiding in the shadows of her heart. It hadn't taken much to reignite the passion and there it was, the reason was clear and there for all to see. Richard knew it too, and Fran justified her thoughts with the recognition as to why Richard had given in so easily to the split. Sighing, she had never meant to hurt him but there had been no going back and all three of them knew it. Sarah had been a complication and Fran felt betrayed to a certain degree but still Richard deserved happiness. She carried on applying the minimal make up that she always wore and tied her hair, as always, into a ponytail. She looked sideways and front on in the mirror, narrowing her eyes at the Fran that looked back and then on a whim wound the curls high into a bun on top of her head with titian tendrils curling around her face. Looking in her drawer she found a black velvet bow on a hair tie and held the escaping curls in place. She had never worn her hair like this before and she liked what she saw. The Fran who looked back at her now looked different, young, and yes, dare she say it, pretty, and smiling she stood up to leave the room. The phone was ringing, and she ran down the stairs to pick up the receiver. It was probably her mother asking her to say goodnight to Emily. She patted her tummy, "you have one hell of a pair of grandparents little one" and smiled.

She glanced at the clock as she left her room and frowned, time was ticking on and Robbie had not made it home yet, she really didn't want to see Sarah on her own. The phone rang off but then started again; rather breathlessly she picked up the receiver and spoke;

"Hello, Fran Taylor speaking".

"Hi Fran, it's me......look I am really sorry, but we have had several emergencies in, and I have to go to theatre. I am so sorry!"

She knew he meant it, but his timing was dreadful. She didn't know what to say, so she didn't say anything.

"Look I know it is not ideal, but perhaps you can put them off and make it for another night".

"It will be too late for that; the meal is ready and besides they will be on their way by now. Crap this is all I need!" She could hear his name being paged and heard him speak to a nurse about some medication and softened the edge to her voice. "I suppose it can't be helped.... See you later then!"

"Sorry Bean, I truly am......Yep, what? Yes I am coming now. Sorry Bean got to go!"

With that he was gone. Fran sunk onto the bottom step of the stairs. She didn't want to do this on her own but .... The doorbell rang.... She didn't have any choice.

With niceties over, she ushered them through to the sitting room, she noted Sarah's distain as she removed Emily's rather well-loved teddy from the sofa and brushed crumbs away before sitting; Richard remained standing looking as handsome as ever.

"You are looking well Fran, how are you"?

"Thank you, but getting a bit tired now, otherwise we are well.". Richard noted how she rested her hands on her swollen stomach and felt that she had never looked so beautiful. She smiled at him, her green eyes twinkling; her red hair against her white skin looked vibrant and the curls framing her face gave her a youthful look. He hadn't seen her wear it like this before and it was very becoming. His thoughts were interrupted as he felt Sarah's hand reach up and hold his own. He looked down at the perfection, of sleek hair and blue questioning eyes and smiled at her. She was indeed beautiful but there was something about her perfection that put him on edge.....Fran was speaking, and he needed to pull himself together.

"So, I am afraid that is the situation....." Fran finished.

"What is?" said Richard, confused.

"Richard! Where did you go to then?" drawled Sarah "It's Robbie he is held up in theatre, he won't be here tonight."

"Oh that's a shame, never mind at least you girls can chat." He meant it without a hidden agenda but looking down at Sarah, he could see his innocent comment had not pleased her.

Awkwardly Fran answered, breaking the friction. "Let's go through."

Richard was pleased to see the effort made with the dining room set up, there were fresh flowers as a centre piece, and noted with pleasure, that the best china was present. He had always liked this room and coming from South Africa, it seemed the quintessential English styled room. Fran had dressed it well with colours calming and furniture comfortable. "I have always loved this room; it looks lovely Fran, it really does. The colours are so peaceful arn't they Sarah."

Fran smiled at him, a genuinely happy smile. Once again Richard saw the beauty in her eyes and once again Sarah's voice cut into his thoughts.

"It is lovely, Fran. Not my style but so...... so...what's the word I am looking for? ...Quaint. That's it, so very English and quaint." Fran looked at Richard, trying to ignore her patronising comments and saw that Richard was staring at Sarah with astonishment and embarressment, which she ignored.

"So this is the famous Robbie!" She had picked up a photo that sat on the buffet and was gazing at it, tracing her finger over his face, smiling up at her. "And Emily, how nice. She is your spitting image Franny." Fran crossed the room and took the photograph from Sarah. "Yes, we are very much alike, everyone says..."

"And so like her father..... oh don't look so surprised Franny, Richard told me that Robbie is her actual father..... it's Uncle Robbie, isnt it?"

Fran set the photo back in its place and looking at Richard with a quizzical look, asked them to take a sit. "Please make yourself comfortable, dinner is ready, I won't be a minute. Richard please pour the wine for yourselves. No not for me, just water thanks."

In the kitchen Fran leant against the wall and took a deep breath to steady herself. There was no doubt in her mind that Robbie had been right about Vanessa Brooks and that somehow Sarah was part of the triangle. Sarah's reaction to Robbie's photo had unnerved her and for the hundredth time she wished that Robbie was home. Taking the dish out of the oven, Richard's voice sounded behind her....... "Can I help you?" With relief she passed the heavy pot to Richard, "Thank you," she felt suddenly very weary, and his help was much appreciated. He put the pot down and put a reassuring hand on his shoulder, she leant against him for just a minute, feeling the familiarity of him, and breathed. Sarah's words cut through the roon like ice, making them both start. "Wow, how cute! It is truly great that you all can still be friends considering....." She was leaning against the door frame, with her wine glass in hand. "Sarah!" Richard berated, let's go through." Richard carried the dish through and Fran saw him whisper something in Sarah's ear as they sat. She did not look happy but behaved through dinner and conversation flowed pleasantly. The food was well received, and the wine flowed. Francesca noted that Sarah although polite in her conversation, seemed quieter than normal and the banter was mainly between herself and Richard, regaling stories from the past. It wasn't until the discussion turned to the current state of Mackenzie Taylor, that Sarah perked up, and by then she had drunk more than her fair share of the wine.

"I understand you now have an investor in the company?" Fran spoke with a confidence that she didn't actually have. She saw Richard, stop, with glass midway to his mouth, and looked up, eyebrows knitted with concern.

"We sure do!" Sarah slurred, "and a good one too, hey babe!" Richard didn't answer but stared intently at Fran. He he has seen that look on her face before, one of stubbon determination, and there was no stopping her once she started. Fran's voice was cold but her smile remained, the green eyes glinting. He turned his head and looked at Sarah, she seemed oblivious to the conversation ahead and was pouring yet another glass of wine.

"I know it is of no consequence now, as the deed has been done but as an Executive of the company, I was surprised that this fait du complet was done before the board meeting and subsequent discussion."

Sarah smiled, took a gulp of her wine, and put her glass down, and misjudging the table, spilled the remaining contents. "Oops, sorry". She dabbed at the table with her napkin and continued "You see, Franny, you need to strike whilst the iron Is hot. The opportunity arose when no one else could be bothered to back us. It is a good decision I think".

"A good decision for who, because the way I see it, it doesn't seem to be benefiting anyone, particularly those who are employees!"

"Franny, you of all people must know you how it is. In the time of adjustment, you lose some people along the way. It's business and survival."

"I don't agree. The apprentice program, for example, has seen some fabulous designers spring up and go on to build the industry further. Without it, Mackenzie Taylor is just another manufacturing company, like all the rest."

"Yeh and they in turn become competition.... wake up Franny, these people milked the company at our cost."

"Like me? I was an apprentice; did I milk the company?"

"No, but you did marry the boss!" Sarah laughed at her own joke.... Richard sat stony faced aghast at her behaviour. Fran jumped to her feet, grabbing the main dish, her face a furious shade of red.... "What the hell....."

Richard interrupted...... "It is only temporary, until we get on our feet. A lot of the industry has canned the programs. It's just not viable at present to have those extra wages."

"But in the meantime, Richard, we lose staff and our good name. That's if we keep the name. Perhaps a new name change is in order, what do you think Sarah, Mackenzie Taylor Brookes?"

"You know Franny, that's not a bad idea!" Her answer hung in the air and like the frost forming outside, the atmosphere became cold and uninviting. "What do you think babe?"

"I think you have had a little too much of this!" He removed the wine bottle from her reach, "Enough now!" and removed the bottle from the table. Fran walked out of the dining room going back to the kitchen. Through the wall she could hear Richard's voice, clipped and angry and in return Sarah's simpering tones. Taking the apple pie out of the oven she realised, too late, that she had made Richard's favourite and had a sudden vision of smashing it into Sarah's beautiful, perfect face. She smiled at the thought and returned to the dining room.

"Apple pie anyone?"

"My favourite.... don't' suppose you have made the lemon custard that I like?". Fran put down the jug and duly pushed it towards him.

Sarah's blue eyes darkened and narrowed as she looked at Francesca. "How sweet of you. Is it Robbie's favourite too? ... No not for me, got to look after my figure".

Francesca ignored the comment and sat. "I am interested so please enlighten me, but where did you find Brookes Shipping"?

"I floated the shares on the Stock Exchange, and they contacted me. I had actually known of them in LA and it was a fairly easy transition."

"Funny, I couldn't find them on the Stock Exchange Business Register, probably looking in the wrong place knowing me. So, you knew Vanessa Brookes from back home?" Fran watched as Sarah's head inclined towards her ever so slightly. "Vanessa Brookes?"

"Yes, I noticed her signature on the contract, that you had witnessed." Richard put his spoon down with a clatter, and muttered, "sorry!" but did not pick it up.

"Actually, I went to school and university with her. She is well known to our family and as I said, it was an easy transaction. It's who you know in this world Franny." Sarah seeing that Fran didnt look convinced, carried on, "Look Franny, whilst you were getting up to all sorts of things, I was left to work and work I did, bloody hard actually. You made it quite clear to me that you wanted nothing more to do with the company and did you or did you not ask me to take over your role. Yes, I had to make changes, and on the fly, because otherwise poor Richard would have gone under, but not without plenty of decision making and thought. It's man eat man out there and those that opposed or stood in our way, were removed. Don't you see Franny dear, it was for the best." Francesca looked at her blue eyes, the firm jaw and manipulative charm, that Richard had stupidly fell for and matched her stare. Coldly she spoke, slowly and deliberately. "Do you mean someone like Hazel?... did Hazel get in your way? Did Hazel guess that your decision making wasn't completely kosher?" Sarah's hand lifted and wound its way around Richard's arm. "Hazel was tired and nearing retirement. She mentioned that the work had gotten too much for her and had begun to make mistakes. Rather than pull her up and embarrass her, we moved her to another area. She is still with us and I believe quite happy and due to retire soon".

"To dispatching I believe?"

"Wow, you are very well informed!" Sarah made a mental note to bring the retirement date forward, Richard was so busy he wouldn't even notice. "I suppose being an Executive, you still have that finger of yours on the pulse."

"Exactly, very much so, which is why I still have difficulty in understanding why I was not involved in the decision regarding an investment company. However, as you say, it is man eat man, out there in the textile world and we have to move forward. For that reason I think it would be judicious to meet your Vanessa in person and listen to what she has to say about moving our company forward. What do you think Richard?" She turned to look at Richard, and saw a mixture of admiration and something else in his eyes that she recognised as longing and regret. She felt fire in her belly and was ready for battle. "Preferably in the next month.... I already resemble a beached whale and travelling into London is not getting easier for me, what do you say?"

"Great! Sarah let's invite her over, I am alsointerested in hearing what she has to say and should have done this earlier." Sarah was looking from Fran to Richard with a look of disbelief but calmly continued "Sure, no stress. You do understand that as an investor, she will be a silent partner." "A silent partner, who is putting money into a sinking company will still need to have confidence in what has been backed, don't you think Sarah. I for one, want to meet this wonderful person. What say you Richard?" "I am with you Fran, and totally agree. Sarah can we leave this with you......say...in the next two weeks." "I will see when she is available, although she travels a great deal and it may not be possible, given the time frame. It's nice to have you back on-board Franny, quite like old times." The smile was false, and the words, cutting. Turning to Richard, Sarah stood unsteadily, "Honey, if you have finished drooling over Franny's apple pie, perhaps we should make a move. We have a long day tomorrow and Franny, dear, you are, quite frankly, looking done in."

Richard stood and started to clear the plates… "Please leave that Richard, Sarah is right, I am done in, but as you know, I like to clean up the kitchen myself. I have to stay up for Robbie anyway."

"Well if you are sure."

"Richard, she's sure, now let's go!"

Fran walked to the door, retrieving coats from the pegs. Richard shrugged his on and then assisted, a rather swaying Sarah, into hers. "Thank you Franny, what an interesting evening. Such a shame that Robbie couldn't be with us. Maybe next time. Richard, hunny, we must arrange it soon."

"Thank you Fran, the meal was lovely." Richard said as he ushered Sarah out of the door. Fran, leaning on the porch, spoke "Oh just one thing before you go", they both turned expectantly, "Sarah my name… my name is Francesca not Franny" and with that she smiled sweetly, said goodbye and with mumbled pleasantries from Richard followed by an awkward kiss on the cheek, they were gone.

Francesca sank on to the bottom step and promptly burst into tears.

An hour later, having cleared the table and the kitchen, Fran sank into the sofa to wait for Robbie to come home. She felt too wired to sleep and although exhausted couldn't face her empty bed. Something blue stuck out from under the cushion; it was Sarah's cashmere scarf, she could still smell the perfume infused into it and threw it on to the coffee table, annoyed that anything of her was left in her home. The baby flipped and she rubbed her side. "You didn't like her either did you. It's okay she won't bother us again." Fran sighed and shifted her position getting comfortable; it had been an interesting night.

During the drive home, Richard steered the car in stony silence. Sarah's behaviour was disgraceful and embarrassing to say the least. "Richard!" He turned to see Sarah looking at him intently. "What is it Sarah?" "I didn't know you liked apple pie so much?" The sarcasm was barely hidden, "you practically drooled over it. Actually it wasnt the only thing you were drooling over!"

"Shut up Sarah!"

"It's a shame that Robbie wasn't there, he could have joined in. I am sure he had some good old yarns to tell as well, it would have been a great reunon. Oooh like the one about how he got Fran, I mean Francesca pregnant and then left her...only to find her again...and then just for good measure got her pregnant again. Ahh the memories!"

"I said shut up....you have had far too much to drink!"

"You still love her don't you Richard. It must of killed you seeing her, so …so vulnerable and pregnant."

Richard drove on holding back a retort. He felt really tired and truth be told, Sarah wasn't that far from the truth. There was no point replying and in his refusal to answer Sarah's continual taunts she gave up looking stonily out of the window.

When Robbie finally came home he found a sleeping Fran on the couch. Covering her with a blanket, he caught sight of the blue scarf laid across the table. He picked it up to hang it in the hall and as he moved it, Sarah's perfume wafted up from the folds of the soft material. The fragrance of Gardenia evoked memories that had been long buried, unlocking a fear that he never thought he would feel again. The delicacy of the perfume held the air, and swirled around him and with it came a plethora of feelings attacking his senses. He stopped still, heart beating fast and brought the scarf up to his nose. The soft material enveloped his face and there was no mistaking the scent that sent him spiralling back to the pain of the past. He smelt it again, there it was, no mistake and in horror he dropped the scarf to the floor. There was only one person that he knew wore that scent and it was too much of a coincidence for it to be anyone else.

He poured a whiskey, knocked it back, and then poured another. His thoughts were a jumble and the more he tried the more confused he became. It had after all been a dinner with Sarah and Richard, and there was no reason why Sarah couldn't wear the same scent but there was a nagging gut wrenching feeling that would not go away. He reasoned that he had had a very dramatic day and night and maybe he was over sensitive but something felt wrong, very wrong. Leaning back in his chair he looked at Fran sleeping, it must have been a difficult night for her and wished he had been here.

Robbie got up and walked into the kitchen and flicked the switch on the kettle. He would have a tea and calm himself down. Perhaps he was just overreacting, the scent evoking a memory didn't mean it was reality. But what if......no this was ridiculous, none of this made sense.

Deep in thought he didn't hear Francesca come into the kitchen, "Robbie?". Startled he dropped the cup he was holding .... "Shit! Sorry about that. Hey, how was tonight"? He bent to clear up the broken cup and clean up the mess.

"It was horrible actually, Sarah got drunk and Richard was Richard. I didn't find out much more and I really could have done with you here!"

"And no one else came?"

"What? Of course no one else came. What are you talking about?"

"That scarf...."

"Yes, Sarah left it behind, I will give it to Richard next time I see him. Odd really, I don't remember her wearing it at all and found it under the couch cushion. Come to think of it she didn't sit on that seat and coats and scarfs were hung up before they came through. I can't for the life of me understand how it got there!"

"Unless it was planted"!

"Planted? Robbie you are not making sense?"

"What if it was planted on purpose?"

"But why?"

Robbie stormed out of the kitchen and into the hall without answering.

"Robbie, why?"

Francesca followed Robbie into the hall. It was cold and she shivered, she didn't like this, Robbie was acting so strangely. She found him holding the scarf, turning it over as if looking for something. She watched as he dropped onto the bottom step and held out the scarf to her....

"What is it Robbie?"

"Look, there," and seeing her confusion, "Look at the label."

Francesca stared at the writing and read – "Scarfs by Orion for VB". Confused, she looked from the scarf to Robbie.

The fog of thought began to clear.... Vanessa, his ex wife had always liked labels, designer labels and would get her initials added to every accessory; bags, shoes and scarfs she thought it made them unique.

"Fran, Sarah isn't Sarah!"

"What do you mean she is not Sarah? Robbie you are scaring me!"

"Do you remember me telling you how Vanessa had several aliases and was a manipulative bitch who would stop at nothing? Well Sarah isn't Sarah! Sarah is Vanessa Brookes, my ex wife! I am telling you that they are one of the same. Vanessa who wears Gardenia, which, incidentally, isn't sold in London, only in LA, this scarf is covered in it; Vanessa who has her initials on every accesory that she owns..... Planted and left on purpose for me to find it. Vanessa is here and you can bet your bottom dollar that she is syphoning money from the company into her own account. Vanessa Brooks of Brookes Shipping! Richard has played straight into her hands!"

"Bloody hell Robbie, what now!"

"We play her at her own game but for now, let's get some sleep!"

Neither slept well and over coffee they continued the conversation, thankfully Emily was still at Mary's for a sleep over as neither felt they could deal with a 5 year old and her questions.

"I just don't understand; if Sarah thought she was meeting us for dinner, wouldn't you have recognised her as Vanessa? How would she have explained that to Richard? I just don't' understand what she is playing at!"

"You don't know her. Her game plan would have been clever and well thought out. The question is what shall we do next." Robbie drained his coffee cup. "I didn't sleep much last night thinking this over, and as I said before we must play her at her own game. By now she would have expected that her scarf will have been found. She will presume that eventually I will have worked it out, the perfume and initials, yes?" He shot a look at Francesca... "Do you see what I am getting at Fran?"

"I think so....... go on."

"If the scarf is not mentioned, it will frustrate her and then somehow we need to trick her into her next move!"

262

"Shouldn't we let Richard know?"

"No! I think the less people that know, the easier it will be. My bet is that in her frustration she will start to make mistakes and then it will be easy to make the hunter, hunted."

"Clever, I like it."

"Thank you. I want you to continue to push for a meeting with Vanessa, if you stop now, Sarah and probably Richard will become suspicious. Ask Hazel to get her son to investigate fraud on the Stock exchange, it must be a crime to not only impersonate but to embezzle in the name of a non floated company; one way and another we will flush her out".

"If it wasn't happening to us, it would be exciting but to tell you the truth, this is the type of madness that you would read in a book not live it in reality! I don't like this at all! I feel violated somehow!"

"It's okay, we will be alright, and I will do whatever it takes to end this situation. Please don't worry." Robbie kissed Fran on her head. "However, I am sorry, but I have to go to work in a minute. Will you be okay?"

"Mum is bringing Emily back and I might ask her to stay a while, I don't feel like being on my own."

"Just remember mum is the word, and I mean that quite literally." He kissed her again and gave a huge bear hug before sauntering out of the room.

Fran watched as he got on his coat and picked up his bag. He turned and saluted her, making her smile. and she blew him a kiss as he left for the day. Fran hoped that Robbie was right; she felt vulnerable and tired. The last two days had been too much and she wasn't sure how much more she could bear. She wandered into the kitchen to wait for Emily's return and just in case locked the back door.

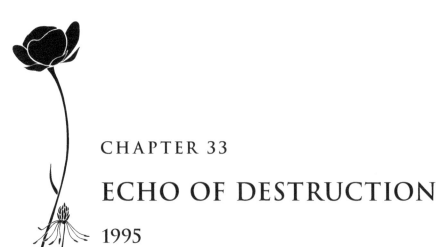

CHAPTER 33

ECHO OF DESTRUCTION

1995

Sarah woke feeling sick and groggy. She groaned and rolled out of bed. Looking at her watch, she realised that not only had she not woken in time for work, but she had also missed an important meeting. Why the hell hadn't Richard woken her? He of course had already left for work.

She vaguely remembered a monumental fight the night before, but she couldn't remember if he came to bed. She presumed that she had blacked out.

Staggering into the bathroom, she looked into the mirror; her reflection confirming the result of the night before. "Shit, shit! Sarah sank to the cold floor and crawled to the toilet, her head spun, the room swirled, and she vomited.

"You asked for this lady! Why did you drink so much? You are not as young as you used to be and you really can't take it. You never could. Yes I know you wanted to make a point, but he wasn't even there. You made a right fool of yourself, didn't you?"

"Shut up Vanessa. I was disappointed that's all."

"And if he had been, how were you going to explain yourself, or didn't you think that far ahead. We have worked too hard to mess this up!"

"I had a plan."

"Not without me, you didn't. Did you leave the scarf like I told you to?"

"Yes of course, now leave me alone." Sarah got up from the floor and dragged herself to the sink. She splashed water onto her face and looked up. "Please Vanessa don't look at me like that, I will do better next time."

The face looking back sneered at her. "It's my turn now, what a mess you have made of this. You will never get Robbie to notice you this way and anyway it is me he wants. Not you!"

"Stop it!"

"It's time to go Sarah! Time to join the others."

"Please Vanesa, I am not ready to go.What about Richard and Mackenzie Taylor? I am needed there."

"And you think I am not? You are simply not needed anymore. You are too emotionally involved and that is dangerous!"

"I am so close to being with Robbie again, and......."

"And what? He is mine, not yours, he never was, and I cannot wait to touch that beautiful body again. You can't have all the fun!"

"Vanessa, please don't make me go......I'll be good I promise!"

"Look at yourself." The face in the mirror was pale and sweaty with makeup congealed in the corners of her eyes. The expression was one of sadness and defeat. "You are pathetic and no longer of any use!"

"No Vanessa. Please leave me alone, I dont need you, I can do this!"

"Really!" The laugh that followed echoed around Sarah, bouncing off the walls and physically attacking her senses.

Sarah turned away from the mirror and she sunk down on her knees holding her hands over her ears. The voice taunted her over and over until when silence decended it became ominus and sitting on the cold floor, she screamed, a long high pitched noise. "Leave me alone, I can do this!"

Standing she washed her face vigorously, not looking at her reflection. Turning away from the mirror she picked up her brush and pulled it through her hair, tying it back off her face.

"Oh there you are Sarah, you are in my way and people that get in my way, have to go!"

"No!" Sarah threw the brush at the mirror and the glass splintered and fell out of the frame.

The image, macabre in its fragmented state, sardonically smiled back. The glint of evil in the one eye left showing and an expression of pure hatred poured out into the person left standing.

"No, Vanessa, it's you that has to go!" Sarah pulled the rest of the glass out of the frame and put it in the bin. She then dressed and left for work.

As she walked into Mackenzie Taylor she felt that nothing could or would stop her. She had a job to do with limited time to do it in. She had a new strength and felt focused at the task ahead.

"I am sorry gentleman, but it seems that Ms Burford will not be joining us today after all. Now as I have been saying......."

The doors opened and all heads turned. Richard watched as Sarah entered the room. Her blonde hair tied into a high ponytail, her make up just so and her dress pristine. There was no sign of the crazy, hysterical creature of the night before. Her unreasonable rantings that had kept him up all night and her viscious hands holding around his throat. He held his throat as if in memory. He had been frightened and in self-defence he had pushed her hard and she had fallen off the bed. He had thought her hurt and bent over to see if she was okay only to feel those cold hands around his throat again and this time the vice like grip wasnt letting go. Her voice had been shrill and not like Sarah's at all and in panic he had punched her. Released from her grip, he watched as she had fallen backwards, hitting her head, knocking herself out. Only after he was sure that she was breathing and of no further harm, he lifted her on to the bed. Walking out of the bedroom and closing the door, he was reminded of the discussion with Fran and Robbie, their words running around his head. Perhaps they had been right and uneasiy he had left the appartment.

Now the vision that entered the office, was of the Sarah he knew, but she looked different. There was an edge to her that he had not seen before but christ she looked gorgeous and nothing like the woman he had left behind.

"Of course I am joining you, wouldn't miss it. So sorry for my tardiness, I got caught up. Now gentleman, where were we.........?"

Richard watched as she worked her magic; her beautiful smile and bright eyes mesmerising the clients as they listened to her pitch. Leaning forward and showing enough cleavage and length of her leg to pull them in. She was magnficent. There were times when he just didn't know who she was but if she got this deal for Mackenzie Taylor, he didn't really care.

With the clients satisfied and the deal in the bag, once alone, Sarah launched herself at Richard, kissing him passionately and he in return kissed back. This wasnt the mess that had tried to strangle him last night.

He pulled back holding her hands and pushing her away. Her breath was coming fast, as was his .... "Richard.....tell Stephanie to hold all calls, tell her what you like but tell her now!"

"Sarah, stop! Wait, I mean, what happened last night?"

She smiled at him, and started to roll her dress above her thighs. He looked at her long legs and then up at her face. "What happened last night?"

She smiled again and sat in the chair opposite, opening her legs just enough to show that she had worn nothing under the dress. "That girl has gone, Richard, and she is very sorry." Her voice purred but was almost childlike. "Now stop being a naughty boy and come and play. We have something to celebrate don't we?"

And just like that his concerns and fears from the night before were completely forgotten.

The face looking over her victims shoulder, was cold, calculating and cruel. She would show them all.

CHAPTER 34

AN UNTOLD STORY

2019

It was hard to tell if Francesca took in her surroundings. Since her last attack and psychosis, she had not spoken or in fact acknowledged anyone or anything. Occupational Therapists visited daily, but there was no improvement and everyone working with her agreed that they found it difficult to connect. Caris asked for a weekly report but truthfully with little change or improvement, there seemed no justification to add in more resources. Therefore, in her own time she would pop up to see Fran but always left feeling a sense of failure and a magnitude of guilt.

Like many afternoons, Caris sat having a coffee in the hospital canteen and like on other occasions she would read through Francesca's notes. She hated not being able to assist someone in need, and as before, felt sure she was missing crucial information. Turning the page Caris looked at the beautiful photo of Francesca, prior to the accident. Her bright green eyes and wide smile laughing up at her. Caris traced a finger over the photo and sighed, and asked herself what was the missing part of this story and how did the accident happen? There was more to this than just a tragic car accident, in that Caris was sure. Looking back down at the photo, Francesca's red curls looked luscious and curled around her face, giving the impression of innocence, yet her eyes held no sadness, and her expression was one of intelligence and determination. "What happened to you Francesca and who was Sarah? What did she do to you?" Caris thought she had gotten close to undoing the intracancy of Fran's mind but obviously Fran had been unable to cope with her memories surfacing and the result, was the tragic psychosis which had changed everything. Somewhere, amongst the mishmash of thoughts, Fran had interlocked Sarah and herself as one person but then the reality of her seeing that kiss may have been the thing that sent her over the edge. It certainly triggered something but who knows what that was! And there it was again, that awful guilt.

Caris picked up the photo again and sighed. "Where have you disappeared to Francesca?"

She felt two hands on her shoulders, which made her jump and looked up into the eyes of Robbie Harvey, he still made her stomach flip and mentally she told herself off. He smiled briefly and then looked at the photo Caris was holding... "That photo was taken in 1990. There had been much excitement at Mackenzie Taylor after they had won a lucrative deal and Richard, her then boss, had taken a photo of the group who had secured it. She was so beautiful and so alive with everything to live for. Richard had always liked this photo, and it had sat on his desk, along with some others for years. When I first met her she looked just like that; a wide smile and eyes that twinkled, her laugh contagious. She was just so quick witted and smart, just lovely." He laughed and continued.. "I wish you had known her; I think you would have got on. She was a brilliant designer and even up to the current day she is still being sought after".

"At Mackenzie Taylor, right"?

"Yes. The Company when sold, allowed her to stay on. They knew her reputation went before her and she would be driven up to London once per week and the rest of the time work in her workshop when she was able. But now...... well now, I suppose I will have to let them know what has happened."

270

Caris heard the regret in his voice and smiled a reassuring smile. He had never really spoken in depth about Francesca prior to accident and it was nice to hear. "Now what were you so engrossed in your sigh was so loud that it was audible from the lift?"

Taking a deep breath, she spoke, trying to be professional but failing spectacularly. "Francesca saw us, together, that night in the hospital. It was what triggered her that day in my office. Somehow she thought I was someone called Sarah and attacked me, saying she had seen us kiss. I, we, breached our oath and got involved. We were not professional at all …and".

"And what! Fran may have seen us but what she saw was two friends needing to comfort each other. The Fran I remembered would have understood. The Fran that was there at that time, couldn't make head or tail of anything. So don't beat yourself up!" Caris heard the anger in his voice but carried on.

"And Sarah"?

"Well Caris, that is a whole other story. I had hoped that Fran could have told you because it may have released some of her pain, but it doesn't look like that will happen now." Robbie looked again at Fran's photo laying on the table and picked it up. "She was something you know, full of energy and ideas.

"What was she like, I mean before the accident. Can you talk about her?"

"Well as I said before, she was full of energy and dynamic, in everything that she did. Fran had a wicked sense of humour, and I have to say a terrible temper, but she easily forgave. She loved life to the full and her smile lit up my world. When we reconnected, she was married to Richard, who was bringing up Emily, my daughter as his own. Fran knew it hurt me, but she insisted that Richard remained Emily's father and I became the Uncle……good old Uncle Robbie. It hurt but there was no way I could change her mind she was stubborn and determined like that. I miss her funny ways…I remember watching her in the field,

271

at the back of her house; the field was covered in buttercups and her arms were open wide...."

Caris watched as Robbie opened his arms wide and swung round, eyes closed. She could see him reliving this memory. He stopped and laughed. "She would close her eyes, threw her head back, her beautiful hair streaming behind her as she swung round, laughing. One day, when Katie was visiting, Katie was her niece, she ran down to the field with both Emily and Katie they had all worn yellow that day and holding hands they sang ring a ring a Rosie......then they opened their arms and swung around each other.......it was a beautiful site. All three looked alike, with their red curls flying out behind them.... in fact Emily and Katie could have been twins. I told her after, that I had seen them and that they looked like part of the buttercup field. She loved that she really did...."

Caris shook her head, "It is such a shame that a careless accident can ruin so many lives. I have been through this file so many times and I might be wrong but there is something missing. Robbie, you must know what happened. It is driving me crazy, and I don't feel I can move on or leave Fran until I find out. Is that bad? Is it some sort of self-indulgence? I need to know. I need to know that I did everything I could to help her, otherwise it seems such a waste."

Robbie sat down opposite and took a deep breath, maybe Caris deserved to know, however unbelievable it sounded. He felt tired and old and didn't want to be custodian of this burden any longer.

"The thing is Caris, this whole thing, the whole story was my fault. You can form your own opinions, but the bottom line is, that if I had taken a different action, our baby would still be alive and Fran, my beautiful Fran, would not be upstairs, so damaged and so tormented!"

Caris sat back in her chair. Although still handsome, he looked tired. The lines around his eyes were deep and full of pain and sadness. She watched as he stared past her, trying to make up his mind as to whether this story should be told and with a sigh Robbie started to talk.......

Robbie initially spoke about his past, how he had met Vanessa and how he had found Fran again and the inevitable path they had taken.

He began, with difficulty, to discuss the chain of events that had led to so many lives being damaged and to Caris's surprise, he blamed himself for the ultimate betrayal of trust.

Anyone walking by would have seen two colleagues looking over case notes, drinking coffee and in deep conversation. This was not unusual in such a busy hospital. The cafeteria was buzzing with activity with nurses rushing about or having time out on their break, looking exhausted from their shift. Family members huddled together and doctors and allied health professionals working on their laptops with mobiles at the ready. Therefore, no one took much notice of the two of them, heads bent in towards each other; both professionals, going about their business. What wasn't seen was the pain in one's eyes and the understanding in the others. Caris had been in this same position countless times counselling those who needed her, but this time it seemed personal; this time she was invested in the outcome more than any other case. She watched and listened as Robbie continued, often stopping with difficulty, emotions taking over him, but he kept going as if this purged the pain that he had held for 23 years. She concentrated on every word, piecing together the painful events that impacted Francesca Taylor's life to such a degree that she now lay upstairs in her bed, not wanting to engage with the present and stuck in the past.

"It was the dinner party that truly revealed Sarah as Vanessa; she'd left a scarf you see and that was the catalyst, the roller coaster that started it all. Over the next few weeks Fran concocted a plan to expose Sarah to Richard and hopefully save Mackenzie Taylor. Fran insisted that Sarah fly Vanessa over from LA to meet with Richard and the Executive Board and although she was heavily pregnant, she went back to work."

Caris looked confused. "But Robbie, how could Vanessa fly over, if Vanessa was Sarah"?

"Exactly! There was no way. Fran also asked for closed door meetings with Richard and as an Executive Board Member she had every right to do so. These did not include Sarah, which drove her crazy, her paranoia making her suspicious of every meeting that was had without her, which was exactly what Fran wanted. Richard was pleased to see her back at Mackenzie Taylor and didn't question why the change of heart and although it worried me, you have to remember she by now was 7 months pregnant, Fran knew that naturally Richard would become attentive and caring as he had done before and milked it for all it was worth.

Sarah became neurotic at home, accusing Richard of leaving her out of things and questioning his feelings for Francesca and he of course could not dispute it, although he said nothing.

There was still no word from Vanessa and Fran used to tell me that Sarah's behaviour had become more concerning with each day passing. Staff were terrified of her reaction to things; sudden bursts of tempers were common, and they steered clear of her or resigned. As the year wound up, and Fran got tireder, I put my foot down and told Fran that enough was enough. Christmas was around the corner and Emily was finishing school for the year. Mary, Fran's mum was happy to help but I was concerned about Fran and the baby.

Around about the 15th of December, I can't remember the actual date it all came to a head and that should have been an end to all the games being played but quite frankly it was only the beginning".

"Goodness, what happened Robbie".

"Things got serious, and if it hadn't been bad before, it got much worse".

Caris leaned forward intent on hearing what happened next. "Go on!"

274

Robbie, yawned and looked at his watch, he couldn't believe the time…

Hey, I have been talking for hours – are you hungry?"

"I am a bit." Caris replied.

"Me too, lets catch a bite to eat and I will continue, but I warn you it is not very pretty."

Caris and Robbie, left the hospital and headed across to the local pub. It was cold and it felt like rain, so they huddled up and ran across the car park into the warmth of the White Stag pub. It was a mistake, the wrong place; many of their colleagues were having a drink and it was some time before they sat in a booth and Robbie continued the story. "I am sure that the date was December 15th 1995 because Emily had just broken up from school and Mary and Joe had her for the day. Fran told me that morning, that she was exhausted and promised that this was the last day she would be going into Mackenzie Taylor, which was a relief. They planned to meet with Sarah that day and ask for some clarity surrounding Vanessa and Fran had convinced Richard that there were obvious issues that needed to be addressed, pointing out many discrepancies which forced his hand for the sake of the company......"

1995 – Fran's Story

When Sarah walked in she noticed two things – the ledgers on Richard's desk and Fran sitting in Richard's chair, with Richard standing behind her. The pages were being turned as she walked through the glass doors and they did not look up but instead asked her to take a seat.".

After a time, Fran looked up, closed the ledger with a bang and smiled. "Very interesting reading don't you think Sarah?"

"Sure!" her tone disinterested and edgy.

"I can see at the end of each month, well actually on 24th of every month a sum of money goes from Mackenzie Taylor to Brookes Shipping and then on the 27th of the month a percentage of this payment is reversed and paid to a Vanessa Brookes.".

"Yes that is right, it was set up that way, it is probably to do with tax or something."

"This is rather unorthodox and wondered who gave approval for this to happen?" Sarah looked at Richard and then to Fran and back again. She was still calm, but her voice had a slight quiver to it as she spoke. "Richard, you know babe, we worked it out together! Remember?"

Richard although uncomfortable, said that he didn't remember ever approving this set up. He knew he was sealing an end to his relationship with Sarah, but enough was enough. Fran was right, something didn't feel right and after Sarah's strange behaviour, he had his doubts as to whether she was worth it.

"Sure you do. It was something to do with a subsidiary company off set account."

"No I am sorry Sarah; I just don't remember."

Fran reopened the ledger and tapped her finger on a line of figures - "There is a discrepancy here, here and here. Are you able to explain them Sarah?"

Sarah's blue eyes were blazing, and Fran could see she was getting angry. "Why the hell would I know about the finances Fran?" Richard replied, "Because Sarah, they are to do with your department and the last time I looked your ambit is to manage the budget in Organics and it looks like it is all loss and no profit, how then are you making ends meet with no revenue gain?" Fran turned to Richard, looking astounded. "For god's sake Richard, why the hell didn't you notice"? She gave him no chance to answer but carried on regardless ignoring the angry looks she was getting from Sarah.

"I put it to you, Sarah, you are very aware of what is going on. In fact, although we cannot prove it as yet, we believe that you and Vanessa are working together, and we would very much like to speak with her. Please can you give me the contact number for the company because oddly enough, Richard has no details at all."

"I've told you that Vanessa has not been available", Sarah said coldly.

"Why? Where is she?" Richard walked over to where Sarah sat and looked down at her.

"Richard don't do this to me babe, what I have I done to deserve this?" She attempted to stand up, but Richard moved closer. "Sit down we haven't finished!"

"Well I have!" Sarah pushed her chair back violently and stood up, the chair falling over and slamming onto the floor. "How dare you both talk to me in this way. I don't know what it is like in London, but in the US you are innocent until proven guilty and I am not guilty of anything!"

Richard lent over to his phone and pushed a button "Security. Hi, can you please escort Ms Burford from the building….about an hour, great thanks. …. I am sorry Sarah, but until this mess is sorted, I think it better that you are suspended from your duties here."

"Richard I ……I love you babe, why are you doing this to me, to us?"

"I also think it would be for the best if you move out of the apartment for now. I can send a car to get your stuff, but I want you gone by the time I get home."

Sarah flew across the room; her blue eyes blazing and slammed her hands onto the desk in front of Fran. "It's her, isn't it Richard? It's always been her – You are so clever Francesca! You had them both, Robbie and Richard and you have left me with nothing, well you will pay for this!" Her voice, strangely different, cruel and cold.

"Sarah, I am warning you!" Richard was behind her pulling her off the desk, away from Fran but she twisted her body around and threw her arms around Richard's neck "Baby, please, you know you love me, you said you did!" The desperate voice was Sarah's, in its pleading lilt.

"Don't make this harder than it is Sarah, get off me now and leave with some dignity, please!"

A child-like voice rang out, "She doesn't want to come and play today!"

"What, stop it Sarah!" Richard dropped her wrists, unnerved by her odd behaviour.

The cold, cruel voice was back again, replacing the child…"Sarah's gone, my dear Richard, she left months ago….. thank god! That needy bitch has become surplus to requirement, and now you have me to deal with… are you ready for that…. I don't think so!" The grip on Richard's arms was vice like and he was reminded of the hands that had gone around his throat. "Sarah?" He could see her, but it wasn't her in front of him. The hand that slapped him was strong and hard, her long nails scratched down his face, he felt the pain. "I told you Richard, dear, that Sarah has gone, we won't be speaking her name again, will we!"

"We won't! We won't! She won't be coming back to play with us again. Coz she has been naughty hasn't she!" The giggle that followed was eerie and haunting, but the child carried on speaking. "I have been waiting to meet with you for ages, but she wouldn't let me. My name is May, and I would very much like to play with Emily…." Richard, holding his face looked at Fran as she started to speak, her voice clear and strong, and shivers ran down his spine- "Vanessa come out come out wherever you are! Are you hiding? We won't hurt you; we just want to talk with you?"

"What the hell are you doing Fran?"

Francesca ignored Richard and carried on in a sing song voice "Vanessa, come out come out wherever you are?".

Then a different voice answered. An upper-class American twang with a clipped tone, spoke. "My god, what took you so long? This is so boring!"

Sarah threw herself in to a chair, making a mockery of a yawn. "Sarah, I told you they would find me!" The voice laughed, a cold calculating laugh and continued, "It really wasn't too hard; I have been here all the time but Sarah, wouldn't let me out. She was absolutely sure she could deal with this without me, but as you can see she has made a complete mess of everything. Now what was it that you wanted me to do?"

Richard stared at the woman sitting in front of them, her long legs were crossed over each other and she looked totally unperturbed by their reactions.

"Richard let me introduce you to Vanessa Brookes; in case you hadn't realised she and Sarah are the same person. In fact all of those people were the same person!"

Vanessa clapped her hands slowly "Aren't you clever Francesca. It is Francesca isn't it? Not Fran or Frannie?"

"What the hell are you trying to achieve? I just don't get it! What was the point of all this?" Richard stuttered angrily in his confusion.

"Richard" said Fran, incredibly calmly, "I believe Vanessa is trying to ruin your business and ultimately, I think it is because of me. Am I right, Vanessa?

"Top marks!" Vanessa clapped her hands again.

"But why? You and I had something, why do you want to hurt me and my business, what did I ever do to you?"

"Oh Richard, you were just a pawn on my chess board. It was fun it really was, and Sarah actually thought that you loved her, how sweet." Her awful laugh chilled the room. "But you are so right pretty

Francesca, you see you have the one thing that I want. In fact you have them both, don't you? Rather greedy and unfair, don't you think"? Vanessa stood from her chair and picked up her bag.

"You look so confused Francesca, why? Surely you know that Richard, poor sook, still loves you and Robbie, my Robbie, absolutely adores you?"

Fran remained seated, she felt quite dizzy and looked at Richard for support.

"I think you have said enough Sarah, Vanessa, whoever you are." He picked up the phone and rang for security again. "Brookes Shipping is a sham and is already under investigation by the Fraud Squad. My advice to you, leave my family alone and get the hell out of here before charges can be made!"

"You are quite wrong Richard. Brookes Shipping is still very much a company, my company and getting richer every minute, thanks to Mackenzie Taylor and a few others." She walked towards the glass doors, but then turned back just as they were opened by two security guards. "I will leave, I was getting bored anyway, but when you least expect it, I'll be back; adieu"! She blew them a kiss and then linked arms with the two guards; "Do you skip" the child asked…. "We can sing We're off to see the Wizard, it's ever so much fun" The guards looked back uneasily at Richard who was standing by the door. He nodded at them and they escorted Vanessa out of the office and then out of the building.

Tears finally flowed down Fran's face – "Please let that be an end to this madness".

Richard looked at her pale face and hoped with all his heart that Francesca and Emily would remain safe. Sarah was unhinged that was for sure, but how could he report her to the police, as soon as they found out that he had been her lover and that she had run his business for him, it would be put down as a lover's tiff. It dawned on him, that this was exactly what she had wanted; an alibi, a diversion and Richard had fallen for it, hook, line, and sinker.

"C'mon Fran, it's been a long day, let me take you home".

Fran had never been so grateful; it had been an awfully long day.

CHAPTER 35

COLD DEPRESSION

1996

With Christmas and New Year's over, Francesca looked around her home and sighed. She loved Christmas and having all her family and friends over, but now she was tired and in her eyes her home was one big mess. She had never coped with things out of order, always needing them in place; neat and tidy and it was most definitely not that. The massive Christmas tree, which she noted had dropped pine needles everywhere, had replaced two armchairs which were now squashed together across the room. Emily's new toys were strewn haphazardly and tinsel which has been carefully wrapped over the tree, was now everywhere. Robbie had said he would help clear it up but had been called into the hospital. "Leave it" he had said, "It can wait". But she couldn't leave it any longer. Now 38 weeks pregnant, her nesting driven need for cleanliness was uppermost in her thought's and today was the day. Emily was out with her grandparents with Tom and Nancy's children, and she had the house to herself.

"A coffee is needed before I tackle this." Fran wandered into the kitchen and whilst making her coffee she reflected on the last few weeks. Firstly there were the twice daily calls of the phone ringing and no one on the other end and then there was the late-night knocks on the door that apparently only she could hear. When leaving the house, she felt as if someone was watching her drive off, and she had remarked to Robbie, that sometimes when she was alone, which wasn't that often, she felt the house was being watched. Robbie soothed her and said all the right things, but it didn't help as he wasn't home that much of late, with December and January being the worse months for accidents.

She had spoken to her mother, Mary, who by now knew of Vanessa and the goings on and suggested that Fran moved in with them, but she didn't want to leave her home, her belongings. In fact she had become quite obsessive of where things should be and how things should look and just put it down, to her pregnancy.

Picking up the steaming cup of coffee, she looked out the window, the fields often calmed her but today, the weather made them look bleak. Looking up at the sky, the clouds were oppressive and the chill coming through the slightly open window was enough for her to shiver. Patting her very protruding abdomen she spoke to her baby, as she often did, "I think we are going to get more snow little one".

She closed the window, and as she reached up to secure the latch, a flash of blue caught her eye. She looked again but there was nothing. Maybe it was just a car driving by, but the lane was quiet and didn't get a lot of traffic, and anyway she would have heard it. Looking again and peering through the trees at the end of the garden, she saw it – something tied to the gate. She couldn't make it out so opened the back door and walked down to the end of the path. A blue scarf was tied to the gate post and was flying about in the wind, moving back behind the trees, and then flying forward, taunting the wind, with come and catch me. "That's odd" Fran said to herself, "someone must have dropped it". There were often walkers with their dogs trudging up the path into town, and it was a possibility that someone finding it, picked it up and tied it on the fence for safe keeping. She mused that it hadn't been there yesterday because she herself had walked this way and would have seen it. As she came closer, the chill in the air wasn't the only thing that was cold; small hairs on her arms rose and a shiver went down her spine, this wasn't any old scarf, it was the one Sarah, had left in the house after the dinner party, the one she thought was still on the peg in the hallway. She had never had the chance to give it back and after all that had happened on December the 15th, she didn't feel it appropriate to give it to Richard.

"Pull yourself together Fran, there must be loads of similar scarfs", but Fran knew without looking that the initials VB would be on the label.

She scurried up the path and let herself into the house, locking the door behind her.

She walked tentatively through to the hallway, the peg was empty, and the scarf was missing. Sinking down on to the stairs, she shakily picked up the telephone and phoned Robbie. Thankfully, he picked up straight away. She could picture him in his office smiling into the phone as he answered her.

"Are you okay, is it the baby"?

"No, but can you come home…… now!"

"Is it the baby, is it coming?"

"No! For goodness sake, I need you home, I am frightened!"! Fran went on to tell him about the scarf, but she could tell that he wasn't really listening, after all it wasn't the first time she was sure something wasn't right. Once she had told him that it was just a feeling that she sometimes got and that something felt all sorts of wrong and he had pacified her by saying it sometimes happens in pregnancy.

Another time, he had rushed home from the hospital because Fran had been hysterical, that someone was tapping continually on the door – it had turned out to be the branch of the tree that, now naked of leaves moved freely with the wind and tapped on the glass.

On another occasion, she had cried into his arms because there was a set of footsteps leading up to the back door, showing small, neat footprints in the freshly lain snow. "Look" she had said, hysterically pointing, "It's

a woman's size foot-print, and no one has been here since yesterday.".
Robbie had come home and searching the garden had found a note from
the neighbour written in her sprawling writing. It had said that she had
had to leave in a hurry to see her daughter and would be back tomorrow.
Would they mind feeding the cat that night, which they had done
before. The note continued to say that she had tried knocking on the
front door, but no one had answered. The note must have blown away
attaching itself to the hedge that surrounded the garden. Retrieving it,
Robbie had shown the evidence to Fran but still, she seemed nervous
and not convinced.

"Are you listening to me Robbie, the scarf is not on the peg and is now
wrapped around the post at the bottom of the garden!"

"I will come home soon, but I saw Emily with it the other day, she said
she liked the way it smelt. I had taken it off her and put it in the bin, but
maybe she just took it out again, you know how she is. Stop worrying,
I will be home soon. This stress is not good for your blood pressure."

Perhaps he was right, and she chastised herself for her paranoid thoughts.

That night over dinner, Emily happily chatted away and told them of
her day with Katie and Henry. "It was so much fun mum, and Uncle
Robbie, you never guess what I got given."

"What did you get given?" Robbie said and smiled as Emily got down
from the table and ran off to the hallway bringing back a huge lollypop.
"See!"

"Wow, that is a lot of sugar Emily, Granny doesn't normally give
you things like that, did Katie and Henry get one too?" Fran asked,
extremely surprised as neither her mother nor her sister in law, Nancy,
would normally buy sugary products.

Emily held it tightly to her chest and had an odd expression on her face.

"Emily?"

She said nothing but gripped the stick of the lolly tighter.

"Emily, did granny give you this?" Fran's voice was louder than intended and Emily looked frightened.

"Emily tell me now, tell mummy!" Robbie could see that this was getting her nowhere. Emily's happy face was now looking scared, and she was about to cry.

"Fran you're frightening her." Turning to Emily he spoke quietly, "Em, is this a special secret?" Emily nodded "and did a special friend give this to you?" Emily nodded again, still holding onto the stick tightly.

"So let's play a game, what do you think? Shall we play a game?"

"Yes please Uncle Robbie but why is mummy cross with me, have I been naughty?" her bottom lip quivered again.

"Mummy isn't cross, she is a bit worried that's all, aren't you mummy. Come and sit with me." Emily got up and snuggled in next to Robbie.

"It's okay mummy, I won't eat it all at once will I, its huge!"

"Okay, so I will ask you a question and you can say yes or no, is that okay?"

"Yes Uncle Robbie."

"Did granny buy this lolly pop?"

"No!"

"Did Katie and Henry get a lolly pop as well?"

"No, just me."

"Weren't you a lucky girl." Emily giggled she liked this game.

"The person who gave you this secret, was it a boy?"

"No, Uncle Robbie, don't be silly. I don't talk to boys"

"Oh so it was a girl and was this girl pretty."

"No, it wasn't a girl like me, it was a lady, and she was really pretty, and she smelt so nice, like flowers, and anyway she wasn't a stranger, so it was okay."

Fran's head turned slowly towards her daughter and her eyes held Robbie's. She let out a moan.

"So this pretty lady, gave you a lolly pop, when did she do that?"

"Well, we were all at the park, at the climbing frame. Katie fell off the slide and she cut her knee and cried and cried. Henry was making fun and got told off. Granny told him to sit on the seat and not move, but he did, and granny got cross."

"Where was your grandad when this all happened, Emily?" Fran had found her voice, although she could barely get the words out.

"Oh, Grandad went to the shop."

"Emily did someone come and talk to you when all this was happening?" Robbie steered the conversation back and waited for Emily's to answer but by now she was getting restless and had lost concentration.

"Can I eat it now please Uncle Robbie?" Emily whined.

"No not yet, in a minute okay?" Emily nodded reluctantly.

"So you were playing on the climbing frame and a lady spoke to you, whilst Granny was busy?"

"Yes, I just told you…"

"Emily what did she say?"

"She told me that she knew daddy and you mummy. She said she was an old friend of the family and she even knew you Uncle Robbie. She said she was coming to see you soon. Umm and she wanted to wish me a Happy Christmas and this was my present?"

"Did she tell you it was a secret?"

Emily giggled again, "Oh yes". She put her little fingers to her mouth "Shush. You see she didn't have one for Katie or Henry and she thought it would be unfair. Wasn't that nice of her. Can I eat it now?"

Robbie smiled down at her, "Sugar isn't good for you Emily and mummy and I would rather you didn't, besides it's bedtime for beautiful princesses. Can you give it to me?" Her little hands tightened on the stick and she started to cry. 'But you promised!"

"I know but it is bedtime, oh and Emily, if you see the lady again will you let us know, point her out to us, so we can thank her?"

"Yes I will but it's not fair" Emily shouted and stamped her foot.

"Emily, please!" Fran held out her hand, she hated seeing the tears run down her little girls face but it was necessary, she didn't know what lengths Vanessa would go to. "Come on, up the magic stairway and time for bed, what story is it tonight?"

Once alone, Fran looked at Robbie, "Now do you believe me Robbie. She is not going to stop until she gets you back!". Robbie was quiet and put his arms around Fran. "I am sorry Fran, but I can assure you, I am going to put a stop to this one way or another. The issue being, where the hell do I find her?"

Fran kissed him, "Well she can't be too far away! This was far too close for comfort and you have to stop her, whatever it takes".

Later, as Fran lay sleeping in bed, her red curls spilling over the pillow, Robbie felt he had never seen anything so beautiful, and he vowed he would protect her and his family. He closed the curtains and turned off the light and climbed in next to Fran. He was exhausted, work had been crazy of late, but his mind would not switch off. He felt restless; why hadn't he listened to Fran. He mentally kicked himself, but he could do nothing about it now. He cuddled into Fran, his hands resting on her tummy and just as he was beginning to drift off he felt the movement of his baby kicking his hands up and down. New life! It made him all the more determined than ever to stop this madness.

In the garden, under the moon, next to the old oak tree, stood a figure. The woman looked up as the curtains were closed and the light went off and smiled. Soon that would be her bedroom and Robbie would be closing the curtains for her.

She turned back to the tree and continued carving. She stood back and admired her work. Walking out the gate she looked back and blew a kiss towards the bedroom window. "Goodnight my love, see you very soon".

CHAPTER 36

COUNTDOWN

1996

"Have you been under any undue stress lately, Fran?" Dr York said as he took the cuff off Fran's arm. "Your blood pressure is quite high. Dr Harvey have you not been keeping an eye on your wife's activities?" "John, you know Fran nearly as well as I do, have you ever known her to slow down and by the way once again, Fran is not my wife." Robbie smiled at Dr York, their Obstetrician; Robbie had known and worked with him for years and although due to retire, he had decided to stay on for one last birth, Fran's birth. "Is there an issue here, John?"

"Well I am not happy with your blood pressure Fran; it has steadily increased over the last week. Anything you want to talk about"?

"Just a few issues at home but nothing to worry about!" Fran answered, looking at Robbie. Doubt was obvious on Dr York's face, "You have to look after yourself Fran dear. Your baby is due in 10 days, and you need to rest now. It doesn't matter what is going on around you, isn't that right Robbie!" Robbie clapped him on the back and replied "Absolutely, I will look after both of them. Do you think she will deliver on time?"

"Well the head is not down, so unless it engages, you may be late but due date is still 20th January, ok?"

"Well, it cannot come quick enough, I feel whale like".

"Marry this beautiful girl, Robbie! She is funny, I like her. Now young lady rest up and we will meet next Wednesday. I believe it is the 17th." He consulted his diary, yes it is. We will see where you are up to and with any luck…..." He acted out rocking a baby and they laughed "Ok?"

Driving home, they were both quiet, then Robbie spoke breaking the silence, "Fran, why didn't you tell Dr York, about…" Fran interrupted "Because Robbie, it is our issue, nobody else's. Because when I saw the carving on the tree, a little bit of me died and because I need to concentrate on the new life we made in happier times and not on the madness that is surrounding us now." Fran started to cry, "I am scared everyday Robbie. When I open the curtains in the morning, is she going to be looking up from the garden? When I open the door is she going to be standing there and when the phone rings and there is no one on the other end, is it her? What next? Is she going to lie in wait, with a noose to put ….."

"Stop it Fran, this will not help your blood pressure, will it! Dr York made it quite clear that you had to rest and stay calm. I know you are scared but you need to look after yourself and our baby. Perhaps we should take Mary up on her offer, it makes sense for you and Emily go and stay with your mum and dad. The Police said that it wasn't safe and given the evidence that they presented regarding Vanessa, I agree with them. Fran I think it's time".

"No Robbie, I don't want to leave my home. She is not going to do this to us!"

"But that carving, it was the last straw." Robbie's hands tightened on the steering wheel; at least now the Police were involved".

The car drove into the driveway, Robbie turned off the ignition and then turned to Fran. "I can't bear seeing you like this and as I cannot be with you 24/7 I would feel better if I knew someone was with you and you were safe. So please Fran, do it for me or at least Emily and the baby. Please!"

Fran got out of the car and slammed the door. She stormed up the pathway; she didn't want to leave the sanctity of her home, or leave her belongings, let alone change her routine. Her hands shook as she fumbled to put the key in the door, but the door swung open, it was unlocked and Fran turning to Robbie, fainted.

Robbie had laid Fran on the couch and checked that she was okay, it had been the shock he told himself. He covered her with a blanket as the room was cold and then sat in the chair opposite looking around the room for the umpteenth time. The devastation was there, plan to see. He had phoned the police and they had told him not to touch anything, but he couldn't leave it like this, surely; Fran couldn't see this when she woke up. He stared around the room and put his head in his hands. Photos on the mantle of Fran and Robbie had been replaced with photos of himself and Vanessa. There were photos of their wedding; photos of a laughing Vanessa on the Australian beach, looking into the camera, her blonde her flying in the wind. Photos of a kiss; of a hug and one of Vanessa standing with a new pram, as if pushing the baby that never was. All the photos of Emily and Francesca were gone. The family portrait looking down from the wall of a laughing Fran and Robbie, holding Emily, who was also laughing, was damaged. Spray paint covered Fran's face and the letters RIP had been written in red. He couldn't let her see this, not after the carving found on the tree; that sick, depraved carving depicting a pregnant woman being hung from a branch…..it was too much to deal with and now this.

There was a knock at the door, and Robbie moved quietly to open it – in the hallway he spoke to the police. "Please remove the evidence quickly and quietly, my partner cannot see this, she is 38 weeks pregnant, and we are on countdown now. I just don't know if she can cope with anymore."

"I quite understand sir, but we need to take fingerprints and remove the…….". Screams of anguish came from the sitting room, and Robbie, followed by the police officers, ran in to find Fran holding the photo of Vanessa and Robbie on their wedding day. Tears rolled down her face and as she saw Robbie she threw the photo with all her strength into the fireplace. Then she doubled over; pain showing on her face and hands clutching her stomach.

The young officer took one look at the situation and radioed for an ambulance. Then checking Fran, Robbie took her into his arms, gently reassuring her; rocking her as she cried. "I can't fight this anymore, Robbie. Please make it stop!"! With that she let out another scream and collapsed back into the couch, moaning as the pain of the inevitable took over.

CHAPTER 37

HURTFUL REVELATIONS

2019

"So did Fran have her baby"? Caris sat on the edge of her seat, fork in hand, hanging of every word.

"No, but they kept her in for observation. Her blood pressure was dangerously high and her anxiety higher. They would have kept her until she delivered but Fran insisted that she needed to be home with Emily. In fact she made such a fuss that it was felt medically it wouldn't benefit her to remain. The compromise was that she stayed for two more days, which she agreed to, but secretly they all thought that the baby would come early. What she wasn't aware of was that I had already packed up her and Emily's belongings and taken them around to her mum's house. We had all agreed it was safer to do so even though we knew that Fran would kick up a stink. You see, she had become sort of obsessed with her routine and her belongings being just so. At times it was impossible to please her should one thing be out of place or put away wrongly, but I thought, as did others, that it was due to the stress she was under and that it would sort itself out. Unfortunately, it never did. The police investigating this case had uncovered a trail of criminal offenses, not only in Australia, but also America and the UK. Vanessa has several personalities, and her business activities were being investigated by the fraud squad in LA. There were several missing persons notifications out and several husbands with grievances and business losses. Anytime they had closed in on her, she somehow disappeared along with large sums of money. The HMR.C in England was extremely interested in our case as they were investigating her undercover activities and her many aliases. The net was closing in, but she remained elusive. Remember that in 1996 there was not the technology that there is today, and Vanessa was very clever and manipulative". "Quite the professional" Caris said, absorbed in the story.

The food had been good and now sipping another wine, she had lost count, she felt more at ease in Robbie's presence. The wood fire burnt merrily, with flames licking up the chimney breast, leaving black sooty in prints on the red brick. At any other time this would have been idyllic, but, under the current circumstances, impossible. It was obvious to Caris that Vanessa had a type of schizophrenia but without doing a profile of her, it was hard to tell which. Her disorganised speech differences and behaviours were out of touch with reality and her serious mental disorder showed in her misinterpretation and delusional way of thinking. Caris also thought there was an element of Bipolar. Her manic episodes that Robbie had explained were indeed a symptom, with highs and lows of depressive activity which could last for months if untreated; she would have been as dangerous as a ticking time bomb. Robbie's voice interrupted her deliberations and she smiled encouragingly for him to continue. Once again the strain of reliving the events showed in his eyes as he started to talk, running a hand through his greying hair. "She was on all accounts a dangerous lady and was thought to be schizophrenic in nature". "I thought so" Caris said, "Not only that but I am sure, knowing what I now know, that there was obvious Bipolar evidence which seemed apparent. So what happened next?" Robbie took a swig of his beer and began again, "On the second day in hospital, Fran was extremely distraught, she didn't trust one of the nurses and wanted to go home. It took all my strength to calm her down, but not until I had checked every nurse that had been on duty. Finally she settled and told me that Tom and Nancy had visited that day and had given her a set of photos to cheer her up. One was of Tom and Nancy and their two children Katie and Henry and the other of the two children laughing out at the photographer. We had both exclaimed how Emily was the spitting image of her older cousin, Katie, with both having the same red ringlets. Both girls were the same height although a year apart and both had the same smile that lit up their pretty faces. Fran entrusted me to take the photos home, with strict instructions to hang them on the wall and not leave them on the mantle where they could be taken. She instructed me several times, that they were to be hung in the space above the picture of her parents just before the stairs. I of course agreed to do so. In days to come she often asked if the photos were still there. I didn't realise then, but I should have done, how damaged she was. The situation that she found herself in and the persecution she was suffering would have been enough for anyone to cope with, but I was so wrapped up in keeping her safe that I didn't see. I…I just didn't realise!" His voice had become thicker with emotion and to prevent the loss of control he slammed down his glass with beer spilling onto the table. "Dam it, sorry. It's just that I should have done more; instead, I made it so much worse."

Caris could see that Robbie, was near to tears and was reliving the memory of this tragedy as if it were today. She also realised that he had had far too much beer to drive home. Her apartment was close by and suggested that they walked to it. Leaving the pub, the drizzle of rain had now become quite heavy and neither had an umbrella. So by the time they arrived at Caris's little flat they were both cold and very wet. Dripping on the floor, Caris lit the small gas fire and threw a towel at Robbie to dry himself. Walking home, he had said very little and now he seemed preoccupied. She passed him a man's robe, and he looked up questioningly. "It was my ex's, it's the only thing he left behind. Would you like a hot chocolate? It will warm you up as this little fire, doesn't do much but better than nothing."

"It's fine and yes please, if it not too much trouble." Robbie was actually chilled to the bone and was thankful for the thick robe that she had given to him. He stripped off his wet shirt and then under the robe he took of his wet pants and instantly felt better. His muscular chest had not gone amiss and Caris busied herself so as not to show her obvious appreciation. Robbie smiled and thanked her again. "You truly are good to me, after all we have put you through." "Robbie it's my job, I just wish I could have unlocked Francesca's mind to help her." Caris walked into her kitchen and through the hatch she watched Robbie as she made the hot chocolate. He sat in a chair by the fire, head in hands. He was still handsome, but tired creases around his eyes were deep and etched into his skin. Twenty-three years of caring for someone who could not return the love, who could not express themselves and who was unwell would do that to you. The pain in his eyes and the sadness in his words, triggered something inside of her that had been long gone and as she gave him the cup, she looked into his eyes and smiled. "Here you go, drink up." He put the cup on the table and grabbed her hands. Leaning forward, he said, "Caris, I cannot thank you enough; it has been a long time since anyone cared what I had to say. This has been our battle, Fran's and mine, for such a long time and now it seems that it is nearing an end and I cannot say how grateful I am to have you listen to our story." Caris smiled, "You are welcome. Do you feel strong enough to continue?" He let go of her hands and nodded his head. Caris moved to the chair opposite, sipping her drink. "I do understand if you are too tired, you have been through an ordeal yourself tonight. The spare room is next door when you are ready." Robbie took a few sips of the chocolate and then took a deep breath. Caris, curled up in the chair, leaning forward in anticipation and Robbie started to speak again......

1996

With Fran and Emily safely settled at her parents, Robbie had gone home. It had been a long-complicated day with many tears from Francesca when she learnt of the plan. She had argued the need to be in her own home but with the united force of her parents, she gave in, especially when Emily said she wanted to stay. Robbie reasoned with her that the baby was due soon that we didn't want to risk her getting unwell; nine days that's all it was, and eventually she agreed.

Later, he walked up the steps of the cottage and let himself in. He hadn't remembered leaving a light on in the dining room, but it wasn't out of the realm of possibility. He put his bag down and hung up his coat and scarf. The waft of cooking reached him as he opened the door to the dining room and saw that the table was laid for two. He turned and opened the joining door to the kitchen, his pulse racing. Slowly he opened the door to find Vanessa wearing Fran's apron, cooking at the stove.

"Hi honey, your home, now pour yourself a drink and I will be with you in a second." Her voice was like warmed honey and her manner as natural as any wife greeting her husband as he came home from a long day at work. "What the hell are you doing here Vanessa?" Robbie stood in the doorway, his heart banging in his chest and anger rising.

"I am cooking you dinner of course, silly. How was your day?"

"Vanessa, I repeat what are you doing in my home! You are not welcome and if I were you I would leave before I call the police!"

"Why would you do that? I have been waiting for you for so long and now we are finally together again. Have you missed me?" She undid her apron; he noticed for the first time that she was scantily dressed under it, and advanced towards him with arms open.

Robbie put his hand out as if to distance himself, "I don't know what you are playing at, but I need you to leave! Get out!"

"Robbie! Don't be silly. You can stop the act now! We have the place to ourselves, you are a clever boy getting rid of Francesca. I tried but she is a stubborn one isn't she?"

Robbie said nothing and walked to the telephone and picking up the receiver started to ring the police. The phone was dead. He put the receiver down and looked at Vanessa who was now leaning on the kitchen bench, with a wine glass in her hand. "You cut the bloody phone line, is there no end to your talents?"

"Why thank you. I wanted our first evening together to be uninterrupted. Darling can you get me another drink?"

"Vanessa why are you doing this, we are not legally together anymore, but Francesca and I are! I love her and nothing you can do will change that. I don't want you! I want you to leave!"

"Of course you want me. You always have. Don't you remember every little tiff we had was always made up in the bedroom." His back was turned away from her as he futilely tried the phone again. She came behind him and pushed her body against his, snaking her arms around his middle. "Now stop being so silly and come and share dinner with me in our new home." Robbie untangled her hands and turned round on her and with all his might he threw her bodily across the floor. He didn't care any longer; he didn't worry that his actions could hurt her. He wanted to hurt her, and he was angry. "This is not your home! It is mine and Francesca's! You need to understand that I do not love you, I love Francesca and our children. Do you understand, you bloody witch!" He bored down on her, standing over her. He could hear his voice getting louder and louder, but by now he was past caring. Her blue eyes gazed up at him and she smiled sweetly as he carried on. "You are not wanted here. We are divorced and whoever you really are, get the hell out of my life! Go away and crawl back under the rock from whence you once came. Never come back, do you hear me? I no longer care what happens to you and Richard and Fran certainly do not care, so for god sakes leave or god help me! Do you understand?"

The smile remained on her lips as she struggled to get up, rearranging what little clothing she had on. Behind the smile was a sinister look as she wiped away a trickle of blood that dripped out of the corner of her mouth. For a minute she stared at it, the red smeared over her white skin and sighed. "No can do babe! You see my love, if you don't share dinner with me, I will make Francesca suffer and every time you go off to work or leave the house, her life will get that little bit worse. You will find that sweet little Emily, will suddenly disappear, poof, and eventually you will lose everything that is precious to you. So you see my darling, you don't have a choice. Now wash your hands so we can eat! I am sure you are hungry." Her chilling laugh taunted him. 'Come along, she waltzed passed him into the kitchen, returning with two dishes which she took into the dining room. Tomorrow this room needs changing around, it's a mess."

"There, eat up and enjoy".

2019

I remember having no appetite and just sat looking at her whilst she ate without a care in the world. There was no mistaking that she was a beautiful sexy woman and that any man could fall for her; like my father, like Richard, and I then of course me. "Your father?" Caris interrupted. "Oh yes! But then she had been interesting; kind and sort of vulnerable, but this woman was cruel and so very calculating, watching my every move. To all sense of purpose I was trapped. I couldn't think, my mind was jumbled, and I have to admit, I was afraid."

To Caris's horror, Robbie broke down in tears. She jumped off her chair and held him in her arms; his sobs coming thick and fast as he leant into her chest.

His voice was muffled, "I don't deserve your kindness, I really don't."

"Ssh Ssh," Caris comforted. "It's okay, let it all out." She stayed holding him and he cried as if his heart was breaking. Finally, although still struggling, he started to talk.....

"But it got so much worse and when you learn what happened next, I can assure you that you won't want to hug me, you won't want to know me!"

"Try me! Get it all out, you will feel so much better if you do. 23 years of holding on to this could make a man crazy."

"I was crazy. After this, I swore to never get involved with anyone again, never feel and never love. My actions didn't just kill any feelings that I may have had, but it killed any feeling others had too!"

Caris let go and looked into his eyes, "Robbie, from what you have said, you cannot blame all this on something you did. Vanessa was manipulative you had no choice. Francesca and Emily's lives was threatened, you did what you had to do and if that meant following Vanessa's bidding, then so be it. She put you in an awful position.

Professionally I think you have said enough for tonight and as a friend, I am watching you fall to pieces. Perhaps it's time you stopped and got some rest".

"No, I have to tell you, I have to tell it all!" Robbie shouted and stood up, knocking the hot chocolate over. "Oh god I am so sorry but if I don't keep talking I will never get it out. It's been stuck in here," he thumped his chest, "for so long. I just need to........." He sat down again and stared ahead with a sadness that broke Caris's heart. She quietly got up and grabbed some kitchen towel and mopping up the mess, she looked at him and saw the silent battle going round and round in his thoughts; that personal struggle of anger and sadness screaming to be let out. She had to let him speak, however, late it was. This, she knew, was the outlet that he needed to close this chapter and allow him to get on with his life. Somehow she knew that this new life featured her, and she would be there for him, whatever it took and whatever he said, she would be there.

CHAPTER 38

ERROR IN JUDGEMENT

1996

Robbie sat opposite Vanessa as she ate her meal. Her conversation and questions, a blur and not answered; his meal not eaten. "Oh baby, aren't you hungry, I spent ages putting this together for you. Come on try a little, just for me!" Her voice was sickly sweet, and it made him feel sick. In his mind, he held Francesca. He could hear her voice and saw her smile and he would do anything to keep her safe.

"What are you thinking about honey?"

"Actually, Vanessa, I am thinking about Francesca and how much I love her!"

Vanessa stood and walked around the table to where Robbie, sat. "You see, my love, that doesn't make me happy, in fact it makes me really mad!" Her arms snaked around his neck and her hands began to tighten. "You don't love Francesca, you love me. You hurt me Robbie, when you left me for her, but now Francesca is gone, and I have come back to you." Her voice suddenly changed to that of the child. "And you are not gonna hurt me are you? You are going to look after me. Otherwise I will tell my daddy and he won't be happy that you hurt his little girl!" She giggled, "and he will most probably hurt you or maybe……" she giggled again, "or maybe kill you and we don't want that!"

He shook her off and coughed and took a large swig of the wine. He wasn't sure what to make of this and didn't quite know what to do, especially as she seemed to find this funny and was laughing at him.

Vanessa spoke again, this time in her normal voice – "What shall we do tonight? What about a movie or we could just go to bed, now that's an idea?"

Robbie said nothing and sat staring at Vanessa. She looked the same but the free-spirited girl he had met in Australia had disappeared. In front of him, was a manic freak that he had no control of. The child was back, "Not fair, not fair... you want talk to me, and I am being ever so nice. Daddy hurts people that hurt me. You don't want me to call him do you?"

"But Vanessa, the phone doesn't work, how can you call your daddy?"

Vanessa switched back, "Do you really think, I am that stupid Robbie? Now help me with these dishes and then….."

"And then what? If you think I am going to bed with you, you have another thing coming".

"Quite frankly, Robbie, you don't have a choice. Let me make this quite clear – every time you annoy me, life will get that much harder for Francesca. I know people, who, when called, will act out exactly what I want…well need I say more!"

"What the hell is wrong with you! Francesca is about to have a baby, hurt her you hurt our unborn child. Do you hear me, do you understand?"

Vanessa looked at Robbie and smiled sweetly. She walked back to her seat and lifted the dishes off the table. "Yes!"

"Yes? He took another drink.

She threw the dishes down on the table – "Yes! Yes! Yes! I heard you but I don't care! I don't care about Francesca; I don't care about Emily and I don't care about your bastard. It could be a nurse; a midwife or a doctor, accidents happen. Do *you* understand? I always get what I want! And Robbie, I want you!"

Robbie understood too well. His stomach churned and his head felt as if it would burst. Fran was due in a week and somehow he needed to get out of this mess before then and without any harm coming to Fran.

His pager went off, checking it, he saw that the hospital needed him, perhaps a way out.

"Vanessa, the hospital just paged me. I have to go!"

"Sorry but my needs are much more important" Vanessa picked up the dishes and walked out of the dining room and went into the kitchen.

Robbie burst through the door after her. "What do you think will happen if I don't go to the hospital, Vanessa? Let me tell you! They will ring my mobile and if I don't answer, they will ring the home phone and they will find that the line doesn't work. Then they will ring my next of kin, which funnily enough, is Francesca. Who will tell them that I am here at home……..." exasperated he slammed out of the kitchen and walked into the hall.

Vanessa continued washing the dishes and didn't rush after him but continued humming to herself as she completed the job. He hurriedly put on his coat and hat, but as he picked up his bag, he became light-headed, and he had to steady himself against the bannister. He shook his head and stood again, but his vision blurred. Hearing the kitchen door open, he urged himself to turn as if to walk out of the front door, but somehow his feet would not walk, and he staggered forward. Something compelled him to turn back and standing in the doorway, with the light shadowing her features, stood Vanessa leaning against the door plinth. "I don't think so Robbie, now stop being silly, let's go to bed!"

"What the hell have you done Vanessa?". Robbie's voice was by now slurring.

"Well you may not have eaten but you did have a drink didn't you and baby, you don't look so good, let me help you".

2019

Caris you have to believe me, I never wanted anything to happen, but I was powerless. When I woke the next morning, Vanessa lay naked next to my naked body, my arms were wrapped around her and I could only presume that …..well you know. I tried to get up, but my head pounded, and I couldn't move. I was due at the hospital and I knew I would have to explain why I didn't answer my pager the previous night, but Vanessa had thought of that. She had reconnected the phone and telephoned ahead of me, stating that she was a friend of the family, looking after Fran and both Fran and I had fallen unwell. She went on to explain that poor Dr Harvey was still very sick and unable to work. They quite understood and told her that Dr Harvey's patient load would be cancelled for the next couple of days. They hoped that both Dr Harvey and Ms Taylor would be better soon particularly in Ms Taylor's condition and Vanessa had oozed empathy. I lay there listening to her twittering on with one thought in my mind, that whilst I was here in Vanessa's grasp, Francesca was safe. It occurred to me that Francesca would find it strange that I wasn't visiting her and would try to contact me but then she would put it down to my workload as normal. I was glad she had her parents to look after her but being so close to the birth date and knowing her stubbornness, she may investigate and in doing so she would walk straight into this miserable trap and god knows what would happen.

I lay there thinking things through and all the while Vanessa talked. I didn't really listen to her but could hear snippets of her conversation as she made plans for our future. My head continued to pound but it had begun to clear and then it came to me, the solution was easy; I would play her game.

I gave my body to Vanessa and she used it, any which way she pleased. I became the loving husband that she thought I was, and we played happy families planning our future together. You have to understand that I had no choice but at least whilst Vanessa was busy plotting our life journey Francesca and Emily were protected. I couldn't warn Fran as I didn't have my phone, god knows where that had ended up, but I watched the days go by with Fran getting closer to her due date. However, two days later, on the 14th of January everything changed, and all our lives fractured.

Caris, I have lived with this guilt for 23 years! Caring for a person I dearly love but who cannot return the same and grieving for those who have gone because of something I did has never left me and is a responsibility that has been a burden that I take seriously. Living with a person so radically changed that I don't know her anymore because of an error in judgement is my punishment and for that, I will never forgive myself.

Robbie leant back in the chair, his eyes closed, the pain etched on his face. Caris squeezed his hand. This was too much for anyone to go through, and yet, she knew professionally that he had to. She waited to hear what she had been waiting for – the why; the how and the fractured diagnosis that would close this case.

CHAPTER 39

DISTORTION AND SPECULATION

1996

Mary marked off the calendar, drawing a line through Friday and sighed. It had been a difficult day. Her daughter had come home from hospital that morning and was definitely not herself. Heavily pregnant, she seemed preoccupied with, well, everything. Constantly moving things into place and muttering to herself crossly, didn't seem normal and her anger towards Robbie, was misplaced, considering he had put her with them for her own safety. "Talk to her Joe", Mary said to her husband, when they had gone to bed. "Robbie was only trying to do the right thing and Fran really gave him a piece of her mind. She actually told him that she didn't want to see him again. What are we going to do Joe?"

"Well love, Fran just needs to understand that we are only looking out for her, keeping her and Emily safe. Don't worry Mary, it will sort itself out."

Mary wiped her eyes with a tissue and continued, "and Joe, she didn't even say goodbye to Emily when Richard picked her up. This cannot be good for her or the baby!" Joe, looking at his wife, agreed. He too was worried; his precious daughter should be excited about the birth of her second child but instead she seemed disengaged, as if it were all happening to someone else. Joe liked the simple things in life, and this all seemed too complicated. He also hated seeing his wife so upset but wasn't sure what to say to help but tried by saying, "I will talk to her in the morning, and perhaps, tomorrow, you could speak with Robbie." Mary smiled nervously and agreed, "Ok Joe, good idea."

Joe cuddled his wife reassuringly, "that's it, we just need to get them talking together and they will be back to normal!"

"Oh Joe. I do love you." Mary said and snuggled down feeling much better.

With Emily at Richards', Mary was free to have a heart to heart with Robbie. She left Joe making breakfast for Fran and hoped that he would make her see sense. Fran had seemed more like her old self and even laughed at one of Joe's dreadful dad jokes. Perhaps Joe had been right, and Fran had just been tired.

Driving down the road, she visualised the conversation that she was to have. It was odd that Robbie hadn't rung the night before. He always rang Emily before she left for Richard's when he was at work and she noted that he hadn't spoken to Fran either. Surely he would want to see how she was. She recalled that Fran had shouted at him, that she didn't want to see him ever again, and that he hadn't listened to what she had wanted, but still, it just wasn't like him even if he was busy. Mary reasoned with herself that Robbie had probably been caught up at work and was sure that he was just giving Fran breathing space but with the baby due any day, it all seemed rather out of character. That nagging gut like feeling rose it's ugly head again and gnawed at her as she drove through the pretty village of Little Stockton. She would just have to lay it on the line… the baby and Fran needed him more than ever and bugger the consequences.

She turned down the picturesque lane where Holly Cottage stood, nestled between the large old trees that had probably been there long before the cottage was built and saw a white car outside the house. "Dam" Mary said, he had visitors.

As she neared, she saw the front door open. Stepping out of the house was a tall blonde woman who stood on the step looking up and down the street. In Mary's mind she was dressed rather scantily, particularly as it was so cold and damp. Mary parked the car further up the street and watched, trying to make sense of what she was seeing. The woman walked to the white car, and again looked up the street before opening the boot. She then leant in and took something out, it looked like a holdall, and then before going back inside the house, looked up the street again as if looking for something or someone. She then walked up the steps, went inside and shut the door behind her. Mary thought she had seen her before but couldn't quite see her face as she was hidden by trees that lined the street. Getting out of her car, she wrapped her warm scarf around her neck, did up her coat and trudged down the hill towards the house. There was only one way to find out.

Walking up the steps to Holly Cottage Mary rapped on the door. There was no answer. She tried again but still no one came. "Robbie, it's Mary…..is everything ok?" Mary shouted and then rapped on the door again. Walking backwards down the steps, she looked up at the windows; they stared back at her, with no expression.

Mary walked down to the side of the house, where the white car sat. The car was empty, and she noted it was a rental with no evidence to say who had driven it.

The back gate, normally open, was locked. "Robbie, it's me, Mary, are you home?" Mary shouted again but still no one answered. It started to rain, and the winter wind chilled her to the bone. Walking up to the front door, she opened the letter box and looked through. She could see a lady's coat and lady's boots at the foot of the stair at the end of the corridor; she could see Robbie's doctor bag, which meant he was home, but the house was quiet, too quiet. The rain had become quite heavy now and Mary was soaked through and she decided to leave but she had a very uneasy feeling as she walked back up the hill that she was being watched. Every nerve in her body screamed out that something was very wrong, and she didn't know what to do next. She needed to speak with Joe and see if he had any ideas, he always knew what to do.

As Mary reached her car, the wind whipped her hair across her face and took her scarf from her neck, blowing it across the road. She turned to chase it, the material skipping and dipping in the wind as it flew up the street, eventually dropping into the gutter, wet and lifeless, opposite the cottage. Mary stooped to pick it up and as she did she looked back at the cottage, bleak and dark against the stormy skies, and there, looking out of her daughter's bedroom window was a woman, a woman with long blonde hair. Mary stared at her, trying to comprehend why she was even there; the rain and wind forgotten. Horrified, Mary, watched as the woman slowly took off her dress seductively, pressing her bare breasts against the windowpane. She put her hands on her nipples and twisted them erotically moving her hips backwards and forwards as if in a sexual act. Slamming her hands against the glass she smiled as if in ecstasy and then beckoned to Mary, inviting her to come forward. When Mary didn't move, she threw back her head and laughed. The silent gesture was seen but not heard, it's intent understood. The chill that ran through Mary's bones was not because of the cold but was now due to the fear that gripped her.

Stumbling, half running, back to her car Mary climbed in and locked the door before driving off. As she drove home she racked her brains where she had seen the woman before, but it was not until she stopped at the lights, did she have the realisation of where and more importantly who she was. She shivered and turned up the heater in the car, she was wet and cold and just wanted to be home. Nothing made any sense but one this was for certain she needed Joe more than ever. Perhaps there was a reasonable explanation but for the life of her she couldn't see one and above all else Fran had to be kept in the dark.

Vanessa watched as Mary drove off. She smiled to herself and climbed into bed with a sleeping Robbie. The drugs keeping him sedated helped. He needed to forget Fran and Emily and the life he had before. He loved her, he told her so and soon they would leave this god forsaken place and start a family of their own. Her hands aroused him, and he groaned, "Fran". She climbed on to him and moved rhythmically bringing him to a climax. "Yes baby I am here and always will be".

Arriving home, Mary walked into the kitchen, the welcoming site of her home, brought tears to her eyes. "Joe!" "Joe!" She anxiously called. His voice floated through from the lounge, "In here love". She walked through, and he looked up smiling, putting the newspaper down. "Goodness Mary your soaked through to the skin, whatever happened? Come and sit here by the fire and I will get you a towel."

"Where is Fran, Joe?"

"She's upstairs having a rest. Won't be a minute." He left the room and came back with a towel. He could see that something was wrong and watched Mary, as she stared into the fire. She jumped as Joe wrapped the towel around her shoulders but then leant back into him, looking up as he spoke to her. "What is it love? Did you speak with Robbie?"

"No, I don't think he was home."

"Working then?"

"No, I don't think so".

"So where have you been all this time, your soaked through? Come on now, you don't want to catch a cold". He rubbed her shoulders trying to warm her and Mary told Joe what had occurred. "Joe, I am absolutely sure it was Vanessa…. Sarah or whatever her name is…..but what I want to know is what was she doing in Fran's house and why was Robbie's bag still there if he wasn't?"

"Perhaps we should call the hospital and see if he at work, but my betting is that he was in the house. The question is whether he was there by choice or not. I think we should call the police, don't you?"

Mary was about to agree but a knock on the front door, followed by the doorbell, interrupted them. Joe left to answer it; the doorbell sounding again. "Okay! Okay, hold your horses," he called out.

Returning to the room he held a large bouquet of flowers in his hands. "It's for Fran and Robbie. I wonder why it was sent here".

"Whose it's from?" Mary queried.

"Hang on, let's look and see. There's a card......

Dear Dr Harvey & Fran,
We are sorry to hear you are both feeling unwell.
We hope you will be back on your feet soon.
Best Wishes
Nurses on Ward 5
Ps: We didn't have your address, so we sent it to Fran's mum.
Hope you don't mind."

Joe scratched his head, showing the card to Mary. "Well, that makes no sense at all! Robbie wasn't ill the last time we saw him, granted Fran hasn't been her best and they knew she was here but....." He scratched his head again and then pulled on his chin, thinking. "I suppose it explains why he hasn't been at work though doesn't it. But if he got sick, why is that Vanessa person in his home and as you said, naked; this is all very confusing?"

Joe looked at the flowers again as if they would unlock the mystery.

"I don't know Joe, but I don't like it one little bit. We will have to go to the police but for now get rid of that card so as to not arouse suspicion. That is the last thing Fran needs today!"

"What don't I need today mum?" Fran's red curls poked around the door. "These flowers are lovely; they must have cost a bomb. Who are they for?

"We don't know Fran," her parents chorused.

"You're holding the card dad, what does it say?" Fran asked expectantly.

"It's nothing, don't you worry about it. Now can I get you, a cup of tea?"

Fran sniffed their perfume, it was beautiful. "They are such pretty colours, and the smell is glorious. Are they for you mum? I haven't missed a special occasion have I? Seriously this pregnancy is driving me nuts, I can't remember anything".

"There from your dad, Fran. I haven't been myself lately, and he thought it would cheer me up."

"You old dog you. I have never seen you be so romantic before." She walked over to her father and gave him a kiss on his cheek. "Well they are lovely and so are you both. I am sorry I have been such a grump lately. Poor Robbie, he has been living with my moods for weeks now. Do you know, I became paranoid that someone was watching me! Madness! I feel so much better today; that sleep did me the world of good."

"That's good dear. You obviously needed it". Getting up, Mary finished towel drying her hair, "Now I'm off to have a shower, I got soaked going to the shops and I am rather cold."

Fran watched her mother as she walked across the room. "Mum, before you go," Mary stopped and turned, she wasn't sure what Fran was going to say but she had a good idea and needed to be prepared. "Have you heard from Robbie? I have tried ringing him to apologies but his mobile keeps going to voice mail."

"Oh, he is probably busy, in the operating theatre or something, but no, sorry Fran I haven't."

"That's rather odd. He never turns his phone off, just in case I need him, you know," she indicated the baby, "and today he has clinics and often phones me between patients."

"Well, you did tell him you didn't want to speak with him again. Your dad and I thought that a bit harsh and perhaps he does too. You need to keep that temper of yours under control my girl!"

"For goodness sake mum, don't be so dramatic. Robbie and I have fights all the time, but he knows I don't mean anything by it. It's odd that's all. I am sure I have nothing to worry about but it's not like him and ......"

Joe walked in with the tea and having heard part of the conversation joined in, tousling Fran's hair, as he always had done since she was a child, "Now now, my love. I am sure that there is a suitable explanation. As you mum said he is probably busy, getting things sorted before the baby comes. Here have a lovely cup of tea and perhaps try later."

"Thanks dad." Fran smiled up at him, good old reliable dad. He always made things better, but Robbie's disappearance was worrying her. "The thing is, and sorry to keep harbouring on...I spoke with Emily this morning, before having a rest. She asked to come home because Richard was busy and on the phone all the time. I persuaded her to stay but she seemed upset. When I asked her what was wrong, she told me that Uncle Robbie, didn't call her last night and she didn't have a good sleep. Dad, Robbie never forgets to call. I think there is something wrong!"

"Fran, now stop it. You will upset yourself. Have you thought that Robbie might need a bit of self-time before the baby comes? When I was pregnant with Tom, your dad was in a right lather and wasn't himself at all. Wasn't that right Joe?" Joe laughed, "I am afraid your mothers' right. I was a complete mess. Worrying how I was to juggle work, your mother, and a baby but it all worked out in the end. Now, Fran, your mum, is going to catch her death if she doesn't have that shower so off you go Mary."

Mary was relieved to be leaving the conversation headed up the stairs. Joe always knew what to say but still, she didn't know how they were going to get out of this one; someone was going to get hurt. She knew that they would have to go to the police, but the question was, how? They couldn't leave Fran on her own and she needed Joe to come with her. His calm, pragmatic reasoning instead of her emotional outburst would make the case plausible and perhaps they would listen. Maybe she would ring Tom; if he was free, he could visit tomorrow and then Fran wouldn't get suspicious. Yes that was it.

As the water flowed over her, the stress of the day washed away. She reflected on her life and realised that she was an incredibly lucky woman. Two beautiful children and three, soon to be four, beautiful grandchildren. Both her children's partners, Robbie and Nancy had proven too be very much part of the family and even Richard, after a fashion, was still accepted as their son in law. Joe still made her laugh as he did when they were at high school together, and was, she believed, all a woman could want. Their house was paid for and really, until now, they had not had any worries of great concern, well nothing they couldn't deal with. They had even discussed early retirement with a tidy sum to look after them in their old age. Yes, they had done well for themselves; they didn't want much out of life, just to enjoy those whom they loved around them. Turning the shower off and grabbing a towel, she stared at her face in the mirror. A few more lines around her eyes and her mouth, and with her hair a little greyer, she still looked much the same, as did Joe, and neither noticed the years that had passed. She still loved Joe and he her, as much, if not more, as on the day they got married. She finished dressing and nodded to her reflection; there were not many of their friends that could say that these days. She smiled as she rubbed in her moisturiser and knew that without a shadow of a doubt that her family meant everything to her. Looking at her watch, she realised if they were to have dinner by 6 she would need to get a move on and walked out of the bathroom feeling calm and much better than when she had gone in. However, raised voices pulled her out of her revelry and she hurried downstairs to find out what combat was she to referee now.

Opening the kitchen door, she saw her fiery daughter, red in face and her patient husband looking defeated. "Give me the card dad, I just saw you put it in your pocket!"

Joe looked sheepish but made no effort to retrieve the card. "Dad, please" and more urgently, "Now!"

"Hey what is going on? I leave you alone for a few minutes and I come down to World War 3. Fran, what is it?"

"You have been gone an hour, actually! And in that time, Sheila rang me from Ward 5. Funny thing is she asked me if we liked the flowers? Isn't that funny Mum!" She looked at both of them, their guilty faces giving them away. "She was sorry that we had been so ill; food poisoning was horrible and hoped that it hadn't affected the baby in anyway. She also hoped that Dr Harvey was on the mend and I assured her that all was well. But imagine my surprise when she asked if she could talk with Dr Harvey; that she knew he was off at the moment but was doing the clinic roster for next week and she needed to know if she should book the Locum in or not. I asked her why she was calling me and why she hadn't contacted Dr Harvey on his mobile and she told me that she had tried many times, but his mobile was turned off. She was sorry to bother me but was getting a little desperate". She turned from one parent to another, "Isn't that strange!" With no forthcoming response, she continued rather sarcastically and pointedly, "Is someone going to tell me what is going on?"

"Now Fran, calm down, let's sit down and dad will make us a nice hot chocolate or a cup of tea."

"I don't want any bloody hot chocolate mum; I want to see what is written on the card. Dad, hand it over please". Joe did so and watched as Fran read the contents. Once finished she looked at her parents who by now were sitting on the sofa, guiltily looking back at her.

"I don't understand why you didn't tell me who sent them. Why did you say they were for you mum? Dad never sends you flowers! What is going on and what the hell is wrong with Robbie? Do you know?......... Why did you lie to me?"

Fran was walking up and down, firing questions; her voice getting louder and louder, and all Mary and Joe could do was stare at her. When she finally stopped and faced both of them with hands on hips and her face red and hot, her eyes narrowed "What are you hiding from me?" Tears started to flow, and Joe jumped up and put his arms around her, guiding her to a chair. "I think love, we need to talk, but you mustn't excite yourself, not in your condition."

"Please tell me dad, I can't deal with much more". When Joe didn't answer, her voice faltered, "Mum, please. Is Robbie okay?"

Mary's soft voice began to speak. She worded the sentences carefully without embellishing the details. She had years of practice as a primary school teacher, and it took all her reserves to describe the situation as painlessly as possible. Her reasoning, she told Joe later, was to protect Fran. "Joe, I hope I did the right thing, I couldn't tell her everything could I? Joe had agreed but neither were convinced, and both went to bed with a feeling of foreboding.

"I went to see Robbie yesterday morning. You weren't yourself and I wanted to talk some sense into him. When I got to the house, there was no one there".

"He would have been at the clinic, like normal", Fran added.

"Yes I thought that too, but something told me that he was home."

"Why"

"Call it intuition but I felt a presence there".

"Oh mum for goodness…."

"Let your mum finish what she is saying," Joe interrupted.

"Thank you Joe. So I knocked again and called his name. The wind and rain was blowing up a storm and I thought he may not hear me; so I opened the letter box and looked in. It was quite dark…..."

"Well it would be wouldn't it if no one was there!"

"Fran!"

"Sorry mum, carry on…"

"Anyway, I was just about to close it when I saw, at the end of the hallway, his doctor's bag… I called his name but still nothing, but the floor board creaked upstairs, you know the lose one….but still no one spoke. I have to say, by now I was dripping wet and felt quite spooked. I left and trudged up the road to my car, but my scarf blew down the road, so I chased it, it got all soggy and wet…."

"Mum, what has your wet scarf got to do with Robbie…this is ridiculous!" She saw the look that was given between her mum and dad, "Okay, okay! What, happened next?"

"Well when I caught up with my scarf, I looked up at the house and I could have sworn the curtain moved and I saw someone standing there looking down at me".

"Who?" Fran asked her voice suddenly very strained.

"Well that's just it, I am not sure. It wasn't Robbie, that is for certain. So I turned tail and came home. I was telling your dad, when the flowers arrived and then you came in and well, we didn't want to worry you. The card said that both of you were ill, you see, and we didn't want you thinking the worst."

"Have you thought of ringing the hospital, he may have been caught up in theatre or something?"

"Well that is a possibility of course but have you ever known him to leave the house without his doctor's bag?" Mary exclaimed. She had missed out so much detail that she didn't want to go on for fear of incriminating the lie further.

Fran sat back in the chair, she looked washed out, her brows were furrowed as she thought this through, and her eyes were closed.

"Come on poppet, I am sure there is an explanation, and we will all have a laugh later when we find out, he had popped up the road for something at the shop. Perhaps mum's imagination has got the better of her. Now, I am going to make some hot chocolate for myself and mum, do you want one love?"

Fran barely heard her dad as her mind whirled in every direction. The baby moved suddenly, taking her breath away and leaving her hands on her stomach she soothed it, cooing "It's alright, daddy is alright," but in her heart of hearts she knew something wasn't right at all and as soon as she could find out.

CHAPTER 40

TRAGEDY OF EVENTS

2019

Into the night Robbie talked, sharing his story, telling Caris of Vanessa's cruelty and perversions. He believed that he had been drugged as his mind had been muddled and her lies became reality. The threats towards his family became his living dread and were often; being made to listen to her deranged thoughts, until he cried begging her to stop. This was the Vanessa whose personality was quite mad and cruel; her sudden outbursts of unabated anger regarding the injustice towards her caused her to rant and rave incoherently, but just as suddenly she would then weep becoming apologetic and hating herself, that she didn't mean it and it wasn't her fault; this was the Vanessa who he had known in Australia. It was only then there would be a reprieve from the hate that surrounded him, as she indulge him in remembering a happier time. She would insist on making love, crying out her passion for him. However, it was the child like Vanessa, called May, that caused the most pain with her demands and spiteful actions which left scars that he would always remember. The voice would twist sweetness into a malicious malady which he would, even today hear again and again in his dreams, and now as he relayed the story, it came back to him, making him sob as he continued the story.

"Rob! Rob! Robbie! I want to play Doctors and Nurses…….NOW!" Her voice high pitched and demanding, and when Robbie refused to do the degrading things asked of him, she would hurt him, slapping and pinching, even burning his skin with the end of a cigarette with a taunt that haunted him.

"Poor Dr Robbie fits the crime,
Taking drugs through a line!
Beg me, please go on 1 2 3,
Do what I ask, do it for me
Doctor! Doctor! Doctor!

The depravity of this story made Caris feel sick, it was unbelievable, and dreaded asking but knew she had to, "What did she mean by that?"

Robbie slowly rolled up his sleeve. She gasped as she saw jagged, red, hardened scars, which ran from his elbow to his wrist. She traced them with her finger and could only imagine the torture that he had gone through. She had no idea how anyone got over this sort of behaviour but somehow, he had, and over the years had carried on with some semblance of normality. Tears poured down her cheeks and he gently wiped them away, saying he was sorry. She looked into his gentle eyes and stretched up a hand to his face, holding his cheek in the palm of her hand and as she did, he turned to kiss it, resting his lips. His gesture, caring and gentle, told Caris that someway in reliving the events of 23 years ago, the journey of recovery had begun, and the man long gone was recovering however, hard it may be.

Awkwardly, Caris stood looking down at the broken man and held out her hand. Robbie stood and allowed her to lead him into her room where she undressed him. He neither put up a fight nor refused; too exhausted to stop her. He climbed into bed without thought of the consequence and Caris climbed in next to him, holding him in her arms as he drifted off to sleep. She lay awake for some time, mulling over the experiences she had heard, her mind in overtime. She tried to piece together the tragedy of events that had occurred but without an end she was no nearer to the truth and she didn't know if Robbie had the strength to speak of more. She could not imagine the trauma that Robbie had gone through over those three days and although he had said that he had lost track of time and thought it longer, his story fitted in with the date of the accident on 15th January. Eventually her thoughts blurred, and she too fell into a deep sleep; her mind filled with nightmares and pain. She awoke suddenly interrupted by Robbie's restless cries as he battled invisible demons that taunted his dreams. She tried to comfort him, soothing him with words and stroking his back but he suddenly sprung up putting his hands around her throat. Caris couldn't fight him for he was too heavy but spoke to him over and over telling him her name. At some point, when she was near to blacking out, his hands shifted from her throat and as he released his grip, he snapped out of his trance collapsing on top of her and sobbing uncontrollably. "I'm sorry, so sorry! I thought you were….".

"It's okay, I know I know", Caris comforted him, her voice rasping. They lay side by side panting, both were silent. Eventually, Robbie sat on the side of the bed, head in his hands, sobbing, "It will never end" he mumbled, "Vanessa may be gone but she comes to me at night and the whole things starts all over again…. She said she would never leave me, and she was so right. She said that nobody could love me like she could and anyone who tried would die trying….and for fuck's sake she was right" He was now shouting, his voice hysterical. "My Fran, my beautiful Fran and now you, Caris. She made quite sure that I would never love again didn't she!"

Caris crawled behind him and lay her head on his back. Robbie shook her off and stood up, walking to the window, "I am so sorry Caris, I am a danger to any woman that lays next to me and I don't want to hurt you."

"Has this happened before, Robbie"?

Robbie stared out of the window, it was still dark and there was nothing to see but it was easier to continue without looking at Caris.

"I had renovated the cottage so it would be easier for Fran to get around when she came home from the hospital, moving our bedroom to the back of the house, so she didn't need to climb the stairs and putting in a downstairs bathroom. I think she thought I was her Carer as she was fairly institutionalised having been in the hospital so long. When she initially came home, she was confused and didn't seem to remember me, in fact she had difficulty remembering anyone. She asked after Emily more than once but then just as suddenly she stopped talking about her. I didn't encourage further discussion as this was easier for both of us. We all thought it would be better if she slept alone until her memory allowed me back in, and so I slept upstairs but one night, I couldn't bare it any longer and I climbed into bed behind her…. I missed her so much and I just wanted to hold her". Robbie started to cry again, great heaving sobs. "Go on Robbie" Caris encouraged.

"Fran screamed, terrified. Something inside me was triggered and I put my hands around her throat and squeezed". Caris put her own hands up to her throat, still feeling bruised from earlier. "Fran was choking and hitting out at me but all I could hear was a childish laugh, taunting me and telling me to do it……. I didn't want to hurt her, Caris, I just couldn't help myself."

"Oh god, Robbie! Why didn't you get treatment? I could have helped you…. After all you went through, there would have been no harm in trying. Was Fran okay?"

"She started to fit, and it shook me out of the trance that I was in… It was a massive episode and she ended back in hospital. I don't think she remembered what happened, but how will I ever know. I didn't sleep with her again and to this day I am Robbie the Carer who looks after her, putting her to bed and making sure the house is just as she knows it. Quite frankly I am nothing more to her and what we had, will never came back. We live compatibly but in a sort of vortex."

Caris felt silent tears trickle down her face and wiped them away with the back of her hand. "Don't cry for me Caris. It is no more than I deserve."

"How can you say that Robbie, it wasn't your fault none of it was. Let me help you, or if not me, I have a friend who specialises in this sort of trauma… please Robbie. You need help!"

Robbie let out a cold and chilling laugh - "The revered and respected Dr Robbie Harvey, is in fact a nutter!" He bowed dramatically towards Caris hand sweeping through the air.

"Stop it Robbie, now you are feeling sorry for yourself, and although you have right to be angry, upset or whatever it is you are feeling, I am not about to let you wallow in your own pity any longer."

The telephone rang in the hallway, interrupting their discussion – Caris looked at the clock, it was 7am and the light was beginning to come through the window. She walked out the bedroom and picked up the receiver.

"Yes, he is here, is everything okay?……… I will let him know immediately. Thank you Sister." Caris put the receiver down, conscious that she had just admitted that Dr Robbie Harvey was in her home but in the scheme of things she didn't think it mattered and walking back into the bedroom and seeing the wreck of a man in front of her, she didn't think she cared either.

"Robbie," she watched as he lifted his head, his eyes red from crying and his face, pale. "That was the hospital. Fran has had a massive fit and is unconscious. Sister Mary says you are needed as they feel there isn't much time!"

Dragging on his clothes, he ran out of the bedroom to put on his coat. He turned back in to the bedroom addressing Caris. "please can you come. I can't do this without you!"

If anyone thought that Dr Robbie Harvey looked worse for wear on arrival to the hospital, they didn't say or if anyone questioned that Caris was by his side, they kept it to themselves. The tragedy of the situation and the devotion that Robbie had shown over the last 23 years was undoubtedly all they spoke about.

As he walked into Ward 5, he was greeted by Sister Nora, she looked tired and sad as she spoke, her rich Irish brogue thickened by the emotion that she was feeling.

"Dr Harvey, I am glad you got here so quickly. It was a bad one that is for sure!"

Robbie acknowledged this; he had worked with Sister Nora for many years and Fran was well known to them all, seemingly part of the family. "What happened, she was fine when we left her?"

"Well Dr Harvey, you will never believe this, but she spoke for the first time. We were all so excited and she looked straight at us and uttered a whole sentence or two. Of course, it didn't make a whole lot of sense but nevertheless she spoke, God bless her. Then the poor darling's eyes rolled back in her head and the tremors started. We laid her down, but they got worse and were lengthy, but then just as quickly, they stopped. She hasn't woken since".

"Can I ask what she said Sister Nora?" Robbie asked.

"Well don't be bothering yourself with her nonsense, because that is what it was, just a little bit of nonsense".

"Please Sister Nora, it will mean a lot to me, It's just…..". Caris rested her hand on Robbie's arm, encouraging him to say what he felt. "It's just I cannot bear to think of her tormented or frightened."

"I am sure you don't. Well, let me see. It is such a pity, what a lovely lady Francesca is as well". The old nurse furrowed her brow and then looked up with a smile, "She said something about a flower… daffodils or dandelion or something like that. Now what was it, my memory isn't what it was."

"Sister," Caris said. "Yes, my dear what is it?" "It is just a hunch, and something Francesca has mentioned before, but could the flower have been a buttercup?" Again Sister Nora thought before answering and on seeing a nurse running by, she called her over, "Nurse Rose, come here please dear." The young nurse stopped and smiled. "Yes Sister, what can I do for you?"

"Do you remember what Francesca Taylor said when she spoke this afternoon? For the life of me I cannot remember." "Yes Sister, she said the words buttercup, which we all thought rather strange and then after a while she said something about a bridge…"

Robbie looked puzzled, "A bridge?"

"Yes, Dr Harvey. We thought she was quoting something, like a poem. She had the loveliest of smiles on her face and her eyes were closed…." The nurse closed her own eyes as if remembering…. Robbie and Caris waited with bated breath and then the words tumbled out, a little stilted, trying hard to remember exactly what she had heard. *"Over the bridge and into the field the buttercups danced in the breeze. I see you and you are waiting for me. Yellow faces, smiling up at the sun and my sweet one, I can see you are smiling too. I am coming."* Nurse Rose opened her eyes and saw eyes filled with tears looking back at her. "As I said before we thought that she was reciting a poem".

Caris gently spoke, "Is that all she said, was there anything else?"

"After she spoke, she learnt forward, we thought she was going to fall and we went to stop her but then she put her hands out like this and opened her eyes, lifting her head to the ceiling". Nurse Rose demonstrated her arms stretched out to each side of her "and she repeated, almost in a whisper, I am coming".

Nurse Rose looked at Sister Nora and was rewarded with a smile, "Will that be all Sister; I am late for shift?"

"Thank you, Nurse Rose, run along dear. There, what did I tell you Dr Harvey, just a bit of nonsense. In my experience, it does happen sometimes. Something from a memory pops into a troubled mind and the patient relives it. So very sad!"

They walked quietly into the ward. Sister Nora had no idea of the consequences or importance of Francesca's words but Caris did. She had heard Fran speak of buttercups before in her room and each time she had sounded at peace and Robbie remembered Francesca swirling round in the field full of buttercups below their house with Emily and Katie, their arms stretched out and faces smiling up at the sun. He remembered the laughter as they swung round and round free and happy; their titian curls flying around them like a mantel of fire. This was the memory that would stay with him, not the Francesca who lay, pale and still, the constant bleep of the monitor being the only noise. Fran looked peaceful, as if in a deep sleep and had been washed and put into a hospital nightdress, which Robbie knew that Fran would have hated, and her curls had been brushed and lay around her on the white pillow. Robbie picked up her limp hand, his face ashen.

"Oh my beautiful Bean, wake up and talk to me," but his request was futile. Clinically he knew what the monitors were telling him, but emotionally he wasn't ready to say goodbye. Caris looked at his face, tears pouring down his cheeks and anguish etched his eyes.

"Robbie", Caris whispered, "It doesn't seem right that I am here." Robbie looked up and spoke, "Caris, I don't want to do this alone, but I would appreciate if you could do something for me, if you don't mind?"

"Of course."

Robbie took a crumpled piece of paper out of his wallet and passed it to Caris. She opened it up and looked at the two telephone numbers written on it. She looked up quizzically, waiting further instruction.

"Please will you ring these numbers and all you need to say is that it is time". Caris went to speak but Robbie continued. "The code is for

New York and so it will be about 3 am but I want you to keep trying until you get at least one of them. Once you make contact, please say that Robbie Harvey has asked you to ring and that it is time. It's a sort of code you see. Can you do this for me?"

"Yes, Robbie but who are these people, do I get a name?"

"You don't need a name. They will know what it is about. Please there is no time to ask questions, but I need you to do this for me and soon."

Caris agreed and left the room. She would go to her office at the back of the hospital and ring from there. Somehow these people were part of this story and it seemed that even after all Robbie had said, there were still secrets untold.

CHAPTER 41

THE TIME IS NOW?

2019

It had taken an hour to get through and eventually it was a sleepy American female voice that answered. Caris relayed Robbie's message exactly as she had been asked and in reply the voice simply said thank you and hung up. Caris stared at the receiver confused and then tried the second number but although she tried several times, she was unable to get through and hoped that whoever she had spoken too, would pass on the message.

Returning to the ward she found Robbie still holding Fran's hand but now he was resting back in the chair, his eyes closed. She thought him sleeping but as she approached his eyes flicked open and he smiled. "Did you make contact? Did you say that it was time?"

Caris said that she did, and that she had spoken with a woman but that the man wasn't available. Robbie nodded his head and then whispered something to the sleeping Fran.

A nurse bustled in and did her observations on Francesca and then asked if they would like a cup of tea. Both tired but not able to sleep they said yes, and the nurse left the room.

"I know you told me not to ask, but who are these people? It seems there are still secrets that you have kept from me. Why is that?"

Robbie looked up at her, and then at Francesca, lying so peacefully. He placed Fran's hand back on the bed and leant forward, rubbing his hands across his face as he spoke.… "Because I can't. It's not that I don't trust you, I do, explicitly, but a long time ago a promise was made to protect Fran and I was made the keeper of that promise. I held the key, metaphorically speaking, that kept her safe, locked away until needed You, on my behalf, unlocked it. I only hope that I haven't left it too late".

"Let me understand this; a promise was made to protect Francesca and now a code has been given that unlocks this promise and then what......?" Caris looked puzzled.

"Then they will come. Fran is failing fast and........."

Caris interrupted "and they need to say their goodbyes."

"That the gist of it, yes." Caris thought about what she had heard. Walking around the bed and pulling a chair up close to Robbie, she sat, their knees touching, and picking up his big hands in hers, spoke quietly," Robbie what the hell happened? You say you will never forgive yourself and that it was your fault the accident occurred but how can you blame yourself for all this?" She indicated the sleeping Fran and turned to Robbie, imploring him to speak again.

"I told you that I allowed Vanessa to behave in the way she did to protect Francesca, and how keeping her occupied kept her away from Francesca and Emily."

"Yes". Caris replied quietly.

"Well, Vanessa took great delight in telling me of Mary's visit. I had been so out of it that I hadn't heard Mary calling. Vanessa told me of her performance at the window that had made Mary flee. With glee she related Mary's retreat and saw the fear in my eyes, and she knew what

I was thinking. May then visited chanting three blind mice over and over, skipping around the room, until I begged her to stop."

"Three blind mice? What did that signify" Caris asked. Robbie smiled coldly, his face struggling with emotion. "Three blind mice, three blind mice, see how they run, see how they run, they all ran after the farmer's wife who cut...."

"Oh god Robbie! Mary would have gone home and told her daughter and husband of the events that she'd seen.........three of them would have run back to the house....wouldn't they!" And then as if the realism kicked home, Caris whispered the next part, almost to herself, "*Who cut of their tails with a carving knife*..........she wanted to kill them, didn't she! Oh my God!"

"yes, possibly, but I believe it relates to Fran and our children, 1 2 3 or at least make them suffer. She often talked of a life without Fran and her children and in a way she got exactly what she asked for."

"Did Mary and Joe return?"

"No, but Fran did and at 9 month's pregnant she didn't stand a chance and walked right into Vanessa's trap." Robbie voice cracked as if reliving that fateful day "It was the last time I saw her before the accident!" He put his face into his hands and to Caris's horror he sobbed; great deep demanding sobs, that wrenched at his body, his shoulders heaving. Turning to Francesca he picked her hand and held it to him, "I am so sorry Bean. I did it to protect you, you know I did. I have tried to tell you for years, about what happened, but you wouldn't let me in......I love you my beautiful girl and I am so sorry!"

Caris felt sick. She couldn't leave him like this, but she felt like an intruder. "Can I get you anything Robbie?" There was no reply, his head bowed, tears still flowed, pain etched across his face. Eventually he looked up "Sorry Caris. I need to get out of here for a bit."

They stood and walked together to the nurses station. "Dr Harvey is just popping out. Please page him, should there be any change or concern," Caris reported to the nurse working the shift. The nurse looked up warmly, "Of course," and watched as they walked off the ward. Shaking her head, she carried on writing her notes. There had been so many rumours about Dr Harvey and Francesca Taylor over the years. It was good to see him with another woman, god knows how many women had tried before, but he had always refrained. Dr. Harvey was a gentleman, not like some of the others, to both patients and staff and as far as she was concerned that made him a good sort. There was something about him, however, that no one could ever put their finger on; a sadness that seemed to engulf him, poor man. A bell rang and she jumped up to answer it, her train of thought gone.

They walked in silence, the air was damp and cold, but they didn't seem to notice. The old part of the hospital, on the other side of the car park was now the nurses home and staff recreation centre. It was linked by an overhead enclosed overpass from the main hospital, which was used as a shortcut by many. Once outside they walked over the little stone bridge taking them over a trickling brook, which given the time of year and the amount of rain, was quite full. Robbie hadn't spoken since they left the ward, and it was only now as they walked over the bridge, did he speak again. "Fran used to meet me here for lunch. I would see her from up there", he pointed to the overpass "You couldn't miss her. Her hair would shine in the sunshine, but it was the way she greeted people, her huge smile and her ability to be at ease with everyone." A smile lingered as he remembered. "I think that was the hardest loss of all. I never saw that smile again, her carefree attitude gone and in its place a withdrawn shell of a woman. She went through the motions of living but the person I knew had died long before. I was never sure if she knew me as Robbie, her lover and friend or Robbie who cared for her. Twenty-three years of missed opportunities.

I never knew what she was thinking about, but sometimes she would suddenly remember something from the past and we would talk about it but by the next day it was forgotten, part of having a head injury I suppose. It hit Mary and Joe really hard, well the whole thing did really. I don't think Mary ever got over the tragedy and there was a sadness that affected the whole family. When Fran went back to work, it was the only time I saw glimpses of the Fran I knew, but fleeting memories had begun to come back, which, had become more frequent, which is why I involved you again. Sadly every time there seemed any grasp of reality it was accompanied by a fit, each time getting worse. It was as if her brain didn't want her to remember and fought any chance of normality."

They had reached the old wooden bench at the top of the hill, it was illuminated by a street-light and they sat looking down on the town below..."And now, I think she has given up trying. I would give anything to see those green eyes twinkle and her wide smile again."

Caris linked her arm through his and shivered, it was damp and getting colder. She leant her head on his arm and knew that going forward Robbie would need her support to get over this tragedy. She reasoned that whatever happened they would be indefinitely linked, and that it would take many years to resolve this mess, if at all. The sound of Robbie's voice pulled her out of her revelry as he continued speaking. His words hanging in the air, suspended by the night mist....

"What Fran believed she saw would have caused anyone to doubt their relationship, but it was the aftermath that caused the irreparable damage............."

1996

All night Fran laid in her bed thinking of how she could get back to her house. It was out of the question asking her parents to take her, she had already tried over dinner but the argument that ensued wasn't worth the battle. She thought of asking her father when they were alone but on this occasion, he had sided with her mother. She wondered if she could drive herself, but realistically didn't think she couldn't safely fit behind the wheel, and more importantly she had a feeling that she could be in early labour and couldn't risk it. She concluded that there was no way she would make it alone and felt frustrated and frightened. The thought that she didn't know what was happening with Robbie made her feel sick and knew in her gut that something was wrong. She had to find him if it was the last thing she would do.

When Tom arrived in the morning, it seemed that any effort to leave was thwarted. He told her that Katie had wanted to see her auntie before the new baby came, and anyway he hadn't seen her for a while. It was such a shame that Emily was with her father and Nancy would have come too but she hadn't been feeling too well.

They all must have thought her stupid, for as Tom arrived both her parents suddenly had something to do down in the town and was left talking about nothing with Tom. Fran knew she had to think of something and although she was glad to see her brother, she wasn't sure how much he knew.

Whilst Katie played with Emily's jigsaws, she made coffee in the kitchen; it was now or never, she had to speak with Tom. She didn't even hear what Tom was saying about his new job and how Nancy was doing in hers. It wasn't until she suddenly heard Tom yell her name that she realised she was pouring milk over the side of the cup onto the benchtop, it was clear that she was not acting herself at all.

"What the hell is up with you Franny?" Tom asked, "Here". Grabbing a cloth he picked up the cup and mopped up the mess. "Mum said you were worried about Robbie, but she didn't elaborate, what was going on?"

"Tom, something *is* wrong. For some reason he cannot contact me and if he is in the house then I need to know for myself. This baby is coming, and Robbie wouldn't have abandoned me! Something has stopped him coming to me and that is not right at all. He is not in the hospital and he is not here so something or someone is stopping him.

Tom I need you help?" As Francesca spoke, she was aware that her voice had crescendoed, and tears poured down her face.

"Why is Auntie Fran crying, daddy?" Katie's concerned face looked around the door and ran into Fran's arms, "Please don't cry Auntie Fran, daddy will make it better!" Fran stroked her hair, so like Emily's, and looking over her red curls she addressed Tom, "Will you? Will you help me?"

"Mum said we were to stay here, and anyway they will back soon. I am sorry Fran! Even if I could, I need to get Katie home as Nancy will be worried?"

"But Tom, all I am asking is to go to my house. I need to pick some things up for the hospital and I won't rest until I see for myself that Robbie isn't there. Please, I am begging you, we will be back before mum and dad gets home?"

Tom had never been able to say no to Fran and although he was struggling with his own conscience, he could see how worried his sister was. He argued with himself what was the harm in checking the house and picking up some stuff, but something told him that this was all sorts of wrong. Fran's voice cut through his thoughts, "What would you do if it were Nancy who disappeared? Would you just sit there and wait for her to come home? You wouldn't, you would look for her, so please Tom, please help me!"

"Katie will have to come too, Fran. I can't leave her here on her own and we will have to wait in the car, whilst you go inside. If you are okay with that then we can go."

"Thank you, thank you so much." Fran flung her arms around her brother. Gruffly, he replied, "Well if we are to get back before mum and dad, then we must leave now. Come on!"

Katie was not been pleased that she had left Emily's jigsaw unfinished and consequently had cried and whined the entire time. At six years of age Katie could be rather tenacious at times, and her red hair met her temper. Luckily she could be easily placated and Tom knew it wouldn't be long before his daughter would be giggling again. He reflected that perhaps she had picked up on the tension between brother and sister, she was pretty perceptive like that and Fran hadn't spoken since they left the house. Looking across he saw her head leant against the window, and her anxiety obvious. As they drew near, Fran directed him to to park further up the road, hidden by the trees. He had full view of the house but the occupants, if any, could not see the old Volvo estate parked under the large Oak tree, whose roots twisted and gnarled uplifted the road making it hard to walk on the broken paving stones. The rain, which had threatened, was now gently falling and it was cold and grey. On arrival, Tom had climbed into the back of the car to comfort Katie and was now reading her a book. If he had questioned why there was a need to park so far from the house, he didn't say. One look at Fran's determined face told him that he should leave well alone, but it didn't stop him feeling uneasy. He had rested his arm on hers as they both got out of the car and their eyes interlocked but still he said nothing. Fran looked back before opening the door to the cottage; their heads were bowed over the book and neither looked up. Pushing her key into the door it swung open, which was odd. Had someone left it open on purpose, waiting for her. Tentatively she walked into her hallway; it occurred to her that she was frightened of her own home, which she scolded herself, was ridiculous.

"Robbie! Robbie are you here?" She frantically called as she walked through the house. The heating was on and the house felt as warm and cosy as when she had left it. Coats hanging on the peg, Emily's boots by the backdoor mat looking small next to Robbie's' and letters on the hall table. Someone had been here and if Robbie's boots were at the back door then so was he. As she continued walking quietly up the hall, her eyes fell on the brown leather doctor bag that Robbie took everywhere with him, even when not on duty. "Robbie where are you?" she muttered to herself. A sudden twinge pulled her upright, "Not yet little one, just wait, please, just hang on in there."

With one hand on the banister and one foot on the bottom stair she looked up, the lights were not on and it was dark, and yet she felt that there was someone up there watching her. "Robbie?" she whispered, walking carefully up the few stairs to the top floor. It had always felt welcoming, with its warm colours but today, it felt sinister and not like her home at all. "Robbie are you up here?" A chink of light from under her bedroom door caught her eye and she turned towards door, heart thumping against her chest. Then she heard it, a moan and then squeak of bed springs, followed by heavy breathing, and the squeak of the springs again, now rhythmically moving. There was no mistaking the noise, she knew it well. The second moan was drawn out, it was a woman's voice that she heard followed by a man's. Fran stood just outside the door, barely breathing for fear of being discovered. There was no mistaking the sound of love making, nor that of Robbie's voice and white anger coursed her body. She winced, as once again her body contracted and panting stood against the small rail at the top of the landing until it passed. She heard the creak of the bed as one of them moved and still she stood there, wanting but not wanting to see the depravity of the situation beyond. Her mind tried to make sense of what she was hearing and why it was happening. They had been so happy and even Richard understood why they needed to be together. Robbie was so excited about having another child and this time being known as it's father, and they had talked about it endlessly. She reasoned that she had been difficult over the last few months, but surely that wasn't enough to push him into the arms of another woman, was it? Reality told her, no! He loved her, and he would never have missed shifts at the hospital but at the same time, the little voice answering back told her that just maybe it was a last fling before the baby came. She argued with herself that this wasn't possible, Robbie just wasn't like that. Robbie had been so tender and concerned when she was ill in hospital and was overly protected when it came to her and Emily's safety. He had said that there was no end to Vanessa's cruelty and that he had been worried about them. Perhaps it had all been an act, giving him the excuse to be with someone else, after all hadn't she and Robbie done that to Richard. She looked at her watch, time was ticking, and she needed to know one why another, Tom was waiting for her and her parents would be home soon. With her heart racing she pushed open the door, another painful twinge made her gasp out loudly, and the two naked forms on her bed turned to look at her.

"Robbie!" Fran screamed into the silence. Her anger unabated, ignoring the continual bands of pain.

"Robbie, how could you what are you doing?"

Vanessa climbed off the bed, completely naked, leaving Robbie staring at Fran, the fear in his eyes.

"I wondered how long it would be before you came crawling back from under your stone Francesca Taylor. But you are a bit too late….and life goes on!" Fran watched as Vanessa turned towards Robbie, smiling, and watched as Robbie sunk back into the pillow.

"Robbie, look at me!"

Like a viper Vanessa's head flipped around and she hissed "You tried before to entice Robbie back by providing him with a bastard and now looking at your current state you are trying again with bastard number two!" She laughed at her own joke; a cold chilling sound that ran like ice down Francesca's spine.

"Shut up Vanessa! Robbie, please tell me what is happening here?"

Robbie stared at her and attempted to sit up. "Fran I……" The drugs in his system prevented ongoing speech and he fell back on the pillows again.

"As you can see, sweetie, he is not interested in you, but then can you blame him?" Vanessa ran her hands down her lithe body, leaving her hands resting on her hips. "I ask you, girl to girl who would you rather make love too, me or you? When you think about it, I am indeed his wife, unlike you and it is me he wants to be with. So run along and leave us alone."

Fran stared at the atrocity before her and opened her mouth to speak, but instead she moaned and bent over doubled with pain. Holding her stomach she became breathless.

Finding his voice, Robbie shakily spoke, "For god sake!"

"I know Robbie babe, she's annoyingly dramatic. If I were you Franny, I would turn tail and go before you make a fool of yourself." Vanessa laughed heartlessly.

Fran gripped the door, searing pain coursed through her and beads of sweat formed on her forehead. Through gritted teeth she spoke, slowly and deliberately, "I don't believe this, you and Robbie. Vanessa you live in a fabricated world and if you believe Robbie loves you, I feel sorry for you, because he loves me. Whatever you have done to keep him, hear my words......." Another surge of pain caught her breath and she found it difficult to concentrate, leaning against the door, she pulled her head up and continued...... "You will never wholly have Robbie. I have one thing that you don't have and that is his children...For that reason......" Fran was now panting, struggling through every word... "He will never be yours; he will always be tied to me."

Vanessa had slipped a gown over her and was holding it around her, she had moved to the other side of the bed, closer to Robbie, which gave Fran full view of Robbie's naked body. He did not attempt to leave the bed, his eyes pleaded at her but no words came.

"Robbie, say something, your baby is on it's way, and it needs a father........I can't do this without you. I don't care what you have done, we can talk about it later. Whatever that bitch did to you, we can get over it, but Robbie, I need you. We need you now!" Robbie could hear how desperate she was but he seemed paralysed and found it difficult to form the words. As much as he tried, he could only get single words out, which made little or no sense. They were interrupted by a child's voice which permeated the room and Fran stared at Vanessa, or what looked like Vanessa for she was now sitting cross legged on the bed, plucking at the bedspread... she was staring back at Fran, observing her with her head on the side.... "Have you come to play?" The child like voice was shrill with none of the sweet innocence of a child. "You can if you want to... we like games don't we Uncle Robbie I....but you have your clothes on, take them off... take them off .....take them off"! Her childlike voice crescendoed in her demands as she bounced on the bed and when she got no response- she climbed off, slipped off her gown, and climbed into bed curled into Robbie, suckling her thumb. "Play with me, Uncle Robbie, you know what I like!"

"Fran" croaked Robbie, "Leave!"......... "Now!"

"Don't do this Robbie, I need you".

Fran watched as the child like Vanessa crawled across Robbie, sitting across him, she turned her head and smiled, a satisfied cat-like smile. Pain coursed through Fran's body and she groaned... Again Robbie, spoke, tears welling in his eyes.. "For God sake go! I can't.....". His words stumbled out with difficulty, in one long breath......Fran hesitated, she was seriously in pain now. The cutting voice of Vanessa met her indecision as to whether she should leave or not; the childlike voice replaced with a cold calculation tone, "It's obvious that he chose me not you. If I were you I would go before you deliver that bastard on my floor."

With tears streaming down her face and her hands clutching her stomach, she turned to go and yet something stopped her. She turned slowly, "You may think that you have won, but when this baby is delivered, Robbie's baby, I will have achieved something, not once but twice, that you so far have not achieved. I therefore, have won, don't you think?" The silence was palpable as their eyes met. Gaining strength, Fran continued, "Robbie and I will always have a connection, as will Richard and I. You Vanessa will be left with nothing!" With that she turned, slammed the door and stumbled down the stairs, missing the bottom one she slammed into the wall. Again a wave of pain caught her, taking her breath away. Her wail echoed simultaneously with Vanessa's screams of anger from above; the sounds absorbed into the walls of the house.

Fran stepped out of the house and staggered slowly up the hill, rain hitting her face. She found it difficult to walk and clutching her stomach she pushed forward. From the car, Tom saw his sisters body bend over and stagger forward. He told Katie to stay in the car and got out, running towards her. Fran continued onwards, oblivious of Tom's impending presence and with every step more contractions. She tripped on the root up lifted pavement and as she fell forward, Tom's big arms engulfed her, holding onto her keeping her safe. Fran's body sagged into his and great gut wrenching sobs, muffled into his jacket, seemed uncontrollable. "I've got you! I have got you Franny".

"What's Auntie Fran, crying for"? Tom looked over the top of Fran's head to see Katie looking up. "I told you to stay in the car munchkin......" A scream from Fran, stopped him mid sentence and feeling her hands gripping his shoulders in a vice like hold, meant only one thing, "Fran?" Another contraction, told him the answer and they turned towards the car, Fran, moaning with every step. "Katie, you need to be a big girl and sit in the front seat with daddy, so that Auntie Fran can lay down on the back seat. Is that okay with you?"

Katie's huge blue eyes looked up her daddy, "Mummy won't let me sit at the front, because it's too dangerous."

"I know but just for this once. Like a big girl. It will be our secret ok?" Katie giggled, "Okay daddy."

From the bedroom window, Vanessa's eyes narrowed. She was in a foul mood, Fran's words whirled around in her head. *"Robbie and I will always have a connection, as will Richard and I. You Vanessa will be left with nothing!"*

She slammed her hand against the glass and resting her head against the window, she saw what she thought was Richard and Emily, helping Francesca into the car.

"I spy with my little eye something beginning with three!" Chuckling to herself, she looked over at Robbie. She hadn't wanted to hurt him, but he had been difficult after Fran left and it had been necessary to ease his pain. He was so beautiful and given time he would think her beautiful again. He would understand why he had to be tied to the bed, and why she had given him just that bit more to calm him down. Looking back through the window, she formulated a plan. Robbie wouldn't need to go anywhere if there was nothing for him to go to. 1, 2, and baby makes 3 all gone in one foul swoop. She got dressed, picked up her car keys and got into her car. She waited till Richard's car drove past the house and reversed out of the driveway. Nothing had got in her way before, and this time was no different. Revving her engine she sped up to follow.

CHAPTER 42

REVENGE AND TRAGEDY

1996

2019

Caris shivered and in the silence looked at a spider web jewelled with droplets of water, struggling not to fall. The spider intricately continued to add to the web and Caris felt it was a parody of how she was feeling at that moment. The last few weeks were a confusion of thoughts; two steps forward and one step back, intricately picking through the pieces of information relayed to her, but she knew that Robbie needed her and as she watched him staring into the distance, lost in the past and not really conscious of his surroundings, she leant against his arm to gently remind him that she was there. He turned and looking at her sadly, as he started to speak again....

"What Fran believed she saw would have caused anyone to doubt their relationship, but it was the aftermath that caused the irreparable damage............." He stopped as his mind drifted, it was so long ago, but the pain still haunted him. He looked at Caris sitting next to him, her hands resting in her lap willing him to continue. Somehow he felt connected to her, more than he had with anyone else in the last twenty-three years and he knew he owed her an explanation, but he wasn't sure if he had the strength to relive it again. He thought of Francesca lying in the hospital, she had gone through so much and maybe he owed it to her to finish their story; put the past to rest, but then maybe the whole dam thing should just end with her. He didn't know. He remembered the life they had shared; their laughter and their love and the way that they had talked about their future, but the beautiful imagery of their lives died in the carnage on that cold January day, when she was dragged from the wreckage leaving the Fran he knew behind.

Now, as she fought to keep alive, was it wrong for him to wish an end to her struggle and let her slip into eternal sleep. He didn't know and did he have the right to make that decision when she, herself, to this day did not remember who he was.

Robbie stood up and dug his hands into his pocket and with his back to Caris he related the events that had led up to Fran's discovery of Vanessa's depravity. He was scared that if he turned around he would see the horror and revulsion on Caris's face and remained looking out over the city before him. "Fran thought the worse of course, but then wouldn't anyone! I was so drugged that even though I knew what was happening, which was so awful and wrong, I couldn't have stopped Vanessa. You have to understand, it was the only way I could save Francesca. I tried to warn her, but my words came out all wrong. I just couldn't tell her what I wanted to say and then she left! What was worse was that I knew Fran was in labour, but I couldn't help her! I tried, I bloody tried but the only thing I could do to save her, and our baby was to tell her to leave, to get out and go!" Robbie dropped to his knees, sobbing loudly, with his head in his hands. "I should have done more!"

Caris sat in shock. In all the years that she had been a psychiatrist she had never heard of a story like this. Vanessa's behaviour was an atrocity and Robbie's sacrifice to save Francesca showed his deep love for her. Textbook theory would say that Robbie developed a form of Stockholm syndrome, and although he had been aware of his surroundings most of the time, his survival was due to a developed connection to his abuser and captor, which, then overtook his reality. She could see clearly that professionally Robbie would need extensive help going forward, but for the now she wanted to tell Robbie that she understood; that it didn't matter what had happened and that they could get through it. She called out his name, but he didn't turn, and he didn't reply; so absorbed within his pain that that she couldn't reach him. Forgetting the cold Caris stood and stamped her feet to get the feeling back. She watched Robbie wrestling with a torrid of emotions and as she walked towards him he let out a deep primal roar, releasing years of pent-up pain. She wanted to run to him and say it would be okay, but her gut told her to stay until he turned and came back to her.

Eventually he stood, ran his fingers through his hair and turned, seeing Caris waiting for him. He walked into her open arms crying until there were no more tears to give.

They didn't notice the rain; clothes and hair soaked, but when Robbie's pager went off they knew Fran was in trouble. It was as if she knew and was calling for him. Silence once again ensued as they walked back to the hospital, both deep in contemplative thought.

As they walked into the ward, the machines showed Fran was in distress and when Robbie consulted with the on-call doctor he was informed that she had had several ongoing fits but the last had caused cardiac arrhythmias and the tremors were not settling. It seemed that Fran was still fighting but she had little, or no energy left, and her time was limited.

They sat watching the monitors, the droplets of liquid of the intravenous drip and the rustle of the sheets as Francesca Taylor's body twitched, her life fading from them.

The when, and how seemed to have been forgotten and hours went by as they alternated sleep with drinking coffee; both lost in their own thoughts. As the light came through the window, they were asked to leave the ward whilst the nurse caring for Fran came in to wash her.

Alone in the day room, it seemed a stark contrast to the noise of the ward. There were no noisy monitors and busy nurses to distract them. Left by themselves, Caris finally found the courage to speak, "I know it is difficult, but this story needs to be told. It is the only way that there can ever be closure". He stared at her and shook his head… "Robbie, I think Fran is waiting for you to close this chapter. It seems to me that until you do, she can't leave". Robbie looked out of the window at the dull rainy day and shivered. "If you are right, then we don't have too long. To be truthful I am unsure what was reality or a confused version of reality and can only tell you what I was told."

A young nurse entered the room and interrupted further discussion, "Sorry to interrupt, Dr Harvey, but Mrs. Taylor is ready for you. She has been moved to a private room on the same floor, room 6."

"Thank you nurse."

"If you would like to follow me, I will take you, would you like a tea or coffee?"

"Coffee would be great and thank you. Has there been any change?"

"She is more settled than through the night, but then again the morphine would have kicked in. At least it seems there are no further fits, which is a blessing".

They followed the nurse into a small but comfortable room and sat either side of the bed. Francesca lay still and pale, her beautiful hair brushed until it shone. She looked at peace in her own world, a smile playing on her lips. Robbie looked at her and Caris could see how much he still loved her. Tears shone in his eyes as he held her limp hand. So many years of lost affection and dreams and her heart ached for them both.

1996

When Mary and Joe got home from the police station they found the house empty. It was strange that there was no note from Tom and hoped that Francesca was okay. Joe assured her that Tom would have left a message if Fran had gone into labour and put the kettle on. It was a cold day, and they were soon sitting in front of the fire with their mugs of tea. Outside, the wind howled, and it had begun to snow with the roads becoming treacherous with black ice.

It had been an exhausting exercise with statements having to be written. Much to Mary's disgust instead of being able to go back to the cottage with the police, they were told to stay home, and an investigation would take place only if there was enough admissible evidence to concern them. Sitting in front of the fire relating the events of the morning, Mary had to admit, that it had only been a hunch, a gut feeling, that Robbie was in danger and that her story had seemed rather far-fetched, like something from a movie, but she felt that the policewoman had been rather patronising, "It wasn't even written down!" she exclaimed.

Joe patiently listened again and quietly explained for the umpteenth time that as there was no missing persons' report they were not about to break down the door to search at this stage.

Even the mention of the naked lady in the window didn't raise an eyebrow and it was obvious to Mary that they didn't believe her. It was only when they asked if Robbie was happy in the home did Mary explode and it took quite a while to calm her down.

Joe then took control and explained in his quiet calm way, without any of his wife's emotional outbursts, about Sarah who wasn't really Sarah and gave as much of the back story that he knew. Patiently the police listened but it was only when the name Vanessa Brookes was mentioned was any interest shown. The policewoman had left the room and returned sometime later with a gentleman in a suit, holding a manilla file.

"You could have blown me down with a feather"! Mary exclaimed, "All those photos of that ……..well of Vanessa. That made them sit up and listen didn't it Joe. Wait until I tell Francesca!" Joe patiently sipped his tea, he loved his wife dearly, her passion and imagination, however, could be exhausting.

The detective asked if the lady in the picture resembled the lady in the window and Mary said that it did but that her hair wasn't dark, it was blonde. He then thanked them and informed them that someone may be in touch with them later that day but for now they were to leave the investigation to the police and go home. Mary's protestations went unheard, and they were ushered out.

"I wonder where Tom is. Should I give Nancy a call, perhaps they popped home to her?"

"Leave it love, we have only been home a short while, perhaps they have gone for a drive, after all Fran has been cooped up here since coming out of hospital and she can be very persuasive."

"You're right, Joe. Honestly all this worry has got me absolutely in a tizzy and my nerves are jangling. Truth be known though my gut is never wrong, and something is a foot I can feel it. It's like an ominous thunder cloud ready to burst, you see if it's not!"

Joe smiled affectionately and opened the newspaper to read more bad news, it was never any different these days. Sometime later, he looked up and saw that Mary has fallen asleep, cup in hand. He gently removed it and smiled down at her. "Poor love," he murmured. He got up and switched the light on, it had got quite dark and outside the snowstorm had changed to rain and the sky was grey. Dirty slush had settled on the roads and just looking at it made Joe feel cold. He was only too happy to return to his seat by the fire and soon he too fell asleep.

They were awoken by a pounding on the door. "Tom must have forgotten his house key, Joe, go let them in and I will put the kettle on." Joe got up and looked at his watch, they had been asleep for over an hour, and he felt groggy. Opening the door, expecting to see Tom and Fran, stood a policeman and woman. Joe remembered thinking that they couldn't have been older than Tom, probably younger and ushered them in, out of the cold.

They followed Joe down to the kitchen where Mary was making tea. "Hello Tom, love, where have you been, we were getting worried?" She was in the pantry when they entered and turned looking confused. "Oh sorry officers. I thought it was my son coming home, goodness knows where they all are, I am beginning to get worried, with all that awful weather. Have you come about the investigation?"

The police officers looked awkwardly at the older couple staring expectantly at them. The male constable cleared his throat.

"Unfortunately, no. There has been an accident!"

"Oh dear god, what has happened, is it Tom? Is he okay? Francesca is due to have a baby any day now, and little Katie is with them."

"Mrs. Jacobs, please sit down. The accident happened at the entrance of the roundabout …"

"I have always said that roundabout is dangerous, haven't I Joe!" Joe stood still behind Mary who had now sunk into a chair and patted her shoulders.

"I am afraid we have some bad news." The policewoman moved around and sat in the chair opposite to Mary. Later Mary remembered the practiced concern on the young officer's face and wondered why someone as pretty as that would want to do such an awful job but in the now, she listened with no comprehension of what was going on.

Mary felt Joe's fingers tighten on her shoulder as both heard the words relayed to them. Joe held his breath and didn't release it until he turned away, grief stricken and a broken man. Mary just sat there. The policewoman had got up and made them tea, as she had been told to do. Tea was good for shock, she had been told in her training but the look on the mother's face, was too much and she herself fought back tears. She heard her colleague explaining that the male occupant driving didn't stand a chance and had died on impact. The child was in St Thomas and was not in a good way, she had been sitting in the front you see, and her mother has been notified.

"And my daughter, Fran?" Mary whispered, not wanting to hear but needing to.

"Mrs. Jacobs, Fran was thrown forward and multiple head and body injuries and is on the operating table now. I am so sorry."

"The baby, is the baby ……?"

"We don't know sorry.".

Mary jumped up from her seat and without speaking, walked out into the hall. She brought back Joe's coat and was putting hers on. "Don't just stand there Joe, we need to go. We need to go now!"

"I think, Mr. and Mrs. Jacobs, it would be much safer if we drove you there, it will be much quicker, and the roads are ….." realising too late what she was about to say the young policewoman gently finished by reiterating that it would be safer. She noted that her colleague was speaking into the two-way radio and was nodding with his back to them.

He hadn't signed up for this. He wanted to catch criminals and put them in lock up, not tell parents that half their family was gone. Turning he mustered up the courage to talk and taking a deep breath continued, "I am sorry but the child…….." he looked at the pain filled eyes of both Mary and Joe, willing him to say something positive…. "The child didn't make it; she didn't regain consciousness. I am so sorry."

Mary turned into Joe, sobbing wildly. His face like stone patting her back to comfort her but not really knowing what he was doing. Both officers weren't experienced enough to deal with this amount of tragedy and their comments fell on deaf ears. Suddenly Mary turned to face the police officers her face contorted.

"The child's name is Katie; her name is Katie!" shrieked Mary as she sank back into the chair sobbing wildly.

Nobody spoke as they drove to the hospital to identify their son and grandchild; knowing that they would have to face Nancy and to sit with their daughter who by all accounts may be another statistic. Joe held Mary's hand, looking ahead and not daring to look into his wife's eyes. They still had no idea what had happened to Robbie and now his family, his beautiful family, was fractured. He turned to look at Mary but what he saw was a shell of a woman, everything that she knew, taken from her. Looking through the front window, the rain continued to pour, and the sky was grey with clouds indicating an impending storm and the anger that had been suppressed began to grow. Joe being a mild man, avoided confrontation but now, he wanted to see Vanessa face to face, as he was sure that this was her doing. He vowed that he would not rest until she was punished but then who would listen to him. The police at the police station hadn't and now... and now. Tears coursed down his face and he punched the seat so hard that the police woman asked if he was alright and did he need them to pull over. Even now, he heard himself apologising but then his Mary turned towards him, her face so pale and eyes sunken…..and they cried together trying to come to terms with their impossible grief.

As they left the cottage, Tom drove towards the town, hopping onto the passover that led them down to the M25. The loop road was always congested and with the weather atrocious, it made the journey impossibly slow. It had begun to snow which made visibility difficult, followed by heavy rain. The roads were becoming treacherous and Tom took his time merging into the traffic. He was conscious of cars pushing their way in just to get that extra 5 minutes ahead; the honking cars, which did not help the situation and the tailgaters who felt by closing the gap behind would make things move faster. Thankfully Katie had fallen asleep, which was small mercy and Fran was now quiet too, her earlier hysteria calmed and contractions slower. She had chosen to lay down in the back, as it was more comfortable and mercifully the contractions were too far apart to worry her. Tom hadn't understood much of what she was saying when she reached the car, and for the umpteenth time today, he wished Nancy was here. Looking in the mirror and seeing his sister's tear streaked face, paler than usual, he felt helpless, what did he know about this sort of stuff. He had asked if she had seen Robbie, but her curt reply had put a stop to any further questions. Obviously they had had an argument and he hoped that he would see sense and get to the hospital in time. Tom found Robbie's behaviour out of character, but he didn't dare quiz Fran over it, not now anyway.

Traffic had come too a stand still and Tom looked in the mirror and saw that at last Fran seemed to be sleeping. The panic seemed abated but better safe than sorry. Tom still felt the best place for his sister was in hospital but wish he had taken her to the local hospital and not the city one. Normally only 40 minutes away, this journey was taking much longer. He checked his mirror again and saw that the car behind him barely had time to stop; the driver coming up so quickly that brakes were slammed on and the car skidded to a halt. Tom shook his head and looked over at his sleeping daughter, her face leaning against the window. The car behind honked, the traffic was once again moving. Raising his hand in apology, he took off with the white car behind travelling dangerously close.

The voice on the radio brought him out of his revelry *"On this miserable day let me cheer you up with a song from the 60's.. Build Me Up Buttercup, by the Foundations."* As the music filled the car, Tom chided himself for not concentrating. They were coming up to the big roundabout which divided traffic North and South and he needed his wits about him.

*"I need you
(I need you)
More than anyone, darlin'
You know that I have from the start
So build me up
(Build me up)
Buttercup, don't break my heart
I need you more than anyone, baby
You know that I have from the start
So build me up
(Build me up)
Buttercup, don't break my heart"*

"An oldie but a goodie from our 60's collection. Gotta love those words... Build me up Buttercup" The traffic jingle interrupted the dulcet tones of Tony Haywood, the lunchtime DJ. *"Sorry folks just been informed of a jack-knife lorry on the M25. Wheels went one way and his back end another losing it load over the road; Traffic are telling us of delays, so if you can avoid the area please take another route or better still stay in because the weather isn't getting any easier and it pretty nasty out there. Stay tuned and stay inside".*

Tom groaned and made the decision to turn off at the roundabout instead of attempting to continue. This would lead him back to Little Stockton and he would just have to take Fran to St. Luke's instead. The rain continued to pour, and visibility became worse. Tom swore to himself, what he wouldn't give to have a bowl of Nancy's beef soup, but he gritted his teeth and continued.

From the opposite direction Richard and Emily were having similar problems. They had been diverted twice because of the jack-knifed lorry and were now moving slowly towards the roundabout leading back to Little Stockton. There was nothing to be done but follow the leader which at this moment was at a standstill.

It was slow entering from the South; stop start all the way. As the car in front of Tom, suddenly stopped, Tom had to brake hard throwing Katie and Fran forward. Katie who had been in a deep sleep, woke crying and Fran let out a frightened scream. "It's okay girls, sorry about that!" Tom exclaimed. He tightened his grip on the steering wheel, the tyres were sliding all over the road with the ever worsening rain and the slush left by the snow, there was little traction. Suddenly the car behind slammed into them; once again Tom slammed on the brakes, but the black ice on the road prevented him from stopping and he struggled with keeping the car straight. Katie's tears became loud sobs and Tom could see she was scared. "It's okay Munchkin!"

"Mummy.....I want mummy!" Katie yelled.

"We will be home soon, just keep quiet so daddy can concentrate." Again the car behind slammed into them, shunting them forward into the car in front......the noise of crumpled metal followed by another slam car upon car. "What the......" Tom exclaimed. Fran had sat up and turned to look out of the back window, but the ice freezing on the window had decreased visibility. She managed to rub the glass with her sleeve.... "Tom, it's ....."

"Not now Fran, sit tight I am going to try to get into the other lane and then pull over, I am not sure what's going on here".

"Tom, listen to me" Fran desperately shouted, "It's Vanessa!"

"What! Can you see her?"

"It's the car that was at the cottage......She's trying to kill us!"

"Mummy.....I want mummy!" Katie cried out again.

Tom could hear the fear in his sister's voice and put his hand on Katie's knee. "It's going to be okay. I am going to pull over to the other lane and then got off this roundabout. Just trust me!"

"Well you had better hurry, because this baby is coming, my waters just broke."

Tom looked in the mirror and could see that Fran had laid down again and was panting. At the same time there was the sound of metal upon metal as the car behind, moved into the lane next to them and veered to the right smashing into the passenger side of Tom's car. Katie screamed as she got thrown against the console and then back onto the window. "Daddy" she screamed, her voice terrified, "Daddy I want to go home"!

Tom didn't have time to answer, the white car, smashed again into the side of his car, his wheels could not grip the icy road and he spun out of control into the oncoming traffic, coming in from the north. Around and around he spun, clipping several cars as he passed them. The brakes would not work and there was no traction. Tom pulled as hard as he could on the hand brake, but the front tyres continued to spin sending the back end around. "I'm sorry, I am so sorry! I love you both" shouted Tom as he ploughed into stationary cars waiting to get onto the roundabout from the North. There was a crunch of metal, a screech of brakes and a smell of burning at the impact and then..........`

Hands pulling, sirens screaming, and many voices coming from all directions. "Katie, Katie!" called a female voice. Maybe it was hers, she didn't know. A child screamed from somewhere, and then fell silent. Cold wind and rain swept over her face and then the feeling of being lifted high above the noise, floating above the carnage below. Footsteps running bringing her back down so fast that she gasped. "She's coming back to us", someone said, but she didn't want to go back. She began to float again, and she could see the fields and the buttercups and the little red headed girls dancing, arms outstretched, face upturned, laughing that infectious noise of a child's giggle "I am coming wait for me" she thought she had shouted but it was interrupted again "Resus quick" shouted another voice and she could feel the hands pushing down on her and something being put over her face and pain, so much pain. Red then blue.....red than blue....light then dark; light then dark. It hurt her eyes and she shut them tight. The noise penetrated her senses, seeping into everywhere and everything. She had to go, she couldn't stay here in this awful dark place, she was needed elsewhere, but where; where was it she was meant to go? Hands held her fast again, and then feeling something sharp in her arm she was suddenly falling into a deep dark void. She felt smothered and a feeling of drowning overwhelmed her. Her hands splashed and splashed, was she in the water, was she going to drown? Something was holding her down, she couldn't move. She tried to call out she tried to punch through the water with the instinct to survive taking over but down, down she sank and then nothing, nothing at all.

"She is fitting, another 10mls, quick" came the command.

Richard sitting in traffic, saw the Volvo out of control, and prayed that the poor bastard inside of it would get out of it alive, but he doubted it. He saw the car plough into a stationery van. God help them, he said to himself. He looked at his sleeping daughter and thanked god that they were safe.......

Turning the radio up he waited......it would be a long drive home.

As Tom's car spun out of control, Vanessa, laughed out loud. The fear of losing Robbie was over, he would be hers now with no one to stop her. 1, 2, 3 and baby makes 4. Robbie would need her! He would need comforting and she would be there for him, he would have no one else. Poor soul, losing everything just like that. She would tell him, that she had heard there was an accident on the M25, and she would comfort him as he learnt of his loss. Perhaps, she thought they could return to Australia or maybe LA. No, not LA, she had too many enemies, too many questions. No, they would go back to Australia and start their lives together. Turning the radio up loud, she sang along to the song, not looking back at the carnage caused.

At the roundabout, with the traffic freed up she put her foot on the brake and started to speed towards Little Stockton, a satisfied smile on her face. The rain continued to pour but by now it was so cold that the rain drops had become icicles and visibility was difficult. Turning on the window wipers she could hear the scrape across the glass as ice was removed and with the heat in the car, the window fogged up, making it hard to see. As she turned the corner, the wheels lost their grip as she hit a patch of black ice, the brakes did nothing to help her and gripping the steering wheel, unable to see, the car spun off the road at top speed, mounting the pavement and burst into flames as it hit a power pole.

"This is the six o'clock news with Michael Davenport.

Tragedy occurred at the M25 off ramp at two o'clock this afternoon. A man in his 30s jack knifed across two lanes of traffic into oncoming traffic, causing the death of the driver of a Ford Van. The driver of the other vehicle died on impact and could not be revived at the scene of the accident. One passenger, a 6 year old girl, later died in hospital and the other passenger suffered severe trauma to her face and head with severe abdominal injuries and is now in surgery.

In a separate incident another car leaving the bypass roundabout, spun out of control, and in a dramatic effort to control the car, mounted the pavement and hit a power pole. The vehicle then burst into flames. Thankfully, no pedestrians were present. It is not known who the driver was at this stage.

However, witnesses state that it was this vehicle which drove out of control on the entrance to the roundabout driving dangerously into cars causing the earlier incident. The police are now investigating both tragedies. There will be delays on both the North and the South entrances and exits and detours are in place. Where possible you are advised to take another route or perhaps stay at home, the weather bureau predicts that the weather is only going to get worse.

It is thought that the treacherous weather conditions are the cause of both incidents.

Our thought are with the families at this time.

Now on to other news............"

CHAPTER 43

PIECES OF THE PUZZLE

2019

"Mary and Joe were already at the hospital when I was brought in, and eventually after a week or so they were allowed to see me. With difficulty they told me that Francesca was on life support and that Tom and Katie had died in an accident. They kept asking me why Vanessa had been at the house and in my muddled brain I couldn't comprehend what they were saying. Over and over they asked me the same questions and I could see their anger and pain; their voices raising in desperation. I didn't understand the gravity of the accident, or why they were crying. In the state I was in I didn't understand that half of their family had died. Mary was screaming that she had lost her children because of me, and it wasn't until I heard again that Francesca's life was hanging by a thread that my mind began to clear. I remember asking in confusion if Francesca had given birth to our baby and was the baby all right, only to hear that a little girl had been delivered but had subsequently died, another innocent victim of this whole saga. Mary kept repeating that they were gone, and I just stared at her. She began to hit me, her fists pounding down on me, and I was vaguely aware of Joe pulling her off and of someone running into the room and then they were gone. In the silence one by one the pieces dropped into place, and I threw myself out of bed, screaming that I needed to see Francesca. A policeman had been stationed outside of my door and ran in to restrain me calling for a nurse. Between them they put me back to bed and sedated me. It wasn't until the next day I was able to see Francesca – covered in tubes; machines keeping her alive and her beautiful face disfigured and covered in stitches. I held her hand and spoke to her telling her how sorry I was and how much I loved her but of course there was no response. Even then, hooked up to machines, I felt that I was locked out and I was right. She didn't remember who I was or what I was to her ever again. Over the years, sometimes I thought I saw recognition, but it wasn't Robbie she recognised it was the carer called Robbie, who lived in her house, who advised her and took care of her medical needs. Perhaps my punishment and well deserved. In a way the only saving grace was that her brain damage was such, that she didn't remember the baby or that she had been pregnant. I was too late to bury her but named her Leia. It was a name we had discussed which meant Child of Heaven, I thought it apt."

Caris listened quietly, noticing that he never took his eyes from Francesca's face, holding tightly to her hand and stroking her arm. The sadness creased his face and his voice full of emotion. In their silence the machines continually beeped and when she spoke, she did so in a whisper.

"How did they find you Robbie?"

"The detective who had listened to Mary and Joe's concerns, had been working with Interpol and looking for Vanessa for many years. They broke down the door and found me tied to a bed. In her need to destroy all our lives, she had overdosed me, and I was unconscious and close to death as my heart had gone into cardiac failure. I had to be revived several times but at least I survived. Afterwards there were many times, I wish I had died, I didn't feel I deserved to live, and my punishment was such that everything around me was fractured."

"Oh Robbie I am so sorry and now…. Are you ok?"

"Yes, thankfully no side effects and life, if you can call it that, goes on. I threw myself back into medicine and here we are."

"Bloody hell it is all so difficult to comprehend, but maybe now that your story has finally be shared, you can put it to rest, do you think that is at all possible?"

"One would hope so, but some difficult decisions had to be made to protect all those that remained. I guess, after 23 years any threat to us is over and now I suppose we just have to get on with what's ahead. Over the years, my mind has played tricks on me, seeing Vanessa in many guises and feeling so overwhelmed watching Francesca's struggle that I could have easily given up. But we are okay now aren't we Fran!"

Caris watched as he picked up Fran's hand and kissed it. "Everything is going to be fine,"

It was odd how he spoke as if everything would be okay when they both knew that time was limited. Caris felt that she had some unanswered questions but wasn't sure how much she should push him. After all he had been through she needed to take care how she approached him.

"Robbie, what happened to Mary and Joe? I know I saw them several times at the hospital after the accident happened, but they must be quite old now"?

"Mary never got over her loss. She retired from her job at the school and helped Nancy with her son, as Nancy had to go back to work. Unfortunately after a long illness, she died. Joe still lives around the corner from us, but he is quite frail now and quite forgetful. The loss of half their family took its toll, it did on all of us.

"And did they forgive you"?

"Not a first, but after the funerals for Katie and Tom, eventually the family, or what was left of it, got together to speak with me and decided that there had been too much loss to hate me and that we all should concentrate on Francesca getting better and well. We spoke about what had happened and why it happened. I think they understood and told me it wasn't my fault and in doing so forgave me but none of us ever got over the loss, it was so senseless. Little Katie would have been 29 years old now and like her brother, have a family of her own. The whole mess was down to my misjudgement of the whole situation, and I have enough guilt for all of us". Robbie shook his head and kissed Fran's hand again.

"Life went on and somehow, we all jogged along. The funny thing is Caris, that the kiss we had all that time ago, the one you were so worried about would never have made a difference, as Fran never saw me as anything more than her Carer, she wouldn't have acknowledged it as anything, and it wouldn't have upset her".

"Are you sure about that Robbie, there were some breakthroughs in our consults that beg to differ, and I got the feeling that Fran knew exactly who you were. I suppose we may never know now."

They both looked at Fran, who lay in serenity, a smile on her lips and only the twitching of her body giving away the trauma that she was suffering.

The day ticked on, with little change and as Robbie slept, Caris took her leave. She felt it was in intrusion to continue to sit there. Walking down the stairs to get a coffee, she realised how tired she actually was and yet her mind would not settle.

The jigsaw puzzle was nearly complete, and she concluded, to her frustration, that it might never be finished. Professionally she could see that in order for Robbie to move on he would need help and she was happy just to be there for him but for now she needed space. As a psychiatrist she knew she had gotten to close to the subject matter; she had gone over the professional line and there was no going back. Robbie and Fran's story was so much more than the car accident tragedy that she had been led to believe all those years ago; this was a love story of fundamental extremes. Robbie gave up his freedom to save his partner and child but in doing so had lost everything. It was clear that he had merely existed over the last 23 years and in his self-believed guilt had given up the normality of life. Yet he had existed, he had created a brilliant career for himself and was renown in his field of trauma and head injury. The travesty was that all his success went unnoticed by the very person that meant the most to him. It was so incredibly sad.

Sitting in the hospital cafeteria and sipping her coffee, Caris mulled over all the facts, her thoughts going round and round. She tried to put her psychologist hat on, but she knew she couldn't, she had become to close, and she knew without a doubt that she loved Robbie and would do anything to help him, however long it took. With that realisation she drifted off into a troubled sleep.

The constant bleep of machines crescendoed into a high pitch squeal, waking Robbie from his sleep. Francesca was fitting again; her cardiac monitor showed tachycardia at an alarming rate, and all her vitals were off the chart. Nurses were running and a doctor was giving her medication into her Intravenous infusion. Oxygen was put over her face and concerned faces monitored her. Her body twitched and thrashed about the bed and her eyes, which had been closed, flicked open.

"Robbie, are you there"? Robbie looked down at her in shock and grabbed her outstretched hand. "Yes Fran I am here."

She was looking directly at him, her face swathed in sweat and her hair stuck to her cheek. Robbie gently moved the piece of hair off her face and leant in. Her eyes closed again, "Francesca. Fran, please stay with me" Robbie cried "I love you."

Francesca's eyes flickered and then opened saying "Robbie, is that you, where have you been"?

"I've always been here Bean". The continual movement calmed, and her body became still as her hand tightened oh his.

She repeated the word "Bean" and smiled; her face looking calmer. "I've missed you" Francesca murmured.

"What did you say?" Robbie looked deeply into her eyes, and she smiled at him. Her breathing was laboured; her face hot and her brow furrowed as if trying to think of something. "What is it Fran, try and tell me?" Robbie asked.

Fran struggled with her words but eventually she asked, "Where is Emily, is she coming? What time is it? She is probably still at school or has mum got her?"

Robbie's tears streamed down his cheeks; Francesca had not said Emily's name for 23 years and now she seemed to have returned in the year 1996. She had no knowledge of the here and now and that her beloved mother had passed away some years before. She had no understanding that Tom, her brother and her niece were gone and that their love child never made it. What could he say?

"She is coming, Fran, she will be here soon." He watched as Francesca's eyes closed again and her head nod to one side. "No Fran wake up, don't leave me again!" Her hand clenched his, her grip tightening. Francesca's eyes remained closed, but she continued to talk with Robbie holding on to every word.

"There was an accident wasn't there?"

"Yes that is right but you're here, safe and….." her words interrupted him, they were coming fast tumbling over each other as if she didn't have a moment to waste.

"Was Katie okay, I could hear her call out for her mummy, bless her. I told her she would be alright and to hold on tight but then I didn't hear anymore. There were blue and red lights and Richard told us he loved us…I think…….. but I don't remember anything else".

Robbie listened to her ranting in her breathy voice. If he said it was Tom who died in the wreckage not Richard, it could set her back and the damage could be catastrophic. Her eyes, those emerald pools of green, opened and stared past him as if someone had come in the room, she turned her head as if checking which made him turn, but there was no one there. Tears poured down her cheeks and he gently wiped them away. "Bean you are safe now; I will always be here for you."

She continued to cry, heartbreaking sobs, he stroked her hair and soothed her but when she quietened her eyes searched his face, "It was Tom wasn't it? It wasn't Richard, it was Tom, and, and he didn't make it! I have seen him so many times in my dreams, but then, I have also seen Katie dancing, arms out and laughing looking up to the blue sky, in a field of buttercups. I called her name over and over, but she couldn't hear me. She died too didn't she?" Robbie nodded, not knowing what to say. "I so wanted to be with them, I tried but you wouldn't let me go; You kept me here and they wanted me to go to them. You kept me here like this!" Her voice rose hysterically, and her face twisted into anger as she pulled her hand away from Robbie's.

The treating doctor moved forward with a syringe, "I am sorry Dr Harvey, but she needs sedation before she fits again."

Robbie turned towards the doctor, "Dr Krishinda, please let her talk, she is finding her way back to me. Please don't do this, I won't allow it!"

"Dr Harvey, you know that lucidity can happen after a fit of this degree, but it is short lived. Her vital signs are not good, and this little bit of Morphine will calm her."

"Give me a little more time. What will be, will be but I need this, she needs this, please give us this time together." Hearing his desperate plea the doctor took a step back from the intravenous line. "I will give you a little more time alone but please" he indicated the alarm bell, "press this if there is any sign of fitting."

"Thank you, thank you so much, I will".

Robbie watched as Dr Krishinda spoke to the nurse who had accompanied him. They both left the room, and he was left alone with Francesca.

He looked down at her and watched as she plucked at the sheet. Her eyes stared ahead as if unseeing; had he lost her again? Tentatively he called her name, "Fran can you hear me?" There was no response. He sat down and picked up her hand and linked his fingers through hers "Do you remember when we met", he said, "I nearly ran you over with my motor bike. Gees you went off at me, put me right in my place. I think I fell in love with you right there and then. Later when I saw you at Mary's party in that pretty dress, your beautiful red hair curled, I never wanted to stop dancing with you. Do you remember?" Still nothing. "I couldn't let you go then, and I can't let you go now. I love you Fran, and I always will." Her hands stilled and he kissed them, bringing them up to his cheek. "Come back to me, please." He realised that he was crying, his tears falling unchecked, over their hands. He felt her fingers curl around his and he continued. "I had always intended to come back from Australia when my father died and marry you. I guess I was too late, but we got there in the end didn't we Bean."

He felt her stir and turn her head to look at him, her eyes filled with tears and she whispered, "I remember, I remember it all and I am sorry."

"You're sorry!" Robbie exclaimed, "What have you to be sorry about, I made a right mess of things, but it was to protect you and……". He stopped himself, she didn't need to know about the baby or the loss of it. "All I ever wanted to do was to take care of you, you know that don't you?"

Fran raised her head and whispered her reply, "I know Robbie, I do but…" She faltered and dropped her head back on the pillow. Robbie climbed on the bed and lay next to her and gently put his arm under her to support her. It was the closest he had been for many years without resistance or fear and her head rested easily on his chest. They lay together for some time, until he felt Francesca turn her head up to him. He looked into her beautiful eyes and smoothed her hair from her face, smiling down at her and without looking at the monitor, he knew. Returning his smile with hers, she once again linked her hand in his and in small whispery voice she spoke "I love you Robbie Harvey,

I always have, but it is time to let me go." He didn't reply, or protest because he knew Fran better than anyone and when she made up her mind to do something there was no stopping her. Instead he cried softly into her hair and held her tight as her eyes closed and the last tremors of life passed her over the bridge to her buttercup field and those waiting for her.

CHAPTER 44

REVELATIONS

2019

Caris woke with a start – her coffee cold and still in her hand nestled in her lap. Checking her watch she was amazed to see she had been asleep for an hour. Panicked she jumped up and checked her pager but there had been no calls for her, and she relaxed, sitting back down in the chair. Scanning the cafeteria she began her normal habit of people watching, guessing why they were there whether a patient or visitor.

She focused on an old couple, talking, heads bent in together. The lady smiled as he grabbed her hand and she laughed at something he said. Looking at the walking stick by his side and then at his paler complexion, she wondered if he was the patient and she his visitor. They must be in their late 70's early 80's and she wondered if she would ever find that someone. She thought of herself and Robbie and smiled but then she thought of Robbie and Francesca and the chance that they never had, and her mood changed.

She turned her head acknowledging a colleague and one of the nurses from the ward as they grabbed coffee. Coffee! Yes, she would take one up to Robbie and got out of her seat to join the queue. She liked the noise of the cafeteria it had a life of its own and today was no exception. It was remarkably busy but above the hub bub she heard an American accent asking for "an expresso single shot" and poor

Mrs. Daniels, who ran the coffee shop, replying, "Do what – Do you want a coffee or not"? Another voice joined in the conversation, Caris wasn't sure of this accent – it was English but there was something else hidden underneath it. "Yes mam, a Cappuccino would be lovely, two please.". She watched as a tall distinguished looking man left the queue, followed by…. she couldn't quite see and strained her neck, but her line of sight was interrupted, and she lost sight of her target. The tap on her shoulder put pay to the discovery …… "Caris how are you my dear, I haven't seen you for ages?" Caris turned to see Professor Whitlow, an old friend and colleague. "My goodness! Professor Whitlow, how are you? You are looking well. It has been such a long time; I heard you had retired, what are you doing in our neck of the woods …" The conversation and niceties continued for some time until it was her turn to order. Once ordered she listened to her friend until it was time to say goodbye and with promises to catch up and beverages in each hand she headed up to the ward. As she arrived, she saw the silhouette of a woman, running out of Fran's room into the dark of the corridor, and as she came into the light, Caris saw Francesca running towards her. That couldn't be right and as Caris stepped forward, they collided, sending Caris dropping to the floor with coffee going everywhere. Her assailant dropped to her knees, saying sorry and looking genuinely concerned, and although noticeable upset, assisted in helping Caris up. Looking at the young woman who knelt before her, she found she was undeniably like Francesca, it was uncanny. Not only did she have the same colour of hair, that remarkable titian red, but the same green eyes, which were staring up at her. "I am so sorry, I didn't see you, it's just that we arrived too late." Tears spilled down her cheeks and Caris ushered her to a seat. Caris recognised the accent that she had heard before in the cafeteria. The woman continued "I am so sorry, I am making no sense, but I came to see my mother you see, but we arrived too late. It was the shock that made me run. I didn't know what else to do. Crashing into you wasn't exactly part of the plan".

"That is quite alright" Caris said reassuringly, "I hope you don't mind me asking but are you Francesca's daughter, Emily"?

"I am, my dad and I arrived from Boston today."

"Would that be Richard Taylor"?

"Yes! You seem to know a lot about us."

"I have been working with your father to help Francesca regain her memories. My name is Dr Caris Goodman."

"Do you mean you were working with Robbie Harvey?"

Caris realised her mistake, "Um…. Yes, that would be right."

"It's okay Caris, I know Uncle Robbie is my father, I have known for a long time, but dad is dad and always will be. We got the call to come, and we got here as quickly as we could, but ….. but we were too late." Emily started to cry again. "I mean I haven't seen her since I was a little girl. You probably already know that I wasn't allowed to visit until now. It was just such a shock to find them that way."

"Find them what way, what do you mean? ….. Oh my god"! Even as Caris finished talking, she was up and running down the corridor. Too many thoughts ran through her head; she shouldn't have left him alone. "Robbie?" – she burst through the door to find two nurses washing Francesca. "Excuse me, sorry for interrupting, can you tell me where Dr Harvey is?"

One of the nurses, turned around, "Please leave the room, you shouldn't be here."

Caris tried again, "I am Dr Goodman, I have been treating Mrs. Taylor. Can you tell me where Dr Harvey is please?"

The other nurse spoke, "Sorry doctor! Please excuse my colleague. Dr. Harvey was taken by his friend to the visitors lounge, he wasn't doing too well, what with the situation." She indicated the bed where Francesca lay. Caris looked over towards the bed. "What situation?

What has happened?" Even as she spoke, she noticed the absence of noise and the monitors switched off. The nurse gently took Caris by the arm and escorted her out of the room. "I am so sorry, but Mrs. Taylor, passed away this afternoon. Such a shame that her daughter didn't get to her on time. Mind you, she never visited before now. I believe she lived in America. She found them laying together, you see, wrapped in each other's arms. It took a hell of a lot to get him to move. Who'd of thought. Such a shock!" The nurse sighed and shook her head. "Shall I take you down to the visitor's lounge or will you find your own way?" A soft American voice interrupted, "It's okay, thank you nurse, I will take her. My father and Uncle Robbie are waiting for me." Caris looked up gratefully at Emily and the nurse returned to the room.

"Emily, I am so sorry for your loss!"

"Yeh our timing was off wasn't it. We tried awfully hard to get here but getting flights in a hurry is never easy; red tape and all that. As soon as we got the call, we jumped on a plane but…."

"I know, I was the one who rang you. I didn't know who I was calling, Robbie wouldn't tell me, I was unsure why that was, but I did it anyway."

"There is a lot you don't know Caris, but I am sure my dad, will enlighten you."

They had reached the visitor's lounge and Caris was thankful that no other families were in there. As they walked in, she saw Robbie sitting in a chair, head in hands and a man, who she now knew was Richard standing with his back to the door, looking out of the window.

"Dad!"

Two heads turned to look at her, but it was Richard who spoke, "There you are munchkin, we were worried about you. Are you okay?" He walked up to her and put his arms around her.

"Yes, dad, I just needed some air. This is Caris, she looked after me". Two kind blue eyes looked over Emily's head and smiled. He was very tall, towering over Emily and Caris noted that he was a good-looking man probably in his 50s with his hair greying at the temples.

"Hello Richard, I am Dr Goodman." By habit she stuck her hand out and Richard warmly shook it. "Thank you, for looking after my daughter, it was quite a shock to all of us."

"Yes, Emily told me. It was a shock to me too. I had only left the room an hour before, and she had been sleeping.".

"And you are?" Richard queried.

"Sorry, I was Francesca's psychiatrist, and have been for quite some time."

"Ah, so that is why you know who we are."

"Yes I have been working with Robbie and I know quite a bit about Francesca's story."

"Really!" Richard's eyebrows rose questionably, and he looked across at Robbie, still sitting forlornly in a chair. In the awkward silence Caris crossed over to where Robbie sat. Crouching down in front of him, she asked "Are you alright, what happened. I wasn't gone that long?"

Robbie lifted his head and looked at Caris, although his expression was sad, there was something different about him and a peaceful resignation settled on his face as he told of his last precious moments with Fran. "She is finally at peace with Tom and Katie and knowing Fran she is probably dancing in her buttercup field, arms outstretched with Mary smiling on."

"Oh Robbie, I am so sorry" Caris held his hand and squeezed it.

"Don't be sorry Caris, she certainly wanted to go, and I had no right to keep her any longer. She remembered everything, as clear as a bell and we talked; we talked until there was no more to say. There were no longer any regrets, and we seemed at peace with each other. My beautiful Bean". Tears filled his eyes, as he spoke but a sense of strength has returned to him. Richard came behind his chair and put his hand on his shoulder, supporting him. Looking up at Richard, Caris saw that his blue eyes had clouded over as he held back tears. Standing, she felt out of place, Emily stared out of the window, lost her own memories, and Caris realised that this wasn't her story and she needed to leave.

The nurse who had spoken to her earlier popped her head in the room at the same moment,

"Dr Harvey, she's ready for you."

"Thank you nurse, we will be along in a minute."

As they readied to go and say their last words to Francesca, Caris took her leave, and slipped out unnoticed.

As Caris walked back to her office it was obvious to her that Fran's life had touched many people, her story incredibly sad. In fact her story had embodied and affected anyone who knew her, and she was sure that it would continue to do so for years. Shaking her head, Caris sighed as she walked up the stairs; with the case now closed, Fran's story like others, would be locked away in the archives but still he had a nagging feeling that there was more to this story, and annoyingly she could not put her finger on it.

Once in her office, she took out a file from the locked filing cabinet and opened it. She read again through the history of Francesca Taylor. Turning page after page, going backwards and forwards, scanning pages she had seen before on several occasions, every written word and every photo known to her, but there was something, she was sure, she had missed.

Now, not concentrating on the accident, she noted that Emily, Fran's own daughter, had never been mentioned. Richard had, but although the notation stated that he was the husband, he not been put down as Francesca's next of kin and there was no contact number next to his name. Instead the Emergency Contact was notated as Dr. Robbie Harvey (Carer) and next to his name was his pager number 9409 and not, as usual procedure, his contact number. Maybe it was because he was known by staff at the hospital, but this went against hospital policy, especially as Francesca had been unable to give out information when she was admitted. Then she noticed that there were no addresses for mail out, another unusual fact. In fact there was nothing usual about Fran's personal data at all. It was as if the information has been left out on purpose and not in error. Was it this that was bothering her or was it something else? Although exhausted, Caris carried on reading, starting from the beginning again and working through the file. "What the hell am I missing?" She said out loud. Then as she turned the last page, she saw it. She wasn't quite sure why she hadn't seen it before, but there it was, the answer that begged more questions and had no answers.

Printed in red and in capital letters, a watermark stretched across the whole page –

THIS FILE IS HIGH SECURITY AND CONFIDENTIAL -.
This file is not to leave the hospital. Permission to be sought from
Dr Robbie Harvey before sharing it with any third party.

It had been shared; it had been shared with her! Dr Robbie Harvey had asked for her; a young intern, who yes was making headway in her field but who had no history, as yet, to back up her theory. It had been a great honour at the time, he had painstakingly gone through the details with her and in doing so had formed an alliance, one of which that there was no going back from. She was told she had been hand-picked to look after a difficult case that no one had been able to crack, and she had been so close to doing just that. "Why me?" she yelled out, "Why me!"

Caris sat staring at the back page, staring at the red letters. She then stood, file in hand, and walked backwards and forwards in front of her desk. The answer struck her with such force that she sunk down on the edge of her desk, feeling cold and clammy with shock, the clarity of facts making her feel sick. Dear God, why had she not seen this before, it had been there all along. She remembered the frustration she felt when working with Francesca in those early days with Robbie always there encouraging her, but had it been encouragement, or had it been something else? It now seemed clear to her that Robbie had never meant for this mystery to be solved. The twist and turns were there to protect someone or something, but why had she been called back to help them again, why had this case been reopened, it didn't make sense.

It was hard to comprehend but it was all there in front of her. He had even involved her in a flirty kiss, an elaborate rouse to throw her off the track, knowing it would go against her professional registration and ethics and giving the excuse to get her off the case. Had she got too close to the truth? Francesca's story hadn't only ruined the family's lives but it had also ruined hers and this time she wasn't going to disappear, this time she was going to face the whole family and find out the missing piece of this story.

Caris sat there for a long time before deciding what she should do, professionally, ethically and with determination she would find out the truth. She picked up the phone and rang Robbie's number.

"Hello Caris," she heard his voice tired and strained.

"Robbie, we need to meet!"

"Ah yes. We were expecting your call. When will you be free?"

Caris didn't know what she expected but it wasn't that. With the meeting confirmed and the call finished, she realised that she didn't know Robbie Harvey at all.

CHAPTER 45

THE HIDDEN TRUTH

2019

As Caris drove up to Holly Cottage, it was only her anger that had spurred her on as her courage had abandoned her.

The fact that Robbie and the family had expected her call had added to the confusion and left her with many questions, and over her morning coffee she had been honest with herself that she felt hurt. Robbie had used her for whatever reason, and she had given him her all. She told herself that it was for Francesca's wellbeing, but the truth was that it was also for herself, eventually admitting that she had feelings for the good looking Dr. Robbie Harvey and stupidly she thought it had been reciprocated.

Holly Cottage, the holder of many secrets, stood in front of her. Its neat front garden and pretty facia was welcoming and anyone walking past would think the same, but Caris knew of its hidden horrors and shivers went up her backbone. Nevertheless, taking a deep breath, she marched up the path and then mounted the three steps to the front door, showing more confidence than she actually had. Before knocking, she turned and looked up the tree lined street. It was a lovely bright day, and although cold the sun was shining, and the house was bathed in sunlight. Caris could see why this cottage had once been a home and it saddened her to think of the family that had once lived here.

It was Emily that opened the door, and it struck Caris again how much she looked like Francesca. Her pale skin was clear and looked white against the titian of her hair. Her eyes so bright and green made her face come alive. There was a smattering of freckles on her small, upturned nose and her wide mouth invited a smile. Her accent reflective of her American upbringing invited Caris into the house.

"HI Caris, good to see you again, come on in. Do you want coffee or a tea; I know how you English like their tea". She moved with ease down the corridor towards the kitchen and Caris followed tentatively behind her. The house was well appointed, and she noted that the furnishings were beautiful. Calming colours in pastels were everywhere with vibrant splashes of alternative colour to brighten it up; Francesca sure knew her stuff.

Caris said little and the void was filled with polite chat from Emily who seemed quite at home in a place that she hardly remembered. With her tea in hand, she followed Emily out to the veranda. This area had been enclosed with café blinds and the patio heaters kept it warm, even though it was a cold day. Francesca's touch had made it cosey; coloured cushions lay on the garden furniture with matching sets in the chairs that were around the mosaic table. Hanging baskets filled with ferns and pot plants suitably placed, added to the relaxing atmosphere and the finishing touch was the small water feature trickling in the background. It was just lovely and had it been under any other circumstances Caris would have felt at ease and comfortable. However, as she approached at the table, Caris was greeted by Robbie and Richard and the feeling of peace abated and her anxiety returned.

They both stood as she arrived, and it was Richard who spoke first.

"It is nice to see you again Caris." Caris said nothing. "Please sit down, I see Emily has made you a tea, lovely." Emily arrived with a tray laden with coffee cups and biscuits and proceeded to unload onto the table. Still Caris remained silent but having sat down, was now staring at Robbie, who seemed unable to look in her direction.

Richard attempted his pleasant approach again as he handed out coffee cups and offered her a biscuit. "Caris"?

Caris declined the biscuit and sipped her tea.

"It's hard to believe that our Fran left us two days ago, doesn't seem possible. I said to Emily this morning, that it still feels as if she is here amongst us. Of course Em and I have not been back for some time but nevertheless…" Richard took a biscuit and started to eat it.

"About that"! All eyes turned to Caris as she began to speak. "Why is that? Why haven't you been back? I mean Emily, Francesca was your mother and whatever her state of mind, you her daughter. It could have helped with the healing process". There was an awkward silence, and Caris noticed an exchange of looks between Richard and Robbie. Emily was looking down and her finger was tracing the top of her coffee cup but was first to speak. "It wasn't because we didn't want to, Caris. Fran was my mother and I loved her, it was because it wasn't safe to do so or so we believed at the time. You presume that we didn't care! You presume a lot! I was 6 years old, god dam it, and lost everything I knew". She pushed her chair back and stood.

"Emily it's alright darling". Richard put out his hand and patted her arm, "Sit down, it isn't Caris's fault, she doesn't know the full story and it's high time that she did, isn't it Robbie!"

Robbie slowly looked up, he hadn't drank his coffee and his biscuit lay untouched. He smiled weakly at Caris and nodded. Emily had returned to her seat and rubbed Robbie's arm for encouragement and then spoke, her voice distant as she remembered the events of the past.

"I was only 5 at the time, and dad and I were returning home after my weekend with him. The traffic was slow and weather awful, I had been sleeping thankfully, but as dad tells it, we had been sitting in a traffic jam and a car skidded across the lanes of traffic and ploughed into a white van, right in front of us. At the time, we had no idea who had been driving or indeed who was in the car." Emily stopped then and looked at Richard, who nodded at her to continue. "The traffic was diverted, and I awoke to see ambulances and police cars everywhere. Their red and blue lights flashing and as a child it was all pretty frightening. It took a long time to get home and we had to call into Holly cottage, my home, to pick up some more of my clothes, but when we arrived Holly Cottage was in darkness and unwelcoming, with a police car sitting outside. Dad told me to stay where I was, and I saw him talking to the police officer. Something felt very wrong, and I went to get out of the car just as dad returned. He told me to stay seated and that we were going to drive to Mary and Joe's house. Dad, at the time didn't tell me why but his voice told me not to argue. Later, when I was older, I learnt what had happened to Uncle Robbie and that we very nearly lost him. Of course there was no one at my grandparent's home as they too had gone to the hospital and as there was no one to leave me with, Dad had no choice but to take me back with him. I remember thinking that when I saw mummy again, she would have a new baby because Uncle Robbie, had told me that when mummy went to hospital that would happen. It was all very confusing for a 5 year old".

Richard picked up the story, "It was a confusing time for all of us and it wasn't until the day of the funeral, that Emily was reunited with Robbie and her grandparents again. Of course, she didn't understand what was happening and in her innocence asked Nancy where Katie was, which led to further distress. So after the funeral Robbie took Emily for a walk and explained what had happened to the family and her mother, and that whilst he looked after Fran that she would have to stay with her grandparents until her mummy was better…..little did we know that Francesca's memory had been damaged to such an extent that she was unable to recognise anyone, including her young daughter. It was hard enough explaining to a 5 year old that the new baby wasn't coming but that her mother couldn't remember who she was. It was a very painful and difficult time."

Caris could hear the pain in their voices and see it in their eyes but still Robbie did not look at her. As a gesture, she spoke putting on her professional hat, "I understand that this event would have been dreadful

378

for you all, particularly as Francesca blocked any memory that she had of the past. If it is any comfort, I had started to see glimpses of the person she had been prior to the accident when she began to talk but it was a slow painful process with immense difficulties. Her condition and those like it are always difficult to treat because pushing too hard can set the patient back, and not pushing hard enough, well, achieves nothing. I am sure that the person I worked with, was not the same Francesca that left Holly Cottage on that awful day." Caris stopped and looking directly at Robbie, who was now watching her, she continued, "But I believe Caroline Parsons who continued the work after I left the case, made some great headway in her progress."

"Why?" Emily's voice cut through the silence.

"Why what Munchkin?" Richard asked.

"Why did you leave my mother when you were beginning to make progress. What made you stop?" Her voice sounded bitter, and even accusing. After all she had only been 5 or maybe 6 years old at the time and would have had no idea of what was happening around her.

"My 6ᵗʰ birthday was spent in a hospital, have you any idea how that would have felt. With a woman, who didn't know me from a bar of soap and who couldn't or wouldn't smile! Dad and Uncle Robbie, Grandad and Grandma did their best, but it was awful, and I have never forgotten it......I guess it doesn't matter now!"

"It does matter," Caris said, her voice strained, "None of you will get over this massive loss in your lives unless you face the facts head on and stop hiding behind whatever mask has shrouded the god dam truth!" She put her teacup down and realising that her hands were shaking she stood up, placing her hands on the table, fingers splayed, "I for one, can give you no more of my time, unless you start to open up. Francesca, has gone, and sadly will never come back. Surely now you can come out of hiding. Whatever or whoever it is that inhibits normality can no longer hurt you!"

She picked up her bag, pushed back her chair and made to leave.

"Please Caris. Please don't go!" At the sound of Robbie's voice, she stopped, hand on the doorknob. "We owe you an explanation. Please Caris!"

Not moving, and hand still placed, Caris replied, "I don't think I can. You have embroiled me, into ….this, whatever it is and professionally I feel compromised in so many ways. Robbie, you nearly ruined my career before, I can't let you do it again."

"Please sit down Caris," Robbie pleaded and to the others, "It's time!" There was the noise of general agreement and Caris turned to see three pairs of eyes looking at her. "You see Caris, you are involved, more than you realise and when you hear what we have to tell you, you will realise why you were asked to leave in the first place and why subsequently you were brought back.

Caris returned to her seat and Emily stood. She walked behind Caris and putting her hands on Caris's shoulders, gave them a squeeze. "I think we need something more than coffee, and disappeared inside, returning with wine glasses and a chilled bottles of wine. Returning to the kitchen, she came back out with a platter of cold meats, cheese, crackers and grapes. They had been prepared for a long discussion and Caris settled to listen to what Robbie had to say.

"We all need to stop ducking and weaving around this thing that we are hiding behind." There was general agreement and Robbie continued, "It may not come as any surprise to you, but the one person that disrupted all our lives and has the power to do so again, putting us in further disarray is …." Robbie looked at the others for approval and given, spoke again. "Is…. Vanessa!".

Caris looked at Robbie in absolute surprise, for hadn't she heard that Vanessa had been incinerated; her car hitting a pole. How then, could she continue to wreak havoc from the grave.

"Vanessa?" Caris exclaimed, "but wasn't she killed!"

"Caris, we are talking about someone who knew had to lie; twist fact and get herself lost to reinvent herself again. Vanessa, or whatever her real name was, had multiple personalities and had been the master of disguise, manipulative and creative. She had friends in high places, hidden everywhere and could, I believe, disappear into thin air, which, as it happened was exactly what she did. The reason why a policeman had been placed outside my door was to make sure I was safe. After all I was their main witness to events."

"I am sorry Robbie, but are you saying that Vanessa escaped the fire? She got away?"

"It seems she did, because when they put the fire out there wasn't a body in the car. The door was also open, which seems that the person driving, jumped out before it hit the pole. That is not to say she wasn't hurt but she certainly wasn't burnt alive. The weather was so bad, that no one saw anything other than the car go up in flames. Not only my life, but Francesca's life was still in danger, as was Emily's and even Richards, because he knew too much. As you know it was a long time before Francesca could leave the hospital but by then we were not considered under threat and the police gave no further protection"

"But what was my involvement? I had nothing to do with Vanessa, did I?" Caris questioned.

"Oh but you did, and it will become clearer as I continue. I am sorry Caris, this will come as quite a shock, so perhaps let's pour a drink and have something to eat."

Reluctantly, Caris took the plate of food given to her by Emily and sipped her wine. She shivered, not because she was cold but because the truth that she had hankered after was now a reality and somehow she was part of it. As she watched the party of people around her she wondered how she played a part in this horrific story and readied herself for what she was about to hear.

CHAPTER 46

DR CARIS GOODMAN

1998

The phone rang, and Caris snatched up the receiver in the communal office shared by two other psychiatrists at the hospital. They all had huge workloads, their desks piled high with manila folders, coffee cups and paper.

They had been discussing the dilemma of where to fit another desk as Caris had been promoted and her position was being filled by a young graduate.

The problem, although a good one, had become a heated discussion and Caris was thankful for the interruption.

In 1997 Caris had completed a PhD in head trauma and Post-Traumatic Stress Disorder and to her surprise the hospital had supported her business proposal of working with patients that had been admitted after an accident. Caris's methods had shown good results with her patients healing from within the brain and not just mending physically. Her workload seemingly tripled overnight; being hailed as successful.

Dr Caris Goodman was being noticed.

She turned to her colleagues and putting her finger to her lips shushed them as she spoke.

"Good morning professor, what can I do for you?" Listening she turned to pull a face at her colleagues, signalling them to be quiet, she continued, "I would be delighted. ...Now?... Yes I will be straight up." Putting the phone down, she picked up her notebook and her bag. "Apparently I am being given an interesting project to research... like I can fit anything else in." She groaned and walked out of the office, leaving the chaos behind her.

Knocking on the office door on the 4th floor, her tummy did a flip, nervous excitement kicking in.

"Come in", the voice from within called clear and strong. "Ah Caris, come in. Please take a seat."

"Good morning Professor Kendall". She sat politely and watched as a fat manilla folder was pushed across the desk towards her. Opening it she read about a victim of a motor vehicle accident

Francesca Taylor
DOB March 12, 1967
Female
Age 29 years
DOA 15/01/1996

She read all the personal data and picked up the photograph of a young woman, her wide mouth smiling out of the picture. She was very pretty with her titian curls wrapped around her doll like face, her green eyes twinkled as she smiled.

The personal data went on and on; weight, height etc, painting the picture of a stranger that Caris didn't know. As Caris turned the page, she saw another picture, showing the same face damaged and bloody; so different from the first. Francesca's eyes closed and the body hooked up to machines. A red curl sticking out from a bandaged head, arms cast and leg in traction. The police report read, that on January 15th, 1996, a female was admitted to St Thomas hospital. The white sedan, where she was a back seat passenger, had hit a truck on M25 head on. There was one survivor. A female child later died in hospital and a male was found dead at arrival to the scene. The female was found with multiple contusions and fractures. Evidence of progressive internal bleeding have been recorded. The female was heavily pregnant and unconscious when the paramedics arrived. She was stabilised but critical and during surgery had lost the baby, a girl.

Caris looked up at the professor questioning the content of the file, "This case is two years old, why now?"

"Caris, this is an extremely sad and difficult case. Francesca Taylor has no recollection of the loss of her family, and therefore an extremely sensitive matter. Francesca has Retrograde Amnesia, memories locked away before the trauma of the accident. Although she is now awake, it has taken a long 18 months for her to come back to us. On waking she had remembered her name but little else, and gradually with help from the team, and her parents, certain areas of her life started to return. She still has no recollection of the accident, which, I suppose is a good thing with no idea of the considerable losses in her life. The fear is that when and if she remembers it will be so traumatic, that it will set her back to a catatonic state"

"What about her injuries?"

"She has multiple lacerated scars running the length of her face and remains with a traumatic brain injury due to a decompressed skull fracture which causes immense pressure on the brain. As a result she has become sensitive to light and complains of headaches. Thankfully there is no evidence of epidural bleeding. Having said that she is prone to fitting from time to time and has been back and forward to hospital.

Caris looked up, her brow creased in thought.... This was something that she could really get her teeth into and might be just the break she needed but....

"What are you thinking Caris," the professor kindly said. This case was one that she would never forget and was eager to get to the bottom of the secrets held in Francesca's fractured mind, and if anyone could do it Caris could.

Caris smiled and chose her words carefully as she didn't want to seem ungrateful.

"Interesting case, however, she is post hospital care and out of my jurisdiction and as much as this intrigues me, the time frame makes it impossible I'm afraid." Professor Kendall nodded, "You are right, but the family have heard great things about your work and would like to pay you privately to assist them. This tragedy has taken its toll on the whole family, and even though they have lived through such tragic losses; their son, Francesca's brother, and Katie, their granddaughter, they are trying their best to lead normal lives" Caris blew out a long soft breath. Professor Kendall shook her head "I agree very difficult! Francesca has since moved home with her parents whilst recovering, although she does have a cottage nearby. Her parents feel that it would be good for her to start transitioning back to reality; living in her own home, sleeping in her own bed and they have been taking her there daily to see if she recalls anything. All memorabilia of concern have been removed, however, last week she found a photograph tucked inside the cover of a book. Professor Kendall pointed to an envelope in the side of the file which Caris opened. The photo was of a little girl, standing in a field, hands outstretched, laughing into the camera. She wore bright yellow, and her hat sat at a jaunty angle half off her head, showing bright red hair tumbling past her shoulders. She turned it over and written on the back in bold black ink were the words, "1995 The Buttercup". Mary found her sitting on the floor hugging the photo. I believe that she asked her mother if the photo was of her, and Mary said that it was, but it seems she became very upset, questioning why the photo was in colour. She got quite angry, even violent before becoming disorientated and had to be heavily sedated. Professor Kendall looked up at Caris before she continued. Although she could see the concern on Caris's face, she also saw interest in her eyes and so she carried on.

"Sadly she hasn't spoken since, she understands what is going on around her but not a word has she said and that is where you come in.

Caris, they need you to work your magic and unlock her mind. Are you up for it?"

Caris turned her attention to the photo again. She traced the picture of the little girl, so full of life and asked if it was Katie. "That I don't know, and I haven't liked to ask."

"Will Francesca come here, to the hospital, or will I go to the house?"

"That is entirely up to you. Maybe a bit of both but be warned this will be difficult and something like this would normally be handed over to someone more senior but with your speciality, it is agreed that you are the best person for this case".

"Thank you, Prof…"

"Vivienne, please.".

"Thank you…. Vivienne, for believing in me. I must admit I feel very honoured."

Vivienne leant back in her chair. Caris had always caught her eye. Always bright and full of questions in lectures. She smiled, if she were truthful, it was like looking at a younger version of herself. "Just remember" Vivienne said, "I am always here if you want to run anything by me; it may be with best intentions and all the knowledge in the world that even you cannot unlock this mind, but I know you will give it everything that you've got. Be warned, however, cases like this, with family involved, can become personal and it would be very easy to get too attached. Just take note, okay!"

"Yes, okay and thank you again" Caris replied.

"Oh and one other thing, it's probably not important to the case but you should know that Dr Robbie Harvey is heavily involved with the family and presently lives at Francesca's cottage. So you may need to take some direction from him".

"Dr Robbie Harvey? Chief of….?"

"Yes, the very same. You see prior to the accident he and Francesca lived as husband and wife and tragically it was their baby that was lost"

"No!"

"The sad thing is Francesca does not recognise him as anything more than a Carer, she simply does not remember him in any other way".

"That is just awful"! Caris closed the file and stood up, tucking the file under her arm.

"Please let the family know that I will be happy to take on this case. I would like to meet the parents, without Francesca or Dr Harvey for now as it always helpful to meet close family before I start treatment and I will need to go through the file again before contacting them. Are you happy with this approach"?

Yes, but tread carefully. Dr Harvey is still very closely involved; too closely involved for our liking. There is something that the family have not disclosed and are keeping very tight lipped about. It might be nothing, but my gut says otherwise". Caris pulled a face, "Anything else I should know about?"

"Francesca used to be in charge of Organic Textiles, at Mackenzie Taylor, her ex-husband's company. She will often be found with swatches of materials, which Mary has brought in, of different colours, holding them to the light, mix and matching. This may be a way of getting close to her, breaking the seal of silence. I trust I can leave this with you?" Caris nodded.

"It's your case Caris but I will contact the family today on your behalf. I am pleased and the family will be very relieved".

"Thank you Vivienne,". As Caris made to leave, she stopped and turned back to Vivienne. "Do you not find it odd that she doesn't remember him prior to the accident? If she has Retrograde amnesia and it is linked to trauma leaving her with PTSD, why has she no recall of him prior to the accident; there must be something else locking him out!" She took a couple more steps towards the exit and turned again, "I also do not understand why the family has removed memorabilia if they wish for Francesca to remember – that makes no sense at all!"

"Well Caris, I am sure you will find out" Vivienne encouraged. "Before I forget, you might have noticed 3A is now empty – please feel free to move yourself in. You really need an office of your own now."

"Fantastic! That will make all the difference especially as we have a Grad. joining us".

"Good! I look forward to your reports but now I have another meeting to go to and I have to bid you goodbye".

With the pleasantries over, Caris ran down the stairs, looking in at 3A on her way

She found it to be a decent size and it was all hers. Running down the stairs she gave a little whoop; she couldn't wait to tell her colleagues.

For three months Caris had been visiting her weekly, sometimes more and had used everything she had to open Francesca's mind. She had tried textile therapy, memory games and picture therapy but to no avail. Then a break-through – she had found a jigsaw of an open field, covered with yellow flowers and a blue sky and they had started doing it together. Each visit they completed a bit more with Caris chatting about her life as a child, anything really just to get a response. When they were near to finishing, they found that there was two pieces missing and both searched the box; their seats and under the table but to no avail. "Well Francesca, that's that then" Caris said, feeling defeated. "No o o!" An unsteady 'no' definitely came out of Francesca's mouth. Caris, who was on her knees looking under the chair, came up so fast that she bumped her head on the wooden underside. "Ouch"! Francesca rubbed her own head as she spoke. Again Caris turned her head and saw her to her surprise, Francesca staring down at her, concerned, her words although drawn out, were clear. Caris looked up and said "It's okay" but rubbed her head, nevertheless. "My silly fault. Let's put this away, we can't finish it now". Francesca picked up the bottom of the box, and as she did so let out a sound that was most definitely a giggle; for there under the box were the two missing pieces. The giggle grew and grew until they were both laughing out loud. Picking up one piece she held out the palm of her hand to Caris. "Which piece is it Francesca?" Both looked down at the perfect picture of a buttercup printed on the cardboard piece. "It's a buttercup", Francesca said 'And it goes here, where it should be, it's yellow face amidst the field of green." The second piece then slotted in next to it and the picture was complete. "There", she said, looking very pleased with herself, and with joy, threw back her head and laughed. This was the scene that met Dr Robbie Harvey as he came through the door; it was one he thought he would never see. Caris still down on her knees, looked up at him and continued laughing and Francesca, hands on her hips, a broad smile on her face.

"Well hello there, you both look like you're having a marvellous time. What's been happening?" Francesca's mirth stilled and turned to the jigsaw, she took one look at it and then asked if she could go home. Robbie mouth gaped, "Well done Caris! Well done! Francesca's family will be so pleased. Fran, my love, you have done so well!"

She nodded, serious again. "Yes! I am very tired, and I want to go home."

Caris stood back her head on one side, what had happened between them, for there was no joy, however hard he tried. It was a question she asked herself over and over but couldn't work it out, maybe she would never know.

In the weeks that followed Caris began to see progress. Conversations, although stilted began to flow and Francesca seemed to be coming out of her shell but there was a barrier; a certain something always stopping her from opening up.

The visits which had intensified, were longer and more in depth, leaving Caris exhausted. Her workload at the hospital had increased and visits to Francesca home became fewer so once or twice per week Robbie would drop Francesca off at the hospital for her treatment. They were both busy in their chosen fields, but he always found time to talk with Caris, displaying enthusiasm in the progress and techniques being used. Caris looked forward to these catch ups and felt flattered that he would take time out of his busy schedule to show an interest in what she was doing. She would look up into his intelligent eyes and when he smiled, her heart would melt. Sometimes he would join her for lunch in the hospital cafeteria or join her in the queue to get coffee, always being polite but over time their friendship started to blossom and Caris looked forward to seeing him more and more.

Stella, the new graduate, a rather quiet, shy girl showed immense interest in Caris's work and feeling flattered, Caris asked her if she would like to join her in Francesca's case. However, on these occasions, Francesca would refuse to speak or gave monosyllabic answers, and the atmosphere would change becoming awkward. Stella would feel disheartened and Caris would discuss the importance of introducing another person into the mix, pushing Francesca into reality, and maybe just maybe assisting her to open up further.

A few weeks later, during a rather long session, Francesca had refused to speak unless prompted and had become quite difficult to work with. Caris had noticed a repeat behaviour, where, when tired, Francesca would slap her forehead repeatedly, and this was now happening. "Are you tired Francesca?" Caris asked. In her agitation she ripped the book that Stella was holding and threw it down onto the floor, shouting "No!" leaving Stella shocked at her behaviour. "What did I do wrong", she whispered to Caris, "I was just reading! Perhaps I shouldn't come anymore."

"Actually, I have a feeling that she thinks you are someone else and so we just need to persevere. Don't take it personally, it is part of the job I am afraid, and it is really exciting to see emotions coming out. Do you know, Stella, I believe we are getting somewhere! Perhaps we will get to the bottom of her psychosis."

"Caris, how long do you think it will be before we get a breakthrough." Stella asked. Caris smiled, "Not long. Not long at all!"

The next day, she ran up the stairs to her office to grab a file but as she approached, she noticed her office door open. "That's strange," Caris thought and pushing the door further, she gasped – her office was a mess. Files everywhere, all over the floor and over her desk. The filing cabinet open and her pot plant had been severed, joining the mess on the floor. The armchair was slit open, obviously with a knife, with stuffing pulled out and her colourful rug had red dye thrown over it. Caris looked about her in horror and noticed the same dye decorated the walls. Standing in the middle of all the chaos, her heart beating, she felt violated. This was her space, her sanctuary, how dare this happen. Her anger spurred her to cross over to her desk and pick up the phone to call security. There was no dial tone. She followed the phone wire down to the socket and with a sickening feeling saw that it had been cut. Tears burnt her eyes as she ran out of the room into the corridor. Not looking where she was going, she collided straight into Robbie, who had been coming up to see her.

"Sorry, sorry. I have to …. I!"

"Hey, are you okay, you look, like you have seen a ghost. Are you crying Caris? What is wrong?" he asked.

She turned without a word and kicked open her door.

"Bloody hell, what happened here?"

"I don't know, I just found it like it!"

"Do you have any enemies, because someone doesn't think much of your décor?"

"Very funny Robbie! I need security, there are confidential files in here."

"It's a bloody mess," Robbie said again.

"I really don't care much about the mess, but as I said there are confidential files and documents in here."

"Is anything missing?"

"I don't know. I suppose I had better leave it for the police to check."

"Good idea, Caris. Let's lock it and go downstairs to security right now. Looks like you need a coffee.".

"Thank you, Robbie, but I don't want to keep you. Was there something that you wanted by the way?"

"I was just letting you know that Francesca is not feeling so well and won't be coming today. Of course you will still get paid."

"Oh don't worry about that, not necessary," Caris said awkwardly. "That is a shame, but then, without an office, it would be difficult to meet her here today anyway and it would probably upset her."

"True!"

They walk silently down the two flights of stairs. As they reached the bottom Robbie put his hand on Caris's arm. She looked into his eyes as he said, "If you need anything I am here, you only need to call me."

"Thank you, Robbie," but she knew she wasn't, and tears poured down her cheeks. "Oh Caris, come here, it was probably a disgruntled patient and nothing to be frightened about. If you are worried, you just need to call." He wrapped his arms around her pulling her in tight.

"Thank you, and sorry.". Caris broke away and wiped her eyes. He put his arm on her arm and rubbed it reassuringly.

Robbie's pager suddenly went off breaking the awkward moment, "No rest for the wicked," he smiled and let go of her arm, "Sorry got to go. Are you sure you are okay?" Caris nodded and smiled her colour had returned and she was feeling more like her old self. "Of course, I'm fine and thank you." She turned and headed onwards to security. Robbie looked on as he watched her walk down the corridor. It had seemed an awful long time that any woman looked at him like that ….it was a nice feeling but a dangerous one. Sighing he walked down the corridor in the opposite direction, his pager went again, and he picked up pace.

"The only thing missing was Francesca's file and that really concerns me, Vivienne. There was a lot of personal information in there, including those photographs and what's more all of my notes. Thankfully these were backed up on my computer but even still….. in the wrong hands…. Well it is not worth thinking about!"

"And you are sure that you locked your room" Vivienne asked. 'Yes, I am absolutely sure. The police said the lock had been picked and owing to its age it was quite easy to do so. Who would want to do such a thing!"

"Someone must have been disgruntled, can you think of anyone."

"Well that is just the thing, Vivienne. If someone was disgruntled, I can understand the mess and destruction, but this someone wanted one thing, and that was Francesca's information."

"As you know the family visited me and they were not pleased at all?"

"Yes, the police spoke to them yesterday. They have asked that she continues to see me at my office here twice per week. It was decided not to tell her about the break in as we are making progress. For her things will continue as usual."

"We are making progress are we?"

"Yes, the new graduate, Stella, joins me from time to time. She is really interested in the work I am doing; I didn't think it would hurt for her to get some experience. Is that okay?"

"Of course. Now, are you alright my dear, it must have been an awful shock?" Vivienne looked at Caris with concern. "Do you need anything?"

"It was indeed a dreadful shock, and thank you, but Robbie, I mean Dr Harvey, has been amazing. He mended the broken bookshelf and even bought me a new plant. He has really been helpful."

"You are not getting to close are you? I warned you that this could happen!"

"No, Vivienne, I remain professional."

"Well, let me know if you find out anything else or if you need anything!"

"Thank you, Vivienne."

A few weeks later, with her office back to its former glory, Caris sat at her desk, writing patient notes, when there was a knock on the door.

"Come in!"

Stella walked in with a pile of documents in her hand.

Caris indicated the chair and she sat down. "What have you got there?"

Stella smiled shyly, "I have been looking into retrograde amnesia and I have found some interesting information that might help Francesca." She laid the pamphlets down and said, "I thought you might be interested."

Caris smiled warmly at her, and even though she knew quite a lot about this condition, she thanked Stella. "It is great that you are showing so much interest, and when I have some time, I will be happy to look at these." She indicated the documents with her pen.

"Can't we look at them together now?" Stella asked. Caris noted a hint of petulance but shook her head. "I am sorry Stella, but these reports won't do themselves and they are due by tomorrow, but I will take them home, if that is okay with you, and look through them. Thank you though. Perhaps you can do your dissertation on this subject, there is a lot of information out there."

Stella stood, she picked up the pamphlets that she had laid so carefully down in front of Caris.

"Perhaps if more time was spent on Francesca, we would make quicker progress!"

Her face remained pale but there were two spots of red growing on her cheeks.

"Stella, I am busy at present, but we will spend time going over this case tomorrow if that is okay with you?"

"Is that all Francesca is to you? Just a case?"

Caris viewed the young graduate in front of her and decided, although annoyed at the intrusion and her rudeness, she herself would remain calm.

"Each patient I care for is a case which has different elements. There is a line between becoming personally involved and patient care and Stella, it is important that you learn that right at the beginning. If you think you are getting too close, then perhaps it is time you step back. Francesca is a very special case and needs a lot of my assistance and as you know she is not part of the hospital program,

"I am fully aware, but Caris I think we need to do more!" Stella argued. "I mean you have been at this for a long time now and you still haven't unlocked Francesca's mind. I think she might have a lot more to say if we do, don't you think?"

Caris stopped what she was doing and studied Stella. She was enthusiastic, she could give her that but there was something else that she couldn't put her finger on. An attitude maybe, sometimes that happened with the younger grads, but no, that wasn't it. Caris slowly started to speak, "Stella, you cannot rush this- it's great to see your enthusiasm, but Francesca will talk when she is good and ready and not before. It is your choice whether you stay involved but let me warn you for the sake of Francesca's welfare, we do it my way! I have worked too hard to have Francesca pushed to get a result, because, you see, that could set her back. So it's up to you Stella, if you are happy to come back tomorrow, we will work together to assist Francesca for however long it takes and if you are not, then that's ok too." Caris watched as Stella swung her bag on her shoulder, turn and walk out of her office. "Well I guess that means you are not!" Caris said to herself, shook her head, and picked up her pen, and turned the page in front of her.

Stella didn't show up the next day when she met with Francesca or the next. In fact three weeks went by before Caris encountered Stella again. She continued to meet with Francesca twice weekly and was rewarded by a conversation regarding absolutely nothing but still it was a conversation of sorts and Caris felt that this in itself was a breakthrough. Her friendship with Robbie began to blossom, he was easy going and showed interest in her work asking how she was progressing. His sense of humour and his beautiful smile captured her heart and she looked forward to seeing him, probably more than she should.

She saw Stella one morning waiting in the line for coffee in the hospital cafeteria. She stood alone with her arms crossed across her body. Her glasses kept slipping down her nose and every time she pushed them up, she looked around as if someone would notice. Caris walked up to her and tapped her on the shoulder.

"Hi Stella, how are you"?

Stella jumped and turned and looked Caris up and down before speaking, "Busy!"

"Well that is good to know," Caris replied, taken aback at her rudeness. As Stella grabbed her coffee, she walked past Caris and not saying a word walked into the throng of people and disappeared up the stairs. It was odd behaviour, Caris thought to herself, and she made a mental note to speak to Vivienne and also she would catch up with Felix who now ran the hospital grad. program. Grabbing her coffee she headed off to her next patient, it shouldn't have concerned her that a young graduate, had taken offence at being put in her place but it did. Maybe she could have been less harsh but no, Stella had stepped over the mark and in fact she had felt quite insulted by her attitude and Stella needed to learn. As the day went on, Stella and her attitude left her thoughts; her day was both busy and complicated but that was nothing new.

After work Caris walked down to the underground parking after what seemed like and endless day. It was late, as usual and she was alone. Walking towards her car she had the strangest feeling that she was being

397

watched and was glad when she jumped into her car. Pulling out of the carpark and onto the main road she stopped at the traffic lights and in her mirror saw a car pulling up behind her and was relieved when the lights turned green, and she could pull away. As she drove on the car trailing behind, suddenly revved up and overtook her and then dropped back so that they were level in the two lanes. Ignoring its presence Caris continued to the next set of lights, where the car swapped lanes again pulling up behind her. The black BMW was slick and expensive and could outrun Caris's old car, and yet it remained menacingly behind her. "Change, bloody well change" Caris shouted at the lights, whilst looking in the mirror to see if she knew who was in the car, but the windows had such dark tint that she was unable to see the driver. Caris mentally told herself off, she was being ridiculous with no reason to feel so paranoid, but she felt intimidated and uneasy. As the lights changed to green, she took off at top speed with the BMW travelling closely behind her. Caris decided to change direction, taking a left turn, off the main road, and stopping at her local Chinese takeaway, parking her car in the side street. The BMW continued on its journey, passing her as she walked around the corner to the entrance. "Caris, you are an idiot"! she said out loud and walked into the shop.

Having received her order she left the shop; she still felt uneasy and looked up and down the street before walking back to the car. The night was cold, and she hurried towards the corner, pulling her coat tightly around her. It was quiet, apart from a man walking his dog on the other side of the road and turning into the side street, she walked quickly towards her car. The road was dimly lit and although Caris knew the area well, tonight the shadows felt scary. She shivered and nearing her vehicle, she felt something crunch under her feet and looked down. In the dim street lights she could see shards of glass sparkling all over the road, they twinkled up at her and looking up she saw that the front windscreen of her car had been smashed and the passenger mirror had been vandalised, hanging off the car. On further inspection, her two front tyres had been slashed several times and there was a deep gauged line running the length of the car. Feeling sick, she looked around but there was no one there but still she ran, she needed to get away as quickly as possible.

Running back to the Chinese shop, she threw herself into the warm atmosphere of the shop, blurting out, between tears, that her car had been vandalised. Seeing her distress the owner placed a call with the local police and whilst she waited she found her mobile in her bag and rang the only person who she knew could help her.......

"Caris, how lovely to hear from you, what can I do for you?"

"I need your help Robbie, I am in the Chinese takeaway on Durston street, can you come please?"

"Can't pay for the chop suey, hey?" Robbie chuckled.

"Please Robbie, I am in trouble, please come!"

"Are you okay?" When there was no answer, "I am on my way. Stay put!"

She wondered why she had called him. They were only friends after all, and there were others she could have called, but it seemed the right thing to do. Caris had an uneasy feeling that somehow it was linked to Francesca, she didn't know why, call it sixth sense but somehow, she knew that it was. It didn't take long before a breathless Robbie came flying into the shop to find her. Caris took one look at him and burst into tears. He pulled her up from her seat and wrapped her in his big arms to comfort her. "I am so sorry...." she started to say but Robbie held her closer. "What are friends for," he murmured into her hair, and she knew she had done the right thing and he knew, right then, that he was going to get himself in all sorts of trouble.

After the police had taken a statement and announced that it was probably just kids and there wasn't too much that they could do... She thanked the owner for helping her and found herself with Robbie on the street. Robbie arranged a tow truck through the AA and kept her warm whilst they waited. "Sorry Robbie, I shouldn't have called you" Caris said, "I just didn't have anyone else to ring."

Robbie was looking thoughtful and made no effort to reply. "Robbie, did you hear me?"

"Yes. Yes, sorry Caris. I was thinking." He paused, and then continued, do you not think this is too coincidental?"

Caris looked up at him, his expression was one of concern.

"What do you mean Robbie?"

"Well the break in and a few weeks later, this. Someone seems to be targeting you and I feel that these two incidents could be related. Don't you?"

Caris took a sharp breath in, and was careful how she replied, "It has crossed my mind and I thought, somehow…… no that's just ridiculous!"

"What is it Caris?"

"Just forget it. I am being silly. I am tired and cold; once this car is picked up, I need to book a taxi and get home."

"Nonsense, I will take you!"

"No, Robbie, really I'm…."

"Not another word Caris, you have had a dreadful night and, well it's Drs orders. Now what were you going to say, and if it's a rubbish conspiracy theory we can both have a laugh. God knows we need it!"

"Well I think….." she paused, God, it was exactly that, a conspiracy of sorts….

"Yes……come on Caris, it can't be that bad."

Caris looked up at him, her eyes huge and full of fear she took a deep breath and shut her eyes tight... "That it has something to do with Francesca!" The words came out in a rush and she expected Robbie to burst out laughing but he had stopped walking and was looking down at her with a strange expression on his face. Caris hurriedly continued before she lost her nerve to speak. "Yeh, I know it's stupid. I suppose I am just spooked. The fact that it was only Francesca's file that was stolen in the break-in has concerned me and the fact that my name; my credentials are written all over that file makes me feel vulnerable and quite frankly something just doesn't feel right." Robbie continued to stare at her, his eyes darkened with concern and under the streetlight, his skin looked ashen, and cheeks seemed hollow. "Go on" he said, his voice barely audible.

"It is just a feeling Robbie, but I had a feeling that I was being watched tonight and followed when I drove away from the hospital, and to tell you the truth, I am really scared."

His arms pulled her in and as she looked up into his eyes his mouth lowered onto her own dropping the lightest of kisses onto her lips. "Nothing, I swear, will happen to you. I promise Caris, I promise you!". He then kissed her again and this time the kiss was not tentative but full of passion. Looking back, Caris thought that Robbie had kissed her with a sort of desperation, as if there was no more time to hold back, which, she thought strange, but it had felt so right. She knew it was against everything with her registration at stake, but she didn't want it to stop, she wanted Robbie Harvey, her ethics could wait.

They spent the night together in fact they spent many nights together after the incident, always, of course at Caris's home for obvious reasons. The rather clandestine relationship was kept from everyone and at work they were just two professionals, both in their own way looking after Francesca but at night they shared a passion that Caris had never been involved in before. It had gone past the point of being wrong and had, Caris mused, become part of her normality. She knew she was falling in love with Robbie, and if their passion was anything to go by, he then surely felt the same. It was, they knew, their secret, an exclusive beautiful secret that saw no end.

The normality of Caris's working days became longer and more intense. She often worked late into the night and rarely saw her colleagues and when she wasn't at work, she was with Robbie. Her success in her field had grown and added to her gruelling workload she was asked to lecture at the local university which she did with honour; it didn't seem that long ago that she was a student there herself.

Although busy she still found time for a twice weekly session with Francesca, and slowly Francesca began to come back. Her behaviour towards Robbie, was still distant, but she began to laugh and smile again, and the person that once was came sneaking through getting stronger with every conversation.

Disappointedly, she still had no memory of events prior to the accident and Caris reluctantly told Robbie that she thought there never would be, but Robbie insisted that Caris should continue working with Francesca, and she did so quite happily.

In discussion with Vivienne, Francesca was deemed a success, and although there was still a lot of work to do, Caris felt satisfied with the trajectory of the case.

CHAPTER 47

THE WORM THAT TURNED

1998

As the months went on her relationship with Robbie continued with Robbie seemingly reciprocating her growing feelings and she felt content in their duplicity.

There had been no further incidents in or around the hospital, and the normality of life continued be it rather busy...........................

After a particularly lively session at the university including student interaction, Caris asked if there were any questions. A hand went up at the back of the room....

Caris blinked and stared into the darkness but couldn't see who it was that had spoken for the room was darkened with the only light on the platform where she was standing......

"Can I have the lights changed please?" Caris called out to the technician at the back of the lecture room. Nothing happened and so she continued, speaking to the student with the raised hand, "Yes, can I have your name?"

The student, a girl, did not reveal who she was but started talking, "When you start a case, that is what you call it, isn't it? How long do you usually take to get a result?"

Caris, looked again to see who was talking but all she saw was a sea of eager faces looking at her expectantly.

"Well, it depends. Each case is different, and as for the result it is dependent on the brain injury itself and the willpower of the person within. So the answer is that it takes as long as is needed. You see the brain can switch back on by a trigger or it can just wake up when it is ready. Sometimes, only part of the person returns, something is missing which alters that person for a lifetime but in other cases, there is a win and gradually the whole person returns."

Another hand shot up.

"Yes, can I have your name?"

A male voice, down the front, "Jonathon!"

"Thank you, Jonathon, what is your question?"

"It must be a great feeling to get a person returned to normality and I wonder is there further treatment required and how long does that last for?"

"Great question! It is a wonderful feeling to reach in and find that missing person.

I always think of them as lost souls until this happens, struggling to find their way back, and yes, you are right, there is continuing work, an ongoing program with no time frame, dependent on the individual…… Liken it to a light switch, that can often turn off again, so you have to maintain a balance to keep them in the current. Triggers can be positive to the brain but very often there are triggers that are negative and spiral the brain back into confusion with memory lapses. It takes time and as I have said, each case is different."

There was general murmuring amongst the students. She called out to quieten them, "Are there any more questions?"

The voice from the back called out again, "Amnesia?"

"Are you asking if the memory lapses are called Amnesia?" There was no answer and so she continued. "If that is your question then yes, that is a particular area of damage and very difficult to treat. The brain can close off to things that hurt or when there are frightening reminders of distant thought patterns that cause ill feeling. In doing so shutting out memories that affect the way they think. It is our job to......".

The same voice cut through interrupting Caris mid-flow, "and what do you do about that Dr Goodman?"

Caris didn't know why, but the owner of the voice made her feel uneasy. It was the way she had said Dr Goodman, the way her voice leered as if mocking her answers.

"As I was saying, it is our job as psychiatrists to find the pathway in. There are several ways to treat amnesia and I think I have pretty much tried most of them one way or another, with some success I might add." Again another appreciative murmur..... "However, there is no easy answer that fits all. It really is try, try again in most of the difficult cases, until you get a breakthrough. It can be frustrating for both yourself and the patient but perseverance; patience and empathy is the key..."

"It doesn't always work though, does it!" Heads turned to see the student who had voiced her opinion. "It doesn't matter what's been tried, some severe cases can remain mute or changed forever, wouldn't you agree?" Before Caris had a chance to answer the voice continued, "You haven't always been successful have you, Dr Goodman!"

The voice was familiar, there were nuances that she recognised but couldn't put her finger on and there was something else, an arrogance or an undertone, that made her feel nervous. "You are right! Not every case can be fixed. Some memories can be locked away forever, with the key thrown away but it shouldn't stop us trying. There is a lot of literature on amnesia, and it makes interesting reading. I would suggest you read up on it and next month when I visit, we will use it as our topic. Remind me as I may forget!" The students laughed at her pun, although Caris, hadn't really intended it as a joke. She held up her hand to quieten the room, and as their noise abated, Caris spoke again, "Can I ask who it is that is asking these intriguing questions?" No one spoke, heads turned to see who it was at the back of the hall but all that was seen was the heavy oak door opening and closing. "She's gone Dr Goodman, she just walked out!"

"Do you know who she is? ……Anyone?" There was general discussion, but no one gave up a name. One student spoke out, "there are a fair few external students from the other university Dr Goodman, you are very popular." The students clapped their hands and Caris bowed her head.

"It is very encouraging that the next generation is so enthusiastic. Thank you, I look forward to seeing you all next month".

With the lecture room quiet, Caris started to clear up her things. The auditorium was still in darkness, which felt odd, with the only light being on the stage. She was deep in thought when she heard the noise of heavy doors at the top of the stairs open. "Hello?" she called out…..

The lights were suddenly bright, blinding her as she looked up the auditorium flooded with light……Hello?" She called again.

Caris could make out movement behind the heavy black curtains surrounding the back wall. "Whose there?" she called out nervously.

"I am so sorry Dr Goodman; I didn't mean to make you jump like that" said the technician who came out from behind of the black heavy curtains that adorned the back wall. "I just came in to put the lights on for the next lecture and give it a tidy up. I must admit I thought you had already left."

"Can I ask what happened to you earlier? I asked for the lights to go on at question time as usual, but you were not here. I was practically in darkness!" Caris asked.

"Yes, sorry about that, but It's the oddest thing," the technician said, "I was sitting listening to your lecture in my little cubby up there," he indicated the small lighting and sound room. "It was most interesting, I must say, and then young Terry popped his head in, tapped me on the shoulder and said I was needed in front office. Well as you know it is a far way off, I thought I had time to get back before the end but as you can see I didn't. I am so sorry. Not like me at all."

After her initial annoyance, Caris found herself warming to the old technician, "Well no harm done, just made me a bit nervous to see you hiding behind those black curtains. I hope you got the matter sorted at the front office?"

"Well that's another odd thing, when I got there, I was given this letter to give to you! What is urgent in that, I asked myself. Anyway I took the letter and here I am." She held out her hand...... "So can I have this letter then"?

The letter was duly passed over and Caris popped it her bag.

"Aren't you going to read it?" He said hopefully.

But Caris, had already swung her bag onto her shoulder and was heading off the platform towards the exit. "Thank you, see you in a month" she said and was gone.

Returning to her office, Caris took the envelope out of her bag and laid it on her desk. She didn't recognise the handwriting but that was not unusual and slid a finger under the lip to open it. A small card had been inserted inside and on it, in lavish handwriting seven words jumped off the page and Caris's world once again flipped on its side.....

She sat down heavily into her seat and read the words repeatedly and fear swept through her leaving her heart beating hard in her chest. Picking up the phone she dialled Vivienne's extension...

"Vivienne, it's Caris. Are you free, I have a problem? 4pm, yes that is fine. See you then."

Looking at her watch it was only 3pm

You are another puppet in his game.

What did it mean? She put the card back into the envelope and slid it into her handbag. She had to get out of her office and get some fresh air. Her head was in a spin and she couldn't think straight. What did all this mean? Was this about Robbie? Was he manipulating her? That couldn't be possible, he said he loved her the other night, and she was sure she was in love with him. No, it must have another meaning. Caris left her office, locked the door, and ran down the stairs. Once outside, she walked quickly over the bridge to the public carpark where she had left her car. As she approached, she saw something flapping under the windscreen wipers and retrieved another envelope. With shaking hands she opened it and inside, another card.

Stop interfering in something you can never have.

Caris steadied herself against the car. She told herself it was a silly prank and she and Robbie would discuss it later, but it had scared her. She checked her watch, still another 40 minutes. She walked back to the cafeteria, the warm atmosphere making her feel better and checking her watch again, threw herself into one of the armchairs.

"Well, well! Hello Caris, long time no see!" Caris looked up, it was the last thing she needed right now but there in front of her was Felix from student services. His large smile beaming and his bright red hair and horned rimmed glasses looking down at her. "Do you mind if I join you?" Before she could speak, he had plopped himself down opposite.

"How are you Felix?" Caris asked, mustering normality into her voice.

"Oh busy as usual, so many new students you see, coming out of the damned woodwork….." He carried on talking about this student and that and the difficulties with some "Don't you agree?"

"What, sorry Felix, I missed that?"

"I was saying, we need more students in your department, to help you. You look all tuckered out."

"Yes, I am and that would be good. By the way, how is Stella doing? I haven't seen her around here lately."

"Stella you say?"

"Yes she was a new psych graduate, - tall slender with white-blonde hair and rather large glasses. Now what was her last name….. it escapes me."

"Oh, yes, yes, I remember her now. Poor thing didn't last long. She was only here 6 months and decided it wasn't for her. Came and saw me in a terrible state one day, and then just left. You get that you know, it's not for everyone."

"You must be mistaken, Felix, she was only in my office the other month and prior to that she had been working with me on a rather delicate case."

"Maybe I have, but I don't normally forget a name and in this case, I am not mistaken! However, with the number of students, anything is possible….. leave it with me my dear and I will check. Anyhow, must be off, too much to do and not enough time to do it in. Lovely to see you again Caris."

They said their goodbyes, and Caris, seeing the time, stood to leave. She had an uneasy feeling and none of this made sense. The last time she had seen Stella was here in the cafeteria. She had been on her own and didn't interact with any other staff but there wasn't anything else that pulled attention. She barely spoke when Caris spoke to her and, in her reply, disinterest with derision. Caris thought of what she had said, how she had answered, and it hit her like a thunderbolt, the voice, that cold condescending voice…..the same voice from the university. What had she said….. "When you start a case, that is what you call it, isn't it"? Hadn't she argued in her office about Francesca being known as a case? Caris recalled the words used at the lecture, "You haven't always been successful have you, Dr Goodman!" Her mockery and undertones making Caris anxious. It had to have been Stella but why?

As she arrived at Vivienne's office, Caris felt anxious. She would have to tell her about Robbie and reveal the depth of their relationship. She had certainly stepped over the professional line and didn't know how this would be taken "Shit!" Caris exclaimed to herself "Shit! Shit, Shit!". She reached up her hand and knocked on the door.

"Yes, come in!" ……. Caris peered around the door and came into the room.

"Take a seat Caris.! What is this all about? You didn't sound yourself on the phone.

"Thank you for seeing me at such short notice, Vivienne, I have a bit of a problem!"

"Well it can't be that bad, or I would have heard about it already…. What's up?

CHAPTER 48

CLARITY PREVAILS

2019

Three sets of eyes looked at Caris as she began to speak.

"This case, Francesca's story, had always baffled and intrigued me, which is why I took it back; unfinished business if you like, but I fail to see how I was involved any more than that."

Robbie looked across the table towards her, sadness in his eyes. So many memories, so much pain and as he spoke, Caris could hear all of it in his voice and see it in his eyes.

"Go on, she has to know," said Emily.

"As I said before what we have to tell you, will make you realise why you were asked to leave in the first place and why subsequently you were brought back. Vanessa…."

Caris interrupted Robbie, and glared at the party in front of her……

"Vanessa? You're pinning all this on Vanessa. I never even met her for Christ sake!"

"Caris!", Robbie patiently said, "As I said before, we are talking about someone who knew had to lie; twist fact and get herself lost to reinvent herself again. She could manipulate…"

"Are you saying I met Vanessa? Worked with her…?"

"No, not quite!"

"He looked for encouragement around the table and it was Richard who spoke.

"Caris, it wasn't Robbie, who sent you away. It was me!"

Caris sank to her seat "But why?" She looked at his lean frame and listened to his soft South African accent tinged with an American drawl. He was still good looking, thinning slightly on top, but his tanned skin and searing blue eyes did not escape her.

"When you spoke with Vivienne, after you received the notes, you will remember that she felt that you had got too close, and she dismissed you from the case.

Vivienne telephoned me and told me what she had done; you see she feared for your safety more than anything!"

"What! Do you mean to say that she knew about all of this the whole time. She never let on!"

"No, you didn't and for a very good reason," Richard continued. "What did you find pinned to your office door when you returned from Vivienne's office?"

"Another envelope, but how did you know that?"

"The janitor. He let me know, and how you reacted. You were given leave, were you not?"

"Jim, the old caretaker, you had him on payroll too?"

"Yes. Sorry. But we had to know what was happening at all times, to safeguard Francesca, and subsequently you."

Caris blinked at him in disbelief. Was there anyone else I should know about? It seems my rise to fame had nothing to do with me at all did it? My life, my career, all planned out, has been a bloody fraud!"

"Good God Caris, no, that was all you. Vivienne picked you because you were the brightest student she had had the pleasure in teaching. Your thesis made sense and was perfect for Francesca's needs. All we wanted was to have Francesca back, and the people we put around you, weren't there to spy on you, they were put there to protect you".

"Who else?" Caris's voice faltered, her thoughts all over the place.

"Colleen and Felix. They both knew, but not all of it, and reported back to us, if there was anything untoward."

"Colleen! I studied with her, I thought we were friends and Felix! I do not believe it! Affable Felix wouldn't hurt a fly, how the hell did he get caught up with this?"

Richard smiled, "I have known Felix for years, old drinking buddies. We had lost touch, but when I saw him at the hospital, when Francesca was first admitted, we took up where we left off. He was always trustworthy, a nothing hidden sort of bloke with no ties that could get in the way. He seemed perfect and was only too pleased to help and look out for you. Unfortunately he didn't remain perfect and that was where it all began to unravel. You see, Felix had a bit of a problem that we didn't know about. He gambled, a lot. I always knew he liked to punt, but didn't realise he was in debt, considerable debt actually. He needed funds to bail himself out and needed it in a hurry as he had some undesirables chasing repayment. Somehow he was contacted and was offered money, a large sum of money, which would have got him out of debt. All he had to do was one thing successfully, which, unknowingly changed the safety of Francesca and yourself.

"Felix? I don't believe it! This is so unbelievable, next you are going to tell me there was female spy as well!"

"Well that isn't too far off the truth," Richard replied, looking serious.

There was a break in the conversation, the tension being palpable, and Emily jumped in…. "Anyone for a coffee or something?"

Caris looked up at her, it was like seeing a reincarnation of Francesca. "Or something would be good, I think I need something stronger than coffee."

"Coming right up."

Richard leaned forward in his chair and stared at Caris, "Tell me what you find on your door?"

"Surely you already know?"

Richard did not reply, Caris shut her eyes. She had blanked this out years before but now it was like yesterday, painful, and frightening.

"Caris?"

Caris opened her eyes, she felt exhausted. For years she had felt the victim, and now, perhaps her nightmares would stop, and she could put this all behind her. It was time to get answers and so, with difficulty, she began to speak, reliving it like it was yesterday. The years turned back, and she was once again in Vivienne's office.

1998 -

Vivienne looked down at the cards in her hands and then she looked at Caris. "When you took on this case, I warned you not to make it personal. Not only have you got too close to Francesca, although I must say with great results, but you are involved with Dr Harvey!"

Caris looked up sharply, she had not told Vivienne about her relationship-her face flushed, and she lowered her eyes, unable to look at Vivienne. "Yes, I know Caris and have done for some time. I do not condone this behaviour, but because this work is private, done in your own time and not part of your hospital schedule, I do not have jurisdiction to discipline within the hospital guidelines." Vivienne paused and placed the cards that she had been holding down on the table. Caris looked up and saw the concern in Vivienne's eyes as she spoke again. "What the hell were you thinking? You have gone against everything you know and have been taught. What you do in your own time is your business, but Caris, you have indeed crossed the line.

You have breached your Hippocratic Oath and I find it hard to overlook this. As for these......" she pointed to the cards, "someone has it in for you and I feel you are in danger. These are warning cards sent to scare you off. I believe that they have something to do with Francesca and Robbie Harvey and therefore, for your own sake, I have no choice but to take you off this case!"

"Vivienne! No! Francesca cannot manage without me. She gets very disruptive if we miss a visit. How could I explain this to her? We have got so far, and it may set her back. Please Vivienne!"

"I am sorry Caris, but I will be speaking with the family today. It will ultimately be their decision but given the circumstances and the fact that you have been threatened, your office destroyed, your car damaged, and these messages left for you, it is not safe to carry on. In fact I want you take two months away from the hospital completely!"

Caris stood up and started to pace in the office, "but my case load Vivienne, we are short staff as it is, who will look after these patients?"

"That is my problem Caris, not yours. The longer you remain, the more of a target you will become. As for Dr Harvey, well, I cannot tell you to stop seeing him but ask that you don't. This is obviously directed at your relationship. I should never have gotten you involved in this mess…."

"But no one knew, we kept it secret," Caris cried out interrupting Vivienne mid discussion.

"Did you?" Vivienne opened her drawer and took out an envelope, sliding it across her desk to Caris. "Really Caris, considering I knew, you didn't keep the secret very well hidden." Caris opened the envelope and seeing pictures of herself and Robbie locked in an embrace and another entering her home, she realised the reality and sat down heavily. "Where did you get these Vivienne?"

"The envelope was slipped under my door it could have been anyone. Look it could be as simple as a jealous ex, but Caris, until we know what this is about, keep your distance". Looking at Caris's anguished face, she continued, "I know that this is difficult, but I suggest that your leave starts today. Disappear for a while and come back refreshed."

"Can't I even say goodbye to Fran?".

"No, I think this way is for the best Caris."

Tears poured down Caris's cheek as she tried to talk, "and Robbie, Dr Harvey…I need to……Please Vivienne?"

"He will understand, you have to believe me Caris. Now go and clear out your office and bring me any files you need to handover before the end of the day. You may not like it, but it is the only way. I will explain to the staff that you are taking time off to work on your thesis, its plausible and they will understand."

"But Vivienne…."

"No buts!"

Caris knew that the conversation was finished and there was no point arguing. She watched as Vivienne took a white envelope out of her drawer, and opening it put the cards inside it. She then reopened the drawer and dropped the package inside, locking the drawer behind it. Vivienne looked up and smiled gently, "Thank you Caris.".

Leaving Vivienne's office Caris felt that she had not only let Vivienne down, but also Francesca and if she was honest, herself. Choosing the fire escape to exit, rather than the lift she walked down the concrete stairs, feeing less conspicuous.

The sound of her shoes bouncing off the walls echoed around her and her thoughts pounded in her head; she felt so ashamed. From above she could hear laughter and looked up but seeing no one, she guessed it had come through the various vents in the wall. Then she heard it again, a low sinister laugh that drifted down towards her. Again she looked up and again she could see no one.

"Stop it Caris, you're being paranoid now," she told herself, her voice echoing in front of her. And then another voice joined the conversation, "Caris, Caris, Caris" the words echoed in a whisper crescendoing into the space, mocking her own voice, and then the laughter started again, quietly at first but growing in strength until Caris put her hands over her ears and shouted, "STOP IT!" There was sudden quiet. Caris could feel sweat pouring down her back and her heart thumping in her chest, as she pressed herself against the wall. The hair on her arms stood up and she let out a sob, which echoed all around her. A door slammed above but no footsteps followed, and then below her another slam, another door. The laughter continued and then a silence, which, taunted her, her fear escalating. "Caris Caris Caaaaaris," the voice called her, it seemed to be coming from all directions and then the lights went off, Letting out a scream, Caris stumbled down the remaining stairs feeling her way to the door. With relief she grabbed the handle and pulled, but nothing.

She pulled again, this time more desperately but the door didn't budge. The laughter started anew, it seemed close to her but this time it was that of a child, high pitched and gurgling with glee. "Who is there?" Caris yelled but once again silence. Her hands started to beat on the door; the laughter changed to a sinister cold sneer, and the words that followed chilled her to the bone, "Caris, you didn't listen to me did you; naughty, naughty girl!".

"Please let me out, let me out," she screamed, her voice echoing around her.

"Who are you? What do you want with me?" The childish laughter began again, dark and sinister, taunting her! Caris cried out, terror coursing through her body. She tried the door again, shaking the handle with all her strength and punching the door until her knuckles hurt and then she heard a key and suddenly light flooded in, and she fell forward into the arms of Jim, the hospital janitor.

"It's okay" he crooned, "These old doors sometimes stick, we will have to get this looked at, can't have a fire door sticking can we!" He noted Caris's shaking body and the sweat running down her back as she leant against him.

"You had to use a key, that door didn't stick, it was locked," Caris stuttered. "There was someone in there with me, I could hear them." Tears were pouring down her cheeks and she had begun to shake.

Jim didn't answer but sat her down on a bench on the opposite wall. "We have been having some maintenance done lately, cleaning and all that, perhaps the door got locked but there should have been a sign at top and bottom to prevent people using it. As for voices, well, I don't know about that, but this hospital is old and can creak and echo at times." Seeing her disbelief, Jim carried on "Often you can hear voices from the corridors, through the vents, so perhaps that was all it was. You have had quite a fright haven't you. Come on I will walk you back to your office and get you a cup of tea."

Caris allowed him to help her up, she felt awful, her face pale and eyes watchful. As they rounded the corridor, she saw her office door; normally she felt warm with a sense of pride but the sight of it this time filled her with fear, and she pulled back. "What is it?" Jim said. He watched as Caris pointed to a white envelope pinned to her door.

"It's probably just a message, nothing to worry about." He pulled the envelope down, offering it to her. She shook her head. He noticed her skin had paled further and her eyes held a terrified expression. "Do you want me to open this for you?" Caris nodded. She watched as he stuck his big finger under the lip of the envelope and slit it open, it was empty. "That is odd, nothing in it. Come on let's get you inside."

Once in, she walked over to her desk, her hand threw up over her mouth and she let out a scream. Her head spun, and the ground started to open up and swallow her. Jim reached out but her head hit the floor before he could reach her, and she became unresponsive. He checked her breathing and then standing up he went to the telephone on Caris's desk and there lying upon her paperwork was a noose man's knot with the tarot card of death pinned to it.

"Vivienne, it's Jim here, we have a problem! You are needed in Caris's office right now!"

"Caris, Caris!" It was Vivienne's voice. "Come back Caris, you have had a nasty shock! Caris!".

Caris's eyes fluttered open and saw Vivienne's scared face looking down at her. She tried to sit but her head was thumping. "Thank goodness Jim was with you, it could have been much worse. What happened?"

With assistance Caris was helped to a seat. "Where has it gone?"

"Where has what gone dear?"

"The hangman's noose, it was right here.".

"I think you may have banged your head, there is nothing here Caris".

Caris stared at her desk and then at Vivienne, "You are in it too aren't you, that is why you want me off the case!"

Vivienne sat down opposite Caris and held her hand, "I am only here to protect you Caris. Jim told me about the stairwell, and you have had an awful fright. I think you have been overworking; late nights, no sleep and the added burden of Francesca…" Caris interrupted, "Francesca is not a burden!"

"No but added stress. Now don't worry about the office, I think you need to go home right now. Jim will take you."

Vivienne took in Caris's tired face, the dark marks under her eyes and her pallor and she felt guilty. She had overloaded her with more and more work, and this was the result. She had seen it before, young students trying to prove themselves, but Caris had always been different. Her work, exemplary and opportunities had come her way of her own making. The rest would do her good. She stood up, "Jim will be here soon, don't leave your office until he gets here……."

"But….." Caris interrupted.

"That is an order young lady. Now are you going to be okay? Jim has just popped out for a minute, sorry but I have a meeting to go to?"

Caris nodded but alone the fear crept into her again. She knew that she hadn't imagined the noose, it had been right here. She touched the paperwork strewn across her desk. Jim was probably disposing of it right now. She looked warily around her office but there was nothing untoward and sitting back in her chair, she waited. The phone rang, and she jumped staring at it before snatching it up to cease the incessant ringing, it was Robbie, beautiful calm Robbie.

"Hi, you okay?"

"Eh……yes I am fine". She wanted to tell him but who could she trust.

"Good! I am sorry to bother you but it's just that Fran has had a bad fit; she has been admitted to the ward and had been asking for you."

"Had?"

"She has now slipped into unconsciousness and is now catatonic. The doctors fear the worse. I wondered if perhaps you could come and talk with her. Perhaps your voice will bring her back".

"Robbie, I am not sure I can….. I have….".

"Please, Caris. She needs you!" He quickly told her the ward and room number and then hung up.

Not thinking Caris grabbed her bag and stood, she still felt shaky, but Robbie and Fran needed her and without another thought she left her office.

Arriving at the ward, she nodded to the nurses as she walked down the corridor and then as she neared the room, hesitated. What if this was a roux, another trap? She looked around her but there was normality all around her and she entered the room.

Robbie jumped up as she neared the bed, "Thank you Caris.".

Francesca was pale and the machine next to her bleeped in unison with her twitching limbs. "Francesca, Fran, it's Caris. Can you hear me"? There was nothing. She touched Fran's face and then held her hands but there was no recognition. For a while Robbie was forgotten and Caris squeezed Fran's fingers to get some sort of reaction but still there was nothing. She jumped when Robbie touched her shoulder and turned abruptly towards him.

"Sorry, I didn't mean to frighten you"? Robbie's handsome face looked concerned for her, and she knew she was safe. She stood and fell into his arms, sobbing. He stroked her hair and murmured loving words tipping her face to look into his. He kissed her with tenderness, and she returned the kiss with equal feeling. The machines bleeped on relentlessly and Francesca's body gave a shudder, the machines reacting loudly. Caris pulled away and looked at Fran. Her head had lolled to one side, her eyes open, looking directly at them. There was no life behind them but still those green eyes, staring at them scared her. "Robbie, I can't do this anymore. I have been taken off Fran's case and this……" She indicated their two bodies… "Has to stop now! My life has been threatened and I cannot go on. I can't lose my license to practice because of my stupid behaviour. It is unfair to Fran, unfair to you and definitely unfair to me. Professionally, I cannot help Fran anymore, I have done my best. When she wakes, let her know that I tried and wish you both well."

Robbie slumped in a chair, his sad eyes looking up at her. Caris I already know!"

Caris stared at him, "You knew but you still kissed me, what the…..Well that says everything about this", and with one last look, Caris walked away from Robbie, Francesca, and the whole bloody situation.

As Caris walked out of the ward, she was met by Vivienne and Jim who were waiting for her. None of them spoke as they walked out of the building. She knew that she was leaving all she knew behind her, and she knew for sure that she wouldn't be back; somehow she would build a new life and leave this sorry story behind her.

As they reached the outer offices, Vivienne turned to her and stopped the procession. She grabbed Caris's arms and spoke, hurriedly but with determination.

"Caris, listen to me I knew about the noose and the death threat!". Caris's eyes widened, "but I had hoped that you wouldn't remember, having hit your head". The police have it now, along with the other evidence. Jim has handed them the CCTV footage and it seems that the person involved in this is someone you may know. Stella, Stella Brookes.

Caris opened her mouth in horror. It all made sense, the questions at the University; the voices in the stairwell and easy access to her office, "But why, how. What did I ever do to her?" Her voice was barely audible.

"We don't know, but Jim recognised her and had seen her snooping about your office previously. We checked in with Felix who gave us a lead, quite by accident actually as she matched the description. It may be nothing but hopefully the police will find her, and it will be an end to this stupidity. Now go home and rest. The police will contact you tomorrow. Goodbye Caris, take care". With that Vivienne turned on her heal and left. Jim put Caris in her car and drove her home.

In the days that followed Caris waited for the police to visit but strangely they never came. She also waited for a call from Robbie, but there was no call and no contact. Caris never knew the outcome and even though she tried to put it behind her, nightmares and fears often filled her nights and in the years that followed life never really was the same.

CHAPTER 49

CULMINATION OF FACT

2019

"I finished my thesis which was widely acclaimed, and lectures continued. As you know I opened a successful private practice and life when on......until you phoned me Robbie, until I got caught up in this frigging nightmare again. I can only assume that this cloak and dagger stuff is regarding Stella but for the life of me I still don't see the connection. I never saw or heard from her again, the police never spoke with me, so it seems they got it wrong with their presumptions. I have told you everything that I can remember; things that I never wanted to speak of again. So if you don't mind, I think it is time for me to leave. This has been a painful, upsetting revelation of sorts. You might ask why, after all that I'd been through, did I return your call, Robbie.

Well, I always felt that I had failed the family, failed myself actually, and that there was unfinished business not only with Francesca but also you Robbie. You never contacted me again and at the time I felt alone and frightened, but somehow, I found the strength to rebuild my life and a successful one too. So thank you for the invite and your explanation, which still feels unfinished, but this is where I take my leave." Caris grabbed her bag from the back of the chair...

"Caris, Stop!" Caris turned and looked at Robbie, who was now standing. "Stella Brookes", he paused, "is Vanessa's daughter. Felix got paid by Vanessa to plant her in the graduation program and to infiltrate your work with Francesca."

"But why, I don't understand?"

"She was put there to find out what Francesca knew, because if Fran had returned to us, she would have had enough dirt on Vanessa to put her away for ever. The car crash, my kidnapping, everything! When you couldn't get any further with Francesca, she took it upon herself to intimidate you, so that she could get to me, the only other person that could incriminate her mother and when it became obvious to you that Stella's behaviour was not the norm, Vanessa instructed, Felix to remove Stella from the grad program and things died down for a little while. However, we think that Vanessa, in her manipulation, fuelled Stella's behaviours which then took on another level and the threats towards you got dangerously worse."

Richard continued, his eyes holding Caris's, and she sat down again.

"I spoke with Felix, about Stella I wanted to find out more about her, and her enrolment into the program. When Felix realised that his actions had been part of the atrocities, he broke down. He is not a bad man and had no idea that his kindness had led to this. You see he needed the money to pay off his gambling loans and saw no harm in helping what he thought was a friend. As we now know Vanessa was manipulative and could get people to do anything. Eventually Stella got arrested, but to our amazement with all the evidence made available, no charges were laid, and it was thought that someone higher up was paid off.

"I guess the apple doesn't fall far from the tree; Stella certainly is her mother's daughter". Caris said. Richard, chuckled, "You are right there Caris, but the thing is Stella didn't know her mother, until a year before she met you. What we later found out was that Vanessa was only 18 years old when she gave birth to a baby girl, but her father took the baby away as it didn't fit their plans. It seems that Vanessa, at a very early age, was used to seal her father's business deals, which was probably the catalyst of her mental health disorder. When our lawyer spoke to Stella, he was told that she had met Vanessa quite by accident in a hotel one evening. She was told that Vanessa had been looking for her for years and that in fact she was her mother. Having been struggling for many years, Stella was quick to take the hand of this friendly stranger, and in time they formed a relationship. Stella was showered with gifts, given anything that she wanted and taken to the best places. She was dressed in the best clothes and flown around from one country to another. Stella explained that the whole time she was with Vanessa, she felt that she was being groomed. However, when she failed to get what Vanessa wanted from you, things began to change. Stella was so desperate to please Vanessa and win her back that she went to extremes, which fortunately led to her arrest. However, although the evidence was substantial she was acquitted of any misdemeanours and disappeared from the public eye. I was told later that Vanessa, angry at the failure of her plan completely disowned her, turning her out on the street, saying that she had made an error and that Stella, unfortunately was not her daughter."

"You seem to know an awful lot about Stella's back story, how come"? Caris asked suspiciously.

"Stella had got herself into trouble and sought help through Felix. In turn Felix telephoned me and I came and spoke to her. It was Stella that informed me of Vanessa's next move".

"And that was?"

Robbie took over the conversation, "When you last saw Fran, all those years ago, she was in a dreadful state but did recover of sorts. However, she was in and out of hospital, her fits getting worse. Every time she was admitted to the hospital she become quite paranoid that someone was after her and often asked for you, but of course you had by then left the hospital. She didn't like her new Psychiatrist and refused to cooperate, which ended in frequent arguments. She felt that she was being pushed to say things that she couldn't remember and seemed frightened of the nurses, often becoming abusive, and I would get a call to calm her down. After Richard spoke with Stella, it was realised that the threats that Francesca had spoken about were not a figment of her imagination and the Psychiatrist, although qualified, and a couple of the nurses, were on Vanessa's payroll; Francesca's paranoia a reality."

"So what did Stella tell you?"

"When I spoke with her," Richard continued, "she told me that Francesca's life was in danger, as was Robbie's and Emily's! Vanessa told her that she wanted Robbie to feel the sort of pain that she had felt when she had been left alone and was quite erratic in her behaviour. After Vanessa had helped with Stella's acquittal she had been exceptionally cruel telling her that she was a disappointment. She was told that there had been a mistake and had proof that Stella wasn't actually her daughter and told her to leave. Then Vanessa had simply disappeared; abandoning her without money and nowhere to go. Unfortunately, by the time I found her, she was in a dreadful mess. The poor girl had got in with the wrong crowd and it was easier to sleep the day away, forgetting the past, with the help of a needle. She thought Felix could help her, she needed money to pay for her next hit, but he was too scared to talk with her and passed her on to me.

"What happened to her, is she okay" Caris asked, "Did you help her?"

"Well that's just it, I thought I had, but…..", Richard turned to the others, and they nodded for him to carry on, "You see to get this information I gave her the money she asked for, in fact, paid her more than she actually needed because she swore that she would get off the drugs and make a clean start. I had no reason not to believe her".

"That didn't happen did it?"

"No Caris, unfortunately, a month later Stella's body was found in a skip on a factory site, she had been bashed and quite unrecognisable. I was called to identify her as my number was found in her purse!"

"Oh god, that is awful, how sad! But fairly predictable for drug addicts!"

"The thing is when she was found, the toxicity showed no drugs in her blood stream and for all sense and purpose was clean. She still had her purse on her which contained money and the large wound in the back of her head was a tell- tale sign of foul play. As I say the police contacted me, because my number was found in her purse and after being quizzed for hours, the whole story came out including a theory that poor Stella has been privy to too much and was a risk. Vanessa, or whatever her real identity was, became a wanted woman and therefore, extremely dangerous. She had people working for her, from all walks of life, and it was decided for Emily's safety that I would take her far away and we decided on America, with new identities. It was a difficult decision to make, particularly for Robbie and Fran's parents but we all decided it was for the best. We had all lost so much already and the thought of losing Emily was ……Well let's say Mary and Joe couldn't have taken much more. Mackenzie Taylor was sold, and we disappeared. The four of us; Mary, Joe, Robbie and myself, had a code and the plan was that it would only be activated when necessary. We knew that Vanessa had people everywhere and we needed to go to these extremes to prevent further injury and to keep Em safe."

"It must have been so difficult for you all," Caris said, "but why was I called back, did you feel the threat was over".

"On the contrary, we were separated but the threat was always there, unseen but present. Robbie became Francesca's carer, she knew no different, and was cared for, mostly at home".

Robbie continued, "I changed hospitals and became Chief of Surgery and life continued. Francesca had started to remember certain things, but these caused panic attacks with flashbacks causing ongoing anxiety and a fear of being on her own. She had managed a semblance of reality, as you know, and it helped that she was given an opportunity at her former company, then known as Mackenzie Taylor, with her name proceeding her and returned to work, being driven up to London once per week. It did her good to go back to what she knew, but each drive became more stressful for her, and she felt that she was never safe. The flash backs made her weary and often she would disappear into a memory where I couldn't reach her, but at times I was sure that she knew me and she would look at me as if trying to remember, unfortunately we never got there. The fits were getting more frequent, and the memories were drowning her. What proceeded my call to you was the realisation that for both our sakes something had to be done - I had come home from work and whilst walking up the driveway, I stopped to pick up a buttercup weed that was growing through the path. I held it, looking at the bright petals, turning it back and forth in the sunshine. I admired it's tenacity for staying alive and likened it to myself, strong on the outside but weak within. I looked up and through the window I saw her, her expression one of horror and then she screamed, a high pitched scream and passed out, smashing a mug on the floor. I ran inside, but by then the fit had started, and I had to call an ambulance. As she she came around, she looked directly at me and said, Robbie, where is Emily? I was late home, is she at my mother's?" He stopped, his face pale and tears filled his eyes. With difficulty he carried on, his voice broken, "When I spoke to her, she smiled, the old smile, the one that knew me, and she told me that she was sorry for being late."

He paused again, shaking his head as the memory of that day flowed back. "Caris, she had not spoken about Emily since the accident 23 years ago, and I knew that it was all coming back. I needed you to find her again and open the gateway helping her to remember everything, however painful. It wasn't about her learning to speak this time; it was about getting rid of the monsters that stopped her remembering Tom, Katie and her own daughter, Emily. It was also for her to remember who I bloody was; the person who had loved her so deeply but had hurt her so badly. That was why I called you Caris, only you could help her remember. We all needed your help. Do you now understand?"

Caris watched as he wiped his eyes and put a hand onto his arm to comfort him. Her tears were falling unchecked, such was the tragedy surrounding this family.

"Yes. it all makes sense now. Did you ever see Vanessa again?"

"No! There were a lot of people looking for her after Stella's death, both locally and internationally. Corruptions followed her name like a bad smell and there were several people, other than the police, who also wanted blood. No, she would have disappeared and reinvented herself that's for sure. Richard kept tabs on Brookes Shipping, by using a detective firm to keep him updated, but as far as we know she didn't show up there."

"I also had people on the inside, Richard continued, "And a few years back, the business burnt to the ground with her father inside his office. They said it was a suicide and that he had money problems, but the autopsy report said that the door was locked on the outside adding suspicion of murder to Vanessa's rap sheet. He had been heavily involved with the mafia and had gambling debts and I suppose it could have been anyone with a grudge."

There was silence, and Caris shivered, although it wasn't cold. Emily had poured another round of drinks and set the bottle down with a thump. "All of this to get to one man; our lives wrecked; our family disjointed and my poor mother now dead. She didn't even know I was still alive! I didn't get to see her; I didn't know her, and she didn't get to see me grow up. I didn't even know my grandparents; my whole life a lie". Her voice had risen, and tears flowed. "At the end of the week we bury her, and the story has to die with her. We need to get a semblance of our lives back and stop living in fear".

They rose their glasses to the middle of the table and together without prompting – they called Francesca's name. Their voices flew up and were taken on a breeze, through the house, through the door, and into the garden. The voices called out Katie's name and eventually Tom's, remembering Francesca's brother who valiantly had tried to save them all. Their voices ducked and weaved and as the breeze gained strength, the words flew across the path, bouncing off the gate post, and settled into the large field of buttercups that swayed as if accepting their precious gift.

Anyone looking into the sombre affair, would have seen a family, having a drink, and chatting as normal families do, sitting under the patio, Francesca's flowers all around them. Their sadness went unseen, for as they said the names of their lost ones, smiles spread across their faces as if this acknowledgement had finally laid those lost to rest and in doing so they found the peace that had avoided them for so long.

EPILOGUE

The day was bright, the sky was blue with a breeze that rustled through the trees. It was the sort of day that Francesca would have loved. She would have run down the garden path, opened the garden gate and laughing would have scooped Emily up in her arms and swung her around. She would have then positioned her on her hip, thrown her free hand out to Katie, so like her cousin, who, grinning up at her aunt, would have grabbed it, and the three of them would have run to the field. The beautiful green field, covered with buttercups, which bobbed in the breeze, appreciating the company and the laughter that filled the air.

Instead, a small party of people stood around the grave as the coffin was lowered and Francesca was at last laid to rest. Twenty-three years of pain and mixed-up memories could not bother her anymore, and for the family, twenty-three years of torment, ended. Emily was first to put a handful of earth on top of the coffin, followed by the other members of the family and lastly, Caris. All had something to say but as the tears flowed their strength and unity grew stronger and they held hands as the minister finished his eulogy and each person said their farewells. Her grave was placed at the top of the hill at the far edge of the cemetery, quite some way from the main head stones that guarded their loved ones. The grass surrounding it was rather unruly and not pristinely cut as it was down below, and when the greenkeeper said that he would have it cut back before the funeral, he was asked, ever so politely to leave it as was. It was chosen because daisies bowed to buttercups that sprung up in wild abandon as if to ask for the next dance. A willow tree bent in reverence presiding over the plot as if to protect it, and butterflies flitted through the flowers, kissing each petal as they landed. The family did not leave flowers preferring the natural wilderness that was the backdrop and as they walked back down to the road, although sad, they felt some comfort that Francesca would have loved her resting place.

They said their thank you to the minister who had already walked down to the church, and then, not looking back stepped into the car that was waiting for them. Had they done so, had they looked back, they would have seen the willowy shape of a woman, step out from an adjacent tree, near enough to hear the words of the ceremony but far enough away not to be noticed. She watched as four people walked down the hill and then climbed into their waiting car and left. Turning she walked up the hill with difficulty, her movement slow and unsteady. She was dressed expensively in black, with a veiled hat on her blonde hair, the veil covering her face. As she reached Francesca's resting place, she turned again, but she was quite alone. She held a single white rose and laying it down on the fresh mound of earth, noticeable scars and burns showed across her hand. She stood silently for a short while, and then lifted the veil that had hidden her face. Once beautiful, her bright blue eyes, stared down at the rose she had placed, "I wanted you to see what you did to me, Francesca Taylor, I wanted you to pay but instead, laying here, you win. You escape your jumbled thoughts and leave me with mine. But believe me they will not get away with this, they will pay. One day when they least expect it, I will get them for what they did to me. And when it is done, the love of my life will be alone and broken. He will beg me to stop, and I will be their waiting for him". The words were cruel and mocking, coming out of a mouth that could no longer smile. Her hand reached up tracing the road map of her skin, so ravaged from burns that her once beautiful face was unrecognizable. A siren sounded and she stopped speaking and lowered the veil, stepping away from the graveside. "This is not over Francesca, adieu". She blew the grave a kiss and then stumbled slowly down the hill and out of the cemetery.

2021

There were tears of happiness as Dr Robbie Harvey and Dr Caris Goodchild tied the knot. The marriage on this beautiful day was held in the field below the house and was attended by many friends and family members. Emily was their only bridesmaid, her red hair aflame in the sunlight, so like her mother's. She walked down the path from the house through the gate and as she reached the wedding party, the baby, with the same red curls was giving to her to hold as she arrived and looking up saw her two father's Robbie and Richard smiling at her. Richard stood proud, as the best man, and Tony, Emily's fiancé, winked at her, as he stood as groom's man. She smiled to herself, how lucky was she to have such a supportive family and next year, she too would be married. Waiting, she rocked the small infant and remembered the day that Uncle Robbie became her father. She had needed a blood transfusion after surgery, and it seemed that Richard's blood group was not compatible proving that he could not be her biological father. Richard had apologised for keeping it from her but somehow under the circumstances it didn't matter and here they all were with the only person missing, her mother, Francesca. Her thoughts were interrupted as the murmurs from the congregation became louder and she turned, lifting the babies hand up to wave as Caris walked forward, looking a picture of radiance in white. In her hands a posy of wildflowers, with the centre captured with buttercups. As she reached Emily she leant forward and kissed her on the cheek and gave her the posy in exchange for the wriggling infant. With the baby in her arms, she walked towards Robbie, the smile of love on her lips as she reached him. He leant down first kissing her and then placing a kiss on the baby's head and then the ceremony began.

"In the power invested in me, you may now kiss the bride". As Robbie kissed Caris they were greeted with cheers, clapping of hands, and stamping of feet. The minister, spoke again, "May I now introduce you to Mr. and Mrs. Robbie Harvey". Again there was exaltation of joy enveloping them with love. The baby began to cry, her cries getting louder and louder, and her father leant down, kissing her little red cheeks and said "There, there, Francesca, daddy is here, Ssh now". Just like that her little mouth smiled and her green eyes looked up at him feeling safe and he took her from her mother's arms and carried her down into the throng of people where the celebrations began amongst the buttercups who in the breeze bowed their heads and danced along with the guests long into the night.

Cat Rippon was born in Westcliff-on-Sea, England. In 1990 she emigrated to Australia and has lived here for 32 years, bringing up her family. As a child she always had an overactive imagination and this fueled her joy of writing. The Buttercup is her third book.

Authors note: The Buttercup took two years to write. It was an idea that manifested and would not leave me alone until I got it down on paper. As the characters grew, I got more invested in their story and the twists and turns challenged every word written.

The Buttercup was written using experiences from everywhere in the rich world we live in. The fictional characters pulled me in the more I wrote, and there was no escaping until the very last word. Hopefully this will leave the reader wanting more.

I want to thank my family for encouraging me on this journey and for believing that eventually I would finish. Their encouragement spurred me on.